The Prearranged Plan

BOOK 1

Alyssa McBath

5830 E 2nd St, Ste 7000 #9983
Casper, WY 82609
USA

Dedication

THIS BOOK IS dedicated to my heavenly Father because He carried me through so many things and helped me turn my life around, get out of the situation I was in. He also helped me have a good relationship with my children and broke four or five generations of bad mother-daughter relationships. I honestly would not be where I am today without my faith and my relationship with my Savior. I could not survive without His love, mercy and forgiveness to teach me to love others and forgive those who hurt me.

I also dedicate this book to anyone who has been abused. Though we all face trials and tribulations, some wounds might not heal as easily as others. It is my hope that all will seek and find a relationship with Jesus Christ and know how great is His love for you, that you would grow in knowledge and understanding and deepen your relationship with Him, so you can trust Him to help you heal.

I also want to thank my family and friends for encouraging me to publish the books I wrote. They have been encouraging me for some time now. I could not do this without their love and support. Thank you for putting up with me when I am engrossed in writing, and I'm not present in your lives because I become part of the book when I am reading or writing.

Introduction

ELISA MCVEIGH GREW up in the 1070s in London, England and endured an environment of high expectations, beyond what most were expected to do, followed by criticism, consequences and punishments. Now, she has really high expectations for herself and is used to being in control of nearly every aspect of her life. As she makes her way to the home of her husband, she must learn to rely on him and trust him, learn the ways of his clan and figure out how to be a submissive laird's wife; something she is certain she isna capable of doing after years of taking care of herself and her half-siblings. What she kens how to do is fight to survive and exceed the expectations thrust upon her. She also learns to spend more time praying, studying Scripture and giving her issues over to her heavenly Father, but she struggles with trusting Him because of how her parents and others treated her.

Chapter 1

ELISA MCVEIGH HAD many memories of her trips to Scotland; but, they were confusing. She remembered the details of the route there. She could remember back to when she was about three years old; and although that might be unusual, it dinna seem unusual for her. She sat in the carriage with her parents and watched out the window every minute of the ride. Her parents encouraged her to sleep, but she was always too excited about where they were going to sleep. She leaned against the side of the carriage until her parents mayhap thought she was asleep, but she watched the world go by. She watched as they passed fields and villages and people. She remembered she felt something for the people, but she dinna really ken what it was. She just knew she could feel them, feel what they felt. She smiled at them as they passed by and hoped it was some comfort to them.

As they traveled, she got excited to see the boy who was her husband from shortly after she was born, Ian. He was rather cute as she recalled. Then again, he was ten, almost eleven the last time she saw him, a few years older than her and bigger, taller. She was always small for her age, a tiny little thing. Her excitement changed to confusion. Ian dinna seem interested in her being there. Mostly, he seemed to avoid her. She couldna think of anything she did to make him nay want to be around her, so she just tried to be polite. And sometimes, she followed him around and snuck through the secret passages, even out the tunnel and down to the loch to fish or swim. Other times, she rode her horse through the surrounding woods. Those were the only fun times she recalled ever having; she dinna play as a child. There wasna time for it. She had too much to learn, too many things she needed to know how to do. But, there were always consequences for the few minutes she spent having fun. Since she rarely indulged in anything fun, it was worth the beatings she received when she returned to the castle. Then again, they would have found some reason to beat her even if she dinna leave the castle. Even when she did whatever they asked her to do, she was never fast enough or good enough and they beat her for whatever excuse they could find.

There was always another boy with Ian. They went everywhere together. Her mother would reprimand her or beat her if she even looked at Duncan. Most of her time on the Isle of Mull was spent secluded with her parents and Lady Isobel, Ian's mother. They were always trying to teach her something that she had to remember when she was older. It involved lots of tests and games, and severe punishment when she dinna answer correctly or quickly enough. The trips to Scotland were where the beatings started. And when she arrived home, the tests and games and beatings continued. Until her seventh summer, when she was beaten so badly they couldna return home from Mull until she healed. Ian's nursemaid, Alice, stayed with her night and day and cared for her. The boys sat on the floor in front of her bed and refused to allow anyone near her. It was the only time she could recall anyone trying to protect her or care for her.

When they returned to London, her mother tried to have another child but died during the labor and her little brother died with her. Her father changed after that. He was tough on her before that, but he left her to fend for herself after her mother was gone. It was a blessing, really. She discovered ways to avoid him and his beatings or to feel less, if he did beat her. She made herself feel verra small so the pain would be small. It couldna be any bigger than her or she would focus on a candle flame, which was verra small and she could make the pain feel as small as the flame so it dinna hurt.

She wasna sad about losing her mother. She stood in the church near her father and kept her head down throughout the service. She felt that was the best way to deal with the situation and make it look like she felt what everyone thought she should feel. Thankfully, she wore a black lace veil and no one could really see her face or that she dinna cry. She heard many others in the room crying and felt their pain, but she dinna really feel any loss for her mother. Who would cry for a woman who beat you and then let her friend beat you until you nearly died? What kind of mother could allow the child of her womb to be hurt so badly and nay lift a finger to protect her child? She dinna ken that kind of person at all. She dinna think she could ever allow anyone to be treated that way even if they werena her own child.

She stayed in the church while her father greeted everyone who came to the funeral. She stood near her mother's coffin, but actually much closer to her brother's coffin. She cried for him until she realized the church was nearly empty; and then, she wiped her tears and quietly slipped behind her father and waited for the last few people to leave the church. He placed his arm around her shoulders and walked her to the carriage and helped her in. It almost seemed like he cared about her, except that she knew differently. It was just an act for those that attended the funeral; so they could see his show of affection. No one knew what really went on in their London townhouse, and how her father treated her, except quite possibly her husband's mother and father. She sat facing backwards and folded her hands in her lap and kept her head bowed.

A few carriages followed them home and her father instructed her on the carriage ride home that she was to provide refreshments in the parlor when they arrived and to ensure everyone had a verra nice meal served afterwards. Then, she should retire to the nursery because he dinna want to see her until he sent for her. She acknowledged his request with as much respect as she could muster but continued to keep her head down in submission. She was good at playing the game that was expected of her. She knew she wouldna lose at any game. The beatings werena because she dinna win or dinna perform well enough; she knew it was just an excuse to beat her and so she tolerated it. Really, she was just a child and dinna really have any choice in the matter.

She went to the kitchen and put on an apron and helped the kitchen staff make a verra nice refreshment tray for their guests. The maids brought the trays to the parlor and Elisa poured tea for anyone who wanted tea and whatever drinks anyone asked for. She knew about different drinks and how to mix several. She walked the trays of food around and served everyone until her father signaled for her to leave. She sent the maids back to the parlor to clean up the trays while she returned to the kitchen to help make dinner. The cook praised her choice of menu and thanked her for her help and told her the meal was wonderful. No one seemed to notice that she wasna sitting in the parlor with the rest of them or who went to the kitchen to ensure they had food and drinks. Or perhaps, they just dinna care about a little girl or whether she had all that she needed and was properly cared for. Mayhap, since she was so small, no one really noticed her except when they wanted something from her.

She ensured the maids served the food before she climbed the back stairs up to the nursery with an apple and a piece of bread and a glass of milk. A man came to the nursery later in the day and said his name was Cousin Richard and that if she ever needed him, she had only to send for him. He knelt in front of her and gave her a hug and told her he was sorry for her loss. She remembered thinking he was nice; she wasna sure how she could know that, but he seemed genuine. She would have asked questions about how they were related and why she had never met him before, but they were interrupted by her father, who sent Cousin Richard away. She dinna hear what her father told her cousin, but her cousin left, and she was certain she sensed he was angry.

Her father told her never to see that man again or allow him entrance to the house. She replied, "Yes, Father." What else could she do? She dinna know the man, had never met him before, hadna even heard of him before. Then, her father mumbled something about inappropriate behavior and left the nursery. She was so grateful that there were guests in the house and that he refrained from beating her for the inappropriate behavior.

Not long after her mother's death, her father suddenly remarried. Shortly thereafter, the two of them went to one of his other estates. While they were away, Elisa took over the running of the townhouse and her father's three estates. Really, it wasna that much more than what she already did. She was already doing most of the work around the townhouse anyway. She kept the books and went over all the expenses with the cook and the housekeeper. She helped with all the cooking and cleaning and anything that needed to be taken care of around the property. The estate managers came to her, not realizing that her father wouldna be there for his monthly meeting and she met with them instead. They continued to come see her and review the estate business with her after that. She did her very best to ensure that everything was in order and handled properly. Her father and stepmother dinna return for more than a year and when they came home, Elisa had a little brother named Jonathan. The three of them were inseparable and they seemed happy.

Elisa was happy to be left alone. At least, neither of them beat her like her mother and father used to do. All she could remember from the time she was able to walk was constant tests and games of skill or strategy. She learned to read and do math at the age of three or four. She read about other countries and history before most boys even started their education. By the time her husband would have been old enough to go into training, she had read every book in her parents' house and handled all the finances and balanced all the ledgers. If she made a mistake during the tests or in her studies, they beat her. They beat her if it took too long to answer or perform a task. They always found something wrong with whatever she did as an excuse to beat her. She was not allowed to cry or show any emotions.

Since she learned to take care of all of her father's estates in his absence and he was apparently so besotted with his wife and happy about their son, she continued to meet with his estate managers. She was certainly capable of dealing with reviewing all the ledgers, thanks to all her tests, games and studies. She asked lots of questions about any improvements the managers were interested in trying. She was certain they were quite annoyed with her for all her questions. At first, she was terrified when her father returned that he was going to be angry with her for pestering his estate managers with all her questions. But, he never said anything to her about it. He dinna even seem to notice her after he returned. He was consumed with his second wife and son.

Elisa waited until late at night to go to the nursery to see her little brother, Jonathan. He was a very handsome and healthy boy. She was very happy and spent time every evening and morning petting his head through the crib. She was afraid to hold him. If she got caught near him, she was certain her father would beat her severely, like her last beating on Mull. She caressed her brother's head and prayed for him and his health while she stood there. She prayed every morning for the strength to endure and do whatever was expected of her that day. Every night, she thanked God that He helped her through the day and that she successfully avoided her father's beatings.

One thing she hated more than anything was that whatever her parents taught her, whatever she saw happen, she remembered it all. The newest problem to her life was her cousin, Ken, coming to visit. He liked to hide and jump out from behind corners, furniture, or the tapestries and curtains to scare her. Sometimes, he would grab her, but she was usually alert to his presence and she was pretty good at avoiding him. He liked to delay her from doing what her parents told her to do and then she got beat for it. She tried to explain to her father the first few times, but he beat her worse if she complained; so she stopped complaining and just took the beatings. The worst part was when her cousin touched her. At first, she thought it was accidental, but she soon realized that he did it on purpose. So, she tried to avoid him all the more because she knew that where Cousin Ken touched her, he shouldna ever touch a girl there, especially nay his cousin.

His behavior became more aggressive and he pinned her to the wall or pushed her down on the floor and kissed her and grabbed her inappropriately. When she became more successful at avoiding him, he complained to her father that she wasna cordial to him and Elisa was beat again. She only tried to explain her cousin's inappropriate behavior one time, but that was a mistake and she should have known better. It had been one of her worst beatings since returning from Mull. It severed her ties to her father. She couldna feel anything for him after that. Her cousin realized his power over her and he knew he had her father's support so her cousin used it to get her father to beat her more often. Her father was happy to oblige him. Her cousin, Ken, turned out to be more of a thorn in her side than her own parents.

She devoted herself to the care of the townhouse, estates and her little brother. She woke early to work in the kitchen and she usually fed her brother his breakfast and played with him for a few minutes before she started her studies. She went to the market if the maids were unavailable. When she returned, she helped with lunch. She spent time riding with Sir Colin, their groomsman and gardener. She reviewed the ledgers and made all the necessary entries before she returned to the kitchen to help make dinner.

She usually ate alone in the nursery because Jonathan usually spent his afternoons with his parents and they had dinner with just the three of them. Elisa dinna mind being left alone. It was better than being around her father and risking a beating. Her stepmother was fine, she supposed. The woman rarely spoke to her or asked anything of her, which was better than the tests and being drilled on her studies and beat because of whatever infraction her father could dream up for an excuse to hit her.

When her stepmother became pregnant again, they spent even less time with her. They rarely socialized before; and now, they socialized even less because they seemed worried about anyone knowing they were happy or having another baby. Elisa took a little extra time to be with Jonathan whenever they were too involved in themselves to spend time with their son. She dinna understand how they could just abandon their child.

Then, they had a visitor just before her stepmother went into labor. Elisa frequently slipped into the room to check on her stepmother and bring things for the maid.

She stayed near the door and waited for the maid to tell her what she needed next. She was surprised when the maid left the room. She was going to go after the maid, but she saw the visitor coming down the hall and slipped behind the curtains in the room. For once, she was thankful that she was so small. The man was dressed in rather fine clothing. Elisa knew what fine clothes they were because she purchased her own material to make her own clothes. She saw the man's hands; they were very large and he took one of the pillows and covered her stepmother's face with it. She could hear her stepmother trying to scream but it was muffled by the pillow. What Elisa would never forget was the emblem on the man's ring. She knew that emblem; everyone in the country would recognize it, even from a young age. She stood as still as possible and pretended that she was the smallest creature she could think of being. She took really small, quiet breaths and hoped that no one heard her.

The man left the room and closed the door. Elisa took a few deep breaths to calm down; but she remained where she was for a few moments. She was just about to leave her hiding place when the maid returned. When the maid realized that her stepmother was dead, she ran from the room. Elisa quickly walked to the bed. She had an image in her mind to pull the baby from her stepmother. She took the thread on the table, wrapped it around the chord as tightly as she could and she cut the chord with the knife from the bedside table. She wrapped the baby in the cloth that was setting on the chair next to the table and ran from the room. She went up to the nursery as quickly as she could. She cleaned the baby's face with one of the cloths and then she spanked her on the bottom. She dinna cry so Elisa blew in her face several times and spanked her again. The baby cried and Elisa cuddled her close to her chest.

When the baby calmed down, she washed her up. It was a little girl and she named her Ginger Elisabeth, but she would call her Elisabeth. She hid the baby in one of her trunks that had been given to her. She ran down the back stairs to the kitchen and warmed some milk and snuck back up to the nursery. When she was certain the milk was cool enough to drink, she spooned tiny amounts into the baby's mouth. It took a long time, but Elisa was very patient. She held her little sister to her chest and burped her. Then, she laid Elisabeth on her bed while she changed her. She made a bed for Elisabeth in one of her trunks, but she removed the top so it couldna be closed over the baby.

Elisa started rising earlier and doing her chores even earlier so she could spend a little more time with Jonathan and Elisabeth in the nursery. Her father never came to the nursery. He was obviously upset about losing his second wife. It seemed to upset him even more than his first wife's death. Elisa did her best to avoid him. She feared she would be blamed and beaten. But her father only sent for her once to tell her to care for Jonathan while he went to the funeral.

She told her father, "Of course, Father, I will do everything I can to take care of them and ensure they have everything they need." Her father dinna notice that she used plural words or if he did, he dinna comment on it; so she returned to the nursery. Her father dinna bother about any of the household responsibilities. Elisa wondered if he just dinna care anymore or if he just assumed she would take care of everything as she had been doing for the past few years.

Elisa's day was very busy and she enjoyed it. She liked being busy. She mostly loved to create a schedule and follow it. She made a list of things to do and completed it. She loved her little brother and sister and caring for them. She made clothes for them, which required constant effort to keep up with how quickly they grew. They needed new clothes almost monthly or at least every few months. But, she learned to sew and knit and crochet and she was very good at it, since she was a quick learner and only needed to be shown something once or twice and she could master it. She had a talent that she could see something and she could make it, or she would picture it in her mind and then she could make it.

She woke early and went to the kitchen to make everyone's breakfast. She returned to the nursery to feed Jonathan and Elisabeth. Then, she went to the market to buy what was needed for lunch and dinner. She returned home and fed the baby again and Jonathan. Then, she did most of the cleaning in the main parts of the house before she returned to the nursery to work on her studies and play with Jonathan and Elisabeth. She studied her more difficult subjects while they napped in the late morning and early afternoon. She helped make lunch, but more and more she let the cook deal with lunch. She gave up her riding lessons for now. She could do that later when Jonathan and Elisabeth were also able to ride. After lunch with her siblings, she worked on the ledgers and met with the housekeeper or the estate managers when necessary. Then, she cared for Elisabeth before she helped the cook attend to dinner and she brought her tray up to the nursery and ate with Jonathan and Elisabeth. After everyone was asleep at night, she would sneak downstairs and finish any cleaning that needed to be done. She was always very quiet. She learned to sneak around the house without anyone hearing her. It helped that she discovered secret passages in nearly every room in the house.

That turned out to be the biggest blessing in her life. Her uncle and cousin came to visit more frequently now that her stepmother passed away. Her uncle discussed letting Cousin Ken stay with her father or at least he thought he should spend more time here learning to care for the estates. Elisa knew the real reason her cousin wanted to spend more time here, so she used the secret passages to avoid him. The boy couldna keep his hands off her and it disturbed her. He loved to hide and jump out and scare her, but his behavior was getting worse. She tried to explain to her father, but he called her a liar and beat her. Once her cousin realized the power he had, he pursued her all the more and did things so she would be delayed completing a task her father asked her to do, just so her father would beat her.

One morning, her father suddenly appeared in the nursery when she was trying to study and Elisabeth was not cooperating. She wouldna stop crying and fussing. Elisa walked her. She tried rocking her. She tried laying Elisabeth on her stomach, on her back; she rubbed her back and her stomach. She bounced her. She dinna know what else to do, but she just kept trying everything she could think of to calm her. She changed her and fed her. Nothing worked.

Her father just stared at Elisa while she tried to calm down the baby and work on her studies. "Yes, Father? Is there something you need me to do?"

"Elisa, the maids said the nursery is haunted by my wife's lost baby and they refuse to come up here. They insist that I remove you and Jonathan from the nursery before you are traumatized by the baby's crying."

"There are nay any ghosts up here, Father."

"Where did this baby come from?"

"She was you wife's baby. I brought her up here and I've been taking care of her and Jonathan. I told you I would do all I could to take care of them."

"Give them whatever they need. I will pay for it." That was his only response to her and his only acknowledgement of his children.

"Yes, Father."

"Is there anything you can do to make her stop crying so the maids will stop pestering me?"

"I have tried everything I can think of, Father. She's been fed and changed, rocked, walked, bounced, patted on the back, her stomach has been rubbed. I cuddle her and sing to her. I talk to her. I dinna know what to do. I'm sorry, she's disturbing everyone."

"You are very smart and clever, Elisa. I know you will figure it out. You have always been able to figure out whatever test you were given, so I know you will figure this out too."

Yet, you beat me anyway, she thought to herself, but she was smart enough to nay voice her opinion out loud. Instead, she asked, "Do you think I could take them to the garden when it's sunny out, mayhap just for a few minutes? They might enjoy the fresh air and sunlight."

"Yes, but only if she is quiet; I dinna want her disturbing the whole neighborhood."

"Yes, sir."

Her father left after that. He dinna even acknowledge Jonathan or even look at his daughter. Elisa spent the rest of the afternoon trying to comfort Jonathan as well as Elisabeth. She was very angry with their father. It was bad enough that he treated her the way he did; but now apparently, he was going to be just as cruel to his other children. She did her best to explain that something wasna quite right about their father and that he just missed his wife so much that he couldna stand to be around anyone anymore. She wasna sure if it was an understandable explanation for Jonathan or not.

It wasna very long after her cousin's next visit that her father became ill and she was certain that her cousin poisoned him. But, she couldna prove it and she really dinna have time to deal with her cousin. When she was certain that her father was going to die, she spent time trying to comfort him and nurse him. She knew nothing was going to save him, but she did her best. Her father sent for his lawyer and solicitor and spent a few days going over a number of documents with them. Then, she was called into his room and the lawyer and solicitor read the papers to her and explained everything to her, not that she could really ken any of it. They gave her copies of documents and told her to be verra careful no one found them, to keep them hidden and safe, that she would need them when she went to the Isle of Mull to follow the prearranged plan. She could only think about the fact that her father really was going to die. She chastised herself for even caring; after all the times he had beaten her, she shouldna care whatsoever. But somehow, he expected her to run everything and raise

Jonathan and Elisabeth until she was eighteen and could take them to Mull with her. And just how did he think she was supposed to be capable of getting to Mull? She hadna been there since she was seven.

Part of her was relieved. The man wouldna beat her anymore. But then, she just felt abandoned. Who would take care of them? But there was only one answer. She would have to do what she had been doing since her mother died, and then her father and stepmother had gone away to have Jonathan. She would continue to take care of the household, the estates and her siblings, just as always. Somehow, it was always her responsibility, her job to ensure everything got done, and her fault whenever it wasna done or done to their satisfaction. Well, now it would be done to her satisfaction and there wouldna be any more beatings. She prayed for God's forgiveness and asked for His guidance to help her succeed.

When her uncle and cousin came for the funeral, they were very upset to learn the things the lawyer and solicitor told them. But then, they realized that Elisa was quite capable of running all the estates and they dinna have to do anything except ask for their monthly stipend. It wasna long before her Uncle Kenneth asked her to look at his books for his business. She made arrangements for the maid to spend the day with the children and she met her uncle at his business shop. She looked over the ledgers and corrected all the mistakes.

"Would you be willing to take care of the ledgers for me, Elisa? Obviously, I am not that good at it and it would be less time consuming if you just did it correctly the first time rather than correcting all my mistakes."

"Are you sure, Uncle Kenneth?"

"Yes, it would be a great help to me. Mayhap you could come and help with the inventory too sometimes. You are very good at organizing things, aren't you?"

"Yes, I would be very good with the inventory. I love to make lists of things and organize them. Are you sure I wouldna be in the way? You are certain you wouldna mind?"

"No, I wouldn't mind. As I said, you would be a great help," Uncle Kenneth replied.

"Just send me a message when you want me to come by to help with the inventory. I will need at least a day's warning though, so I can find someone to help watch the children."

"You think of them as your own children, don't you?"

"I know that they are my siblings, but I'm the one who has been providing for them since my stepmother died."

"It's very strange how she died and the baby lived."

"How is it strange?" Elisa asked.

"It's just unusual for the child to live if the mother dies."

"I dinna know anything about that," Elisa shrugged.

She returned home and went straight to the nursery to check on the children before she went to help with the meal. Since it was just her and the children, she dinna worry so much about housework and just asked the maids to keep the master bedroom clean and to have fresh linens ready whenever her uncle or cousin visited. She asked them to ensure the parlor and dining room were always clean. She cleaned the library and the study once a sennight after she finished the ledger entries for the day. She did more intense cleaning when she was up early or stayed up late. Since she slept only a few hours and it helped her to nay think about the nightmares, she was happy to have more vigorous work to occupy her thoughts. She could alleviate some of the cook's and the maids' workload by doing it herself.

She set a schedule and her life settled into a routine. They dinna receive any visitors except the solicitor, estate managers and those her father had done business with, except when she was forced to deal with her cousin and the guests that he brought to the house to entertain.

She and Jonathan thrived on the schedule. Elisa was reluctant to disrupt her routine. She kept detailed lists and organized everything in her life. Her whole life was completely focused on her duties, responsibilities and her education. She had tutors for every subject you could think of including numerous languages.

The only disruptions were her cousin's visits. He showed up at all hours of the night, inebriated and in a foul mood. He pursued her relentlessly and Elisa was afraid to sleep in the nursery because she dinna want the children to see what her cousin tried to do to her. But when she was in the nursery, he left her alone.

On several occasions, he entered the townhouse unnoticed and he lay in wait for her. When he caught her unawares, he pinned her down and took advantage of her. He forced his kisses on her. He grabbed her inappropriately. She protested, but he wouldna relent until he decided he had enough. She tried fighting him but she wasna strong enough. She tried to just lie still, but nay anything made him stop.

As his advances became bolder, he did things she couldna even describe. He beat her and forced himself on her. She suffered through the pain he caused her without a sound, just as her parents taught her with the many beatings they gave her. But it was much worse when he brought his friends home with him. And he made it clear to her that it was his home and she would do as he told her. She had no recourse. She wasna strong enough to fight him or his friends, so she suffered in silence and scrubbed their sin off her as best as she could after they passed out or retired for the night. She stayed in the nursery until she was certain they left the next day, which was often quite late. She went early through the secret passages to the kitchen for enough food for the day and then barred herself in the nursery until her cousin and his friends left.

Within a year of her father's death, her uncle had basically trained her and left her to care for his business. She went once a sennight to the shop and entered everything in the ledger. She took inventory and processed the new inventory that came in. She enjoyed the work and liked organizing things, but she was leery around her uncle and cousin.

Her uncle called at the townhouse one day to complain about how little inventory was being entered into the ledger. She said that whatever was received at the store was entered. She couldna be responsible for anything that happened to the merchandise before it reached the shop.

Her uncle suggested she go with him to the docks to ensure the merchandise was unloaded from the ship to the wagons and then they escorted the merchandise to the store. After a couple months, her uncle started making excuses for not going with her to the dock and she went by herself. She knew how to deal with the captains and their shipmates. The only ones that gave her trouble were those that were friends with her cousin, Ken. Then, they had expectations from her that they insisted she provide to get her merchandise. She was too embarrassed to tell anyone what they did to her and she was responsible for ensuring her uncle's merchandise made it to the store; so she dinna feel she had any choice. Besides, she was just a girl and they would do what they wanted since women had no rights.

In time, she stopped consulting her uncle on the shipments and started creating the purchase requisitions herself. She discussed the routes the captains took and the weather to see if there wasna a more efficient travel route so they would lose less of their merchandise to the weather and pirates. Some of the captains were willing to try her suggestions if it would mean less loss to them. She gave them bonuses when she received better results from them.

She started training with Sir Colin so she could learn to defend herself from her cousin and his friends, whom she now realized were the captains or shipmates with whom he did business. She resumed her riding lessons because she knew at some point the only way she was going to escape the nightmare her life had become was if she found a way to return to Scotland. Somehow, she knew her uncle and cousin werena going to let her go. They wouldna like losing her ability to run the businesses and estates so smoothly and profitably. She made the businesses very successful, just like all the estates were very successful.

She trained with bow and arrows. Next, Sir Colin taught her how to throw a dagger at the target. Then, he taught her how to fight with the dagger; and finally, he taught her to fight with a sword, but it was a smaller sword, designed for a small woman to handle, so it dinna weigh too much for her to lift and swing, but it was strong steel and she learned to counter Sir Colin's blows and defend herself. He also taught her some useful moves that she could use if she was grabbed and she learned to break free of the man's grasp.

Sir Colin trapped and caught little critters in the park and brought them home to their garden and he taught her how to hunt, so she could provide for herself and the children if it was necessary.

Time slipped away quickly with all the things she had to do every day. She was verra busy and she liked staying busy. She still found time to read the books in the library. She had read all of them, but she continued to add to the collection. She loved to read and learn new things. She still had her own studies that the tutors taught her each day, as well. She gave the children lessons in math and reading, as they grew older, she started to teach them about history and she spoke to them mostly in Gaelic, Scots, and English. They were catching on quickly to all the languages. She sang a lullaby to them at bedtime every night.

Once the children were a little older, she started teaching them to ride a horse. Sir Colin helped her. He told her what to do and he worked with Jonathan while Elisa taught Elisabeth. She thought about how long they would have to ride each day and every day she spent more time with them in the garden riding. They wore quite a path around the perimeter of the garden, but she really dinna want to take the children to the park to ride. She was certain it would seem unusual and might be reported to her cousin or uncle. She dinna want to do anything to make them curious about her behavior. Also, since her parents seemed to feel it was important that their births be in secret, she was afraid to let too many people know her siblings existed.

She developed a plan for their escape to Scotland and she started making lists of things to do. She did whatever she could do ahead of time. The problem was that she couldna store food or even clothes for the children because they grew too fast to keep up with them. So, she made one or two extra outfits and kept them hidden in one of her trunks so they would be packed and ready to go when she found the opportunity to escape.

As the children grew, she decided to give each of them one of her trunks. She kept their clothes in the trunks in the nursery and they learned to just live out of their trunks. The only exceptions were Elisa and Elisabeth's dresses. Elisa's, for sure, had to be hung up.

When her uncle started sending her cousin on some of the trips for the merchandise so he could secure contacts and create new business relationships, Elisa realized this opportunity was going to be her greatest chance to escape to Scotland. She waited for a trip when he would be gone at least a few months and far enough away that he would have little chance to come after her before she reached Mull.

She was nearly eighteen and once she turned eighteen at her next birthday, she knew she would have to seriously plan for their escape. She started to design a cloak that would be reversible so they could hide in different condi-tions. She knew late spring could still be cold. They might have to ride through a snow storm. They would be sleeping outside at night and she had to be sure the children dinna get too cold no matter what the weather conditions were. So she made the cloaks from beaver fur since it was very warm and would repel moisture and water. She dyed the fur white on one side and left it brown on the other side.

She searched through the library for books on tanning leather and designed clothes for her and the children. She and Elisabeth could wear breeches and a top under their dresses if it got cold. The additional clothes would provide extra warmth.

She could visualize the trip in her mind. She recalled all the times she had gone to Scotland and she sat watching out the carriage window. She knew the way by heart. She was confident she could get them to Scotland. She stored away what food she could that would last for months. She would refresh the stores every month or every other month until they actually left for Scotland, but at least she would have some things prepared and ready to go.

She consulted Sir Colin on what they could pack for the horses. He assured her that he would take care of it. She gave him three of her trunks, one to store grain and one for waterskins for the horses. He filled one with extra tack and grooming supplies. The water would have to be filled and emptied periodically and refilled to ensure they had fresh water for the trip.

She was ready to go except for the last minute food and water supplies they would need. She knew the route they needed to take, except she had to rely on Sir Colin to get them through London; but once they were outside the city, she could navigate the rest of the way, even in the dark. She could rely on her memories.

She sent her jewelry to be copied over the years. Everything in her room was faux jewelry, but it was very well made and only a professional would be able to tell the difference. All of her real jewelry was hidden in secret compartments in her trunks or stitched into the hem of her cloaks and dresses.

During the day, she tried to continue on as normal. She helped with the cooking and cleaning and spent time teaching the children their lessons. Then, they spent many hours riding in the garden. She went regularly to the docks to ensure the shipments were unloaded and brought to her uncle's shop. She organized all the merchandise in the store and sent the items to people's homes as their purchase orders requested. She ensured everything was entered in the ledgers and accounted for. Under her control, their business was verra successful. She ensured her uncle and cousin had their monthly stipends so they dinna need to come see her for any reason. The less she saw of her cousin, the better.

She usually locked herself in the nursery with the children when her cousin came to the townhouse. She couldna tolerate his advances anymore. She drank heavily to sleep at night because the nightmares were so bad. She couldna forget all the times her parents beat her and now all the times her cousin and his shipping business associates abused her.

She went to the cellar and snuck a few cases up to her room and filled one trunk with a few cases of scotch. She knew that it was produced by her husband's family. Her mother-in-law sent a case every month to the house. She dinna really understand why since her parents were both dead and she dinna entertain any guests. Her parents dinna entertain, even when they lived, but Elisa had taken to drinking a little after her mother died and more after her father died. It was the only thing that could make her forget what her cousin and his friends did to her, so she drank a little more. She knew it was also why she tried to keep so busy all the time, so she dinna have any free time to think about anything, especially nay what was done to her.

She probably dinna need to bring the scotch with because she could drink Ian's scotch if she wanted to drink. But for some reason, she just felt she needed to bring this trunk full of scotch. She knew she would need it. She always just accepted those thoughts and just did it. For some reason, there were some thoughts or ideas that she knew she just needed to do them and things would work out fine. So she followed her instincts in that regard.

There were numerous cases of the scotch in the basement cellar. As far as she knew, she was the only one that drank it other than when her cousin and his friends came to visit. She had no idea what her mother-in-law was thinking sending so much scotch here. There were barrels of something down there, as well as the cases of scotch.

She was sometimes grateful for the supply. It was enough to get Cousin Ken drunk and keep him too inebriated to harm her, but he rarely visited without his friends and they dinna drink themselves into a stupor like her cousin did. He apparently dinna have the ability to hold his liquor.

Elisa could drink a full bottle and more and nay pass out. Sometimes, she wished she could drink enough to pass out from it; but then, she worried about what might happen to the children if she wasna capable of caring for them. So she drank enough to keep the nightmares away and so she could sleep for a few hours.

Usually, she had two or three glasses before bed every night after the children were asleep in their beds. But mostly, she limited her sleep to just a few hours and sat up working on projects, like sewing for the children, since it was difficult to keep up with how quickly they grew. Or, she spent much of the early morning or late evening cleaning house and baking and cooking. She did what she could to alleviate the workload of the staff since she had a bare minimum number of staff for the large townhouse.

She dinna mind the amount of work her parents asked of her. The only thing she minded was that nothing she did ever pleased them. They always found something to complain about or criticize. Then, they beat her. When she thought about those things, she drank a little. After her father beat her for not being cordial to her cousin and she tried to explain what her cousin did to her, she drank a little more. If only she could forget, but she wasna able to forget anything. The worse the ordeal, the harder it seemed it was for her to forget about it. So, she drank a glass or two every day.

She thought about how soon her birthday would be upon her and she reviewed her notes to ensure everything was prepared and ready to go. She started packing away as much food as she could that would keep for at least a fortnight. She gathered everything that she could. She brought what she could to the stable for Sir Colin to keep hidden in preparation for their trip to Scotland. She ensured all their clothes were packed except for the dresses. She was ready except for packing more food and filling the waterskins. The only other thing she needed was a trip for her cousin to go on so they had time to disappear.

She ran through the plan in her mind. She thought about the length of the trip and how far they had to travel, just the four of them out in the open country alone. It would not be easy, but she was not afraid of doing something difficult. The more difficult the challenge, the harder she worked to ensure that she succeeded. This was one time that she couldna afford to fail and so she planned for a very long time and she ensured that she had everything she needed to succeed. The only thing that she could not rely on was the weather. They had to travel a very long distance and sleep outside at night. She needed to ensure that the children wouldna get too cold and then get sick. She did everything she could to prepare for even bad weather.

She could hunt, fish and scavenge in the woods for mushrooms and wild roots and birds' eggs so they could eat. It was spring and eggs would be plentiful and so would wild berries and roots. She had plenty of money so she could send Sir Colin into one of the villages to get supplies when they needed more to eat.

The thing she feared the most was getting through the city streets of London. She had to rely on Sir Colin for that. She did not travel about the city enough to know how to do that. She did not like to rely on anyone else. Sir Colin was good about watching out for her and teaching her things that she dinna know how to do on her own, but she did not like to trust in men, not even sweet, old men; not after what her cousin and his friends did to her. She dinna like anyone to touch her. Sir Colin was careful to nay touch her except to lift her onto her horse. He always spoke to her before he approached her or touched her.

She tried to defend herself against her cousin the last couple times he came to visit. She kept him at bay but he was much bigger than her and it wasna a fair fight. Sir

Colin stepped in when she needed him after her cousin hit her and knocked her to the ground.

So, if she had to trust someone, she supposed it would be Sir Colin. To get out of London, she had to trust him and rely on his guidance. Once they were outside the city, she would be able to get to Mull. All her plans were implemented and she was ready to go. All she needed was confirmation that Cousin Ken set sail for his trip and they would set out for Mull. She prayed all would go well.

Chapter 2

FINALLY, THAT DAY arrived in the spring of 1087. She was at her uncle's office earlier, working on the ledgers. She already logged the inventory from the latest shipment and sent the merchandise to various homes of the nobility with a letter thanking them for their purchase. Her uncle and cousin were arguing about her cousin having to go on another trip. Her uncle was adamant and her cousin wasna happy about having to go. He clearly dinna want to go on this trip. Elisa focused on the ledgers and finished as quickly as she could. She escaped from the office as soon as she finished, while they were both still arguing. She was sure they hadna noticed her leaving.

If it worked out that they could leave tonight, it would be a verra good plan because her uncle would not expect her to come to the shop for another sennight, so they should have at least a sennight for a head start. She prayed this was the opportunity she needed to escape. She asked God to work everything out to their advantage, if it was His will.

When she arrived back at the townhouse, she informed Sir Colin of the news that her cousin had to leave on a trip. She explained about her cousin's argument with her uncle. Sir Colin told her to nay get her hopes up and to just go about her day as she normally would. He said he would find someone he trusted to watch her uncle and her cousin and ensure that the trip was real and actually going to happen and they would let him know when her cousin actually departed on his trip.

Elisa asked if he knew anyone that could truly be trusted to give him this information. Sir Colin assured her that he did indeed know some people that could be trusted to give him honest and accurate information. She returned to the house and went about her usual business until the staff went to bed. She worked in the nursery with the children near her. She really dinna want them out of her sight. She couldna leave without them; she was their parent now.

She put the children to bed, sang to them and hugged and kissed them. She hoped they got a few hours of sleep before they set out. Then, she packed all their trunks with everything that was hanging in the armoires. She had two trunks and the children each had one trunk. She filled one trunk with waterskins, although most of them were empty. She couldna risk spending a long time at the well drawing up water to fill a lot of waterskins; but they needed some water, so she filled one for each of them. In another trunk, she had started storing food, but only things that would keep for a long time, like potatoes, onion, apples, and pears. Sir Colin filled the other trunks with horse supplies. She had nine trunks in total.

Elisa needed to be very quiet as she snuck through the secret passages. She carried one of the trunks down to the kitchen and left it in the secret passage while she filled it. Then, she carried it through the secret passage that ended closest to the garden and the stables. She returned to her room for another trunk and carried it down to the passage just outside the kitchen to collect more food to eat for their long journey. She was glad she knew all the secret hiding places and passages in this house. That knowledge had been so helpful so many times in the past ten years. She prayed for stealth and God's guidance and safety for all of them.

She quickly passed through the corridors and stairwells until she reached the kitchen and cautiously opened the last door and listened carefully for any sounds. Once she was sure no one was in the kitchen, Elisa opened the door a little further so she could look around. The kitchen appeared to be empty. Elisa stepped into the room and quickly closed the door. She walked quietly to the pantry and gathered bread, cheese, fruits, and dried meats and placed them in the trunk. She continued until she had enough food to last at least a sennight. She hoped it would be enough for a fortnight. She doubted she could pack enough to get all the way to Scotland and to Mull. The food probably wouldna last that long anyway. She grabbed a few waterskins which would have to be filled later, after they were far from London.

Elisa carefully made her way back across the kitchen, listening for the sounds of another person. No one. She carried the trunk through the secret passageway and left it with the other trunk near the garden entrance. She returned to the kitchen to ensure that she sealed the secret passage and then she cautiously and silently made her way up the stairs to her room.

She listened carefully at the secret door to her room for any possibility that anyone had entered her room. There werena any sounds indicating anyone was in her room; so, she slowly opened the door. She stood behind the tapestry listening—still no one.

Elisa went across the room to gather her last few items. She already had most of the clothes packed for her little half-brother and half-sister and herself. She already had soaps and hairbrushes and capes set aside. All her real jewelry was already packed. Everything was packed in special trunks that were small and lightweight and had special hidden compartments. She packed the faux replica jewelry in a cloth purse that she could give to someone if they were held up. They wouldna know that it wasna real; and hopefully, she would have enough time to get away before anyone realized it was fake. The marriage contract, adoption paperwork and her father's documents from the lawyer and solicitor were already packed. She carried the trunks, one at a time, through the secret passage to the door closest to the hall that led out to the stable. Then, she returned to her room for the next trunk. She continued until she had the trunks lined up in the secret passage.

Her father decided that if anything happened to him, she and Ian would adopt her half-brother and half-sister. He decided Ian and Elisa would raise them as their own, since she had been raising them since Ginger Elisabeth was born. Elisa was very grateful for the arrangement that her father made. She even thanked him. He told her that he couldna trust his brother to ensure their care and he really loved his children, but he just couldna deal with seeing them after his wife died. She thought it was strange the way he called them his children. She was certain he wasna talking about her. She dinna know why, but she just knew.

When she was only an infant, her parents had prearranged her marriage to her mother's best friend's son. She met Ian several times during the seven summers when they travelled to Scotland to visit her mother's childhood home, family and friends. Both, the King of Scotland and the King of England agreed to the prearranged marriage because they felt it was a good idea to try to keep good relations between the two countries and it would help limit raids. It dinna really seem to work except between a few families. With both kings' approval, her father stood in as a proxy for her during the wedding ceremony. Elisa was told, as she was growing up, that Ian was three and he stood in for himself. He was usually nice to her whenever they visited Scotland, but it seemed all so long ago and so much had happened since then. And some of her memories seemed to conflict with others and the whole thing was very confusing.

She was suddenly flooded with memories from her childhood, memories that Ian dinna want her following him around. Sometimes, they played together, but mostly, it seemed that he dinna want her around. The memories showed Duncan encouraging Ian to be with her, more often than not. She dinna understand any of the memories, but she knew that any time she spent with Duncan always resulted in severe beatings from her mother and Ian's mother. She buried the memories. She dinna have time to think about those things right now and she couldna drink while they were on this trip; so, the best thing to do was to nay think about it. Then, she wouldna want to drink to forget, even though she dinna really forget, but it dulled the memories. She needed to focus on listening carefully to everything that was going on around her and try to be as safe and quiet as possible. She couldna do that if she was remembering things she really wished she could forget.

Jonathan would be called Ian now and Elisabeth would be called Elsbeth. She was glad now that she had been teaching them Gaelic, as well as Scots and English. She called them by their Scottish names all the time and she knew that would help them now that they were finally leaving England and would need to refer to each other by their Scottish names. She and Sir Colin could speak Gaelic during their trip and it would help the little ones pick up the language faster. She recalled her stepmom's death during labor, and how she saved Elsbeth and then Ian and Elsbeth became her charges. She had cared for them most of her life. She had never minded caring for her half-brother and half-sister. They were the happiest part of her childhood. She was certain if her father had known that, he wouldna have allowed it, but then she dinna know who would have taken care of them, because their father certainly dinna seem inclined to do so. She needed to stop these memories from invading her thoughts, but they kept coming.

Uncle Kenneth and Cousin Ken came to visit frequently. Her father told her uncle that she was already wed and that she was the guardian of her half-siblings and that when he was gone, everything would be left to Kenneth and Ken, except for their clothes, Elisa's jewelry and all the horses and tack in the stable, as well as the accounts she maintained with her solicitors. Her father also told her uncle that Sir Colin was Elisa's guardian and that he could go wherever Elisa directed him to go. He was free to come and go as she pleased. Her uncle wasna very happy with all the arrangements, but he had no choice in the matter because it was all documented in legal paperwork to prevent her uncle or cousin from taking anything from his children. Her uncle suggested Ken be allowed to spend his summers visiting and learning to care for the estates. But after the first summer, her father became very ill and died.

Her cousin was not a nice person. He tended towards bouts of severe anger and rage. He clearly lacked any moral character and attempted to harm Elisa on numerous occasions. His behavior was very inappropriate as he often tried to kiss her or fondle her. She washed thoroughly after her cousin visited her and she drank to try to wash away the memories of his debauchery. She hated that she was too weak to stop her cousin; and she hated to even think about what Cousin Ken did to her. It was the worst thing she had ever suffered; worse was that he invited his friends to do the same. It was awful and painful and disgusting. She tried to nay think about it because she usually felt she needed to drink to sleep afterwards. A memory of Scripture came to mind about God destroying Sodom and Gomorrah.

Elisa was very grateful that her father taught her the same things any firstborn son was taught to run the estates and her uncle used her skills to allow her the run of his businesses. She dinna enjoy being around her uncle, but he was better than her cousin. And by keeping the businesses and estates so profitable and successful, she kept her cousin at bay. Her uncle kept his son busy traveling to make new contacts and keep their business interests engaged. It provided for her and her siblings. They dinna live excessively, but they dinna have to scrimp just to provide food and clothing anymore. She put most of the profits aside with her solicitors for their future. Actually, it turned out to be quite a bit of the profits. She knew she was quite a wealthy woman. Her father allowed her a percentage of the profits and she invested as much as possible. She thanked God for the knowledge and skills she had. She was certain those skills could only be a gift from God; so, He deserved all the praise and glory.

As soon as her father became ill, she realized the importance of her education, the benefit of knowing more than just what women were taught to manage the daily household. Since very few people knew she had this knowledge, she knew right away this secret knowledge would be helpful to get herself and her charges to Scotland. Other than working with the maids to cook and clean, no one other than Sir Colin really paid any attention to what she did.

It dinna take long to realize the need to defend herself from Cousin Ken's perverse advances. Thankfully, Uncle Ken needed him more than the estates needed his involvement, which were well-run because her father carefully selected well-educated, honest men to run each property. She only needed to review the ledgers with them once a month and if there was some major repair or something new they wanted to try, she discussed it with them and made a decision after asking numerous questions. She was grateful that she had such a good memory so she could follow up with them to determine how the project was going. She mostly ran her uncle's business. She made most of the decisions and organized everything. The only thing she couldna do and wouldna do was deal with anyone from overseas. But, it seemed as long as the funds came in, her uncle and cousin were mostly satisfied and stayed away from the townhouse.

Elisa only had to deal with Ken when he came to town during the London seasons. Unfortunately, these social events led to drinking and betting and he became drunk and belligerent at these events. Her guess was he was then ejected from people's homes and sent packing. At which point, he apparently decided her home was the place to retire to take out his frustrations on her. Apparently, the best way to assuage his temper was to abuse her.

At first, she was afraid to hide in the nursery for fear of what her cousin would do to Ian or Elsbeth; but, she soon learned to bar the nursery door and stay with the children. Ken apparently had no desire to be around any children besides her. So, the nursery turned out to be a safe haven for her. When she needed to get about the townhouse, she utilized the secret passages. But now, Elsbeth was about the age Elisa was when her cousin started chasing her about the house and she was verra worried that the nursery might not be a safe place to hide anymore; or worse, it might lead her cousin to do something to Elsbeth; and Elisa could not bear to think that she might have had any influence in her cousin hurting Elsbeth. The best thing to do was to make her plans and to leave this place. She hoped that getting to her husband in Scotland would keep them safe.

She worked diligently on the preparations, trying to ensure she planned for every possibility during their travels. Most of the groundwork had actually been done in the last year. She knew all her preparations must be kept secret. She wasna sure why or how she knew, but somehow she felt her cousin and uncle wouldna let her go. It made no sense to Elisa for she knew they cared for no one but themselves, and she was already married. Everything already belonged to the two of them, so keeping the three of them here was only costing them money.

Through all the memories, Elisa saw only one person that she trusted and relied on, Sir Colin, their gardener. He also cared for the horses in the stable. She knew that he was a trusted member of her father-in-law's household. Her father-in-law sent Sir Colin home with her after the last summer that she had been in Scotland. She received a very severe beating from her mother; and then, Lady Isobel continued to beat her. She was laid up in bed and cared for by the nursemaid, Alice, for the remainder of the summer. Sir Colin came home with her at the end of the summer. It was his job to help protect her and get her home to Scotland. He protected her from Cousin Ken several times. She knew her cousin had Sir Colin watched closely. This was partly why she suspected Uncle Kenneth and Cousin Ken wouldna let her go.

Elisa's plan relied on Cousin Ken being sent on a long trip for his father's business. Then, Sir Colin, Ian, Elsbeth, and she would set out for Scotland. But first, they needed to be absolutely certain Cousin Ken actually left on his trip and wouldna double back to catch them leaving. For that, she had to rely on Sir Colin and trust that his contacts would actually provide reliable information, even if she dinna like to rely on anyone else, especially a man. For that, she prayed that God would help her to trust Him to provide for all their needs and also that He would help her trust Sir Colin to get them safely through the streets of London.

In the meantime, she had plenty to do while she waited to see if it was going to be safe to set out on their trip to Mull. She got to work making all the preparations while Sir Colin ensured Ken went to the docks. Once Sir Colin was certain Ken was indeed aboard the ship and it sailed, Sir Colin would return to the townhouse for them. Elisa needed to be ready, which meant waking the children in the middle of the night, dressing them and then watching for Sir Colin's return.

Thankfully, it was early spring and this would give them several months to get through England and into Scotland. She wasna really sure how long this trip would take with four of them travelling by horseback and several horses carrying all their trunks of clothes and food and water. Elisa was grateful her father had stipulated in his will that she owned the horses and not her cousin. He provided for them as best he could, she supposed. If they could just get to her husband in Scotland, renew their vows, and sign the adoption paperwork, then they would be free of her uncle and her cousin.

Elisa quickly made her way through the secret passages and stairwells to the nursery. Listening carefully for any sounds, she let herself into the nursery. She wasna expecting anyone to be in the nursery as she was the only one who cared for Ian and Elsbeth, but she needed to be cautious anyway. She certainly dinna want to be caught leaving London and she dinna want anyone to know about the secret passages. It was the only thing that kept her safe from Cousin Ken most of the time when he was visiting the townhouse.

Elisa quietly barred the nursery door. Then, she gently woke the children and helped them dress. She brushed out their hair and braided Elsbeth's hair. She told them they had to be quieter than they had ever been before because their lives depended on it. They couldna tell anyone what they were doing or where they were going. They were eager to go on a trip after she told them they were going on a secret mission for the king to bring some important documents to her husband. They were very cooperative. As soon as they were dressed, they watched through the window for Sir Colin's return to the garden. She opened one of the windows just slightly so they could hear any noises from the garden. It wasna long before she saw Sir Colin cross the garden and head to the stables. He gave a bird call.

She called back to him with her own whistled bird call and closed the window, removed the bar from the door, and ushered the children into the secret passageway and they made their way to her storage room. She put the children's cloaks on them and clasped them before she gave them each a satchel, a bedroll, and a waterskin. She showed them how to drape the items over their shoulder so they could carry everything easily and still have their hands free to carry a trunk. Then, she put on her cloak and gathered the satchels, bedrolls, and waterskins for Sir Colin and herself.

She stacked everything on top of one of her trunks and carried it down the stairs. The children worked together to carry the other trunk. She stressed to them again the need to be very quiet, so they couldna drop the trunk or let it bang against the wall or the stairs. If they needed to stop and rest, they should whisper quietly to each other and very gently set down the trunk. They quietly made their way through the secret passages to the hall nearest the garden. This was as close as they could get to the stables secretly. Elisa carefully made her way from the passageway down the hallway to the garden door. She verified the hall was clear and checked for anyone in the garden before she returned for Ian and Elsbeth; and then, they made their way to the garden. They stayed in the shadows as much as possible until they reached the stables. She made several trips back to the passage to get the remaining trunks.

Sir Colin saddled the horses while he waited for Elisa to bring the children to the stable. They added their bundles to each saddle and tied the waterskins to the pummels while Sir Colin tied the last two trunks onto the back of one of the horses. Then, Elisa and Sir Colin helped Ian and Elsbeth mount their own horses. Sir Colin helped Elisa mount. As soon as he mounted, they set out through a private path and a secret gate in the garden.

Elisa did her best to trust Sir Colin to get them through the streets of London as she rarely left the house. She was terrified they would be accosted, or worse, they'd be caught by her cousin or one of his men. Again, she said a prayer for their safety and success reaching Scotland.

Sir Colin assured her Ken had indeed set sail on the evening tide and also they wouldna have to worry about the man who watched Sir Colin because he was tied up and staying with a close friend of his. This did verra little to alleviate her fears. She was quite certain she wouldna feel any relief from her fears until she was within Laird Ian's keep on Mull.

Sir Colin agreed that they should travel without stopping the first few days. This would allow them to go at an even pace but anyone following would likely stop at night to rest. Pursuers would probably ride hard after them, but they would have to stop frequently for fresh horses. Since they had been riding for long periods of time every day in the garden, the horses were also accustomed to the increased activity. Luck would have it that the weather was clear and the moon was nearly full, so they would have a full moon or nearly so for several nights while they rode without stopping. It was a good thing and Elisa prayed. She thanked Him for the timing of the full moon, her skills and abilities to prepare ahead of time. She prayed for His will to be done as she hoped God was on their side.

She wasna sure if she could trust anyone within the household so she had no way of knowing if anyone would try to send a message to Ken or if someone would pursue without his orders. Or perhaps, they already had orders to track her down if she was missing. They could only hope no one knew they were gone until breakfast time. They would at least have several hours head start.

Since Elisa packed enough provisions for a fortnight, they wouldna need to stop at inns along the way to eat. They could travel for a sennight or two before Sir Colin would need to enter a town and replenish their food stores; and, the two of them could hunt. They could travel smaller roads to avoid towns and limit their contact with people, which was fine with Elisa because she was too afraid of being caught and dragged back to London. She had no doubts about what her cousin would do to her if he caught her and brought her back to London and she wasna sure how much more of his abuse she could take. She just wanted to get across the border to Scotland.

Sir Colin led the way through the city. He tethered the horses carrying the trunks to his horse and they provided a buffer between the children and the side of the street. The children each rode their own horse in the center of their little party. Elisa rode last and tried to be alert to anyone following them. She watched the streets and alleys around them for anyone who might attack them. She really hoped they could get through London without any incidents or attacks. The streets were mostly dark and the shadows in the doorways could hide anyone. She was terrified, but she couldna let it show. She couldna let it rule her emotions, so she boxed up her feelings in one part of her mind and shut the box. She envisioned the box was locked and buried deep.

Once they were outside the city limits, Elisa took the lead and tethered the horses to her saddle. They rode for three nights and three days only stopping to attend to the horses and their personal needs. They only stopped long enough to unsaddle all the horses, brush down the horses until they were cool and then let the horses eat and drink while the four people took care of private matters and ate a little food from their satchels and drank a little water. Elisa ensured all the waterskins were filled and packed in the trunk and each of them had a full waterskin on their saddle. Elisa brushed out the children's hair and braided Elsbeth's again. Then, she took care of herself while Sir Colin ensured the horses were saddled and everything was secure before they set out again. When Sir Colin was tired, they stopped and rested for two to three hours. The children seemed to be so excited about the journey, she wasna sure they would be able to sleep. But, she was able to get them to lie down and close their eyes. Eventually, they fell asleep while she sang quietly to them. She felt badly about waking them, but they needed to keep moving. They had to put as much space as possible between them and London each day and night as they continued on their journey north.

They often rode double so little Ian and Elsbeth could sleep. This allowed them to keep going because if the horses were tired, they just doubled up on the children's horses. Elisa did her best to stay alert and watch around her as they rode. She wished more than anything that she had a hundred guards surrounding them. They had to be alert and listen for anyone else traveling near them. Then, they needed to duck into the woods around them and out of sight. Thankfully, it was still too early in the year for people to travel and they dinna run into many people.

The children were verra cooperative and played along with their secret mission for the king. This kept them occupied and kept them from complaining too much. She made it a game for the children and she told them stories and asked them questions about what they should do in different situations to keep the children occupied and interested, but also to keep them thinking about how to handle any situation she could think of that might happen to them while they were on this trip. She also asked them questions about the direction they were heading and explained how they could tell the direction based on the time of the day, the shadow on the ground and where the sun was in the sky.

They made good progress and had a good routine going. She was always up and prepared their breakfast before the sky even turned gray. They ate and took care of themselves and their private needs. She and Sir Colin saddled the horses and loaded the trunks on the other horses.

They mounted and set out just as the sky was turning gray each morning. They rode for a few hours and stopped for a bite of fruit, bread or cheese or dried meat and a drink before they switched horses and set out again. Then, they rode for a few more hours before they stopped for a lunch break. They switched horses and set out again and continued with three hours of riding, a break and then, they switched horses before they set out again. They rode until dark or if they had enough moonlight, they rode until midnight. Elisa helped unpack and unsaddle the horses and brushed them out before she ensured the children and Sir Thomas had food if they were hungry. Then, she took the first watch if they stopped early, so Sir Colin could sleep. Then, she slept two or three hours before she woke and let Sir Colin sleep again while she did as much of the preparations as she could without assistance.

She was still anxious to reach the border, but she couldna help but have a little hope as each day passed and no one caught up with them to try to take them back to London. Each morning, she prayed God would keep them all safe and the weather would not hinder them and they would be able to follow the prearranged plan, if it was His will. Every night, she thanked God for His safety and protection and guidance.

The children were thrilled with being outside because so much of their life so far had been confined to the nursery and the garden. They were privileged to have a very large garden even though they lived in the city, but it was nothing compared to the open spaces they rode through each day. They stayed mostly to the west as much as possible and kept to the least populated areas. As much as she was able,

Elisa tried to ride in the woods so they wouldna be seen by anyone else. Elisa pointed out landmarks and homes of the nobility that she knew. It helped to entertain the children and keep them alert. She couldna help but appreciate the beauty of the landscape they rode through. She loved being out in nature. She felt close to God being out in His creation. She loved all different areas, the marshes, the coast, the mountains. She especially loved the mountains.

They tried to cover the open fields during the night, hoping no one would see them. The woods during the day were beautiful with the sun's rays descending through the trees, the light dappling her face with the breeze blowing through the branches. It was difficult to focus on watching their surroundings. She thanked God for the beauty of His creation and for all His guidance and help as they travelled and also for the good weather they were having and for everyone's safety and health. She hoped and prayed that she was following His will and not just her own plan.

The beautiful woods reminded Elisa of her last summer in Scotland, but then the other memories tried to invade her mind and she envisioned boxing them up and locking the box in her mind. She couldna allow her mind to be overrun with memories that would prevent her from paying attention to where they were going or make her too fearful to want to go on. Her memories of Mull werena exactly the best of memories either and many of them conflicted with each other and confused her, so she tried to nay think about it.

She wasna sure what to expect when she showed up on Mull to make her marriage to Ian official; Ian hadna exactly welcomed her with open arms when she visited, and her parents and his mother spent most of the day trying to teach her things and beating her for any little infraction. She couldna determine exactly what her husband would think or feel about her arrival; she wasna sure if she would really be welcome, but she knew she wouldna tolerate little Ian and Elsbeth being treated as she was. She blocked out those memories. She couldna allow any distractions that might prevent them from getting to Mull.

They travelled as much as the horses would allow each day. She tried to keep the pace as steady as possible and switched horses after three hours. It worked well to ride double and let Ian and Elsbeth sleep and then switch horses every few hours to let the other horses rest. She just wanted to cover as much ground as possible in a day and get as far from London as possible. She really dinna want to be caught. They mostly slept in forested areas where it seemed safest. She kept watch most of the night and only slept from midnight to about three. She slept in the top of a tree with a rope suspended around a couple of branches to create a hammock. When she woke, she climbed down with her things and let Sir Colin sleep a few more hours while she prepared the camp for departure. Sometimes, she looked for eggs for their breakfast or she hunted for small game they could eat for breakfast or their dinner that night.

When they stopped for the night, she helped Sir Colin take care of the horses. Then, she made dinner for all of them. If water was nearby, she refilled their waterskins and swapped out the fresh ones with the waterskins in the trunk. Then, she ensured she and the children took care of their needs before she climbed high in a tree and wrapped a rope around two branches and placed the cape with the brown side down between the branches over the rope and tied the cape to the branches creating a pocket between their cape and their plaid to sleep in. Then, they covered themselves with their blankets from their bedrolls. This way, they couldna really be seen from below and they were away from the ground, attackers, and predators. She and the children slept up in the top of a tree with each of their beds set up between two branches.

The white side of the cloak was so they could travel through the highlands if they dinna get to Mull before the snow melted or after it started again in the fall. The white side of the cloak would disguise them a bit, especially if they needed to hide on the ground or among the rocks during a snow storm. They would be warm from the fur and also disguised inside their white cloaks. They could sit verra still and nay be seen if it was necessary.

Elisa did her best to plan for any situation. She carried many daggers hidden in her clothes and even in her hair. She had a bow and a quiver of arrows so she could hunt for small game or use for protection. She had a small sword that she could use if necessary. She had two pins that held her bun in place, but they were really daggers that were verra sharp and she could pull them free and stab an attacker if it was required of her. She sometimes thought about what she might need to do if she needed to protect herself or the children just to be sure she was prepared. She was certain she would do anything she had to in order to protect Ian and Elsbeth. She would nay ever allow them to be treated as she was treated. However, she would gladly suffer whatever she must to protect them.

She woke early in the morning and looked for a stream. She hunted and provided something for the four of them to eat. She built a small fire, cleaned and cooked whatever she hunted. Some days, it was a bird or a rabbit or even fish. She knew if it was necessary she could hunt a deer and prepare it. She would need a bigger fire so she could cook all the meat and then she would put it in the trunk in the satchels. She really dinna want to ruin her trunk's interior, but that would be the only way to carry such a large amount of meat. They might need the meat, but they dinna have time to dry it so it would last longer.

The days and miles passed slowly and Elisa was both anxious about how long it was taking and excited about how far they had come. She wouldna feel comfortable about the distance between her and London. She refused to let down her guard. She still tried hard to keep alert to anyone on the trails around them. She really dinna want to come across any other parties that might say something about how unusual it was to see an older man traveling with a young lady and two children and horses loaded down with trunks. They were too obvious and recognizable if they were seen. It would be too easy for anyone to describe their party to her cousin and he would be hot on their trail.

She kept to smaller trails that ran parallel to the main roads. She skirted around any towns. She tried to explain to the children where they were or what towns they were near. She traveled until late at night before they stopped and set up their camp. Thankfully, she was so accustomed to only sleeping about three hours a night that she could take the first watch while Sir Colin slept. Then, she would sleep a few hours and wake up. She would tell him to sleep a couple more hours. When she knew he was sleeping, she would slip out of the tree and pack up her things. She would take care of her private needs and then hunt or prepare their breakfast.

She was a really good cook since she spent a great deal of her time helping in the kitchen. She dinna have a lot to work with, but she gathered eggs from the nests in the nearby trees and made fresh eggs for the children and Sir Colin to eat for breakfast. Sir Colin rarely asked if she ate anything. She supposed that he just assumed that she took care of her needs. Since she was so small, she assumed no one really paid that much attention to what she did, except her evil cousin, but his reasons were for his vile purposes.

She ate, but it was usually a minimal amount. She dinna usually prepare herself the same thing she made for Sir Colin and the children. They were more in need of sustenance than she was. She was used to going without or making do with what little she had. She usually ensured everyone else was fed before she ate and if there wasna enough to eat she would just eat an apple and a bit of bread or a piece of cheese. At lunch and dinner, she would eat some meat, either the dried meat she packed in her trunk; or a little of what she hunted and cooked, if there was enough for everyone. Since it was spring, the small game tended to be small; so she went without more often than not.

The eggs were plentiful. She looked for mushrooms and herbs and added them to the eggs that she scrambled up and fried with a bit of meat and cheese. Sometimes, she sliced the bread thin and cut cheese to set between the slices and heated it over the fire. It was actually very tasty fare for their traveling situation.

By the end of the second sennight, the children were getting a little bored with their travels and Elisa asked them to name as many things in nature as they could. Then, she asked them to tell her the same thing in Gaelic and Scots. She turned their travels into lessons to keep the children occupied. They dinna complain much after that. She wasna sure how much of her life they understood, but they seemed to sense that it wasna easy for her and they rarely complained because they realized that she made their life much easier than hers was. Elisa was glad to do for her little brother and sister.

Elisa tried to keep Ian and Elsbeth occupied by having them use each word in a sentence. Then, she asked them to try to use all the words in a conversation. When they questioned her, she explained that it would help them understand the people they would be living with when they reached Mull. Most people might not realize that they understood what they were saying and they could learn what others were saying and gain information or knowledge or they could surprise them with their knowledge and speak to them in their language.

The children liked the idea of keeping their skill to themselves and gaining information or knowledge. They said it went along with their mission to serve the kings. Elisa then explained that it would be fine until they reached Mull; but then, it would be dishonest to keep it a secret that they understood what others were saying. These were people with whom they were going to live and they would be their family and clan, so they shouldna want to keep secrets from them, at least not that they understood them.

She enjoyed listening to the children speak in Gaelic and she helped them to get their accent right. Sir Colin was very helpful in that area and he was glad to speak in his native tongue. She could tell by the smile on his face and the tone of his voice; it was just full of happiness. And, she could feel it, but she dinna ken what that really meant; only that she knew he was happy to speak Gaelic and to be returning to Scotland. Elisa enjoyed riding along listening to the three of them talk. She was warmed by Sir Colin's accent. It just made her feel like she was almost home.

During the third sennight of their travels, they knew they were very close to the Scottish border and they spoke almost entirely in Gaelic. Elisa camped just north and west of a village. She stayed with the children and set up their camp. She hunted and prepared their dinner. She took the children to the stream and let them bathe. She asked Ian to keep watch while she helped Elsbeth undress and bathe and Elisa washed Elsbeth's hair. Then, Elisa helped Elsbeth dress again and sat brushing out Elsbeth's hair while Jonathan washed. She brushed Elsbeth's hair until it was completely dry and then she braided it and tied a ribbon around the end of her braids. Then, she held Elsbeth close to her while she listened for any noise around them.

Jonathan hummed their bedtime lullaby so Elisa knew that he was still there and safe. She knew that he was old enough to want some privacy while he dressed and she wanted to be sure that he gave Elsbeth that same courtesy. She wasna concerned that he would try to hurt his sister, the way Elisa's cousin hurt her, but she dinna want to encourage them to watch each other change either. She just preferred to be careful and cautious.

Sir Colin took the money she gave him and their satchels and skirted around to the far side of the village to purchase more supplies. They were running low on food and the horses needed more grain. They wouldna be able to fill up her trunk with food again; so now, Sir Colin would have to stop in a village for supplies every few days. She made sure she was armed and prepared while Sir Colin was gone.

She dinna like being away from Sir Colin; she had become quite attached to him without even realizing it. He was more of a father to her than her father had ever been. Well, her father taught her a great many things. She was well educated, beyond anything most other women would ever know. But, he beat the knowledge into her and the best lesson she learned from him was how to take a beating without crying or making a sound. She learned to be quick and unnoticed as much as possible. She learned that being small could protect her and it meant that her father had a smaller area to aim at when he was beating her.

She learned the things her parents wanted her to learn because she liked learning and she enjoyed knowing how to do so many things. She challenged herself to read every book in the library, which she did; and, there were hundreds of them. She knew how to do many things. She could tan leather. She could cook and clean. She could make candles and soap. She could knit and crochet and sew. She made her own clothes and the children's clothes, including breeches for them to wear when they were out-of-doors or training. She could sheer sheep and card and clean the wool and make it into yarn with or without a spindle. She could take a couple sticks and rub them together to make a fire or she could whittle them down to make her own knitting needles or crochet hooks. She could shop in the market to provide food for the family or hunt and fish and clean the meat and prepare it to store it for winter. She was just as capable in a kitchen as she was around a campfire.

Her favorite things to do were to maintain the ledgers and to inventory and organize the merchandise that came to her uncle's shop. She enjoyed taking the orders and making the list of purchases the captain would be required to acquire on his trip and then, ensuring it was delivered to the person who acquired it. She had really improved the ability of the captains to get more purchases in their ships and get their ships back to London more often. She talked to them about the weather and the currents and discussed different routes and times of the year to travel to certain areas. They may have been annoyed with all her questions, until her suggestions paid off. She rewarded those that were willing to cooperate with her and do things her way. She liked when things were planned out and organized and done her way. She did the same thing with the estate managers to improve the estates and the crops and the breeding of the livestock so that everything was verra profitable. She profited from that and invested her savings. The people on the estates, the ship captains, and her uncle and cousin benefitted from the improvements she worked towards. Her uncle and her cousin really only had to rely on the captains and the estate managers to continue on as she did and they would still be verra profitable. They dinna really need her, if they would but put in a little effort.

She accomplished a great number of things that others werena able to do. She even spent time in the garden with Sir Colin and learned about plants. He had a friend that taught her how to use different plants and herbs to heal wounds and injuries. She dinna really have anyone to practice on but she knew the knowledge would be there when she needed it, since she never seemed to forget anything she saw or heard or read about.

She dinna really ken it, but she dinna feel proud of her accomplishments. It was all tarnished by the fact that her parents beat her and she felt like somehow she didn't do what they wanted or she didn't do it as well as she could have.

She broke free of her morose thoughts and envisioned stuffing them back in the box and locking it shut. She needed to figure out a way to stop letting her mind drift back to those memories; stop ruminating on the past. She gathered their belongings. They returned from the stream to the camp she set up and waited for Sir Colin to return to them. When it got close to dark, she helped the children up the tree, set up their beds, and tucked them into their bedrolls. She sang the lullaby to them in a low voice. She really dinna want to sing out loud, but she sang to the children every night before bed without fail.

She stayed in the tree and was quiet after the children went to sleep. She tried to watch the woods around them and in front of them. Mostly, she listened for any sounds that anyone was approaching them. She dinna relax until she heard a bird call that she was certain was Sir Colin letting her know that he was near. She whistled her own bird call and was silent again.

Sir Colin stepped into the little clearing near the base of the tree she was in. Elisa climbed down to meet him. She unpacked the satchels and packed things the way she wanted them organized. She put some food in each satchel so they always had food with them. If for some reason they were separated, they each had food and water available to them. If necessary, Ian and Elsbeth could survive without them, although they wouldna know how to get to Mull, but they could continue on the path until they reached the next village. Then, Elisa served Sir Colin dinner and let him go to sleep. She packed up the supplies and ensured everything would be ready if they had to load up the horses and ride quickly. She really couldna afford to leave the trunks behind. They contained something verra valuable that she dinna think anyone knew she owned. She wasna sure where the heirlooms came from or how they were given to her, but they were hidden in compartments in the bottoms and sides of each of the trunks. Things she was certain were worth a lot of money, but also were verra significant, even if she dinna ken the significance of the items. Because really, how many jewels and crowns and tiaras did a young lady need? She, personally, dinna need any of them. She never wore such things.

She let Sir Colin sleep for three hours and listened for the sounds of anyone nearby in the woods or approaching them. She woke him so she could sleep for a few hours. But, she woke herself up before the nightmares could start and she told Sir Colin he could sleep until they were ready to ride in the morning. She never liked to sleep more than three hours because then she had nightmares about the beatings she received from her parents and Lady Isobel.

She dreamed about the tests her parents put her through and the nightmares always ended with the things Cousin Ken and his friends did to her. She couldna make them stop and she hated that she couldna control it. The only control she had over the nightmares was to sleep for only three hours. Then, she wouldna have them. If they dinna start, she wouldna cry out or thrash about in her sleep. She wouldna wake anyone else and she wouldna try to hurt anyone for trying to wake her.

She got out of her bed and stood on a branch in the top of the tree and took apart her bed. She climbed down, careful to nay fall and also to ensure the branch would support her weight before she continued down to the next branch. She put away all of her things and brushed out her hair and braided it again. She pinned it up with her dagger pins. She put away her brush and put on her sword and daggers. She took her bow and quiver and went towards the stream so she could look for anything they might have for breakfast.

She returned to camp and prepared breakfast. She got the children up and helped Elsbeth get ready for the day. She let Ian go off by himself to get ready, but she warned him to be close enough he could call for her or whistle to her if he needed help.

Just because they hadna encountered anyone yet, dinna mean they wouldna. She dinna want the children to be captured and used to get to her. She wasna entirely sure that her cousin was sane with his erratic behavior, so she wasna sure what harm he might do to the children.

Once the children were ready, she woke Sir Colin and had his breakfast waiting. She saddled the horses while he ate and had some privacy. She would have tried to load the horses with the trunks, but she couldna hold the trunks and tie them down at the same time, so she waited for Sir Colin to help her. They worked together to load the trunks on the horses. Then, they helped the children mount and they mounted and set out for the day. They were usually on the trail an hour before the sunrise. Then, the routine of the previous day began again; ride for three hours and take a break and eat and drink a little something and then switch horses and ride for another three hours. She helped Sir Colin brush out the horses while they took a break before they saddled the horses and set out again. They continued until dark or later.

Chapter 3

ONCE THEY REACHED Scotland, they added their plaids to their attire. She started to relax just a little; but now, she had another fear. If there was some kind of clan feud, they might be in danger if they met other clans out on raids. But mostly, their travels were going well and they continued to make good progress, for which she thanked the Lord. She dinna want to think about it too much. She needed to learn to trust God to provide for her and her family. She was grateful that the weather had been good so far on their trip. She wished she could spend more time enjoying the view of the countryside, but she dinna have the luxury. She saw the landscape and it was beautiful but it was vital to watch her surroundings for attackers until they got to Laird Ian's and away from Cousin Ken; so he couldna hurt her anymore or try to hurt Elsbeth or harm young Ian. Before she allowed any of those thoughts to settle in her mind, she envisioned the black box and put the memories into the compartments and shut the box and locked it. She focused on the landscape to identify where they needed to go and to ensure no one was lurking in the woods near them. She listened to the noises of the woods so she could hear if the animals gave away their location, or let them know of another's location, or if it was too quiet.

She kept to her routine of rising early and preparing everything so they were ready to go as soon as Sir Colin woke, ate and was ready. She thrived on routine; that and keeping so busy her mind dinna have time to think about the memories that became her nightmares.

She was beginning to feel the stress of worrying about being followed and whether they might run into any other clans before they reached Laird Ian's keep. She felt very tired from the emotional stress. She wasna entirely sure how she would be received and she couldna allow herself to think about the times when she visited Mull in the past. For some odd reason that she couldna ken, she felt like she wasna following the prearranged plan and she was doing something wrong. She dinna like to be wrong. As far back as she could recall, every time they went to Scotland, they went to Mull, to Ian's family to visit and continue her education and discipline. That was the only place she knew to go; so, that was where she led them.

They reached Argyll Woods and set up camp for the night. Elisa was a little excited about making it this far. It meant they only had a couple more days to ride. But, she was fearful of the dense woods. There were too many places to hide. They could ride into an ambush before they realized they were in danger or even realized they were being watched. She tried to bury her fear and focus on watching and listening to their surroundings. She reminded herself that Ian and Elsbeth relied on her and that she couldna let her fear show. She had to be strong for them and ensure they reached the safety of Ian's castle.

After dinner, Sir Colin convinced Elisa to drink a little bit of scotch. He insisted that she needed to sleep more than her usual three hours since she would meet her husband in the next couple of days. He insisted she climb the tree and settle in her bed for the night and he would cover the watch. He climbed up the tree behind her to ensure she dinna lose her balance. Then, he helped the children into their beds and he warned them to nay drink from the waterskin that he was leaving with their mother. Then, he told them only to leave the tree to attend to their needs and to return to their beds as quickly as possible before he ensured they each had a full waterskin and their satchels were full of food.

"Ian, some men will come and surround the tree you are in. Dinna be afraid of them. I will tell them who you are. They are your cousins, so they will keep you safe until I can return with Laird Ian. When they arrive, give them your whistle. Then, they will respond with my whistle. You remember what my whistle sounds like?"

"Aye, I remember what your whistle sounds like. I will try to be brave and ensure Elsbeth is safe when she needs to climb down from the tree."

"You should stay in the tree until the men arrive to guard you."

"Aye," the children replied.

Sir Colin left them and made his way to Laird Argyll. He asked if he could send a few men to guard Lady Elisa and the children and when Laird Argyll agreed, he gave him a description of their location. Laird Argyll said he knew the place and would lead the men himself, but he would ensure they were nearly invisible after initially announcing their presence. Sir Colin explained what they would have to do to announce themselves so the children would know they were there to guard them and nay a threat. Then, Sir Colin set out again for Mull. It took another day to reach Laird Ian.

Laird Ian and his men set out the next morning to meet up with Laird Argyll and Lady Elisa. They arrived at the camp just before nightfall. They spoke with Laird Argyll and his men and enjoyed a big campfire and dinner with their cousins before they set up their bedrolls around the fire for the night. Laird Argyll agreed to keep the watch since they had the least distance to travel and that would allow Laird Ian's men to be rested for their longer journey.

In the morning, the men made breakfast and broke camp. Ian thanked Argyll for his protection, especially for watching Lady Elisa and the children and eliminating their enemies. Argyll's men returned to their keep before Ian decided to wake Lady Elisa.

One morning, she overslept. The sun was bright and well past the horizon. She was awakened by an unknown male voice. She drew her dagger to protect herself and held it firmly out in front of her with the blade pointed at the man. She was so tired. She dinna want to wake up. But she had no idea who this man was that was talking to her. His words just couldna reach her because she was too tired to think straight. But then, she heard another voice speaking. It took a few minutes for the sound to penetrate the fog in her brain and she recognized Sir Colin saying from below, "Be careful, she doesna like anyone to wake her and she is always armed. Dinna get too close or she will stab you." She couldna imagine who Sir Colin would share this information with, because if this man intended to harm her, Sir Colin wouldna warn him.

"Aye, Sir Colin, thank you for the warning, but tis too late now," he chuckled and the men below laughed as well. He wasna worried about disarming such a wee lass. He focused his attention on Lady Elisa and watched for an opportunity to relieve her of her dagger.

Sir Colin's comments helped Elisa to crawl out of her grogginess. She opened her eyes to a really large and muscular man. He was quite handsome and a little rugged looking. His chest was probably twice the width of her shoulders and his arms were the size of the branches with which she anchored her bed. He was like a wall, all muscle from the tightness of his tunic. He had a smirk on his lips which told her he likely had a mischievous streak. It completely disarmed Elisa. Her stomach did a flip. She was shocked that her body responded to him. She avoided men except for those she was forced to deal with for business or estate matters. The only man she really liked was Sir Colin. She dinna have time to deal with men, especially men with a mischievous disposition. She dinna need any trouble that might cause a problem for her husband and his family. She needed to wake up and put this grogginess behind her and pack up so they could be on their way to her husband.

Elisa was so embarrassed because she couldna imagine what she looked like. She always woke with her hair in complete disarray. It couldna be pretty. Perhaps, this was what gave him the smirk; or mayhap, it was seeing her wake with her dagger drawn. She dinna know what caused him to smirk, but the attraction it caused her was alarming. She was certain she wouldna have a chance against him. "I am pretty good with this weapon, sir," she warned.

He said in a deep voice, his Scottish accent a thick brogue, "Good morning, m' lady. Aye, I am sure you are pretty good with that weapon, especially if Sir Colin trained you; but you wouldna be any match for me. I am Laird Ian McVeigh. I am sorry to wake you and startle you, but we must be going."

She dinna know if Laird Ian could tell how much she was affected by his good looks but his deep brogue made her speechless and her stomach was all aflutter. Her chest felt tight and she had trouble taking in enough air to actually breathe. She wasna affected by any other men who came to her father's estates and certainly nay her cousin, Ken. But this man was her husband and she was apparently deeply affected by him.

"M' Laird," she squeaked out, as she sat up and patted her hair. "I will need a few minutes to get ready." But he just kept looking at her. So she looked around for her brush and started working on her hair until it could be braided and pinned up. There wasna much else she could do about her appearance until she climbed down from the tree, but first she needed to loosen the ropes that held her cape. "You can climb down now, m' laird. I need the branch you are on," she said. He moved to a different branch. She folded her cloak over her shoulder and rolled up the rope and climbed down the tree after she used the rope to anchor her cloak and satchel in place. Elisa hadna any idea what her husband thought of her behavior, but she was sure it wasna the proper behavior of the laird's wife.

Nay exactly the way she wanted her first meeting in many years with her husband to go. It had been eleven years since she had seen him last. When her laird husband climbed down from the tree, he was busy talking with his men and making preparations to be off. She needed to eat; but more importantly, she needed a bit of privacy even though she was afraid to go off alone. She was nay sure how Ian would react. She also dinna know if she should offer to feed him and his men. She hadna any idea how long they had been waiting for her to wake up.

She couldna wait any longer, she needed her privacy. So she started to walk away from all the men. Sir Colin and she had such a good routine. He had been her only friend for a long time, but now he seemed like one of her husband's men. It saddened her at the first realization, but then she buried her feelings and remembered that she had been taking care of herself since she was eight and she dinna need anyone. Men were nay her friends, but she wouldna let anyone know her feelings. She was good at keeping her expression whatever she wished people to think she felt, happy, compliant, submissive. She was fine. She dinna need anyone. She survived for ten years without anyone to take care of her or her siblings and she certainly dinna needed the childhood that she had, but it taught her what she needed to do to survive, so she thanked God for the trials that taught her to be so strong and self-sufficient.

As she walked away from the men, she realized how quiet it was. Then, Sir Colin said, "Wait a moment, m' laird. It will be alright. She just needs a bit of privacy. No one will harm her. She is prepared to defend herself if it's necessary."

While she had a few moments of privacy, she straightened her top and her riding habit, checked her hair again and returned to her horse. She gathered all her things and arranged them on the back of the saddle and tied them down. She just looked at Laird Ian until she caught his eye.

When he approached her, she asked, "Have your men broken their fast? Do you want me to make something for everyone?"

He chuckled, "Nay, m' lady, we have all eaten, but you should eat and then we should depart."

She replied, "Aye, m' laird. Have little Ian and Elsbeth eaten?"

"Aye," he said.

"Thank you, m' laird," she said. "I dinna usually sleep so late, I dinna ken why I did so; and now, I am still a little groggy. I am sorry that I am delaying our start."

"It's quite alright, m' lady," He said and returned to his men.

Elisa ate an apple and shared a bit with her horse, Magnum. Then, she had a few bites of bread and cheese. Afterwards, she went to Elsbeth and ensured she was ready to go and had everything she needed. She asked her, "Do you want to ride your horse or do you want to ride with me?"

Elsbeth said, "I want to ride with you, Mother. It's a little intimidating around all these big men. It's kind of scary."

"I know just what you mean; it makes you feel uncertain when before, you were quite confident," she replied. So, Elisa walked Elsbeth's horse to hers and tied the reins to the pummel of her saddle. Then, she lifted Elsbeth up onto Magnum.

Suddenly, she felt hands on her waist. She quickly turned around with her dagger drawn and told Ian, "M' laird, I know we are married but we dinna really know each other. I havena seen you for many years. I dinna blame you, but you must never approach me quietly, dinna sneak up on me. It is verra likely that I will try to harm anyone who tries to touch me without my permission. You mustna ever do that again because it might be bad for both of us. I am sure there are consequences for challenging the laird of the clan, but I dinna grow up with your ways so I dinna know all your clan rules. You dinna know what I have been through and you need to respect my need to be aware of your presence before you approach me."

Ian gently clasped her hand with the dagger and replied, "We will discuss all this later. Are you ready to mount your horse and be off?" He noticed she dinna relinquish the dagger, but still held it firmly in her grasp. He was glad that she seemed well trained.

"Aye, m' laird," she said and she tucked her dagger back in her sleeve and turned towards Magnum. Ian lifted her up so she could swing into the saddle. Sir Colin was helping little Ian onto his own horse and soon everyone was mounted. And then, they started out on their journey to Laird Ian's keep.

Sir Colin stayed near Elisa most of the day, except if Laird Ian asked him to ride with him. They seemed to have a lot to talk about. Occasionally, Laird Ian would glance back at Elisa. She wasna sure if he was checking to see if she was still there, seeing if she was doing alright, or if it was just the natural thing to do because they were talking about her. Laird Ian probably had many questions about his wife and her unusual behaviors.

Elisa only had a bit of correspondence with her mother-in-law, Lady Isobel, after her mother died. She gave her letters to Sir Colin and replies were received through him, as well. She never questioned how he got the messages back and forth, but she knew he was never away from the garden long enough to deliver them himself. Elisa dinna realize he had friends he trusted so close by in London. She just never thought about it. She only knew he was always there for her and he did his best to protect her from her abusive cousin. She was very grateful for his protection.

Now, she wondered how much he really knew and what he would tell the laird. Would he keep her secrets? Would he tell if she asked him to? It was then she realized that she would have to tell her husband about what her cousin and his friends had done to her or she wouldna be able to go through with their marriage. She also needed to be sure he knew about the adoption papers and ensure he agreed to all this before they reaffirmed their vows. She would have to find time to talk to him privately about these things before they arrived home. Mayhap, he wouldna want to marry her after all she'd been through.

Home. That was a nice thought. She might finally be home. What was his home like? She had never been there. She had only been to his parents' home. She hoped he had his own home and she wouldna have to live in the same keep as Lady Isobel. She dinna really think about that before she set out on this endeavor.

While Sir Colin rode with Laird Ian, Sir Duncan rode on her left and Angus rode on her right. They asked casual questions about their trip so far. Sir Duncan asked, "Do you like climbing trees and sleeping up in the top?"

"Well, I climbed trees when I was a girl and I felt it was safer than being on the ground. I just preferred what felt safest, out of harms reach. It might have been better to travel with guards, but I dinna know whom we could trust; so I felt it was best to travel with just the four of us. We havena had any trouble so far. I dinna know what would be normal weather, but it has been warm enough to sleep out overnight and it doesna seem that cold to me. We havena had any rain, only sunshine throughout our trip. We even had clear nights the first few nights when we left London, which was a good thing because it was near the full moon and we were able to travel all through the day and night for several days, only stopping to rest the horses and brush them out. Then, feed and water them before we saddled them again and packed the trunks on the others and started out again."

Angus said, "Little Ian said that you are always armed. Is that true?"

"Aye, it is true. I have been in situations that I had to defend myself, so I have found that it is easiest if I have some kind of weapon. Women's clothing provides lots of cover for weapons."

Sir Duncan responded, "That is interesting. You should fit in quite well with Laird Ian's life. You can ride and protect yourself. Sir Colin said you did most of the hunting during the trip so far and you had breakfast ready every morning when he woke, except for today."

"I dinna ken why I slept so much last night or why I was so tired and groggy this morning. I dinna want to wake up at all. That never happens," Elisa said. She dinna see the two men glance at each other over the top of her head since they were so much taller than her.

Angus said, "Aye, Sir Colin said you sleep verra little most nights and you took most of the watches and he slept quite comfortably. He even said you did most of the preparations for the trip. He also said you did a wonderful job keeping the little ones going and they hardly complained because you kept them interested by making the whole trip into a secret mission for the king. That is amazing."

Sir Duncan said, "Aye, Sir Colin said this morning was the only time he heard you complain about being tired."

Elisa interrupted, "I dinna remember saying anything about being tired."

Sir Duncan responded, "M' laird said you might have been talking in your sleep. He said you dinna look awake and he said he was pretty certain you were asleep when you said that because you had a very specific response when you woke up."

She answered, "Sir Colin is full of praises for me, but the truth is, I couldna even make it out of London without him. Sir Colin made it possible for us to even get started. He ensured my cousin, Ken, actually left on his business trip and that it wasna just a ruse to catch us leaving. Then, he ensured that the one person who could have prevented us from leaving was tied up and held so we could get away. He led us through all of London. It is verra likely I would have gotten lost or mugged. I dinna spend much time traveling about London. I only went to a few specific destinations; straight there and then home."

Angus chuckled before he said, "It sounds like you two made a good team and I've known Colin a verra long time, we grew up together, and he only tells the truth, which is why I think you will be a good wife for m' laird."

"I hope so, but there is so much I dinna know or ken about your ways. I am afraid I will make a terrible mistake and be an embarrassment to m' laird husband," she paused for a bit. Then, she asked, "Do either of you know the plan for our day's ride? Sir Colin and I have mostly been riding double with the children, so they can sleep. We ride one horse for two to three hours and then stop for a quick break and switch horses," she said.

Sir Duncan replied, "Lady Elsbeth is asleep already."

Elisa looked down at Elsbeth in her arms and pulled her closer to her. "Aye," she replied, "the sway of the horse's gate puts her right to sleep. I dinna think she could have ridden her own horse even if she wanted. She might fall off after she fell asleep." Elisa caressed Elsbeth's cheek before she looked up again at the trail, nay that she could actually see the trail with all the guards that closely surrounded her. She hoped that she wouldna be so closely guarded once they reached the castle. She was used to having the freedom to do as she pleased. She had been running her own life for about ten years now and she dinna think she would take it verra well if she was expected to do the bidding of another.

Sir Duncan offered, "If she gets heavy, I would be happy to carry her." But, he was certain Lady Elisa wouldna accept his offer. He could tell by the way Elisa drew Elsbeth closer to herself that she wouldna release the child to anyone else's care. She was verra protective of the child. He smirked when he heard her response.

"I appreciate the offer. I will keep it in mind." They continued on in silence for a while. But before long, she asked Angus if he would ride forward and ask if Sir Colin could come back.

When Sir Colin rode back to Elisa, he asked, "Aye, m' lady? What can I do for you?"

She asked, "Can you ask m' laird if we might stop for a while? I need a break. I am getting verra tired again."

"Of course, m' lady," he said. "It has been a verra long journey." Then, Sir Colin rode back to the front with the laird and they stopped shortly after that in a large clearing where they could see around them for some distance.

Laird Ian dismounted and came over to Elisa. He took Elsbeth from Elisa and carried Elsbeth over to a grassy spot in the shade at the base of a tree. Then, he returned to Elisa, "Are you ready? May I lift you down?"

"Aye, m' laird," she replied. "Thank you." Laird Ian lifted her down from the horse but her legs gave out when he set her down. He quickly swept Elisa up into his arms and carried her to the shade of the tree and set her down next to Elsbeth.

Ian looked down at her with concern. Elisa looked up at him and said, "I am sorry, I dinna ken why I am so tired and weak. This is nay normal."

He replied, "M' lady, you have been going for a verra long time on verra little sleep. This would be a verra tiring journey even if you stopped nightly at inns. You will ride with me for the rest of the day."

"I canna, I have to carry Elsbeth," she pleaded with him.

"Nay, you willna argue with me about this. You will ride with me and Elsbeth will ride with Sir Duncan or Angus," he insisted.

Elisa cried, "But she doesna know them. I canna put her with complete strangers. I dinna trust them."

Ian knelt down in front of her. "Elisa, you will have to trust me on this. I know them and I trust them; therefore, you can trust them. We are nay going to discuss this any further. You will obey me and you will nay argue with me."

She mumbled, "That will rarely ever happen." But, Ian rose and went to take care of the horses. Elisa snuggled up to Elsbeth and soon fell asleep. Little Ian came over and leaned up against the tree near them after he attended his horse.

All too soon, Ian was telling her he was there and it was time to wake up and to set out again. She still hadna had time to speak to Sir Colin about what he told Laird Ian, but Ian seemed to understand her fears. He asked Sir Colin to ride to his right and Angus rode next to Sir Colin. They were talking and reminiscing and catching up about the years Sir Colin missed while he was in London. Ian asked Sir Duncan to ride on his left, so Elisa could see Elsbeth any time she needed to assure herself that Elsbeth was safe. Elisa, of course, rode with Laird Ian, but she soon fell back asleep.

They stopped for the night. It was still early evening. Laird Ian and the men took care of the horses and set up camp. Sir Colin said, "We should go see what we can find for dinner." So she grabbed her bow and quiver of arrows and they set out. It wasna long and they had a few birds and a couple rabbits. When they returned to camp, the fire was lit and she cleaned the birds and rabbits and prepared dinner. She cut as much of the meat off the bone as possible and put the fowl in one pot and the rabbit in another pot. She added potatoes, carrots, and turnips to the pots, some herbs and mushrooms that she found while they were out hunting. Elisa covered everything with water. Then, she mixed together some dough and added little balls of the dough to the stock pots to make dumplings. She made another dough and spread it out over a skillet. She cut up most of her remaining apples and pears and added them to the pot and added some sugar and cinnamon and wrapped the dough over the top of the fruit. She set it on the fire to cook.

The men kept the children preoccupied with stories as they sat by the fire, while she cooked. She wasna sure if this was really to entertain them or more for her peace of mind. But, she was grateful and mouthed, "thank you" to Ian. He gave her a quick smile in return and her stomach did a flip. Her body reacted the same as it had when he woke her earlier that morning.

After they ate and she cleaned up the dishes, she asked Laird Ian about where little Ian, Elsbeth, and she would sleep. They walked together to the tents. Ian's and Elsbeth's things were in one tent. And her things were in Laird Ian's tent. When Ian and Elsbeth were ready for bed, she went in to say goodnight. She told them she was verra proud of how brave and well-behaved they had been on this trip. Little Ian told her that Laird Ian said they would probably arrive at his castle the next day.

Elisa replied, "Good, I am tired of travelling for a while and I will be glad when we finally arrive." They agreed and were soon asleep while she sang to them. She was just about to doze off when Laird Ian cleared his throat to let her know he was there. He escorted Elisa to his tent where they prepared for bed. He assured her that guards would be set around Ian's and Elsbeth's tent and they would be safe. "Sir Colin, Sir Duncan, and Angus will take turns sleeping at the door just inside the tent when they are not on guard duty."

She told him they must talk first before they went to bed because there were things she had to tell him and things she needed to know from him before they reached his castle. So they sat down and she told him everything about her concerns about her uncle and her cousin, Ken, following her and coming after her or the children. Then, she did her best to explain to him a little about what Ken had done or tried to do, and that was why she dinna trust people and was so worried about the children. She was strong and dinna cry while she told him about her cousin. But she couldna bear to explain that Cousin Ken had invited his friends and they had done the same to her and even more than one of them at once. She was too ashamed and embarrassed about the whole thing. Then, she told Ian about the adoption papers and told him she needed to be sure he agreed to adopt Ian and Elsbeth before they could renew their vows.

He replied, "It doesna matter now."

Elisa asked, "What do you mean? It matters to me. I canna renew our vows if you dinna want to adopt the children because I need to be sure they will be provided for and they willna be in danger of Cousin Ken trying to take them from me."

Laird Ian replied, "You dinna know or ken our ways, but we have already renewed our vows according to Scottish law."

"I dinna ken," she said.

"You called me 'm' laird husband' while you were talking to Sir Duncan and Angus today. All the men around you heard you. And I called you 'm' wife' when I was speaking to Sir Colin. So, we are married according to Scottish law because we have both referred to each other as husband and wife. But to reassure you, aye, I will adopt Ian and Elsbeth. I would never let your uncle or cousin have any say over any of you. They are nay to be trusted. I dinna think you have any need to worry about them coming for you. But if they do, I willna allow them to hurt you or take you away from me."

"I hope you are right," she said. After a little pause, she asked, "Will I have to remain within the castle walls or always go about with an escort?"

"For a while, but that might be the case anyway, depending on relationships with other clans," he answered.

After a bit, Ian suggested, "We better get some sleep. We still have a pretty long ride tomorrow. I will go do my rounds about camp and then I will join you."

Before Ian returned, she laid out her bedroll at the foot of his bedroll and covered up under her cloak and plaid. She was tempted to take her rope and find a tree, but she was sure that would irritate her husband. She supposed he would be offended that she dinna trust him to protect her. He wouldna ken her inability to trust anyone after everything she had been through.

Soon, she was deep in her sleep and she dinna remember when Ian returned. But early in the morning, Elisa awoke with a large body snuggled up around her. She struggled to get free, but his arms just tightened around her. The more she tried to free herself, the more tightly he held her. His arm, that her head was resting on, was now wrapped around her and his hand was pressed into her chest.

Ian breathed on her neck as he whispered, "Shh, m' lady, dinna move. It will be alright." His breath on her neck made her freeze. Her whole body was humming like the vibration of a stringed instrument. She had never felt anything like it before.

Then, he whispered, "Relax. I willna hurt you, but I need you to lie still." He pulled her hair loose from its braid and pulled her head back towards him. Then, he kissed the back of her neck.

Elisa reacted instinctively because she knew nothing so such behavior. She had no ability to think, her body just reacted. She no longer struggled to free herself, but rather, she struggled to move closer. She dinna ken how her body could react this way? She always had her guard up around men. She dinna like that he could so easily have this power over her. She was grateful they were both fully clothed.

Ian caressed her shoulder and neck. He continued to kiss her neck. His breath made her shiver. As he ran his other hand down her spine, she moaned again and arched her back even more. He wished they were completely alone.

"M' laird?" she asked.

"Hmm, m' lady?" he asked.

"I think we should stop," she said, even though she really dinna want to stop at all.

"Aye, m' lady," he said between kisses. "You are right." He kissed her. "We should stop." Kiss. "We should wait," kiss, "until after the church wedding," kiss, "and all the paperwork is signed," kiss. "and dispatched to the King of England," kiss, "and the King of Scotland." Kisses. "Then, we shall have to sit through our marriage breakfast." Kiss. "And all day there will be celebrating." Kiss. "And finally," kiss, "late tomorrow night," kiss, "we will be alone together," kisses, "and we can continue this."

"It willna be that bad, will it?" she asked.

"Aye, it will be that bad and worse," he said.

"Ian, you dinna seem to be stopping," she said with a laugh.

"Uh huh," he mumbled between kisses and caresses.

After a few moments, she asked, "Will your mother and father be there for the wedding?" The mention of his parents stopped his kisses and caresses and he pulled away slightly.

"I imagine they will be waiting for us when we arrive. A messenger was sent to inform them of your arrival as soon as Sir Colin came to get me. My mother is probably making all the wedding and celebration arrangements. The whole castle is most likely in an uproar. After we arrive, I dinna doubt I willna see you again until you walk into the chapel."

Elisa turned towards him, but crossed her arms over her chest, and said, "I am sorry our arrival is causing such chaos in your life. Little Ian and I dinna like chaos; it makes us irritable. Elsbeth doesna seem to mind so much. She is much more social than Ian and me." She paused for a minute; then added, "I think I need some time to sit and think."

"And what does a pretty lady need to sit and think about?" Ian asked as he kissed her cute little nose.

"I am much more than just a pretty lady chasing after a handsome man, m' laird," she replied.

"I dinna say you were chasing me," Ian said with a smirk.

"Well, I think I did just chase you clear across England and half of Scotland. The truth is I have taken care of myself since my mother died when I was eight, before Ian was born and I have taken care of the children for quite a long time, since Elsbeth was born. I havena really needed anyone since my mother died. I have been taking care of myself and my siblings and running three estates, a townhouse and two businesses. And it scares me, the way I responded to your touch. I wanted you to touch me and caress me. I have always been verra cautious around men and I have never wanted or needed anyone, especially a man; especially after the way my cousin hurt me. I dinna like that you have this power over me."

"Slow down, m' lady," Ian said. "You dinna need to think about it so much. We have grown up knowing we were married to each other. What happened between us is good. I think it is a sign that we will get along well together."

"Perhaps, I guess I will have to trust you in this matter, for I havena any experience in these matters, except for my cousin's evil ways. And I havena any desire to experience anything like that again."

Elisa could hear hushed voices outside the tent. Little Ian wanted to come see her but wasna being allowed. "I am sorry, m' laird; but our time alone is up. Little Ian will nay be detained for long. He is used to seeing me first thing in the morning. We usually break our fast together and I help them with their studies. I spend a good portion of my day with them. We have been together all day every day this entire trip. Last night was the first time they have been away from me since we set out on this journey."

Elisa dressed as quickly as she could in a clean dress. She was thankful that she wore breeches and a top underneath so she wouldna have to strip out of her clothes in front of Ian. She brushed out her hair and braided it.

Laird Ian wrapped his arms around her waist and nuzzled her neck as he said, "You dinna need to braid your hair for me."

She quickly turned her head to the side so her braid thumped him in the chest and said to him, "I dinna braid it for you. What would your mother think of me, if I rode into the keep with my hair all tangled and flying about me? It wouldna be a good impression of me as a lady or the laird's wife."

He captured her in his arms and held her to him as he replied, "Aye, mayhap, but I dinna mind." He bent his head and kissed her gently for several minutes before he left the tent to check with his men. Outside the tent, he knelt down and spoke with little Ian, "Your mother will be ready shortly, but you and your sister mustna ever enter our tent or our room without our permission. We are married and we mightna wish to be interrupted. Do you ken my meaning?"

"Aye, m' laird, I ken. I am sorry if I was giving your guards a difficult time, but I am nay used to nay being with Mother. I will try to do better."

"It's quite alright, we should have explained to you where we would be and what to expect before you went to bed. I have to check the guard and then we should eat and pack up and be on our way shortly. You can wait here until your mother is ready."

Elisa was glad to have this bit of playfulness between them but she was still verra worried about her role and expectations. She may have been raised to care for and run her father's English estates, but she hadna any idea what was expected of her as a Scottish laird's wife. She could only hope for some time with her mother-in-law so she could ask for her advice; although, she wasna sure she really wanted to speak with her mother-in-law. Lady Isobel wasna nice to her when she was growing up and she wasna sure what to expect now. But, she dinna know anyone else to ask these questions about what to expect or what would be expected of her as a laird's wife. She wasna sure her husband was going to allow them very much time together. She had the distinct impression he was going to be much happier when his parents returned to their home. But at least, she wouldna have to live with Lady Isobel. That news made her verra happy.

She slid her feet into her boots and added a dagger to each boot before she gathered up all her things and packed them in her satchel and rolled up her blanket and bedroll. She packed up all of Ian's things too and placed them near the door of the tent. She brought all her things with her as she left the tent, hoping to bring them to the horses and leave them near her saddle. Little Ian led her to their saddles, where she left her things. Then, they returned to the children's tent to gather Ian's things and pack them in his satchel. Next, she helped Elsbeth dress and brushed and braided her hair. Finally, they packed Elsbeth's things so they could bring their satchels and bedrolls to the horses before they returned to the fire to prepare breakfast. The children were anxious to get riding because they knew this was the last day of their journey. By tonight, they would be in Laird Ian's castle, their new home.

Ian ate with his men. So, she drew the children a little way away from everyone so she could talk to them privately. "Remember when I said we were going on a secret mission for the king?" They nodded. "Well, our mission wasna just a story to entertain you and keep you going on our journey. We are going to live with Laird Ian. He is my husband. We had a proxy marriage."

Little Ian asked, "What is a proxy marriage?"

Elisa said, "A proxy is someone who has the authority to do something for you. In this case, the person, our father, stood up for me and made my wedding vows for me because I was not able. I was too little to make my own vow. Now, Ian and I are married by Scottish law because I called him 'm' laird husband' and he called me his 'wife'. Tomorrow, we will be officially married in a church. This is part of our mission for the king. Our marriage will help strengthen the ties between England and Scotland and help to stop the fighting between our countries. Also, Laird Ian and I will adopt you and you will officially be our children. This will eliminate any claim Cousin Ken, could make to take any of us back to England with him. We will be safe from him in Scotland; although, none of us should go about without some of Ian's men for escorts. They will help protect us and keep us safe. So, the other part of our mission was to get the adoption papers here and signed by Laird Ian and he will send copies of them and our marriage license to both kings."

"So keep being brave another day and we shall complete our mission. I am so proud of you both for being so strong and brave throughout this trip. You have been verra good. Tomorrow, Laird Ian and I will be married and we will spend the rest of the day celebrating our marriage and your adoption. Then, I think we shall rest for a day and get to know where everything is in the castle and the keep. But the day after, we should get back to your studies."

"Ah," they replied.

"Now, I willna listen to any complaining after having all these days off from your studies and a great adventure too. It's been nearly a month. We must hurry and finish eating so we can get started on our last day of travels. I will be glad of a day without a horse under me."

She helped to clean up after the children and took care of cleaning up around the campfire. Then, she saddled the children's horses and helped the children ensure everything of theirs was tied to their saddles before she helped them mount. Soon, they were ready to go. Elsbeth decided to ride her horse for a while. Elisa warned her to let Angus, Sir Colin, Sir Duncan, or her know right away if she started getting tired because she dinna want her to fall asleep and fall off her horse. Then, she asked Angus, Sir Colin, and Sir Duncan to keep a close eye on her.

Elisa saddled her horse and tied her bedroll and satchel to her saddle. Ian helped her mount. She mostly rode in silence because she had feelings of anxiety and excited anticipation. She worried about learning what she needed to do to be a laird's wife and hoped that she wouldna be an embarrassment to her husband. She wished she felt better about the situation she was riding into and that she dinna have such conflicting emotions, because she dinna handle things well when she had conflicting emotions. Conflicting emotions always made her cry and she hated it when she cried. It was a sign of weakness and she wasna supposed to show her emotions in front of anyone, especially cry-ing. How many times had she been beaten? She couldna even count that many, probably. Well, that wasna true; she could count verra high and she was verra good at math, so if she wanted to count all her memories, she could count them all, but she dinna wish to remember that. The point was that she wasna supposed to show her emotions pub-licly and she had been beaten many times to teach her that lesson. She was supposed to suffer in silence.

She listened as some of the men talked of getting home to their wives and families. But mostly, she kept an eye on Elsbeth because she worried she would fall asleep and fall off her horse. She tried to keep her thoughts on anything going on around her rather than her memories or her worries about being good enough for Laird Ian and being a good wife, which she really dinna think she would be a good wife since she dinna like to be told what to do or have to follow another's orders. How could she possibly do that when she had been taking care of herself for over ten years? She dinna know the answer to that and she dinna think she would figure it out any time soon.

Elsbeth rode for a couple of hours but Elisa reigned in nearer to her to pull her feet from the stirrups and she pulled Elsbeth onto her lap. She carried Elsbeth for about an hour. Sir Duncan reigned in next to Elisa and said he would be happy to carry her little bundle for a while. "I am really quite fond of her already."

She was sure he had seen her shoulders and back slumping over from her exhaustion. She really dinna ken why she was so tired; she wasna ever tired, even when she got no sleep for a couple days. She was always able to rise at her normal time nay matter what time she went to bed, nay matter how little sleep she got. But, she reminded herself that Laird Ian trusted him completely; and therefore, she could trust him too. She struggled with what to do for several minutes before she convinced herself that she would trust Sir Duncan and let him take Elsbeth from her. Elsbeth cuddled right up to him and was quickly sound asleep again. Elisa was a little disappointed that Elsbeth was comfortable with Sir Duncan and happily fell right back asleep. But, she also dinna want to spoil the girl from trusting her guards either, so she tried to nay let it upset her too much; well, at least, nay outwardly. Even if she was terribly upset, nay any of their party would ever know about it because she wouldna allow her emotions to show on her face.

Elisa did everything she could think of to relieve the stress in her back, neck and shoulders. She shrugged her shoulders and rolled them forward and then back and she shifted in her saddle trying to stretch her back. She was vaguely aware that Sir Duncan and Angus were riding verra near to her. But soon, she was drifting off. A little while later, she was aware of being lifted from her horse.

Chapter 4

Elisa drew her dagger and fought to free herself from the strong grip around her waist. She was so tired, too tired to fight; but she had to fight or who knew what her cousin would do to her this time. "No, blast it. Get your blasted hands off me. You're nay going to touch me, blast you; nay ever again, you bastard."

Ian had no choice but to drop the reins and protect himself. She was skilled with her dagger and had drawn his blood. He needed both hands to hold her on his lap and capture her hands. It was too late now to heed the warnings he was given. Once he held her hands, he spoke to her to try to calm her down. He spoke in a quiet and soothing voice, "Elisa, it's Ian, your husband. Stop fighting. No one is trying to hurt you. I only wished to hold you while we ride because you were falling asleep in the saddle. I willna hurt you. I just thought I could pull you onto my lap and tuck your head under my chin so I could hold you while you slept. I dinna mean to frighten you or scare you. I wouldna ever do anything to hurt you." He just repeated himself until she calmed down. It took quite some time before she calmed down and was fully awake.

All Sir Duncan could do was drag her horse away from the fight so Magnum wouldna rear up. The last thing

Duncan wanted was for Elisa to be trampled if she somehow broke free from Ian's grip and landed on the ground.

It was several minutes before Elisa was calm and actually awake. She shook her head to clear the cobwebs and fog away. She still couldna ken why she was so tired and even when she was awake she felt like she was groggy and walking in a fog. She dinna ken it. Finally, she turned to Ian and said, "I warned you, to nay sneak up on me and to announce your presence, Laird Ian. I told you I was pretty good with a dagger. Sir Colin warned you to be careful because I am always armed and that I dinna like to be woke up. You should have listened to us."

"Aye, you did. I realize, now that it's too late, that I should have heeded your warnings and Sir Colin's. You are so small. You hardly weigh anything, I dinna expect that you could do any real damage. I will be more careful in the future. Now, tell me where you learned such language? You sounded like you worked on the docks."

"Aye, the London docks, m' laird."

"Oh, so now you are going to act like a lady?" he chuckled, teasing her. "And what were you doing on the London docks?"

"Protecting my shipments and ensuring they made it to their proper destination, my shop. Well, my uncle and cousin's shop actually. Apparently, sailors dinna have any honor." Elisa barely registered the gasps the men around her made before she continued on. "If I wasna present to ensure my merchandise was loaded onto the carts, they would have pilfered half my shipment before it was even loaded on the carts and the other half would have disappeared before it reached my shop."

"Who let you go to the docks to supervise the unloading of your ships?" Laird Ian asked. "It's no place for a woman, let alone a young girl."

"No one lets me do anything. I do what I want when I want. No one tells me what to do or where to go."

"Well, you ken now that you are here and you have a husband that is nay going to be the case anymore?"

"Nay, I dinna ken any such thing."

"I see you really dinna ken our ways." Ian paused and took several deep breaths to calm down. How could he explain to her without upsetting her and making her fight for her freedom? "Elisa, why did you suddenly decide to come to Scotland by yourself?"

"I told you; to get away from Cousin Ken."

"I see. We are going to have to discuss that in more detail later, but nay here, and nay now. Can you reach my reins?" Elisa nodded and leaned over the horse's neck to grab his reins; then, Ian pulled her up again. Once he was holding the reins again, he pulled her into his chest and tucked her head under his chin. "Try to stay relaxed and calm. I dinna want to upset you with what I have to say; but I dinna think you are going to like this. You ken the only way to protect you and the children is if we marry?"

"Aye."

"Once we are married, you will be expected to obey me."

"To do what you say, when you say, how you say, where you say," she said in a verra low, calm voice. Ian thought she sounded like when she was a little girl, sweet and innocent.

"Aye," he replied in a low, calm voice.

She lowered her voice to a whisper, "I dinna think that is verra likely to happen, m' laird. I wouldna get your hopes up."

"It is for your safety and the clan's safety, Elisa; to protect you and the children and all of our family and clan. Isna that what you will say in your vow, to love, honor and obey?"

Elisa dinna answer him. She couldna say she would do something unless she intended to keep her word. So she rode in silence for a long time thinking about her situation.

"Are you sleeping, Elisa?"

"Nay, just thinking."

"You dinna answer my question."

"I canna answer your question until I know the answer."

"Dinna your parents teach you that you would have to obey your husband?"

"Nay, my parents dinna teach me about what would happen when I was married."

"Well, what did your parents teach you?"

"They taught me to run the household. I learned to manage my father's townhouse and his three estates. I met with the housekeeper and the estate managers and made all the decisions and paid all the bills and reconciled all the ledgers. And after my father died, I ran my uncle and cousin's shipping and merchandise businesses. I ordered all the merchandise, handled the inventory, shipped it to the buyers and did all the ledgers. I have made all the decisions in my life, and my brother and sister's lives and all the decisions regarding the estates and businesses. I decided what improvements to make and what risks were taken. I met with all the managers and captains. I gave the orders. My mother's been dead since I was eight and my father since I was twelve, but he rarely had anything to do with me since my mother died, except to train me to take care of things, and to," but she stopped before she said what she was thinking. No one needed to know everything about her childhood. She kept silent after that. She breathed slowly and deeply until she was calm and could smile again. No one needed to know what she went through, what they did to her.

After several minutes of riding, Ian whispered to Duncan, "Is she sleeping?"

"Nay, Lady Elisa isna sleeping."

"How does she look? Does she look upset or angry or sad?"

"Nay, she looks perfectly normal."

"Like she used to look after her parents beat her and she returned to the nursery as if nothing had happened?"

"Aye, exactly like that."

"It doesna sound like her life got any better over the years after she returned to London when she was seven."

"Nay, it doesna. Something awful has been done to her from the way she fought to get away from you and what she said."

"Aye, and I dinna think she told me everything. Probably what she told me is the least of the transgressions. Make sure the other guards ken to nay touch her unless it's absolutely necessary to protect her life. Dinna sneak up on her and be sure you announce your presence. I imagine if she wasna on her horse and asleep, she might have fought much harder and mayhap done more damage."

Duncan whispered back, "I will be sure the men ken and they will obey your command. No one will touch her except if it's absolutely necessary to protect her life." He glanced down at Elsbeth. "Do you think anything happened to little Ian or Elsbeth, like what happened to Lady Elisa?"

Ian continued to whisper, "Elisa dinna say anything happened to the little ones. Mayhap, that was why she decided now was the time to come to Scotland before something did happen to them."

"Aye, quite possibly," Duncan replied. "Can you lift your arm away from Lady Elisa? I can wrap a cloth around your cut to stop the bleeding until you can have it stitched later."

Ian lifted his elbow out to his side towards Duncan. Duncan folded a strip of material and placed it on Ian's arm before he wrapped a second strip around his arm and tied it over the first linen. He made sure he dinna touch Lady Elisa at any time while he worked on Ian's arm. Then, he moved his horse away from his laird. They rode in silence after that.

Elisa must have fallen asleep during their ride at some point, but she dinna recall. She only recalled her conversation with Ian and then nay wanting to say anything about what happened to her and she stopped talking in the middle of her sentence and snuggled into him and took several deep breaths to calm down. She remembered breathing in Ian's scent and listening to his heartbeat. He held her tightly to him and she felt safe, safe enough to fall asleep watching Elsbeth sleep in Sir Duncan's arms. She woke to a bright room. It was quiet and the bed was comfortable. She dinna recall arriving at Ian's home, nor did she remember meeting his parents or going to bed. But now, she sensed someone was in the room. She drew one of her daggers; but then a little boy said, "It is alright. I just wanted to see my new momma."

"And who are you?" she asked.

"I am Ian's son, Hawk," he said.

"Ian's son?" she asked.

"Aye, my mother died when I was a baby and he is my father; so I came to live here at the castle with him. I met Ian and Elsbeth in the nursery yesterday when you arrived and they said their mother was marrying the laird. So I wanted to come see you. I know I wasna supposed to come in without you saying so, but I was too curious to wait. I am sorry."

"Well, it is alright now. But you should always knock before you come in and wait for your father or me to say it is alright to enter. Especially, because I always keep a dagger near to protect me, so it mightna be safe for you to startle me or scare me. Do you ken? Can you promise me you willna do that again? It's for your safety, so I willna hurt you. I dinna like anyone to wake me or startle me or scare me. I am afraid that if you did that I might react and hurt you."

"Aye, m' lady, I promise," he said.

"Good. Now, Hawk, do you know where your father is?"

"Aye, m' lady, he is getting ready for your wedding. Grandma is making him annoyed with all her preparations; so, he is hiding in the room next door and soaking in the bath so she willna bother him. She willna go in his room or there will be consequences." Little Hawk laughed, then said, "Sorry."

"Nay; you dinna have to be sorry. I ken that this family likes its consequences." She paused for a moment before she asked, "Do you mean I am getting married today and no one thought to wake me?"

"Aye and nay, Grandpa said you just have to learn to wait for women. They always take forever to get ready. He said you just have to accept that that's the way it is with women. You just have to learn to live with it."

"And by Grandpa, I assume you mean Chief Ian. Well, would you like to go on a secret mission for me?" she asked. He nodded his head excitedly. "Go find out how much longer before your father is ready, but dinna tell him I am awake or that you saw me or talked to me, alright?"

He nodded and was out the door.

She rose from the bed and straightened the covers. Then, she quickly found a basin of water behind the dressing screen with which to wash. There was a tub as well, so she brushed out her hair. Then, she undressed and stepped into the tub and poured the basin of water over her head as she knelt in the tub, slathered in soap, and rinsed quickly before Hawk returned. She wrapped a towel around hair and dried off and wrapped in another towel. She was thankful for the dressing screen.

Hawk snuck back into the room and said, "No one saw me leave or enter the room. Father is still in his bath, mainly so he can hide from Grandmother; so, he intends to stay there until the priest comes to tell him he must dress to go to the chapel."

"Good," she replied. "Now, I need some privacy to dress, but then I need your help to sneak up to the nursery."

"Nay," he cried, "you dinna want to go up there. Grandmother is getting little Ian and Elsbeth ready. Ian is giving her a fit. He said he isna dressing until he sees you. Then, he told Grandmother that he dinna need any help from her to dress and he'd scream if she tried."

"Well, how about if you go tell Ian to come down here and distract Lady Isobel so he can escape. Perhaps, some disaster in the kitchen and they could both escape to come see me. This will give me the time I need to get ready, get rid of Lady Isobel, and we will all sneak out to the chapel. So make sure they have everything they need to go to the wedding."

"Excellent plan, Momma. I will head straight to the kitchen and then to the nursery to let Grandmother know she is needed in the kitchen."

"Just let yourself in, I will be ready." she quickly brushed out her hair and started braiding it to put it up. Once she had the braid tied off and wrapped into a bun, she used her dagger pins to anchor the bun in place so it wouldna come lose. Then, she dressed as quickly as she could. A dress hung on the dressing screen and she supposed it was her husband's clan colors. Some jewelry was laid out too and she added it to her ensemble. She took a quick look in the mirror and thought she looked passable, presentable at least.

She searched through her trunks for the marriage license documents and the adoption documents, but they werena in her trunks. She supposed Ian took them and put them somewhere he considered to be safe. She realized that meant he knew how to open all her trunks' secret compartments and that he might have seen all her jewelry and such. He may have read some of the other documents that were hidden in the compartments. But, she dinna have time to think about that.

Soon, there was a loud crash below. Then, she heard splashing and swearing next door. Apparently, Ian was out of his bath. Elisa chuckled to herself. She dinna realize that one small boy could cause so much trouble. Then, there was screeching upstairs. Lady Isobel and Ian were making their way to the kitchen. A couple minutes later, the children entered the room.

"Hawk, do you know if your father took any important papers to his room?"

"I know where he keeps all his important papers. I will be right back with them."

"Wait a moment, please. Can you read?" she asked.

"Aye."

"Good, I only need one parchment. There should be six of them together: three are copies of our marriage license, and three are copies of Ian's and Elsbeth's adoption papers. I need one of the copies of the adoption papers. And be careful, I believe your father may have spilled water when he was getting out of his bath. I dinna want you to slip and fall if there is a puddle of water in the room. Quickly, and dinna get caught. I am sure we dinna have much time before they start searching for you."

In five minutes, Hawk returned with the adoption paper she requested. She grabbed her writing desk, and said, "Lead us, as secretly as possible, to the chapel. Quietly, everyone." Hawk showed her where the secret passage was and how to trigger the latch. Then, they followed him into the secret passage, and downstairs, and soon they made their way to the chapel.

Elisa quickly set up the blank parchment and started copying the adoption papers but put Hawk's name on the document. As soon as it was complete, she asked Hawk to send the priest out to the chapel, but to be sure he knew he was on a secret mission.

A short time later, the priest entered the chapel. He was shocked to see Lady Elisa and said so. "Good morning, m' lady. I am Father Patrick. I am surprised to see you are ready and waiting out here. Everyone inside is complaining because they think the London lass is sleeping the day away."

"So I heard, but obviously, I am ready and waiting for all of them." She flashed a smile at him. She wasna really upset with her father-in-law and his comments. She realized he was probably just complaining to be complaining or to tease her, knowing his comment would get back to her. He probably thought it would cause some tiff with her or get her moving, as it had done. She was momentarily disappointed in herself for allowing herself to fall into his trap. She chuckled and then continued with Father Patrick, "But first, I need you to witness my signature on this document. And when my husband arrives, I need a private place to discuss something with him."

She signed the adoption document and then Father Patrick witnessed it. Then, he showed her where his office was. She asked, "Will you please go tell my husband you think he should dress and gather everyone in the chapel immediately to wait for me here? If possible, let them keep thinking they are waiting for me. Since they think they are waiting on me and complaining about it, I think it will be funny for them to discover that I'm waiting on them."

Father Patrick laughed, "Aye, m' lady, that will be verra funny and certainly Chief Ian will find it so, since he is the one complaining the most. I will be happy to help with your ruse."

She turned to Hawk, "You can return this document to where you found it. Then, you three should return to the nursery. Thank you for all your help. I will do my best to ensure you dinna get in trouble for any of this."

Elisa sat in the first pew and waited patiently for everyone to arrive. She prayed for God to give her the right words to say to her husband and for patience to listen to what he had to say about Hawk being his son and the courage and strength and understanding to accept the situation. The first to arrive was her mother-in-law, Lady Isobel, with the three children sulking behind. They were followed by her father-in-law, another Ian in the family. How many Ian names does one family need? Elisa wondered; Jonathan, who would now be called Ian; her husband, Laird Ian; and Chief Ian.

She stood and curtsied and said, "M' lady." She thought Lady Isobel might faint, but she quickly recovered and went off on a tirade. "Stop, Lady Isobel, you may run roughshod over your children and grandchildren, but nay me. I willna be disrespected in this way. When I want your advice, I will ask for it. I know I will need your advice, for I wasna raised to ken your Scottish ways after my mother died. If you see I need assistance or am about to do something wrong or against your ways, you may approach me and say, 'May I make a suggestion?' or 'May I speak with you privately about this?' Otherwise, you will nay treat me like a child, but with respect. And, you will do much better with Ian and our children, if you do the same with them."

"Well, I never," lady Isobel started to say.

Elisa interrupted again, and said, "I am sure no one has ever dared to stand up to you. However, I have been running my own life and raising two children since my stepmother died six years ago. Now, is there anything I need to know about the ceremony that is different from an English ceremony?"

"Nay, it is basically the same," Lady Isobel said.

"Verra well. I have one more thing to say. I need to speak privately with Laird Ian when he arrives and I would appreciate your help entertaining the guests while we talk privately," she said.

Verra soon, Sir Colin entered with two bouquets, one for Lady Elisa and one for little Elsbeth. Elisa told him, "Thank you, Sir Colin; that was verra thoughtful of you." Elisa and the children waited at the altar. Little Ian stood on the laird's side and Elsbeth and Elisa on the other side. She asked Hawk to wait in Father Patrick's office.

Then, Laird Ian entered the chapel complaining, "I dinna know why we need to be all dressed and waiting here for my wife." But then, he saw her and a smile broke out on his face and a laugh escaped him. Her heart leapt at the sound and she could feel a big smile formed on her face, in response. She wasna as surprised this time when her body reacted to Ian's smile and laugh. It was intoxicating and she was verra drawn to him. She hoped that he was correct that this meant they would get along well together, but she was still concerned about their night together. She had mixed feelings about the situation and she dinna see any way to work that out in her mind. She dinna think she could forget about what her cousin did to her and she dinna think she wanted to be with her husband with that thought in her mind. But, she dinna have time to think about that now.

Ian asked, "Where is Ha?" but his voice trailed off. He mumbled, "Only he could have pulled this off, the little sneak."

"Where is who, m' laird husband?" she asked innocently. "Mayhap, we should have a private talk; now, before the ceremony," she demanded.

"Our guests have waited…" he started to say before she interrupted him.

"They can wait a little longer. We need to talk *before* the ceremony."

Elisa entered the priest's office and turned around in front of Hawk to try to block Ian's view of him. Then, she asked, "Is there something you want to tell me that mayhap you forgot to tell me, or mayhap there wasna time, or mayhap you were nay sure how to tell me? Because, it would be best if you just came straight out with it."

He stepped closer to her and touched her in the hopes it would get her to stop talking. But then, he saw Hawk over her shoulder and tried to sidestep her. She blocked his move by stepping to her side and in front of him. "There you are," Ian said. "I knew you were involved in all this. You disobeyed me and went into her room, dinna you?"

"Aye, Father; I'm sorry, but I was too curious to wait after all the excitement that Ian and Elsbeth were talking about their mother marrying the laird."

"Wait, m' laird," she said. "He and I have already worked all that out and I enlisted him in my scheme, so please dinna blame him for any of this. I wasna happy to hear that everyone was complaining about waiting for me while I slept all day, when nay anyone bothered to come wake me." Elisa turned to Hawk, "You may go sit with Ian and Elsbeth so your father and I may talk."

"Well, what do we need to talk about if you already know Hawk is my son?" Ian asked. "I am assuming that is what you want to talk about. I wasna trying to keep any secrets from you. I just dinna think about it when we talked the night before last and then we were involved in the things that you shared and discussing them. I'm sorry; I dinna mean to keep it from you."

"I wanted to hear it directly from you. What really happened?" she asked.

Ian turned to ensure the door was shut securely. Then, he lowered his voice to tell Elisa, "Hawk isna really mine, but his mother was killed in a raid and we dinna know who the father is, so I just said he was mine because people would be less likely to pick on him for being born out of wedlock if he is the laird's son. They willna speak out against their laird. It is a rule you might nay know about," Ian added, sarcastically with a raised eyebrow and a smirk. "Hawk doesna know he isna mine and I dinna want him to know otherwise."

"Thank you for telling me. I will do my best to nay ever bring it up again. He will fit perfectly into our family. We are nay even married and we already have three children. Who knows what people think of us?"

Ian stepped closer to Elisa and held her in his arms. She wrapped her arms around his waist and laid her cheek against his chest for a few minutes. Then, she released him and said, "Thank you for telling me this. It helps me feel I can trust you to protect Ian, Elsbeth, and me. If you would do this to protect Hawk, then I know you will protect us too." Ian kissed her then, which made her stomach flutter. She just wanted to melt into him and remain there. She really wasna looking forward to the ceremony and celebration; she dinna like to be the center of attention, nor did she like large crowds of people. They made her feel self-conscious. She worried again that she would make some terrible mistake and embarrass her husband.

Ian suggested, "We had better get back to the wedding." He held her hand as they returned to the chapel.

Elisa took her bouquet from Elsbeth and they stood on one side of the altar. Ian and the boys stood on the other. He stood facing Elisa throughout the ceremony. Ian clasped Elisa's hand to place a ring on her finger and then he kissed the palm of her hand and folded her fingers closed over the kiss. He said, "This kiss is protected by your hand, just as I vow to protect you and our children." Then, he turned her hand over and kissed the back of her hand and said, "This kiss is my vow to cherish you and to respect you and to trust you and to share all that I am able with you." Then, Ian kissed Elisa on the lips and said, "This kiss is my vow to be faithful until my last breath."

Elisa was so overwhelmed with emotion that she hardly heard the priest pronounce them husband and wife. Father Patrick turned to Ian and said, "You may kiss your wife, again." Ian kissed Elisa verra passionately.

Then, Ian and Elisa turned to their family and hugged and kissed the children first and told them to nay leave the chapel because they had something else to share with them when everyone else returned to the great hall. Then, they greeted Ian's father, Chief Ian, and his mother, Lady Isobel, followed by most of the household staff and all of Ian's men that werena on duty. Elisa did her best to nay let her feelings for her mother-in-law show. She should probably try to get over the past hurt. She tried to commit to memory all the names of the staff and guards that were introduced to her. It seemed it would be late in the day before they finished.

Finally, when everyone returned to the hall, Father Patrick took out the parchments so they could first sign their marriage contract and write the entry in the family registry. Then, Ian took the other parchments, but was shocked when the top one was already signed by Elisa and witnessed by Father Patrick. "What is this?" he asked, as he looked more closely at it.

"I thought Hawk would want the same from me as Ian and Elsbeth will have from you," Elisa said. Ian chuckled, which made her stomach flutter. He signed the document too. Now, Hawk was officially their son.

Ian turned to the children and informed them that the papers they were signing would officially make them their children and they would all be adopted now. "No one can ever take you away from our family." The children were verra happy and waited patiently for them to sign all the papers. Then, Laird Ian told Hawk the truth about his coming to be his father and how he did it to protect him and provide for him and that he loved him as his own son, but now it would be official. Elisa wasna sure how Hawk would take this news, but he dinna seem to be upset.

Elisa opened her arms to give Hawk a hug and told him, "I wanted to adopt you so you would be mine, just as the laird is adopting little Ian and Elsbeth. This way you will feel as much a part of our family as they do and no one is left out. I hope you ken and are nay upset with me."

Hawk shook his head and gave his new momma a tight squeeze. Then, they walked back to the great hall to enjoy their meal and a day of celebrations. The children ran around, nay taking a direct route back to the hall. After eating, which included many toasts, the bailey would be set up with games and music, tables of food would be added later in the day. The celebrating would continue late into the night and early morning. She kenned why her husband was concerned that he wouldna be allowed to be with her until the wedding and then they still couldna be together until late this evening, nay that she was certain whether to look forward to that or nay. She admitted to herself that she was attracted to her husband; there was definitely something between them, but she was too worried about her past to think about anything more that would occur later. She just dinna know how she would feel about that or if she could actually follow through. But, she dinna have to think about that just now, she supposed. That could wait until after they ate breakfast, lunch and dinner and celebrated with her husband's family and clan all day.

All through their breakfast, Ian's hand rested on Elisa's back. He grasped her by the waist and pulled her closer to him and massaged her lower back. His hand drifted lower and lower and he pressed his thumb into her dimples. He made her shiver and it was all she could do to nay squirm. Elisa only hoped her face wasna burning with embarrassment. She tried to press her elbow into Ian's rib to get him to stop; but, that only lasted a little while before he started in again. It seemed that her husband couldna keep his hands off her.

Elisa took a bite and wiped her face with her napkin. She laid it on her lap and moved her hand to Ian's leg and trailed her fingers up and down his leg. She could feel his leg flexing as she squeezed, so she pressed harder and ran her hand from his knee up his thigh. His leg jerked and hit the bottom of the table, upsetting their drinks.

Elisa quickly grabbed her napkin to slow the spread of the drinks. She set the cups upright and stood up. She quickly excused herself so she could go to the kitchen to retrieve more rags to clean up the table. She desperately hoped her face wasna red when she returned to the table. She took a couple deep breaths and headed back to the table. Elisa should have realized she was in trouble by the look on Ian's face, but she was too focused on appearing calm as she walked back into the room.

She did her best to mop up the mess without looking at or touching Ian. But when Ian grabbed her arm, she dropped the rags and let out a little shriek. He pulled her down onto the bench next to him and said, "We have maids who can do that." He leaned closer and whispered in her ear so only she could hear, "You will pay for that later."

Elisa looked up at him through her lashes and replied, "I dinna ken what you mean?"

"Dinna play the innocent with me; you knew exactly what you were doing."

"Nay, I dinna," she answered. "But you could have stopped before it went this far. Did you expect me to sit there and take it and give nothing back?"

"Aye, actually, I did," he replied.

"Well, your expectations were unreasonable," Elisa said and turned to speak with Lady Isobel.

Then, Ian's father said, "I believe you will have your hands full with your wife." When Elisa turned and glared at him, he raised his cup and said, "A happy marriage to you." Elisa responded by raising her eyebrow as if to say, doubtful. Seriously, these men thought they could just dictate to her and expect nay anything in return. It was ridiculous. They dinna ken her at all if they thought she wouldna respond. She supposed she shouldna allow herself to take the bait.

After Ian took a sip in response to his father's toast, he said to Elisa, "You have to drink to the toast, dear."

She replied, "I dinna have a drink because you spilled my cup of ale on the table."

Ian handed his cup to her, but cautioned her, "You can drink from my cup, but be careful; it isna ale."

"I am well aware of what you are drinking, dear. Lady Isobel kept our household well supplied from your father's stores. Is it the same recipe?" When he nodded, she tipped his cup up and drained the remainder of his cup.

Elisa turned to Lady Isobel and said, "You should gather the other ladies and the children and start setting up the games outside." Lady Isobel rose from her chair and with a wave of her hand, the women and children joined her. Many of the men rose to help, as well. When Lady Isobel looked at Chief Ian, Elisa said, "M' lady, I am certain Chief Ian will join you in a few minutes."

When they were out the door, Elisa took her husband's cup, which had already been refilled, and raised it, and toasted her father-in-law, "To the laird of the clan, my father-in-law, who seems to love to instigate the best in me." She drank most of the cup, leaving only a swallow for her husband to drink for the required toast; and then, she handed the cup to her husband.

After he took a drink, a maid refilled his cup again. Elisa took the cup back, raised it, and toasted her husband, "To my husband, who hasna any idea how much trouble I can be." In a lower tone, she added, "But I think you are about to find out." She downed his newly filled cup, leaving him only a sip to toast, but some of it ran down her chin and throat. She stood up between the bench and table and pushed the dishes away behind her and said to Ian, "I seem to have spilled a little and I dinna have a napkin. Mayhap, you could help me out, m' dear." She sat down on the table in front of him and put one foot between her husband's legs.

Ian growled at her and all the other men laughed and jeered at him, which Elisa completely ignored. Ian roared at the men and everyone cleared the room, except Ian's father and Sir Duncan. Elisa pulled on Ian's shirt as he stood up. She leaned back on the table, pulling him down on top of her. She hoped he would kiss her. She could see he was irate, but it was his own fault because he drove her to it. He stood up, picked her up and stormed up the stairs two at a time. He kicked their bedroom door open and dropped her on the bed. "Elisa, you will stay in this room until you sober up. Then, and only then, will you come down to the celebration. You will behave as a lady should. You will obey me, do you ken? Otherwise, I will nay be responsible for what happens to you."

"I dinna think that will happen, m' laird husband."

Ian stormed out of the room and slammed the door. He marched down the stairs and told Duncan to wait for Lady Elisa to come downstairs when she sobered up. He asked a maid to go up and see if his wife needed anything. Then, he left the keep. He walked to the stables and vigorously brushed out his horse. He would have preferred to saddle Talon and go for a gallop. The nerve of that woman, did she have to throw herself at him like that and try to entice him to kiss her breasts in front of half his men? He let himself rant in his mind for several minutes before he forced himself to calm down. When he finished brushing Talon, he gave him a little oats and took several deep breaths to calm his irritation before he joined the celebration.

He was first accosted by the children, who were full of numerous questions about their mother and where she was and what she was doing and when was she going to join the celebration. He calmly waited for the children to finish asking all their questions before he tried to gently answer them, which of course, led to more questions from them. He tried to be as patient as possible with them. He kept his thoughts to himself and blocked anyone from sensing what he was thinking. He certainly dinna need the children to know what their mother just did. Although, he doubted he could keep it a secret from them. You couldna keep secrets from these people for verra long. It seemed to be the curse of the gift of sight, that everyone knew everyone's business.

"Your mother will join us in a little while, children. Why dinna you go and join the games and enjoy yourselves? I am certain she will come and find you as soon as she comes out to the celebration."

The children ran off to play and he went to ensure that all was well with the guard. Then, he mingled with their guests. Everyone asked about Elisa. He told them his wife was resting for a few minutes; that she had a verra long journey and needed to rest for a little while before she joined the celebrations. She was causing him trouble from the beginning. He dinna need these frustrations. He was willing to accept his responsibilities. He had grown to care for her; he was certainly attracted to her. It seemed he couldna keep his hands off her. But, he dinna want this disruption to his life. He supposed it would take some time to get used to having someone that he needed to consider before he made decisions and ask her opinions of various situations, to consider her feelings or needs. He dinna think he was a verra patient man and he wasna sure how much time he had to make the changes that would be necessary to accept his marriage and adjust to this change in his life.

He dinna ken his mother's plans, or schemes more likely, and he knew it would be bad to interfere, but his wife's behavior had always been too complex for him to deal with. She could do everything they asked of her, exactly as they asked and they would say she was too slow or find some imperfection to excuse their desire to beat her. He couldna stand to watch it or hear it; nay that she ever cried. Nay, she bore it all in silence and then walked away as if nothing even happened. Often, she would skip away like she was happy and lighthearted. He dinna ken her at all. And if Cousin Daniel came to visit, she might sit with him for a while afterwards. He would hold her on his lap and rest her head under his chin until she fell asleep. He would hold her until she woke up. Then, she would skip out of the room, like this was the happiest place on earth. It irritated him so much. He knew his father, the chief, thought he was irresponsible, unaccepting of his marriage and basically, just plain selfish; but the truth was that he just couldna stand the way they treated her. What was he supposed to do? Sit and watch it. How could any man bear to watch them beat her when she tried so hard to be exactly what they wanted her to be and do everything they asked her to do? He dinna ken how they could crush her spirit the way they did. Obviously, they hadna crushed her spirit; they had only made her stronger.

He contemplated killing his mother on several occasions, but it wouldna help Elisa when he could do nothing about her own mother and father treating her like a punching bag.

He stamped down his anger. He shouldna allow himself to think about their childhood. He dinna do anything to change it then and it was too late to change it now. He couldna allow his guilt to bury him. It was best to nay even think about it. He would try to keep his mother as far away from Elisa as possible and nay allow her to do anything to hurt Elisa. He could only do his best to protect her, even if it meant sacrificing himself for her or the children. He would be strong enough to forfeit his life for her.

In the meantime, he would try to enjoy what time they were allowed to be together. He dinna know how long that would be. He knew Duncan had already seen their futures. He dinna ask because he dinna want to know any more than the glimpse he'd seen. He dinna want to be part of any of his mother's plans, schemes, he corrected. He ensured that his father would ensure Elisa's safety if anything happened to him; so Chief Ian went to the king and bargained with him to have contracts drawn up so that Duncan could marry her immediately following his death. He did what he could to ensure her safety. He could only hope it would be enough.

He would try to be happy with the time they had together and hope that Duncan would find happiness with the situation when Ian was gone from this God-forsaken, miserable land. He shook his head. What was he doing thinking about these things on his wedding day? He should be thinking about his wife, celebrating and receiving congratulations from all his clan. She was rather attractive and fit quite nicely against his body and he verra much enjoyed the times he held her the past few days. He was looking forward to their night together, with the exception that he had to get her to tell him more about what her cousin did to her.

When he saw his father approaching him, he swore, "Blast."

"What are you doing off by yourself, m' son?"

"I dinna want to talk about it, Father. You should return to the celebration and leave me alone."

"You are nay still fighting this marriage, are you? I thought you had accepted the situation and even welcomed it."

"I have accepted my marriage, Father. That wasna ever the issue. I told you I dinna want to talk about it. Just leave me alone."

"You would think you might be happier than this if you have accepted your marriage. Are you upset with Elisa's behavior at the table? You know it's my fault; I pushed her too far."

"I was at first, but nay that isna what I am upset about. Please, just let it go, Father. I dinna want to say. I dinna want to say anything that is going to hurt anyone's feelings. I will work it out on my own. I dinna want to think about it and I certainly dinna want to discuss it."

"So, this is about her childhood, then?"

"Blast it, Father. Why do you have to keep pushing? You are so blasted stubborn and determined. It's so irritating sometimes."

Chief Ian laughed, "Like Elisa?"

"Aye, like her; she's just like you. You should be verra proud of yourself and her. It's just that the more she acts like you, the more she incurs Mother's wrath and I am nay going to tolerate that. I canna bear to even think about what was done to her or what plans lie ahead. She never needed to be treated like that. She was more than willing to do all that was asked of her without any of that. It was completely unnecessary to treat her like that."

"I dinna think you will have to worry about that. You willna have to see your mother verra much if you dinna wish to. This is your home and you can deny her entrance if you wish."

"You had better ensure that she kens to nay lay a finger on my wife, because I willna be merciful to Mother after everything she has done to Elisa. I dinna think I could stop myself from killing her if she hurts Elisa."

"I ken. I will ensure Isobel kens as well. You dinna have to feel guilty about her childhood, Ian. It was my responsibility and I will take the blame and bear the responsibility for everything that happened to Elisa. I was serious when I toasted my wish that you have a happy marriage, even though Elisa took it as a challenge. She is strong; she stood up to Isobel as soon as Isobel started to lecture her in the chapel. I was verra proud of Elisa for standing up to Isobel and making it clear that she would be treated with respect. She told Isobel that she would do well to treat you and the children with more respect too."

"I am sorry that this causes so much conflict for you, Father; but I canna tolerate Elisa being mistreated anymore. I canna bear to see her in pain like the last time she was here. I know that you love Mother, but I canna love a person who treats my wife the way she treated Elisa. Elisa never did anything to deserve the mistreatment she received. I canna hide behind the excuse that I was a child and nay big enough to do anything to stop it, for I know I never tried. I probably hurt her feelings because I dinna want her to follow us around, but I knew what they would do and I couldna bear to hear it or see it. She probably thinks that I am as bad as them."

"Do you ken what it was like after she returned to London? The reports came back that she was doing well and she was good," the chief said.

"I dinna know who sent those reports to you, Father. I dinna think things were good for her in London. I dinna think they improved any and I dinna think she has told me what happened. I dinna think she will tell me. You can ask Duncan his opinion if you dinna trust my assessment."

"I trust your assessment, Ian; but I might ask Duncan his opinion even so. You willna take it the wrong way, will you?"

"Nay, Father. I willna be upset with you for asking Duncan his opinion about Elisa. But, you had better be careful. You know that he loves her verra deeply still and I dinna need any issues in that area. I have been faithful to my marriage and I plan to continue to do so. I expect Duncan to respect my marriage. I appreciate his feelings for her and I know that because of his feelings, he will do everything he can to protect her. I need his help to protect her. And, I appreciate that you made arrangements with the king so that if anything happens to me, Duncan can marry her immediately afterwards. I know that he has always loved her and will always love her and he will protect her and take care of her. He will treat her kindly. I can rest in peace knowing that he will be here for her."

"So, you still think that will come into play?"

"Yes, Father, I still think the vision will come into play. Has anyone ever been able to change the outcome of a vision? I intend to make the best of my marriage for whatever amount of time I'm allowed with Elisa. I'm sorry for what it will do to Duncan, seeing us together; but I think he kens. I am even sorrier for what my death will do to Elisa, but there isna anything I can do to change the vision. All I can do is make the best of the situation, whatever time we are allotted. You should return to the celebrations, Father. I dinna feel like celebrating without my wife by my side."

His father clapped him on the shoulder and turned and walked back to the men gathered together having a few drinks. Chief Ian poured himself a scotch and took a healthy swig. Then, he buried his conversation with his son and focused on the conversations with the men. He did his best to appear that he was enjoying himself. He wasna happy to hear that his son mightna be with them verra long, nor the pain it would cause Elisa. But, he wasna sure there was anything that he could do about it. He couldna change Ian's future. They might delay it, but they couldna change the outcome. It would happen just as the gift of sight showed it would happen. Trying to interfere would only cause him more problems with Lady Isobel in his already problematic marriage, nay that it would stop him; but, he dinna see any way he could change things for his son and Elisa. If he thought he could do something to help or prevent the loss of his son, he would move the high-lands to make it happen. But, he knew how the gift of sight worked. You couldna change the outcome of a vision; nay anyone ever had.

He let his love for Isobel rule his decisions back then; mainly, because he was young and stupid and thought that love was all that mattered. He knew better now. Unfortunately, he had already sown all the damage before he realized the true nature of his wife. He couldna regret having Ian and Duncan for sons, nor Elisa for his daughter-in-law. They werena his own flesh, but adopted orphans, but they were his sons, nonetheless. They were raised as twins in his home after Isobel miscarried; but as far as he knew, she dinna know this; at least, nay for certain. Ian was raised as his firstborn and Duncan as his commander of the guard, young Ian's first in command. They both knew all they needed to know to be the laird; and one day they'd be the chieftain. They could use some educa-tion in that regard, but he hoped he had some time on this earth before they needed to be trained to be the Chieftain of the Highlands.

He wouldna regret his efforts to better the country and to help put a better man on the throne that would help their country, especially in the event that England wanted to try to rule Scotland, which seemed to be the consensus. Most of the lairds that gathered on Mull every summer for the tournaments and the lairds' meetings all agreed that at some point, England would try to conquer and rule Scotland. They were determined to conquer every-one around them and to grind any resistors under their boots. The lowlanders and the marshes might tolerate and cooperate with England if they felt they were treated well enough, but nay highlander would ever accept the yoke of a Sassenach. It wasna to be tolerated. The clans might fight each other for women or old feuds or even just for the sport of it, but when England marches on their soil they will unite and fight back with all their might. He would do everything in his power, and he had a great deal of power as the Highland Chieftain, to ensure the men of Scotland stood together, unified in their efforts to thwart the English and kill as many Sassenach as possible.

Chapter 5

Elisa sat on the bed just long enough to hear the front door to the keep slam shut. Then, she moved to the chair by the fire. She should have recognized his mood when she returned from the kitchen to the hall after her actions caused him to spill their drinks. But, he should also ken that she wasna going to back down from any kind of a challenge; clearly, his father dinna expect her to back down. He seemed quite amused that she accepted his challenge. She supposed she carried things too far by lying back on the table and trying to entice her husband by pulling him down on top of her and saying what she had about the scotch dripping down her chin and nay having a napkin before his father and some of his men. She chuckled to herself for a moment remembering the scene she made.

After a couple minutes, there was a knock at the door, "Enter," Elisa said.

A maid asked, "What can I do for you, m' lady?"

"I assume m' laird sent you up to take care of me. I dinna know why he sent you to me, when I havena used a maid before. I dinna really need anything, but I suppose you could take out a dress, so I can change; but really, I can do it myself. There is one thing you could do for me; would you be kind enough to bring me a pitcher of water and a goblet as well as a bucket of water, please? Do you think it would be too inconvenient to have water sent up in two or three hours so I could have a bath?"

"I will ask the cook to have water ready in two hours. It's nay inconvenient. Which dress would you like to wear, m' lady?"

"Just a day dress for now. Mayhap something purple for later, since purple brings out the green in my eyes. That may help to catch the laird's attention and put him in a more forgiving mood. I am afraid I behaved rather badly."

"I am sorry, m' lady, the kitchen staff was gossiping."

"Nay, dinna be too hard on them; it is my own fault for nay controlling my emotions and actions. I should have behaved more appropriately."

"Aye, m' lady," the maid said and laid two dresses on the bed. "I will be right back with your water."

Elisa said, "Thank you and I would appreciate it if you could ensure that a bucket of water is set by the hearth every evening before bed. I will use it to wash in the evening before bed or when I wake in the morning. It will be warm enough if it sets on the hearth all night."

"Aye, m' lady," the maid replied as she left the room.

Elisa rose from her chair by the fire and crossed the room to her trunks. She opened one and pulled out a pair of men's breeches and a man's style top. She quickly undressed and then dressed in the breeches and top and then she slipped the day dress over the top and fastened it. She put on a pair of boots and slipped a dagger into each one. She waited in the chair by the fireplace for the maid to return with the water. She asked the maid to bring her the pitcher of water and leave the bucket near the fire for later. When the maid left again, Elisa drank several glasses of water. Then, she tucked a couple daggers into both the front and back of the waist of her dress. She allowed herself to take a verra short nap. She knew she would be completely recovered after a fifteen minute nap.

Elisa returned to the great hall where she discovered Sir Duncan was obviously waiting for her. He couldna have been more obvious if he tried from the way he leaned against the table with his arms crossed. She said, "Sir Duncan, you dinna have to wait for me. You could have gone out to enjoy the festivities. But since you are here, I have a great favor to ask of you. I would like you to escort me to the stables and then ask some of the guards to escort me to the loch; however many men you feel is a sufficient guard. Then, I would appreciate it if you would ask Sir Colin and Angus to keep an eye on the children. I would be verra grateful if the three of you watched them while I am gone to the loch."

"M' laird willna be happy."

"Mayhap, but I will have the required escort of your wise choosing and I will be confident the children are cared for in my absence, if the three of you are watching them. And I promise to nay be gone more than three hours. Will that satisfy you?"

"It isna me you have to satisfy, m' lady."

"Aye, I know. But, I am nay disobeying m' laird's rules." They reached the stables and Elisa asked Sir Colin to saddle her horse, Magnum. Then, Sir Colin helped her mount. She asked if there was a less obvious way from the stables to the loch. Sir Colin told her the escort would know the way and for her to be careful. While they were talking, Sir Duncan brought several men to escort her. Elisa waited patiently while Sir Colin and the stable hands quickly saddled the guards' horses. They were off and the guards led her out a secret gate in the garden wall and through the woods to the loch. It only took a short time to get to the loch.

Once she dismounted by the loch, Elisa asked one of the escorts to watch from one direction and another to watch from the opposite direction. She asked two other guards to stand with their backs to her and hold the corners of her cloak creating a bit of privacy. A minute later, she had stripped off the dress and tucked it into her saddle bag before she entered the water in her breeches and top. "You may put the cloak down and carry on with your watch. I will swim for an hour out and an hour back," Elisa called, as she turned her back to them and swam off. She thoroughly enjoyed swimming; it reminded her of when she visited Scotland when she was a child. Going to the loch and swimming or fishing had been the only times she could remember that she played as a child; the only fun she had. Well, occasionally, she rode through the woods, but that usually occurred after she and Ian had some disagreement and she would ride off to be alone, even though she wasna ever alone. She always had numerous guards surrounding her, even when they snuck out of the castle. Come to think of it, she recalled that she wasna ever truly alone with Duncan; and therefore, there wasna ever any real danger of doing anything inappropriate with Duncan. So apparently, the beatings were really just because her parents and Lady Isobel wanted to beat her and they just needed some excuse for why they were beating her. She tried to put aside her thoughts and enjoy her swim.

After Elisa left the stable with her escort, Duncan asked Sir Colin and Angus to come with him and to help watch the children until Lady Elisa returned from the loch. They were happy to be of assistance even though they dinna feel it was necessary because they dinna think anything would happen to the children inside the castle walls. Duncan explained that it was Lady Elisa's request to ease her concerns for the children in her absence. They were happy to be of help for Lady Elisa. He smirked at how easily it worked.

When Ian saw Sir Duncan with the children, he headed straight for them. Sir Duncan turned to Sir Colin, "You better go saddle Talon quickly. M' laird is most likely going to desire to follow Lady Elisa to the loch." Sir Colin headed to the stables, glad to be away from the laird's anger.

"Why are you out here, Sir Duncan? You are supposed to be waiting for my wife to come down to the celebration."

"M' laird, Lady Elisa has already come down and she asked the three of us, Sir Colin, Angus, and me, to watch the children."

"I dinna see my wife."

"Nay, m' laird, she isna here. She asked for an escort to the loch; so I sent Sir Thomas, Sir Scott and several other men with her. She assured me she wasna breaking any rules as long as she had an escort with her. She said she would feel confident that the children were cared for by the three of us in her absence," Duncan smirked.

"Aye, she is nay breaking any rules, if she goes out with an escort. However, I told her to stay in her room until she sobered up. You saw how much she drank, Duncan; she shouldna be near the loch. And, it isna funny; so wipe that smirk off your face. If anything happens to her, I will hold you responsible."

"Aye, m' laird," Duncan replied, but he couldna stop the smirk from forming into a smile. He knew Lady Elisa wasna drunk. She dinna stumble or stagger at all when she came down the stairs or walked with him to the stables. She dinna slur her speech at all either and that was what he told Ian. "She isna drunk, I assure you."

Ian shook his head and headed off to the stables where he found Sir Colin had already saddled Talon and was waiting for him.

"M' laird, may I make a suggestion?"

"Aye, Sir Colin, you may."

"I think it would be best if you werena too angry with m' lady. She has basically raised herself since she was eight years old and little Ian and Elsbeth since she was ten and twelve. She has run her father's estates, of which he had several. She is well-educated and independent and so she is used to being the one who runs her life and gives the orders. I believe she should only be given a few rules at a time and a lot of patience from you. You also need to ken the violent people her mother, father and cousin were. She will never trust you if you respond in that way. You need to find a way to get her to do your bidding without her feeling like you are telling her what to do, make it seem like it was her idea. I have one other thought for you to consider, m' laird," Sir Colin paused.

"Aye?" the laird asked.

"Why do you suppose the two of you are at battle with each other so much? I dinna think you would be in such conflict unless you had some feelings for each other.

She will need to know how much you care for her before she will open up to you with her feelings because she willna want anyone to try to use that, to have any power over either of you. She will think it is for everyone's protection. She will likely be verra confused about her feelings and she doesna handle conflicting emotions very well, if you will pardon me for using her own words."

"Aye, I will consider all you have said. You have been around her much more than I have been able to be there for her and I imagine you know her best. Thank you."

"Well, then, you had best be off, if you want to get her out of the loch before dark. She loves to swim and ride; so you two at least have that in common. I am sorry her father dinna send her and the children here as soon as he got sick. It would have been better for her." Sir Colin patted Talon's neck while Ian mounted.

"Aye, I suppose so; but according to my father, nay as much fun for me. Although, I think it is he who is entertained. He admitted that he was to blame for her behavior earlier as he instigated it. Thank you, again, Sir Colin, for everything that you have done for Elisa and for your advice." Then, Ian was off at breakneck speed.

Elisa was starting her swim back, when the laird reined in his horse at the shore of the loch. "How long has she been out there?"

"She has been swimming just over an hour, m' laird. She is a verra good swimmer. She doesna have your power and strength, but she can hold her own."

"Let's just hope she doesna need saving after how much she drank at breakfast, or I may drown her myself," Ian chuckled.

"Nay, you wouldna drown her, m' laird. You are having too much fun, I think."

"She undermines my authority with her plotting and scheming and she is a bad example to others," Ian commented as he dismounted and handed the reins to the guard.

"Nay, m' laird, we all know and ken that she wasna raised with our Scottish ways. She will come around. She just needs some time and patience."

"Well, if you want to move the men back to the woods, I think I will join her for a swim."

"Aye, m' laird." He and the other men moved just into the tree line.

Ian quickly undressed and headed towards the water. Elisa had made good progress coming back to the shore; it wouldna take long for Ian to reach her. He covered the distance in a couple minutes. The water was verra calming and refreshing and it greatly improved his mood. He was surprised at how quickly his mood changed. At first, he chocked it up to the water, but he soon realized it was also due in large part, he chuckled to himself, because of his desire for his wife. He did feel it was a good thing they both wanted each other. It would help them in getting through the awkward beginning of their relationship, even though they had known and been married to each other all of Elisa's life, eighteen years. He was surprised how much he cared for her and desired her when he hadna seen her in eleven years and their parting hadna been on verra good terms. He dinna think it would be possible to tamp down his desire for Elisa, but he should at least try, especially given all the bad things she had been through. He really dinna need to scare her. Tonight was going to be difficult enough for the two of them.

When Ian reached Elisa, he said, "You swim verra well, m' lady. Are you enjoying your swim?"

"Aye, m' laird, I am. You are nay angry with my?"

"I was at first, but I was reminded that you hadna broken any rules since you had an escort; and also the water has greatly improved my mood."

"I ken exactly what you mean. I am sorry I behaved so badly before."

"It was partly my fault. I realize now, I pushed you to do it. Sir Colin had a few thoughts on the matter and I realize he knows you better and so he is most likely right. I will work on my approach."

Ian and Elisa stared at each other, treading water for a while. His gaze was as intoxicating as the scotch she drank earlier. She allowed her body to drift closer to Ian until he grabbed her and pulled her up against him. To keep their legs from becoming entangled while they both tried to kick around in the water, he pulled her legs up around his waist so she straddled him. As he kicked his legs back and forth to tread water, his thighs brushed against her. Elisa wrapped her arms around his neck. Shock waves shot through both of them.

Ian bent his head down and covered her lips with his. Elisa wondered briefly how they could stay afloat if they stopped treading water, but she soon lost all thoughts and just focused on the feelings Ian invoked. Ian floated on his back with Elisa on top of him. Elisa wanted so much more, nay that she knew what that really meant, but she knew she couldna get her wet breeches off, especially while they were in the water. She wanted him to touch her.

"These blasted clothes," Elisa said without realizing.

"What are you wearing, anyway?" Ian asked.

"I am sorry, I dinna realize I said that out loud."

Ian laughed, "Aye, ye did."

"Sorry. These breeches and top are made out of fine leather and treated with oil so the water runs off. They dinna get so heavy when they get wet, and it helps me to glide through the water."

"You will have a hard time getting them off while they are wet."

"Aye, they willna come off until they dry, but they are so comfortable, especially for swimming." She leaned down to kiss him but hesitated.

"Aye, my brave lass, go ahead and kiss me," Ian encouraged.

"I dinna know what to do."

"You will figure it out." So, Elisa leaned down and kissed him; and when he started to kiss her back, she stuck her tongue out and flicked it across his upper lip. He groaned and held her tighter. Her stomach was aflutter and she moaned into his mouth. "I would love to continue," he grumbled. "But, we have to get back to our wedding celebration or my mother is going to be verra disappointed."

Elisa ran her hands up from his shoulders to his neck, and then she squeezed her legs tightly around his waist as she reached up and pulled his face to hers and kissed him again. "Must we?" she asked.

"Aye," he groaned. Then, he held her gently by the waist and set her away from him as he let his legs sink into the water. He held her for a moment and looked into her eyes before he kissed her again. Then, they swam back to shore.

They decided it would be easiest to just wear her cloak over the wet clothes as it was going to be too difficult to change or even get the dress on over the wet clothes. Ian took what he needed from his saddlebag and dried off and dressed. He approached Elisa and asked, "Are you ready?"

"Aye," she answered, looking into his eyes, captured in his gaze.

He stepped closer and slid one hand slowly and gently across her cheek until he wrapped it around her neck. The other, he slid around her waist and pulled her tightly to him before he bent his head down and kissed her hard. He was most likely bruising her lips, but at the moment he dinna care. He needed some control, but he wasna sure where that was going to come from. He dinna have any. The three days they had been together, sleeping together in his tent and holding her on his lap while they rode and everything that happened today was creating too much anticipation. He wasna a patient man. He was big enough and strong enough to take what he wanted and he wanted her, but he wouldna treat her that way. He had to find some control before tonight.

When he ended the kiss, he pulled slowly back from her, still looking into her eyes. He guarded his thoughts when he realized that things had changed since they were children. He grew to care for her and so much more, but he wasna sure that he should share that with her, at least nay right now. When he broke the gaze, he moved his hands to her waist and lifted her onto her saddle. Then, he mounted his horse. They returned the way Elisa had come and snuck back into the stable. Ian helped her dismount and went to the door to see if it was clear. He instructed the men to distract his mother if she started to approach as they headed to the house.

Meanwhile, Sir Colin gave Elisa a wink and then took care of all the horses. She rewarded him with a big smile. She thought to herself, if only she and Ian could get along this well, she would be so happy.

Then, Elisa walked with Ian to the house and up to her room. Ian bent his head down to hers and kissed her again, but verra gently this time. Then, he gently turned her and nudged her into her room and closed the door and left her to get ready. She stood in front of the fire until her breeches were dry enough to remove. She stripped as quickly as she could. Then, she rinsed in the tub that the maid had ensured was filled in her absence and washed out her hair. She brushed it out and braided it and pinned it up. Finally, she put on her purple dress.

Ian knocked on the door and entered, "Are you ready, m' dear?"

"Aye, I just need to find some shoes."

"Nay if you dinna want to."

"Really?" she asked. "I could go barefoot? That wouldna ever be proper in England."

Ian chuckled as he nodded. He took advantage of their time alone and kissed her again. He was gentle and in control this time; it was too tempting with their bed just a few feet away. Then, he tucked her arm in his and escorted her down the stairs and out of the hall to the ongoing celebrations. They were immediately accosted by his mother. Ian squeezed her hand and turned and winked at her as they approached Lady Isobel, "Mother, there you are. We have been looking everywhere for you. Lady Elisa is all rested and ready to behave herself for the rest of the celebrations."

Elisa could hardly contain her laughter as she tried to apologize. "I am so sorry, m' lady; for my behavior earlier; I am nay sure what came over me; I must have drunk too much scotch."

Lady Isobel replied, "It's quite alright, dear. These Ian men tend to drive a person to drinking. As for you, Ian, dinna think I dinna know that you instigated the whole thing, you always were the one to start it."

"I dinna force her to drink, Mother."

"Dinna you? You dinna tell her she would be insulting your father, if she dinna drink to his toast? You manipulated the whole thing."

"But I dinna make her drink the entire pint, three times."

"Humph. Dinna play the innocent one with me," she said, and turned, and walked off.

"Come, m' lady, let us enjoy our celebration," Ian said as he turned and looked at Elisa with a huge smile on his face. He gently squeezed her hand in his.

"Can we find the children first, m' laird?" she asked. She just wanted to be sure they were alright and she was certain they would feel better if they knew she was alright too.

"Aye, they will no doubt be reassured that all is well with us."

"Did they pester you with questions about me and why I wasna with you?" she asked with a smile.

Ian inhaled deeply; her smile was dazzling. She was verra beautiful. He tried to control his response, but he couldna help smiling back at her. "Aye, they had several questions and so did Father."

The children came running towards them as soon as they saw them. "Momma, is everything alright?" "Are you alright now?" they asked.

"Aye, I am fine. What have you three been doing all day?" she asked as she hugged the three of them. The children were so excited and told them all about the games they had been playing. The children couldna seem to stop talking.

They talked with the children for several minutes before they ran off to play another game. Then, Ian took Elisa's hand and wrapped it around his arm and escorted her through the crowd. Everyone stopped to speak with them and wish them well. Elisa was verra gracious and accepted their congratulations. She asked how they were related and about their family; everyone was happy to answer her questions and share about their family with her. Ian let her get to know their clan until he was nearly famished. He excused them so they could get something to eat.

He found a place to lay out a plaid for their family to sit on and then they rounded up the children and went through the line for food. They had a picnic dinner together as a family. The children told stories and asked lots of questions, which Ian had to answer the majority of them. Then, Ian asked Elisa, "Do you have an idea of what you want to do tomorrow?"

"I was hoping to sleep verra late, as we English lasses apparently tend to do," she replied with a completely straight face, not a hint of humor. Ian was amused. "But then, I thought you could give us a tour of the castle. Mayhap, if there is time, we could bring the children with us to the loch and have another picnic lunch and even go swimming."

"That sounds like a fun day, but you three will have to be verra good and let us sleep in," Ian said to the children. "Three of you have had a verra long journey, your mother especially as she dinna sleep much while you were travelling here. And, remember the rule to nay enter our room without knocking first and waiting for our permission to enter."

"Aye, we will," they cried.

Elisa enjoyed seeing that the three of them got along very well. The boys even seemed to include Elsbeth in everything they did. She dinna allow herself to reflect on her childhood and compare this situation to her childhood when she came to Mull. She needed to try to make the best of this situation. She couldna have any hard feelings about that time; they were children then. She dinna want to let it affect what would be expected of her now. She couldna expect them to protect her when they were just boys. Her own parents dinna protect her, so there wasna any reason to expect anything more from young boys. She envisioned boxing up the memories again. She had to figure out how to block the memories from popping into her mind at the worst possible times. She needed to have better control of herself. She quietly took a few deep breaths to try to control her emotions. She'd prefer to walk away and be alone, but she knew that would just start an interrogation and she dinna want to answer any questions right now. If she had to explain, she was sure she would cry or say something hurtful and blame them; and she really dinna want to do that. She knew she shouldna blame them. She tried to breathe slowly and deeply for several minutes until she could control her emotions again, but without making it obvious to the others that she was upset.

Ian noticed the change in Elisa's mood, but he dinna want to draw attention to her; so he dinna say anything to her about eating more. He could ask her before they went to bed if she was hungry and ensure that she ate more then. He continued to converse with the children until Elisa joined the conversation again.

After supper, there was music and dancing and a lot of visiting with Ian's parents and more of the clan. Elisa felt overwhelmed and wondered if she would ever remember all their names. As the laird's wife, she was sure it would be expected of her. Ian asked her if she would like to dance. She apologized to him beforehand, "I am nay sure I know how to dance, m' laird. I canna recall ever dancing before."

"We will start with something easy and something where I can hold you close and lead you around. If you prefer, we can move away from everyone and find a quiet place to dance."

"That might be best. I dinna want to embarrass you. I am nay sure I can be led. I dinna think I ken how to follow." She thought to herself, I dinna think I have followed anyone anywhere since I left here eleven years ago. You might say it was beat out of me. But she kept her smile on her face and dinna say anything out loud. She kept her emotions in check as Ian led her away from all the people; although, buried was probably a better description.

He found a place in the shadows and pulled her into his arms. They could still hear the music, but it was just the two of them. "Just try to relax and let me guide you where

I want you to go. Think about us swimming in the loch again. You let me pull you into my arms and position your legs where I wanted them and you let me hold you while I kissed you and we floated in the water. It will be a little like gliding through the water together."

Elisa couldna answer. She was caught in his gaze and couldna break free. She was mesmerized by him and she could feel everywhere that his body was touching hers. She was tingling everywhere he was touching her. She wasna even sure if they were moving, until she felt the cold stone wall behind her and suddenly he was kissing her and the wall dinna even feel cold. Actually, she felt warm all over. She was completely unaware of anything but his kiss.

She dinna know how long they stood against the wall in the shadows. The music played in the distance and the only thing she was aware of was the way Ian kissed her and she kissed him back. She felt so much. She felt like she was strumming like a guitar string that vibrates after it's been plucked. Her stomach was aflutter and her chest was tight. It felt glorious. It was wonderful.

Ian held her tightly. He kissed her. He wouldna allow himself to be out of control. They would wait until they were alone in their room. He needed to ask her a few questions before he could pursue any further with her. He was unsure what she had been through with her cousin. Until he knew that, he needed to proceed with caution so he dinna hurt her unnecessarily.

She was verra beautiful in her purple dress, the way it brought out the green in her eyes, which sparkled like emeralds in sunlight; except every once in a while, her eyes lightened and then a darkness appeared at the edges, and something changed in her mood. She looked verra hurt. He could tell she was hurt even if she continued to smile. But after a few minutes, she took a few deep breaths and then, she appeared to be fine again. He wondered if she remembered something, but dinna want anyone else to know her thoughts and then, she tried to cover it up.

He continued to kiss her. He looked deeply into her eyes and she seemed to be caught in his gaze and unaware of anything else. He meant to dance with her, but he only took a few steps before he gave in to his desire to kiss her. Then, he had gently danced her to the wall and pressed her up against it. He dinna need to pin her down. He was certain it wasna necessary, but the cool wall against his hand and arm at her back helped to keep him in check. He wanted to be gentle and go slow. He thought perhaps he could kiss her all night and nay ever get enough.

He moved her hand, which he held in his to his chest and held it there for a long time. His other hand he used to draw her body snuggly to his and keep her there. He played with her dimples. He pulled back long enough to lift her hand to his lips and kiss each finger and the palm. Then, he folded each finger one at a time over his kiss and kissed each finger again. He turned her hand over and kissed the back of her hand before he rested her hand on his chest again. Then, he dipped his head down to hers as he moved his hand to her neck. He slid his fingers behind her neck and caught them in her hair. He turned her head slightly to the side so he might continue to kiss her and he proceeded to slide his tongue into her mouth.

He thought of kissing from her cheek to her ear and down her neck and shoulder, but before he could get that thought into action, he heard the children calling to them. So, he lightened the kiss and just gave her sweet, gentle kisses on the lips. He dinna think she heard the children or he would have expected her to push him away, especially, since her one hand still rested against his chest where he left it.

Elisa vaguely heard someone call out, "Here they are." But, it dinna register who it was or that they were looking for Ian and her until Elsbeth pulled on her skirt.

"Momma?"

Elisa dropped her hand from around Ian's neck and gently pressed against his chest. He broke the kiss and lifted his head. He started to step back and tripped over the boys.

"Pardon me," Ian said, "I'm sorry, boys. What can we do for you three?" He only just realized that Elsbeth had a hold of Elisa's skirt and was looking up at the two of them, first Elisa and then him and back to Elisa.

Elisa knelt down and put an arm around Elsbeth, and asked, "What is it, m' dear?"

"I'm tired Momma, and I want to go to bed. What were you and Father doing? You dinna hear us when we were calling for you?"

"I'm verra sorry, dear, that we dinna hear you."

Ian knelt down to Elsbeth too, "Were you scared?"

"Nay, Father. Mother said you and your men would protect us from now on."

"Aye, Elsbeth; that is verra true. We will do our verra best to ensure all of you are safe from now on."

"Thank you, Father. I am just tired and I want to go to bed. Will that be alright? It willna ruin anyone's fun, will it?"

"That is fine if you wish to go to bed. It's perfectly alright and it willna ruin anyone's fun. The clan will celebrate late into the night. Actually, it will be early in the morning before most of them go to bed. We can go up to bed now if you wish. How about you two? Are you ready for bed, Ian and Hawk?"

"We are happy to go to bed now," Ian replied for the two of them.

"Are you sure that is Hawk's opinion as well, Ian?"

"Aye, Father; I'm sure."

"Verra well. I will lead all of you up to the nursery then. I can show you a way around the crowd so we dinna have to stop and talk to everyone. It will take quite a while if we have to go back through the clan. Everyone will want to wish us well. It's rather embarrassing." He made a face and rolled his eyes.

The children laughed, and Elsbeth asked, "You get embarrassed, Father?"

"Aye, sometimes, but nay verra often" He lifted Elsbeth in his arm and took Elisa's hand in the other and led them around the bailey towards the stables. They entered the side door and took a secret passage up to the nursery level.

Elisa chuckled, "You may have just spoiled any chance of them falling asleep now."

"What did I do?"

"Secret passages are verra thrilling and exciting." She lowered her voice, "Now, they will be thinking about how many other secret passages there are in the castle."

"Well, if they are good and go to bed, mayhap, I can show them some more tomorrow."

"Oh, Father, that would be more fun than riding for nearly a month to get from London to the Isle of Mull."

"And here I thought I planned a great adventure for you," Elisa said, disappointed that they were more excited about secret passages than all the time they had spent together. She pretended to pout.

"Dinna pout, Mother," Ian said and hugged her.

She laughed, "I am only teasing you, dear."

"How could I nay like the idea of exploring a castle and all its secret passages and tunnels?"

"I ken how exciting such things are, Ian. I was a little girl a very long time ago and I enjoyed it too. It's a lot of fun." But she was thankful they were at the nursery door and she could devote her time to helping Elsbeth undress and put on her nightgown behind the dressing screen. She spent several minutes brushing out Elsbeth's hair and finally braiding it. She wrapped a ribbon around the bottom lengths and tied it tight. And then, it was time to tuck the children into bed. Then, she pulled Elsbeth to her and gave her a verra tight hug.

The whole time she was helping Elsbeth get ready for bed, she reminded herself not to think about her childhood. She dinna need to think about the few hours of fun that she had when they all resulted in very painful beatings and then she would be reminded of all the difficulties of her childhood. That would end with the horrible memories of her cousin and she definitely dinna want to think about that just before she was going to go to her room with her husband. So, she thought about putting the memories back in the box that she envisioned them being in. Then, she kept her focus on her children.

She hugged and kissed them before she sang the lullaby to each of them. She helped Elsbeth into bed, hugged and kissed her, and sang to her. She kissed Elsbeth's forehead before she rose from the edge of the bed and moved to Hawk's bed.

When she sat with Hawk, he asked, "Are we nay a bit old to have a lullaby sung to us at bedtime?"

"I dinna have to sing to you, if you dinna want me to, Hawk; but I sing to Elsbeth and Ian every night. I have since they were very little. It helps them relax and fall asleep with a happy thought. I want them to know they are loved every night before they go to sleep."

"Is that because you werena loved when you were a little girl?" he asked.

"What would you know about that, Hawk?"

"I dinna know, but I just know it's true."

"Well, I dinna want any of you to be treated the way I was treated. I dinna think there is anything wrong with that."

"You are very sad, Mother; even though no one can tell when they look at you. You are verra good at hiding your true feelings so no one will know how you really feel. You are afraid to be happy because you think something bad will happen then."

"Well, Hawk, if that's true, it's for me to deal with and you dinna have to worry about it. Do you ken?"

"Yes, Mother, I ken. You dinna have to worry."

"Thank you, Hawk. I will try to remind myself all the time of what you said. Now, do you want me to sing to you before you go to sleep?"

"Yes, Mother; I want to know that I am loved before I go to sleep," he answered with a wink and a grin.

"I think you are a scamp, young man," Elisa said as she ran a hand through his hair and then she sang the lullaby to him. When she finished, she ensured his blankets were tucked up under his chin and kissed his forehead. "I love you," she told him as she hugged him; and then, moved to Ian's bed.

When she leaned down to hug Ian, he whispered in her ear, "I love you, Mother. Thank you for everything you have done to take care of Elsbeth and me and to ensure that we knew we were loved. Thank you for bringing us to Mull so we could have a father who would protect all of us. I hope that you will be very happy now that you are officially married and we made it here safely. Thank you for adopting all of us and making us a family."

"You are welcome, Ian. I love you." She sang to him and tucked the blankets up under his chin. She kissed his forehead before she rose from the bed.

Then, Ian kissed each child on the forehead and told them, "Goodnight, I love you." He took Elisa's hand and looped it around his arm and led her back downstairs to their bedroom. Ian's things had been moved back to their room. He ensured the room was safe before he led his wife into their room and closed the door. He turned to her and asked, "You dinna eat verra much dinner; do you want something? I can send a maid to bring you a plate of food."

"Nay, Ian, I am fine. I dinna think I can eat anything right now. That's verra thoughtful of you; but you dinna have to worry about me." She dinna add that she had survived on much less. He dinna need to know. It wouldna serve any purpose, but to hurt people's feelings or make them feel guilty. It wouldna change what was in the past. She took a few deep breaths and tried to calm down and block out the memories.

She walked to one of her trunks and opened it and took out her hairbrush and brushed out her hair. She envisioned digging a deep hole and burying the box of memories in it and covering it up with all the dirt. She pictured herself packing the dirt down by hitting the shovel on the dirt pile until it was hard and firm again. She hoped the memories would stay buried this time. She was thinking about it far too much lately. She supposed it might be for several reasons. For one thing, she wasna drinking every night. For another, she wasna getting up as early as she normally did and working until well past dark, keeping too busy to think about the memories or anything else. She wasna working hard like she normally did. Things were much too casual here. She needed a rigid schedule to adhere to; then, she would be too busy to think about the memories. She had to come to terms with the things that happened when she visited here when she was a child. She thought it verra unlikely that she would forget the memories; so the only option was to find a way to control her emotions to having the memories. It was best to nay have emotions and feelings; then, they wouldna be out of control.

She was determined to be in control of her emotions, so she inhaled slowly and held her breath for a couple seconds and exhaled slowly until she was calm and in control. She finished brushing out her hair and put her brush back in her trunk.

She tried to nay think about what was going to happen next. She would prefer if someone explained each step and then she could think of it as a list and check off each step of the list. She liked everything organized and scheduled and then, she was in better control of her emotions if she stuck to her schedule.

She couldna control what was done to her when she was a child, and really, it wasna that long ago what her cousin and his friends did to her. Since she couldna control what all those people did to her, she tried to control everything else in her life that she could possibly control. She supposed it was irrational to try to control everything. One couldna actually control everything. Sometimes, things happened that you couldna account for or control. And nay only that, but she needed to accept that her life wasna her own; she was God's child and she was supposed to surrender her life to doing His will and let Him be in control, but she doubted that was something she could actually do.

She should probably set aside some time to meet with Father Patrick and mayhap try to speak with him about her control issues. Mayhap, he could help her to think of some verses that would remind her to let her heavenly Father be in control, nay that she thought she would be verra good at it, nigh impossible. It was difficult to think of God as her Father because her father had been so abusive; so, she couldna accept that God was a loving Father when she dinna know what that was. She supposed she should at least give it a try, even if she dinna think she would have any success at it. She knew it was the right thing to do. Why was the right thing always the hardest thing? Mayhap, she would ask Father Patrick that question too and he could give her an answer, something other than the Scriptures about life's trials and tribulations. She had enough of that in her life. Where was the loving and merciful Father in all of this, that's what she wanted to know?

Chapter 6

Elisa was verra anxious and tried to nay think about what was coming next. She tried to focus on their afternoon at the loch and all the feelings Ian made her feel. But, she was verra scared and getting more scared as she heard Ian undressing behind her.

"Elisa," Ian said as he approached her. He gently touched her shoulders as he stepped into her from behind. Then, he ran his hands down her arms. "Are you alright? Are you nervous?"

Elisa nodded as she turned towards him and hugged him. He cupped her chin in his hand and tilted her face up to his, "It will be alright. You can trust me. But, first, I need to know something more about what you told me in my tent because it doesna seem to explain why you reacted the way you did when I tried to lift you onto my horse; nor what you said."

"What do you mean?" she asked. "I'm not sure what I said as you tried to lift me onto your horse. I was asleep."

He repeated her words, "No, blast it. Get your blasted hands off me. You're nay going to touch me, blast you; nay ever again, you bastard."

"I'm sorry, but I'm still nay certain what you are asking me, Ian. Just say it plainly."

"You told me in my tent that your cousin, Ken, would hide and jump out and grab you. That he would tickle you and pin you down and try to kiss you or touch you inappropriately, but you were much more violent than your behavior warranted. Did he do something more to you?"

"Do we have to talk about this now?"

"Aye, Elisa, it matters as to how I will treat you when we are together. Did your cousin force you? Has he lain with you or are you still untouched?"

"I dinna know how to answer you, Ian. I dinna think I can explain it to you, even if I knew the answer. But, I think the answer is yes to all your questions." Elisa pushed away from Ian and stepped back. She couldna look at him. She moved to the chair by the fire and pulled her knees up to her chest. She buried her face. She was so ashamed and dinna know how she would find the courage to say what she had to tell him. She dinna know how to explain to him about what was done to her. She had no desire to discuss this, especially right now and she certainly dinna want to think about it or remember what her cousin and his friends did to her. But, she couldna forget either. She hoped being with her husband wouldna be like that because she dinna think she could bear it.

Ian followed her to the chairs and sat down in his chair across from her. After several minutes of watching the fire, he slid the footstool closer to her and moved to the footstool. He placed his hands on her arms, which were wrapped around her knees. "Elisa, I dinna ken how your cousin could lie with you and force you and you could still be untouched. But, if you are, I know that I must go verra slow and be cautious. I dinna want to hurt you, but there will be pain when we are first together. But after your body recovers in a couple days, it shouldna hurt when we are together."

"Cousin Ken said he couldna take my, I hope you know what I mean, because I was married; but he still forced himself on me. I canna explain it to you. Only that what he did hurt. It was extremely painful and it dinna get better with each time."

"I think I ken now. Do you want to talk more about what your cousin did to you?"

Elisa shook her head, "Nay, I dinna want to talk about it or think about it ever again."

"Do you ken what will happen between the two of us?"

"Ian, my mother died when I was eight, there wasna anyone to explain anything to me. I ken what animals do to mate, but that is about the extent of it. I dinna think I can bear to do this. I certainly dinna want to discuss anything with your mother."

"Did you enjoy this afternoon at the loch?" he asked.

"Aye, verra much."

"Did it make you feel good?"

"Aye, I wanted more. I wanted you to touch me."

"I am pretty sure you enjoyed me kissing you after we danced. I'm sorry I pressed you into the cold wall."

"It's alright, Ian; I dinna notice the cold while you kissed me. I dinna mind."

"So, just focus on that and remember how good you felt," Ian said to calm her.

Elisa nodded. Ian kissed her then. He lifted her in his arms and carried her across their room. She stood there while he put out most of the candles in the room. When he returned to where she stood, he kissed her to distraction. She was lost in her feelings.

He enjoyed her response. "Just be brave a little longer."

He pulled his lips away from hers and whispered, "Open your eyes and look at me, Elisa. I really need you to trust me now. It will be alright, I promise. I want you to ken that I dinna want to hurt you but I have to do this. I need to tell you before I hurt you so you will know that you can still trust me. It willna be like what you are remembering and thinking; I would never hurt you that way."

Elisa was verra scared and started to struggle to get free from under Ian. "Shh, my brave lass. Remember, I said you had to be brave a little while longer? So now, you need to be brave. Do you ken?"

She looked at him a little bit calmer, "Will you kiss me again?"

"Aye, I will if you will let me, but keep your eyes open. Will you try to nay bite me?"

"I canna promise that," she answered and he chuckled. He kissed her again and she tried only to feel his lips on hers and the flutter she felt in her stomach as he caressed her. She dinna pull away or fight him as he continued. She never guessed anything could be so wonderful.

Ian nuzzled her neck and kissed her and when he pulled back, he said, "I am sorry I had to hurt you, m' sweet, brave wife."

"It's alright. You also made me feel wonderful."

Ian hooked his right foot around her left leg and rolled onto his back, turning her towards him so her head was on his chest, his arm around her neck. Her leg was draped across his leg with her foot nestled between his calves. He held her tight and said, "Sweet dreams, m' sweet wife." She barely heard him, before she drifted off to sleep.

Elisa awoke with a start in the early morning. It was never a good thing when she woke with this feeling. She realized her head was resting on a verra solid arm, another arm was draped over her, and a leg had her legs pinned down. She panicked and struggled to get free.

"Shh, m' sweet wife, it's only me, your husband, Ian. It's alright." He gently pulled her closer and pressed his chest into her back. He drifted back to sleep, but Elisa lay there awake for a long time. Part of her was afraid, but the rest of her was tingling wherever Ian's body was touching her. She discovered that she could override the feeling that something bad would happen if she focused on the feelings she felt where her husband touched her. She preferred his caress to the bad feeling that was waiting to spoil her day; so she tried to focus on the feelings that Ian's touch made her feel. When she became restless, she pressed backwards into him. Ian moaned in his sleep. She pressed into him again.

She tried to roll over towards Ian, but she was too pinned down under him. She pulled her knees up towards her stomach to try to free her legs. As she started to roll towards Ian, he shifted onto his back and pulled her to him. She rolled on top of him, and she lay still for a minute, but then she was brave enough to pull her knees up. She kissed his chest and her hair cascaded around her and covered his chest and arms. She dinna know what to do, but she wanted him to show her.

She worked her way up his chest, kissing him until she could kiss his mouth. He moaned into her mouth.

"Uh huh," she said. And then, he was finally awake. He kissed her deeper than before. "Elisa, m' sweet wife, you are amazing."

"It frightens me to see how much effect you have on me."

"You shouldna be afraid of the attraction between us. You have just as much effect on me; I would have thought that was obvious at the table yesterday morning, when I reacted to your hand on my leg."

"I hadna any idea that you would react like that. How could I know? I just wanted you to stop rubbing my lower back; you were making me crazy with wanting something more from you but I dinna know what I wanted. I just thought if I touched you similarly to how you were touching me, you might feel what I was feeling and stop. I hadna any idea your leg would be so sensitive. I was mortified, especially since I was pretty certain your father was aware of what was going on."

"My father was quite amused by the whole incident. And my mother pretends to be outraged, but she is actually happy to see us so happy together."

"Oh, yesterday was about our happiness? Because I thought it was about me being annoyed with you and you saying you are in charge and I have to do whatever you say," she replied.

"Well, think about it, Elisa, when was the last time you did anything playful or fun? Your life has been all about surviving, protecting yourself and the children, and planning your escape to get here. But yesterday, dinna you have fun planning your surprise on me and my family, so that we thought we were waiting on you when you were really waiting on us? Dinna you enjoy plotting with Hawk to make it all happen? You were playing for the first time in years."

"I suppose." They laid there holding each other for a while.

Then, Ian asked, "Do you wish to sleep anymore?"

"Nay, I dinna need any more sleep. Why?"

"Well, about our plans for today. I need to change things around a bit. I need to get the men back to the training field. Then, I thought we could have our picnic at the loch and swim. We can tour the castle when we return."

"Aye, that would be fine, but could I come with you to the training field and bring the children. I will keep them away from the men, but they need to begin training too. I have already been training Ian a little."

"And Elsbeth, will you bring her to the training field too?"

"Aye, Ian, she is going to have to see it some time. The life of a Scotsman is a life of fighting. These kings may approve of marriages between our countries in order to reduce the raids but dinna fool yourself, the King of England willna leave Scotland alone until he conquers it. Besides, Elsbeth has to be prepared to dress the wounds. I am nay going to allow her to run around unarmed and defenseless."

"So, you intend to train her so she can protect herself, rather than trust the men around her to protect her?"

"It isna about trust, Ian. You canna be by my side all the time. You have seen that I can hunt and live out in the open and provide for myself. Would you want Elsbeth to be helpless if she was lost in the woods? Would you want her to wait to be rescued or find her way home on her own? What if you or your men werena the first ones to find her? Would you want her to be capable of defending herself against her attackers? I have some skill, m' laird. I am nay as strong as you or your men, but I have other resources and I will use whatever is necessary to my advantage. My whole life has been about surviving, even the worst of circumstances and believe me, when it comes down to it, I will do whatever is necessary to survive or protect the children."

"Verra well, you may bring the children and come to the training field." Then, he asked, "Do you wish to dress now?"

"Nay, after you go, I will wash, and then dress." She wrapped in her plaid and stood by the window looking out at the day. Something was stirring up a lot of dust a couple hills away. "Ian, have you seen out the window? I think you had better take a look." The feeling was creeping back in.

He came to the window and stood behind her. He rested his hands on her upper arms while he looked out the window. "It is probably visitors to a neighbor, but I will send out riders to investigate, before I head to the training field." He leaned around her and kissed her for a long time. He was verra happy with her response, so he deepened the kiss. He moved one hand down her arm and slipped it under her arm and around her waist. He gently pulled her back against him. He moved his other hand to her cheek and caressed it. He knew she needed some time to recover.

As soon as Ian left, she quickly washed with the bucket of water she asked the maid to keep near the fire. She opened her trunk that she kept many of her weapons in and she strapped several weapons on her body. Then, she dressed in her leather breeches and top, and then covered that with her plaid. She brushed out her hair, braided it, and pinned it up. Next, she armed herself with her bow and arrows, her small sword, and several more daggers on the outside of her clothing.

Then, she left her room and went up to the children's nursery. She told Ian and Hawk, "Dress quickly in something you can work hard in and get dirty. We are going to the training field. Then, gather your wooden swords for practice."

She turned to Elsbeth, "I will help you get dressed behind the screen. The laird has agreed to let me train you, as well." Elisa gave Elsbeth a set of breeches and a top to match. She helped Elsbeth dress. She spent a long time brushing out Elsbeth's hair and braiding it and pinning it up, so it would be out of Elsbeth's way while she was training. The last thing the girl needed was her hair in her face while she was trying to fight men who were much stronger. She was very happy to see Elsbeth's reaction to her hard work in creating her outfit.

"Momma, these are so soft," Elsbeth exclaimed.

"I know. They are verra comfortable and the best thing I have ever made. But you can only wear them for training and swimming. Otherwise, you should dress and act as a lady. I dinna have anyone to teach me those things, so we'll probably have to ask a maid to help you, because I dinna know what to do myself, let alone to teach you."

"Alright, Momma," Elsbeth replied.

Elisa wrapped her in a matching plaid and gave her a wooden dagger and a wooden sword for training. "You must treat these as real weapons. They are nay toys. Do you ken? Girls need more weapons and resources than boys because girls are nay as strong as boys, so they need to be cunning."

"Aye, Momma, I ken."

"One day, you will have real weapons," Elisa said to all the children as they headed down the stairs and out to the training field. "You must remember that weapons should only be drawn to defend yourself or another who isna able to defend themselves because a weapon can kill yourself or another person. This is a verra serious responsibility. One that you mustna take lightly. Do you ken?"

"Aye, Momma, we ken," they all three replied in unison as they descended the stairs to the main hall of the keep.

As they walked to the training field, they could hear the men's swords clanging together. "First rule of training is for you to listen and do exactly what you are told. We will stay near the wall and away from the men. If I say 'down', you drop to the ground as quickly as possible. If I tell you to stay, you stay exactly where you are."

About halfway along the wall, Elisa heard the hissing of air. She froze and said "Down." The children dropped to the ground as quickly as she did. A long dagger made a loud thump as it landed in a board in the wall about three feet ahead of them. Elisa rose from the ground, walked to the board, and wrenched the handle of the dagger up and down a few times to loosen it from the wood and pulled it out. She told the children to stay there and sit against the wall. She walked towards the men and asked, "Who threw this? Which of you dared to threaten the laird's wife and children?"

A young lad meekly looked at the ground and mumbled, "I did, m' lady. I dinna think women and children should be on the training field. I only wanted to scare you off."

"Well, since you challenged me, defend yourself." Elisa took a defensive stance with the dagger held out before her.

"But, you have my weapon," the young man complained. "What am I supposed to do?"

"I guess today's lesson is that you shouldna relinquish your weapon so quickly to another." She stepped towards him and he took one step back. She whipped her left leg out, hooked it around his right leg as she shoved her hands into his chest and knocked him to the ground. As he rolled to one side, he rose up on his hands and knees and she used the flat of the blade to spank his bottom. Several of the men laughed and jeered at him. But one lad was offended and drew his sword. She used her foot to push the one on the ground away from her by placing her foot on his hip and shoving him away.

"Well, that is fine on an unarmed lad, but how are you against an armed man?" he asked.

Elisa turned slightly towards him, keeping the other one in her peripheral vision. When she was sure the lad on the ground wasna going to trip her, she turned squarely to her new opponent. After a few clashes, the second lad realized he was quite equally matched and he wasna going to dissuade her so easily. She was able to withstand his assault and block each blow since he was a young lad and nay a wall of muscles like Ian and some of his other guards. But, she was used to training with a strong warrior, since she always trained with Sir Colin.

Then, behind her, she heard Ian's loud voice booming, "What is going on here?" The lad nearly dropped his sword. Elisa used the opportunity to step in and disarmed him. "Enough!" Ian insisted. "Somebody had better start explaining this."

"I was walking the children along the wall, as I said I would, when I heard the hissing of a blade coming towards us. I quickly yelled for the children to get down, which they did. Then, this dagger," she held the dagger up, "stuck into a board in the wall just a few feet in front of us. I pulled it from the wall and came over here and asked who threw it. This lad," she pointed to the young lad who had thrown it, "said he threw it and I confronted him."

The second lad spoke up, "She knocked him to the ground and used the flat of the blade to spank my brother. The men started laughing at him and making comments; I became angry and I drew my sword on her in defense of my brother, m' laird. I am sorry; I should have been in better control of my emotions, but I am responsible for protecting my brother."

"You both should have been in better control of your emotions," the laird said.

"If someone tries to harm me or our children, I am going to do what I can to protect them," Elisa said in her defense.

"Lady Elisa, would you please check on the children? I will join you in a few minutes. I need to speak with the men for a few minutes first." He gave her a look that she was certain meant she had better obey him. He waited for her to obey his command, even though he knew that wouldna be what she wanted to do. She already told him she dinna think it would be in her nature to follow; and that she wasna sure she could be led.

She hesitated for a moment, but then curtsied to Ian and said, "Aye, m' laird." She handed him the boys' daggers before she turned and walked towards the children as gracefully as she knew how, knowing her breeches would emphasize every movement.

Ian informed the men that his wife and children had his permission to train away from the men; then, he gave the men instructions for their training, which they carried out immediately. Then, he pulled the two boys aside and spoke with them privately. "I realize that you dinna know Lady Elisa had my permission to bring the children to the training field. However, it isna your place to deal with this, nor do I appreciate that you threatened them with a weapon. You will return to your quarters for today. You may return to the training field tomorrow morning; but in the meantime, I want you to think about how you should have handled the situation and let me or if I am unavailable, then let Sir Duncan know your response. You may go." Ian watched them walk towards the barracks. He could tell from their posture the older was verra upset with his younger brother. The younger one was trying to apologize but the older one dinna want to hear it.

Ian turned and walked towards Elisa and the children. He hoped this dinna make the problem worse. He hoped it dinna create an issue with his wife. He couldna tolerate them trying to do anything to harm his wife or children. He hoped they dinna think to retaliate against her.

As Elisa returned to the children, she saw little Ian grasp Hawk's arm as he told him to stay where Mother had told him. Hawk remembered and obeyed.

"Ian, thank you for reminding Hawk to obey my orders. And Hawk, thank you for heeding your brother's advice and obeying me. Ian and Elsbeth know to always obey me, but I know it's new for you to have a mother to listen to. But, I realize now that I made some mistakes yesterday by not listening to Laird Ian. It was wrong of me and worse, it was a bad example to you children and the other members of the clan. So now, I need to tell you, you should always obey me except if it conflicts with the laird's orders. If you dinna know which orders to obey, then you must ask us. Do you ken?"

"Aye, Momma, we ken."

"Come on, let's move down to the end of the wall and start your training." Ian and Hawk ran ahead and got there first and started sword fighting. Ian instructed Hawk if he did something differently than how he was taught. Elsbeth and Elisa walked along slowly. Elisa dinna want to hurry because she was in a mood, a verra bad mood. The bad feeling was getting much worse and she dinna like it. It was going to ruin their plans for the day. She dinna like when the plan changed, especially if there wasna anything she could do to control the situation. It always made her irritable, more irritable than the feeling was making her feel.

Elsbeth looked up at her. When she saw the look on her mother's face, she took her hand in hers and asked, "Momma, what is wrong?"

"I dinna ken what is wrong, Elsbeth; I am just in a verra bad mood and I dinna want to talk about it, alright?" When they reached the area where the boys were training, Elisa gave Elsbeth a few instructions and then watched her do what she said. In her current mood, Elisa knew she couldna train with Elsbeth because she might injure Elsbeth since she was so distracted by the feeling that she knew something bad would happen today. After several minutes, she said, "Can you sit and watch your brothers until your father joins us? Hopefully, he willna mind training you. It wouldna be safe for me to train in my current mood. I might be too distracted and hurt you and I wouldna ever want to hurt you."

"Aye, Momma."

When Ian finally joined them, it only took a glance for him to see something was wrong with Elisa. She said, "I dinna want to talk about it, can you please work with Elsbeth?"

He nodded, but said, "I only wanted to say thank you for doing as I asked. I also wanted to tell you that you dinna do anything wrong. Those lads have needed a set down for a while, but I dinna ken how to go about it because they are orphaned and the oldest lad just tries to protect his brother. His brother needs to learn to nay get into trouble to begin with. I want to give them some leniency because of their situation, but it's frustrating that the younger one constantly gets into some scrap and the older always tries to defend him or take the blame for his brother. He doesna see that he isna helping his brother. His brother needs to be responsible for his behavior. I sent them back to their quarters for today and asked them to think about how they should have handled the situation. I will allow them to return to training tomorrow if they have an answer to my question."

Elisa replied, "More orphans? Do you take in all the orphans in the county?"

"Aye."

"Aye? And how many would that be?"

"Thirty or forty."

Then, Ian went and sat with Elsbeth and they talked for a while. He asked Elsbeth, "Do you ken what is wrong with your momma?"

"Nay, Papa, she only said she was in a verra bad mood and she dinna want to talk about it and that it wouldna be safe for her to train in her mood. She asked me to watch Ian and Hawk until you joined us. Are you going to show me what to do?"

"Aye, I will teach you. What has your momma taught you?" Ian asked.

"Rule one is to listen and do exactly what I am told. If I am told 'down', I am to lie down as quickly as possible. If I am told to stay, I have to stay exactly where I am. She also said this is a weapon," Elsbeth showed her new father her wooden sword. She continued, "Weapons are nay toys. They can kill people, myself or someone else. And I should never draw my weapon except to defend myself or someone else who isna able to defend themselves."

Elisa was filled with pride that Elsbeth remembered everything. Then, she showed Ian the wooden dagger and told him, "Momma gave me this too. She said girls need more weapons and resources than boys because girls are nay as strong as boys, so they need to be cunning. I think Momma is verra cunning; she is stronger than those boys because she was able to disarm both of them and knock them down. Momma is also verra smart. She can find creative ways to pay for things without Cousin Ken, finding out. She even made me these verra soft breeches to match hers."

Ian said, "Aye, I think your momma is verra smart, and creative, and mayhap cunning, and sometimes she can be sneaky when she needs to be, but I dinna think she would have done things that she shouldna do unless it was absolutely necessary for your survival."

Elsbeth thought for a few minutes while she trained, then said, "Why would you tell Momma you took in thirty or forty orphans? She is going to make them all something and I will have to help her."

"Like what?" Ian asked.

"She will make all of them clothes and a blanket."

"Elsbeth, come here, please." Elisa called.

"Aye, Momma."

Elisa lowered her voice and said, "I really dinna want you to tell Ian everything about me; and remember, I told you we need to be thankful for what we have and show our gratitude by giving to others who have less than us."

"Aye, Momma, I remember now. I am sorry."

"It's alright, honey, just remember to add that to your prayers tonight."

"Aye." Elsbeth said and she bounded back to Ian. Ian gave her instructions and showed her what to do and then watched her do it. He guided her gently. He was a good teacher, patient with Elsbeth if she dinna ken how to do something right away.

Elisa sat and watched them for a long time. The feeling was growing stronger, which meant that whatever was going to happen would happen soon. She shouldna have allowed herself to be happy that she made it to Scotland and her husband. Then, mayhap what was going to happen wouldna happen. She knew from her experience that any time she was happy or had a bit of fun, there were always severe consequences. She should know better than to try to have fun or be happy; nothing good could come of it. How many times was she beat as a child when she went off with Ian and Duncan? She shouldna need any reminders to know that nothing good would come of her having fun or being happy.

She knew how to handle the pain and suffering. She should just accept that was what was expected of her and nay try to have the other. Then, she wouldna have to deal with her emotions being pulled first in one direction and then in the other and she wouldna get so upset with others or herself for nay being capable of controlling her emotions.

Ian was right, she had fun planning her trick on him and his family; but if she thought about it more clearly, she would have recognized that she did it because she was angry they dinna awakened her for her own wedding; and then, they had the nerve to be upset with her because they had to wait on her to wake up and dress. It wasna as if they sent a maid to wake her or to help her dress. She was irritated by their comment when she felt it was their own fault. However, she knew from past experience that no matter what she did, it dinna matter because she was still to blame and she was the one who was punished.

She should have known better than to try to turn the table on them and give them a dose of their own. She should have just accepted that she was at fault and taken the blame and nay enjoyed giving them a bit of what they deserved. Then, mayhap, she wouldna be dealing with this feeling that something verra bad would happen today.

Given what she expected would happen, they shouldna go to the loch. It would be best to put everyone's safety first and stay within the walls. She shouldna be trying to have fun anyway. She could find a maid to plan something fun with the children and nay try to be any part of that; then, these things mightna happen.

She was determined to change her behavior. Now, she just needed to convince Ian that it would be best to nay go to the loch. She wished she had recalled that something bad would happen if she had fun or was happy before she married Ian; and then, mayhap, he wouldna have married her, but she might have been able to convince him to take in the children for their safety, since he dinna seem to mind taking in all the orphans in the area.

She sighed quietly to herself. She was frustrated that she dinna remembered this before now. She was disappointed in herself and her failure. She dinna like to be wrong, do something wrong; failure meant punishment.

After several minutes, she forced herself to stop thinking these depressing thoughts. She just had to accept that she would have to do whatever was required of her. She focused her breathing for several minutes and then she rose from the bench she was sitting on and approached Ian. "I am alright now. I can take over Elsbeth's training, if you wish, m' laird."

"Are you certain? I dinna mind working with Elsbeth; I am quite enjoying myself."

"It's up to you, but I could work with Elsbeth and you could work with the boys or return to your men."

"I will work with Elsbeth; you can work with the boys. I can train with the men afterwards or even tomorrow. I really dinna mind, m' lady; I am enjoying myself."

"Verra well, m' laird," Elisa replied. Then, she walked towards the boys and worked with them. She was usually verra patient with the children. She dinna really ken where it came from; she had certainly never been shown any patience. She was very gentle when she corrected them and she tried to be encouraging and supportive. She supposed it was because she dinna like anyone to be treated as she was treated. She just couldna ken how her parents could do what they did to her. They were so kind to Jonathan when he was little; but then, they just abandoned him when his mother became pregnant with Elsbeth. She couldna ken it.

She ran through the same routine that she usually worked on with little Ian and they stopped frequently to explain to Hawk so he would ken each direction before they started. Then, the two boys would train and Elisa would only stop them if they needed correction. She tried to teach them everything that she recalled Sir Colin taught her.

Usually, she worked with one boy at a time and trained with them; then, she would work with the other; and after they both seemed to ken what she was trying to teach them, she let them train with each other for a while until she wanted to show them something else.

She worked with the boys for over an hour. She explained to Hawk the exercises that Ian did, so the two boys could work on them together. She knew the boys needed to run so they would have more stamina and there were exercises they could do to help build muscles, exercises she did every day to make herself stronger. The boys couldna just spend their time swinging a sword or pulling the string on their bow or tossing daggers at a target if they really wanted to grow up to be stronger. They needed to exercise to grow stronger, but she knew it would also help them be more attentive in the classroom when they worked on their studies if they spent more time getting fresh air and exercise. It was good to have a balance between academics and outside excursions and exercise.

Suddenly, she felt a sharp pain and the bad feeling was much stronger. She bit her lip so no one would know what was going on with her. She did her best to cover up the pain so no one could see it in her features. She wasna supposed to let anyone know that she got these feelings that something bad was about to happen. She took several slow, deep breaths to recover.

She only had to focus on the memories of her childhood for a couple minutes and remember all the times that she was beaten by her mother or father or Lady Isobel. She was able to just take her punishment and pretend like it dinna bother her or affect her. She could just continue on with life like nothing happened and they couldna get to her, nay the real her, nay who she really was on the inside, deep inside her. Sometimes, it felt like the real her was so deep inside that she wasna sure if even she knew who she was anymore. None of them knew the real her and how determined she was, determined to survive whatever was thrown at her, whatever she had to endure.

She would endure it all because she knew the least little bit of affection was worth it all. And Ian had shown her that his kisses and caresses, his affection could banish the bad away. She dinna think about the memories of her childhood or what was done to her by her cousin and his friends or even the bad feeling she had this morning when he held her or kissed her. She began to realize the need for affection when she took Elsbeth from her mother and started caring for her and Ian. She knew she had to keep that to herself. She instinctively knew that her father wouldna allow her to raise the children if he realized that she cared at all for them and especially nay if he knew that she gained anything in return from taking care of them. She loved when they snuggled into her and wrapped their arms around her or laid their hand in hers. There were so many things that she loved about them, too many to think about right now. And she returned her thoughts to the boys and their training and ensuring that she covered her feelings about the bad feeling that she knew meant something bad would happen today, back to reality.

She watched the boys in her peripheral view while she looked out over the training field. She wondered just how many men Ian had here because the training field was really big. It was quite a distance from one corner to the other. It would be a good distance for the boys to run from one end to the other. The archery targets were along the far wall so if the boys stayed along this wall, they should be alright running between the two walls. Although, she would be sure to explain to them that they shouldna be running along this wall if anyone was practicing with the targets.

Chapter 7

ELISA INTERRUPTED LITTLE Ian and Hawk's training to tell them, "Remember to do your exercises, Ian, and show Hawk what to do before you do it, so you can do it together. Also, this is a big training field so you can run from this corner to that far corner," she pointed to the other end of the wall, "and back. But never run behind any archery targets when they are set up or when they are doing target practice. I will talk to Laird Ian about getting each of you a bow and a quiver full of arrows." The boys nodded; so, Elisa started walking back to the keep.

By the time she reached the entrance, she heard a bird call. She figured Ian was calling someone to him so they could watch the children, which meant he would be right behind her. She dinna even make it across the bailey.

Ian called, "Elisa, please stop so I dinna have to grab you and upset you even more."

Elisa froze and thought to herself, does the man have to have such long, muscular legs that he can cover the distance in so short a time?

Ian pleaded, "Please, Elisa, just turn to me and trust me with whatever is bothering you."

She turned to him. She knew he could see the tears on her face but she dinna want him to touch her, so she held up her hand to him. "Dinna reach out and touch me no matter what happens. I need to feel what I am feeling and if you touch me the feeling will go away. Do you ken?"

"Aye," he agreed.

"First, I am nay supposed to tell anyone when this happens. By telling you this, I might be putting you and the clan at risk, but you are my husband and I suppose you have a right to know. I should have told you before we were married, but I really dinna remember it until it happens. All I can really tell you is that I get a verra bad feeling and then something bad happens. I dinna cause the bad thing to happen nor do I want it to happen, it's more like a warning to be careful. My parents said that other people would think I was a witch, so they told me to nay tell anyone about things when this happens to me."

Elisa paused for a moment, and then continued, "Earlier this morning when I woke up, the bad feeling was there. It startled me awake and I was afraid. I tried to wiggle free from under you, but you held me even tighter. I tried to lay still for a long time, but I dinna like lying in bed when I am awake and I know there are other things I could be doing. Then, I noticed that the tingling that your touch gives me made the bad feeling go away. I dinna want to feel the bad feeling, so that is why I worked to get you to roll over and laid on top of you. But then, when I was watching out the window and saw the dust, I knew the bad feeling was back and nay going to go away. That is why I wanted you to see the dust rising over the hills. Something verra bad is going to happen and I am verra afraid. I feel that the bad thing is going to involve you and I am verra worried about you being hurt. I really dinna think we should take the children to the loch for our picnic and swimming; even though they are going to be verra upset, especially little Ian. Something snaps in him whenever we have to suddenly change our plans. He often has a fit of rage, but I can usually calm him down. Other times, he just needs to do something physical to work it out."

Ian asked, "What if we increased the guard and that way we could still have our picnic?"

"I ken that I am supposed to trust you and your men to protect us, so I will do my best to try to trust you, m' laird. But, you need to know that I will do whatever is necessary to try to protect you, your clan, and especially, the children. I am saying I might nay follow your orders."

"I ken that already, m' sweet wife," Ian chuckled.

"I need to ask a favor of you, m' laird."

"What is the favor, before I can say 'aye' or 'nay'?"

"If Cousin Ken comes here, I need your assurance that you will listen to me about how best to deal with him. If something happens to you, I need you to tell Sir Duncan that I am in charge."

"Nay, m' lady, I canna do that because the men wouldna like taking orders from a woman, especially one they hardly know."

"I know him better than any of you. What if I gave the orders privately and then you give the men the orders?"

"I will give you my assurance that I will listen to your advice, but that doesna mean I will follow your orders. I will ask Sir Duncan to do the same in my stead. Verra well?"

"Aye, m' laird husband. We ken each other verra well." Elisa replied. "I will go and organize our picnic provisions and you can return to your training. I am sorry you have missed your training because of the children and me."

He smiled down at her and drew her closer, "I have verra much enjoyed my morning. I dinna feel I have missed anything, Elisa." Then, he turned and went back to the training field. Elisa turned and went into the hall and into the kitchen. She busied herself with gathering food and filling waterskins. Then, she started towards the great hall to return to her room. Unfortunately, Lady Isobel was walking through the great hall towards the kitchen just as Elisa was leaving the kitchen. In her current mood, Elisa knew this couldna turn out well.

She tried to just walk past her mother-in-law, but Lady Isobel stopped in front of her, forcing Elisa to stop. Lady Isobel said, "Why must you dress in men's breeches and behave like a man? It isna verra ladylike. Dinna you ken your husband's position? His father is the chieftain; he will be the chieftain one day. Everything you do reflects upon your husband and the chieftain."

Elisa yelled at her, "Mayhap, because I was raised by a man, in a man's world, with a man's education, to follow men's rules, and trained to defend myself against men. One might have expected my mother's best friend, m' lady, to teach me the way a lady should behave since my mother and my stepmother died, and there werena any other female relatives to do the job. I am sorry I am such a great disappointment to you. I am sure you had much higher expectations from your son's wife considering his high ranking position." She stepped around Lady Isobel and stormed off. Out of the corner of her eye, she saw

Ian and the children standing in the doorway. She swore, "Blast it," and ran up the stairs to their room and slammed the door closed.

"Stay right where you are, Mother," Ian demanded. Then, he turned to the children. "Ian, do you know what your mother would expect you to do to get ready for a picnic and swimming?"

"Aye, Father, I will see to it. We will be ready verra soon." The children were followed up to the nursery by Sir Duncan, Sir Colin and Angus.

Ian turned to his mother, "Mother, what have you done to upset Lady Elisa, now?"

"Ian, why do you let her dress like a man and behave like a man? It isna ladylike."

"Mother, let me make this verra clear to you, I dinna want you to criticize my wife again. How she dresses or behaves is my concern now, nay yours. I quite like her leather breeches."

His mother interrupted, "I know what you like about her breeches and dinna be vulgar with me."

"Enough, Mother. This is *my* home and she is *my* wife. She and I will work out our marriage between us. No more criticism from you. I finally got her to open up to me and she was in a better mood and now you have ruined it. If you continue to interfere in my marriage, I will not allow you to come here again. You will not see your grandchildren. You better heed my warning because I willna tolerate you hurting Elisa anymore." And with that, Ian turned and went upstairs to see to his wife.

He knocked first before entering. His wife stepped from the tub and wrapped in a robe and walked to the window. He strode to where Elisa was standing. He stood behind her, as close as he could be without actually touching her. "Are you still worried about the dust you saw this morning, or angry with my mother?"

"Nay, Ian, I am angry with myself for losing my temper and yelling at her again. I canna seem to control my emotions at all since I arrived here. Your mother is right and I dinna want to admit it, but I really dinna know anything about behaving like a lady. I havena had any training in that area. Everything that I have been educated on has been what a firstborn son would learn and need to know to run several English estates and businesses. I havena had any feminine influence since my mother died. My stepmother had nothing to do with me at all, which frankly, seemed like a blessing compared to the way my mother treated me. Honestly, I dinna think my mother spent any time explaining to me how a lady should act. Mayhap, she thought she would have time for that later."

"First of all, you are correct; Mother should have come to help out your father. Father and Mother should have gone to get you when your father died. And worse, I should have gone to get you long before now. Then, you wouldna have been forced to face all the things you had to endure. On top of all that, you had to travel a great distance on your own and provide for yourself and the children, when I should have been there for you. No one could have done better, Elisa. You should be proud of yourself, nay angry for losing your temper or being emotional." He paused, then added, "Now, Mother has been informed that she isna to criticize you, nor is she to meddle in how we work out our marriage."

Elisa turned to him, "Thank you, Ian." She leaned into him and wrapped her arms around his waist. He enveloped her in his arms and they hugged for a long time. Then, Ian went to the tub, stripped out of his training clothes and washed with the remaining bucket of water.

While he was getting ready, Elisa went to her trunk and pulled out several daggers and laid them on the bed. She began strapping them on, one around each calf, one around each thigh, two at the back of her waist, one on each forearm and upper arm. She put on her pendant that allowed her to carry a dagger concealed at the back of her neck. She pulled her hair loose from on top of her head, took out the braid, and re-braided it. She pinned it up with two needle-like daggers.

Ian watched, fascinated, "How many daggers are you going to wear?"

"Twenty and my sword," she answered.

"I only counted thirteen." He was nay amused that she felt she needed to wear so many daggers to feel safe.

"Well, another dagger will be strapped to my waist with my sword. There is a dagger in each pocket of my cloak and two more are stitched into the hem of my cloak and one in each boot." She began dressing and added her sword belt to her waist. Then, she put on her boots and slipped a dagger in each boot. Then, she walked across the room to get her cloak.

Ian put his arm out to pull her to him. He gently cupped her chin in his hand and turned her face to his. He lightly kissed her and then said, "You ken this doesna look like you are trusting my men and me to protect you?"

"I trust you, Ian; I am just going prepared for the worst." She stepped out of his embrace, put on her cloak, and reached for the door. "I will see that the children are ready and meet you in the hall." She went upstairs to the nursery.

The children were ready. Little Ian strapped his dagger to his waist. Elisa asked Hawk if he had a dagger, but he dinna. She ducked behind the screen and removed her breeches part of the way. She untied one of her daggers from her thigh and redressed and emerged from behind the dressing screen. Then, she tied the dagger around Hawk's waist. Next, she clasped Elsbeth's cloak around her daughter. She carried the boys' cloaks and they headed down to the hall. Ian was emerging from their room as the boys ran past.

Little Ian called out, "Father, we will race you to the door of the hall."

They were all three off at breakneck speed down the stairs. She knew her husband wouldna allow the boys to win a challenge against their laird. When Elsbeth and Elisa reached the top of the stairs, Ian and the boys were playing near the door. Elsbeth ran down the stairs to join the fun when she saw them. Ian tossed them in the air, caught them and spun them around. Elisa just watched in awe, her heart swelled to see how happy they were. He could give them the love they hadna received from their own father. Something she had never had either. But she remembered how her father had doted on little Ian before his mother died. She knew he probably dinna remember the time he spent with his parents because he was too young, but she remembered; she also remembered that her father dinna treat her that way and he never had. Before she started crying, she buried her emotions and stuffed the memories back in the little box that she envisioned them in and locked the box in her mind. She tried to smile.

Then, they headed to the stables, Ian approached Elisa to help her mount, but first he pulled her close and briefly kissed her. Then, he asked, "Are you going to share anything with me about these minutes of sadness that come over you occasionally?"

"Nay, I dinna want to discuss it. I am sorry; I canna seem to make the memories stop popping into my head."

"Elisa, I am your husband and I dinna mind listening if you would share with me."

She shook her head slightly, "I will be alright."

He wanted to shake her or at least sigh in his frustration, but he supposed she needed to know him better before she could feel comfortable about sharing with him. "Are you ready?"

"Aye."

He lifted her on her saddle and helped her get situated before he mounted his horse and led them to the loch. Ian increased the guard at the castle and their escort. She tried to be comforted by this knowledge. She knew nothing good ever came of these bad feelings that she sometimes got. These things never ended well, but she knew she should try to trust her husband and his guards. She would try to trust them, but she would also be prepared for the worst. She also knew she should trust God, so she prayed that He would protect all of their family.

The guards spread out along the shore and in the woods. Ian and Elisa took the kids swimming first. They were all having fun and she kept her feelings to herself for their sake. Then, they returned to the shore to have their picnic. The children sat and ate quietly, which was a relief. She wanted to hear every sound around her; but then, she nearly jumped every time she heard a noise in the woods. She couldna eat; she was so on edge. Ian couldna do anything to ease her discomfort.

Ian tried to get her to eat something, "Just a little piece of bread, please, Elisa. Try to relax and enjoy our picnic." He tried to feed her a little piece of the bread. She ate the bite and then took the bread from him and continued to eat it. He shared his cup of ale with her every few bites. She took a drink to wash down the bread. When she heard the clash of metal against metal, she stood up, grabbed Elsbeth and was just about to the horses when she heard Ian say, "Put Ian with Sir Thomas, Elsbeth with Sir Colin, and Hawk will ride with Angus. You three will stay with the children until I say otherwise."

"Aye, m' laird," they replied and did as they were told.

Before Elisa could reach her horse, she felt two strong hands lift her up. And then she heard Ian say, "You will have to find a way to forgive me, m' sweet wife." He handed her up to Sir Duncan, "Dinna let her off your horse until you are inside the castle walls. Dinna let her out of your sight until I return. She is your first priority. Take the tunnel, quickly now, I'll hold them off."

"Aye, m' laird," Sir Duncan replied. He wheeled his horse about and they were off. She tried to look over his shoulder at her husband. Ian reached his hand out to her and clasped his fingers shut over his palm. She knew instantly what he meant; this was his way of protecting her.

She returned the gesture and she stopped struggling on Sir Duncan's lap.

Once they were in the tunnel, torches were lit and they continued to ride on to the castle. Elisa said, "Sir Duncan, I can ride my own horse."

"Nay, m' lady, the laird said you ride with me until we are inside the castle walls. I willna take any chances that you will hang back and try to return to the laird."

She groaned, "Verra well."

A minute later, she asked, "Should we talk about the plan or wait until we reach the castle?"

"You may make your suggestions, m' lady, I will listen, and then we will decide if it is a good plan or nay."

"Well, I want the children protected first and foremost. Is there a secret room to hide them in? If so, I want Sir Colin and Angus and five other men hidden with the children, with as much food and water stores as possible. If possible, I would feel best if there is a suitable woman to stay with Elsbeth. One who would be a comfort to the children and nay become hysterical if the room was broken into. I just need to know they are safe."

"Consider it done, m' lady. Angus' wife, Alice, would be a good choice. She was Ian's nanny."

"Verra well, I shall have to trust your judgment on the matter. Thank you. I havena any idea what to expect will happen to Laird Ian. I would imagine he might be killed, but I think it's more likely he will be captured and used for ransom or an exchange. At least, I hope that is their intentions."

"You dinna have to trust my judgment of Alice being a good choice to watch the children. You could trust your own judgment, but mayhap, now is nay the time to think about those memories. But if you wish to recall, she was there for you when you needed caring for. And why do you think m' laird might be used for an exchange, m' lady?"

"If this is Cousin Ken, he will exchange Ian for me, I think."

"Alright, so what would your plan be?" Sir Duncan asked.

"I would invite him into the castle, but only my cousin, none of his men. I would have him stripped and searched for any weapons, which I would relieve him of all weapons. His men can camp in the field outside the castle. I would offer him food and ale and see what he wants. He will want to taunt me just so he can see my reaction and if he can scare me. He likes that sort of thing. Then, I would escort him to a chamber for the night, preferably a room that hasna a secret passage and set guards at his door. I would mayhap have him escorted to the dungeon until he tells us where he is holding Laird Ian."

"In the meantime, I would see if my father-in-law could get more of his soldiers into the castle or I might plan a raid on Ken's men. Chief Ian's men can use the trees for cover until they attack. If they attack during the night, I would guess there would only be a few guards and most of his men will be asleep in their tents. It wouldna be a difficult battle at all. I dinna think he would be that prepared for a battle. He is a merchant; but even that, I did most of the work for him and his father. He is too lazy to bother to do any real work. I dinna think you will find his men prepared for an attack or any difficulty during a battle because I dinna think they are soldiers or guards as all your men or Chief Ian's men will be."

She continued, "I would slaughter all but one. I would allow him to speak with Ken and send the one survivor to bring back Ian or else we will kill Cousin Ken. If possible, we should have the man followed so we can deal directly with the captors or rescue Ian ourselves. Hopefully, they will agree to exchange Ian for Ken. I might agree to the ransom if I felt it would encourage them to return Ian and return home to England."

"I am verra impressed, m' lady. That is a verra good plan. M' laird already asked Chieftain Ian to gather his men to him and he already doubled the guards on the castle walls. I believe he respected your warning and has already started preparations for a battle and a siege."

"I must tell you, Sir Duncan, I doubt I will sleep until m' laird returns. I sleep verra little anyway; but now, I willna sleep until he is returned. I also wish to speak with Angus and his wife before the children are brought to the secret room. I must speak with the children to give them my love and encouragement. Then, I would like to go up on the parapets to await some word as to what has happened to m' laird husband."

"M' lady, we are about to enter the castle now. I just want you to know I think you are verra brave and I willna leave your side, nay even for a moment. You will be protected as long as it takes to get m' laird back home. Now, dinna let the children see you are scared when we go into the sunlight," he whispered this last part.

Duncan lowered Elisa to the ground and dismounted. Once everyone was dismounted, the children were brought into the castle. Sir Duncan and Angus stayed with Elisa until Alice was brought to them. Elisa took her aside and said, "Thank you for doing this, Alice. I appreciate it and I am relieved to know the children will be well provided for. I intend to see them now and try to explain what I can. I just need to know if you think I should come see them or if you think that would be harder on them if I came and left again each day."

"I am glad to help you, m' lady. And rest assured, the children will be well cared for and protected. I think you should talk with them now, explain what is happening and then, dinna return until this is all over. I feel that will be best and also what is safest, m' lady. We wouldna want the wrong person to see where the children are hidden."

"Verra well. Would you go to the kitchen and ensure you have all the provisions you will need. Then, let us get them settled." The women returned to Sir Duncan and Angus and were led to the children. Elisa told the children what she could. "You will have to hide out with Alice and these guards until it is safe for you to come out; alright?"

"Aye, Mother," they replied.

"I canna tell you much more than that except that it is so we can protect you. You must be verra brave and quiet and nay complaining. I love you all very much. I will miss you, but I canna come see you until after this is all over; otherwise, it might give away your hiding place. I will pray for all of you and your safety and we must all pray for your father's safety and his quick return." Then, she gave them each a hug and a kiss before she walked out of the secret room and the door was closed and locked and barred from the inside.

Elisa and Sir Duncan returned to the main hall. She busied herself talking with the cook and the maids to ensure food was provided to all the men on watch at regular intervals. Meanwhile, Sir Duncan talked with the men about the plans. Then, when all the orders were given, he escorted Elisa to the parapets. She just stood there, staring out over the hills, waiting.

As evening approached, Sir Duncan approached her, "Lady Elisa, you should return to the castle. You shouldna let yourself become chilled."

"Nay, Sir Duncan, I am staying here until my cousin comes. If you wish to send someone for my cloak, you may do so. But, be sure they dinna approach me without announcing their presence and waiting for my acknowledgment that I ken they are there; and, they mustna touch me. Be sure everyone knows for I willna be responsible for my reaction. Do you ken?"

"Aye, m' lady, the men already know. I will send for your cloak." He turned to one of the men nearby and gave the order.

"Sir Duncan," she asked, "is there anything I could be doing to help? Anything the laird's wife would be expected to do?"

"I dinna think there is anything else for you to do, m' lady. I believe you already did all you can. We just have to wait and watch now."

"What will you do for sleep if I dinna sleep?"

"If you willna sleep, then I willna sleep. I dinna require much sleep, at least nay for long periods of time. I can catch up later."

"I dinna think that is a good idea. I need you to be clearheaded and rested so you can give the orders until m' laird returns. I give you my word, I willna leave the castle,

I willna try to rescue Ian on my own. I will stay within the main keep while you sleep, if you provide another to protect me."

"Verra well, but only if you keep your word. If you betray me, I will have you locked up with the children. Do you ken?"

"Aye, I give you my word," she said and turned back to the wall. She continued to look out over the hills for any signs of riders. Duncan occasionally spoke with her to get her attention and then he took her arm and walked her to one side or the other of the parapet. After a while, she realized it was to keep their legs from cramping and to stay alert. Elisa dinna need the exercise to stay alert. She just focused on the task she needed to do and she was alert to that one thing. Usually, that was all she was focused on, just the one task. But, she let him lead her around the parapet because she dinna want her legs to cramp from standing still in one place for so long and then be told she had to return to the keep. She wouldna take being treated like a child verra well, nay after raising herself and running so many estates and businesses since she was eight years old.

She buried the memories back in the box and locked it before they could really form in her mind. She dinna want to think about that time of her life anymore. That was the last thing she would ever want to do is think about what her cousin and his friends did to her. She was barely capable of explaining it to her husband and she only told him the bare minimum. She just couldna bear to think about it because she was ashamed and embarrassed and disappointed in herself for being too weak to deal with the situation herself.

She focused on steeling herself for what her cousin might say. She knew he liked nothing more than to catch her unaware and startle her. She had to be prepared to face anything that he might say. He was the type of person who would gladly humiliate her in front of others.

She was certain that was why he brought his friends to the townhouse. She supposed it made him feel like a big, strong man to humiliate her and force her to be subject to his vile debauchery. She couldna think of anything more humiliating than the things he did to her, except inviting his friends to watch or join him.

Ugh! She had to bury all these thoughts and stop thinking about it or she wouldna be able to face her cousin. If he saw the effect he had on her, he would taunt her. She had to be strong; show no signs of any weakness. She had to figure out a way to get her cousin to return the laird to them. She had to be strong enough to sacrifice herself for the clan if it was necessary; and with her cousin, it would be necessary; but hopefully, she could convince him to leave the children here and she wouldna have to worry about her cousin hurting them. If they were safe here and she had to return to London, at least she would be comforted knowing that her cousin couldna use the children to force her to do anything.

She was always good at doing whatever was necessary; so she would just have to do what was necessary to get Cousin Ken to return the laird. She wouldna think about what that would be; what he would do to her, require of her when they returned to London. She would just focus on negotiating for Laird Ian's return; and hopefully, she could convince Cousin Ken to let the children stay here. She thought about the cost to feed and clothe them; how often they needed clothes because they were growing so quickly. The loss of income was the best way to deal with her cousin, since he cared so much about drinking and gambling. She would miss little Ian and Elsbeth terribly, but she wouldna think about that right now. She could think about that after the laird was returned to his clan and she was on her way back to London. She would just think about their need to be safe from their vile cousin.

It was too late now, but she should have tried harder to convince Ian that they shouldna go to the loch. She should have explained to him that she shouldna have fun or try to be happy because something bad always happened afterwards. She had the feeling that something bad would happen and she let him convince her that he could protect them and keep them safe. And now, he had been taken captive. She hoped and prayed that he wasna killed because she felt it would be all her fault.

Sir Duncan glanced at Lady Elisa frequently. He dinna want to try to know what she was thinking. He dinna know what gifts she had, if she had any, but he assumed she must have them. She wasna his wife, so he had no right to know her thoughts. She seemed very serious, but he could also tell that something was upsetting her too. He wished he could comfort her and tell her that everything would be alright, but he dinna know her cousin. They dinna know if her cousin was the one who had Ian, but it seemed the most likely circumstance. It was verra unlikely to be a coincidence that their laird was taken the day after he remarried Lady Elisa.

She clearly dinna like any man to touch her, given what happened on the ride when Ian lifted her onto his lap and the warnings she had given them that no one should touch her or she wouldna be responsible for her reaction. Clearly, her reaction would be a violent one after how she reacted to Ian lifting her off her horse and onto his. Several of the men had seen and commented on it later, but he had told them to nay discuss it, except to ensure everyone knew to nay touch her without her permission unless it was required to protect her and keep her safe.

She seemed certain her cousin was involved in this plot to take the laird and that he would exchange the laird for her. He needed to trust that she knew her cousin best and that she would ken how he would operate. Her plan was good; it had merit. He would trust that it would work. Once they had Ian back, he could eliminate her cousin. The more Duncan thought about her behavior, the more he wondered what exactly her cousin had done to hurt her. She was very calm and emotionless on the outside, but he could sense her turmoil. She kept her feelings and emotions buried and hidden. It was very much like when she was beaten as a child and then she pretended like nothing had happened. She never cried. He supposed they beat her emotions out of her.

Ian had warned him to watch her closely because she told Ian she would do whatever was necessary to protect the family, especially, the children. It was obvious that she cared very much for them. He hoped she would keep her word to nay leave the castle or try to rescue Ian. He really dinna want to lock her up with the children. She wasna a child; that was obvious. She had grown into a very beautiful woman. He still loved her just as much as he had the first time he saw her lying in the crib in their nursery, the first summer she came to visit. He sat beside her crib and held her hand and caressed her cheek or hair. They had a marriage ceremony between her and Ian. She was Ian's wife and he had to keep his feelings buried; but he couldna control his attraction to her. He wanted to be around her as much as possible when they were children and her family visited here. Something about her warmed him, nay just on the outside like a fire does, but to his core. He felt compelled to seek out her warmth. He couldna explain it, but he had to be near her.

But, Ian dinna want the responsibilities that were forced on him and he dinna want to spend that much time with Elisa. They shared the nursery and had lessons together when she was visiting, but Elisa was much smarter than they were. He found it a little irritating and studied harder in her absence; but every year when she returned, she increased her knowledge even more than he and Ian. So, he challenged her in other ways. She wouldna show any fear, no matter what he did to challenge her; she always accepted the challenge and usually she exceeded his expectations.

He needed to put his feelings aside. He couldna think about his feelings for her. She was his brother's wife, even if she dinna know they were brothers. He dinna ken the plan. He thought the whole thing was ridiculous, but Ian was his brother, she was his brother's wife and the rest was none of his business whatever their mothers planned. There were consequences for interfering in his mother's plans. His responsibility was to command his brother's guards and ensure his family's safety. Elisa was his first priority, especially in his brother's absence. There was no place in his life for feelings and emotions. Killing was cold business, so no place for warmth.

He couldna have what he wanted because she belonged to another. He needed to bury his feelings and keep them buried. If something happened to Ian, then he would marry her; but he couldna allow anything to happen to his brother. He would be hurt too deeply to allow that. They were verra close. Their bond grew even closer since Lady Elisa's last visit and return to London. He did all he could to ensure he knew what he needed to do if he should have to be laird one day and also what was necessary to command the guard and protect the clan. He was very good at protecting the clan. He just needed to ensure that he kept his feelings for his brother's wife buried and closely guarded so that he dinna do anything inappropriate. He would ensure that he was never alone with her or if it was necessary, then it was only for the very briefest amount of time and that the door to the room was wide open. The best thing to do would be to ensure that other guards were always with them; then, he wouldna be alone with her.

Duncan did all he could to encourage Ian to accept his marriage and his responsibilities to his wife. He dinna want to see Elisa hurt because Ian dinna love her. He hoped for Elisa's sake that Ian would love her, even if it caused him a great deal of pain. Duncan would persevere to see her happy and loved.

But for now, they had to wait to see who held his brother and see what they wanted for a ransom. He should have left two of the guards in the tunnel to follow Ian's captors. But, it was too late now to think of that. If they dinna hear anything by morning, he would send his best trackers out to follow the trail. If they went out just before the sunrise, the fresh tracks would likely be full of dew in the woods. The trail should be fairly easy to pick up and follow, unless Ian's captors were clever enough to backtrack and run false trails; but from what Elisa described of her cousin, he probably wasna that clever. He was from London and probably not much of a woodsman. But for now, it was just a waiting game. So they would wait. He was verra patient. He would remain calm and strong to ensure that Elisa would find some comfort in his strength and calmness.

He was impressed with her knowledge of her cousin. She clearly had to deal with quite a lot on her wee shoulders since she left here eleven years ago; most of which, he was certain wasna good. But, she stood here, calm and collected and waited patiently, as if nothing and no one could get to her. She was a pillar of strength; a rock.

He decided to pray while they waited. He thanked God for returning Elisa safely to their clan. He thanked God for keeping her safe, especially during her journey. Then, he asked God to guide him in the right path to take in regards to finding his brother and asked the Lord to return Ian to them safely and quickly.

When he finished his prayer, he walked Lady Elisa around the parapets again. First, he walked her to one side and all along the wall from one end to the other. They spent half an hour at each end of the wall watching the woods for signs of movement. Then, he walked her back across the front of the wall to the far wall and to the far end. They spent another half hour watching out over the wall before he walked her to the other end of the wall and then back across the front of the wall. After a half hour at each corner of the wall, he returned to the center above the gate.

They resumed their vigil, but he would have preferred if he could convince her to go inside and warm up and eat something. He doubted she could eat in her current mood, so he dinna waste his breath trying to convince her. He was certain she would prefer to stand on the wall until there was some word from Ian's captors. He would have to think of some reasonable excuse to get her to go inside if there wasna any word before the night was full upon them. He dinna think that was going to be an easy task, so he prayed Ian's captors would send some word soon.

He saw that food was sent out to the men while they stood watch. He assumed Lady Elisa ordered it, so he asked her about it. "Did you ask the kitchen staff to provide food for the guard, m' lady?"

"Aye, I just dinna know what would happen and how long they might have to stand guard. I know we are nay under siege, but I thought if something happened, they might nay get relieved when they normally would, so it would be best if they were well fed during their shift."

"Are you sure you werena raised in the clan ways? That would definitely be something a laird's wife would ken to do," Duncan complimented her. He knew that she was concerned she dinna ken her responsibilities and would embarrass Ian, but she seemed to ken what to do and did it. He imagined she would have no qualms with doing the work herself if it was necessary. He knew that would definitely be something expected of the laird's wife.

"I dinna think my time here when I was a little girl had anything to do with learning to be a laird's wife or a lady, at least nay that I can recall. I only remember playing strategic games and being tested. The few times I did anything fun, I am pretty sure I was beat for it. My father dinna spend any time on educating me to care for a clan. He expected me to run the townhouse and his three estates. He never talked about coming here until he knew he was going to die and then he had his solicitor and lawyer draw up the necessary contracts to provide for us, so my uncle and cousin knew what belonged to me and what I was allowed to take with me when I returned to Scotland to marry Laird Ian. I dinna know for certain, but I think he worried that his nephew or brother might try to harm little Ian and Elsbeth and he wanted to be certain they were cared for and protected and provided for; so he ensured I had everything I could possibly need to provide for the children and protect them."

"What about you? Did he care for you and provide for you? Did he ensure you were protected?" Duncan was certain he already knew the answer to these questions was nay and it made him extremely angry, though he couldna allow it to show.

"I dinna need anything. I could take care of myself."

Duncan couldna say what he wanted to say. He knew it would push her too far and it really wasna his place. And if he made her cry, it wouldna be appropriate to hold her and comfort her. He had to let it go. It was a good thing her father was already dead, or he just might ride to London and torture and kill the man himself. But for now, he needed to keep his composure and focus on her safety, the clan's safety and do all he could to ensure his brother was returned quickly.

He tried to tamp down his anger to at least a simmer. It wouldna do any good if he let his anger get the better of him. He had never kenned the reasons that Elisa had been beaten for every little infraction, except because her parents just enjoyed that sort of thing. Neither he nor Ian were ever punished for going to the loch to fish or swim or to go riding or even for sneaking out of the castle; nay even when they slept out overnight. It was only Elisa who received a beating. But, then again, they beat her for nay performing to whatever their expectation was for all their tests and games. Although, he supposed they couldna really be called games as they werena for fun; at least, nay fun for Elisa. Her childhood, from what he knew of it while she was here on Mull, was all about performance and punishment.

He dinna ken that either, because she usually completed whatever task was asked of her, but then they claimed she dinna do it quickly enough. So the only conclusion he could draw from that was that they just enjoyed beating her. And therefore, he could only conclude that the beatings continued when she returned to London.

It would explain why her father allowed whatever happened between Cousin Ken and her too. The father likely dinna care what his nephew did to Elisa because he obviously dinna care about her. And from what he could sense about Elisa, something bad was done to her and he was pretty certain that her cousin was the one who did those things to her. It was indisputable after the way she reacted to Ian pulling her from her saddle onto his lap. And her language; nay any young lady should spend any time on the docks for any reason. What she said to Ian indicated that she was speaking to a specific person, presumably, her cousin. That made sense considering her immediate reaction to the attack was that it was her cousin and that she expected he would ransom Ian in exchange for her. The question was why Cousin Ken thought he could have Elisa when she was married to Ian. What could he possibly hope to gain from having her when she was married to another?

Duncan glanced at Elisa to see how she was doing. She appeared fine on the outside. She was composed and in control of her emotions. If she could maintain her composure, so could he. He would do his best to ensure that she was protected. He dinna really like the idea of allowing her cousin inside the castle walls; it put her at greater risk. He would have to ensure that she was closely guarded and protected while the man was within their walls. He'd have to ensure Ken wasna allowed to escape or do any reconnaissance to report back to the people with him. He couldna allow him the opportunity to be alone with Elisa or to abduct her. Her safety had to be his first priority.

But once they had him in a dungeon cell and Ian was returned to them, Duncan wasna certain that he would be able to control his anger and he was certain that Ken was going to receive the brunt and brutal force of his anger.

He quietly took a few deep breaths so he could try to tamp down his anger again. He needed to be alert and in control and put Elisa's safety first.

Chapter 8

Finally, Elisa saw dust rising over the hills. The moment of truth was here. Who was behind this plot? Was Ian alive and only a captive, or dead? "Sir," Elisa called to Duncan. She noticed that he stood there, verra still with his eyes closed. She supposed he was praying for his brother's safety and return. She quickly prayed for the same and for His guidance to help them do the right thing in dealing with Ian's captors. She prayed He would give her the strength to endure what she must. Elisa stepped back and let Sir Duncan give the orders. She dinna want to see. She knew Cousin Ken would call out his taunting demands if he was behind this. He loved to humiliate her and abuse her. She had to steal her emotions, so he couldna see any fear or anxiety. "Ho, my lady, let your cousin in to congratulate you on your wedding nuptials." Aye, just as she suspected, her cousin was behind this evil plot. She couldna deny the cleverness of his plan to come under the guise that he wanted to congratulate her on her wedding.

She touched Sir Duncan's arm and nodded to him.

He gave the orders, "Only you, Cousin Ken, will be allowed to enter the castle, but your men are welcome to set up camp outside the castle walls."

As they descended the stairs, she told Sir Duncan, "I would prefer to be within the main hall to greet my cousin."

Arrangements were made for several men to guard her cousin and search him and every garment and to strip him of everything but his breeches and a shirt. Then, Duncan led Elisa back to the main hall, where Elisa sat at her place at the head of the table.

The guards followed their orders and thoroughly searched every garment that Cousin Ken was wearing, including his boots. He was quite put out to be stripped down to nothing and have every inch of his clothes searched. He protested greatly, but to no avail. There were several guards surrounding him with their swords drawn; so there was nothing he could do but wait patiently until he was given back his breeches and shirt to dress. Then, they searched the inside of his boots and the soles closely before they returned his boots to him.

Her cousin entered the hall, "Cousin," he called, loudly and obnoxiously, "it's so good to see you." He rushed towards her, but Sir Duncan blocked his way.

"It's alright, Sir Duncan," Elisa said in a very calm voice. She rose from her seat and curtsied briefly to him. "Cousin Ken, welcome to my home. I am sorry my husband canna be here to greet you." She was as calm as could be on the outside while she sat up straight on her bench like a regal queen. She pointed to the seat next to her. "Please, come and sit. Let us have supper and catch up. You can share what news there is from London." She turned to one of the kitchen maids, "Please tell the cook to have supper served for the two of us. Thank you."

Cousin Ken said, "Lady Elisa, I wish to congratulate you on your wedding. How were your travels? Not too difficult, I hope?"

"Nay any difficulties, cousin, our travels were a wonderful adventure," she answered as supper was served.

"That is very good; glad to hear it. I know your husband could not be here, but I might be persuaded to return him if you would be willing to return to London with me."

"I wouldna return with you without seeing m' laird husband safe within these walls, Cousin Ken. So you'll need to send word to your men so they can bring him here, if you wish me to go with you."

"You would prefer that option to another more painful option for you husband, wouldna you?"

"I would prefer if you had stayed in London to take care of your businesses and estates. I thought your father sent you on a business trip. Did you complete your meetings so soon or did you abandon your responsibilities to come gallivanting across England and Scotland to search for me?"

"I was informed a few short days after I set out on my trip that you left London and headed north. I knew exactly where you would go; so I changed my ship's course and sailed here. It dinna take me as long to get here as it took you, but we ran into some obstacles on the way. You were well guarded, which I was not expecting."

"What are you talking about? I traveled with Sir Colin and the children. I dinna have any guards until two days ago."

"I am not sure, but we arrived ten days ago and anchored in a bay a little south of here. We have been sending the men out to scout for you. They were attacked five days ago."

"Who are *we?*"

"You know who *we* are. Milliner wants you as much as I do, perhaps more." He grinned at her.

His evil crooked grin, she thought to herself, but dinna say anything. Nor did she allow any emotion show on her face. "How many men did you lose?" Elisa asked.

"Half my crew, but I have enough men to camp outside your walls until you are ready to bargain for your husband and concede your safe position here. I will not leave here without you, Elisa. I need you to run Father's businesses and my estates. I certainly do not have the ability to do so, nor would the people wish to work for me. I do not have the patience to work with people, as you well know. But they are all willing to work for you and everything is so profitable."

"How many men did you bring with, Cousin?"

"A thousand, I dinna expect you would actually allow me entry into the castle and I expected to have to lay siege for some time, but with my ship, I can send for more supplies for quite some time if necessary."

"Do you mean there are a thousand men outside our gates or only five hundred since you lost half?"

"I still have a thousand men after losing half trying to find you on your way here."

"What did you do?"

"I told you, our travels dinna take as long as yours. We arrived before you did and we sent some of the men into the area to pretend to be tinkers and such and traveling merchants, which wasna far from the truth if you think about it. Their purpose was to discover if you had arrived yet and you had not; so we worked our way back towards Glasgow, but we were attacked in the woods about a day's ride from here."

Elisa wondered about that, but dinna comment on it. "So you made your way back here and looked for an opportunity to take m' laird captive so you could exchange him for me?"

"Yes, cousin; it was a rather clever plan, I think. Dinna you agree?"

"Nay, I dinna think it was so clever. You cost one thousand men their lives. If you put as much effort into taking care of what you own, what actually belongs to you, your townhouse and estates and businesses, you could learn to do all the things necessary to run them successfully, if you but put in the effort to do so, Cousin Ken. You are being as pleasant as can be to me right now, because you know you must. You just have to do the same with the estate managers."

"You know that I cannot maintain this façade for very long. It never lasts for very long."

"You just have to try harder. You could do it if you wanted to. You use your weakness as an excuse to continue to behave as you do. Mayhap, you should try going to church until you learn to lean on God and He will help you learn to be in control. You dinna need me; you only need to turn to God and He will help you. You would force me to give up my children? I am the only parent they have ever known. Ian was too little to remember his father. I couldna bring them back with me to London and you wouldna want the expense of caring for them and providing for them anyway; besides, Laird Ian adopted them and they are his children now, so I couldna bring them back to London anyway."

"You could help me. Come back to London with me and I will return your husband. I know what you care about more than anything is protecting the children. I will let the children stay here so they will be safe. I will have no need of them, if I have you and you promise not to run away again."

"I canna leave here until Laird Ian is returned. I willna go with you until I see that he is alive and well and safe within these walls, Cousin Ken."

"Well, we shall have to see what arrangement can be made. What value does your husband have? Laird, soon to be Laird of all the Clan, he must be worth quite a bit. And you know how I always need money."

"You can have whatever amount of money you wish. I will gladly pay so these people can have their laird back. I see now it was futile to try to escape, for you will always come for me, willna you? You will just keep following me."

"Yes, I will always come for you. I will never let you go. And, why do you insist on speaking like them? It is barbaric."

"Why, cousin? Why canna you let me go? It only costs you more money to provide for me."

"Yes, that is true, but the estate managers willna work for me. You can make them work and they do a fine job for you. You can make a lot of money for me. Your father did a wonderful thing for me when he *educated* you. He never guessed that it would be so *beneficial* to me." Elisa knew just what he meant the way he emphasized the words educated and beneficial.

She continued to converse with him until he finished his meal. She was exhausted and she wasna even sure if she ate or just pushed the food around on her plate. Then, she said, "Well, cousin, I've had a rather busy day learning my duties as the laird's wife. So, I hope you will be kind enough to permit me an early evening. One of the men will show you to your room. I shall ask a maid to bring you a bottle of m' laird's finest scotch. I know you are accustomed to it since you've been drinking the same in London."

"That is very kind of you," he said. "I shall see you at breakfast, then."

"Rest well, Cousin Ken."

Cousin Ken stood and bowed to her, then followed his escort to his room. As soon as he stepped out of the main hall, he was surrounded by several guards with their swords drawn and he was escorted to a room and locked in. The guards took positions in the hall outside his door.

Ken was surprised when the door opened again and a maid brought a tray with a bottle of scotch and a mug and set it on his table. Several of the guards entered the room with her and one walked between her and Ken as she placed the tray on his table and the guard turned as he left with her. The guards left the room and locked his door again. The maid returned to the kitchen as the guards took up their positions in the hall again.

Elisa sat at the table until Ken was out of sight. She folded her hands in her lap and prayed that Ken would believe her and that God would forgive her lies and that He was on their side and would work out their plans. But mostly, she prayed that Ian would be returned safely to his clan. She tried to nay think about what she agreed to because she wasna sure that she could keep her word this time.

Elisa sat there praying until word was brought to Sir Duncan that her father-in-law's men had arrived and awaited their orders. Chieftain Ian was brought to the hall. Elisa asked Sir Duncan to have a chair placed near the hearth. She sent a maid to bring food and ale for all the men. Chief Ian assisted her to her seat by the fire. She was too shaken to walk at the moment. "Thank you for providing more men and for your assistance, Chief Ian." Then, the men sat at the table and discussed their plans.

Several hours later, Elisa's father-in-law approached her. "Daughter, Sir Duncan told us everything from when you left the loch until now. You are verra brave and strong. I couldna have asked for a better wife for my son."

Elisa stood and curtsied, "Thank you, m' laird. Is there anything I can do to help? Anything you or your men need? Does Sir Duncan need me to go anywhere with him?"

"Nay, my daughter, he will stay here with you. I will lead the attack on your cousin's camp. You just get some rest. We will do everything we can to eliminate these men and ensure Ian is returned."

"I willna rest until Laird Ian returns. I couldna possibly sleep while he is being held captive." She turned back to the fire and sat down. She continued to pray until Sir Duncan wanted to return to the parapets. She pulled her cloak tight about her and walked with him. The flight of stairs seemed to go on forever. She revived herself, telling herself she must keep a brave face and show the clan that she was strong and brave like her father-in-law and husband believed her to be. She refused to be like the London debutantes that faint at the least little fright. She wasna prone to sleeping until noon. She wouldna faint because she was strong enough to endure this. She would persevere. She would suffer whatever was required of her and continue on as if nothing was wrong. That is what she had been raised to do and she would continue to do it, just as she had been trained to do. She knew God carried her through these difficult trials and He deserved her praise. He deserved all the glory. Well, His will be done, she thought.

They stood on the battlement. It was too dark to see anything, but after a while you could hear the battle. It only lasted a short while. Then, Sir Duncan escorted her back to the main hall, where she resumed her place by the fire. A man was escorted in under guard. Sir Duncan questioned him and explained what was expected of him. He was brought to Cousin Ken's room and allowed to speak with Cousin Ken to try to convince him to give him directions to find the men who held Laird Ian captive.

The man explained to Ken that their camp was attacked while most of them slept in their beds and he was informed that he was the only survivor. They insisted that he find out where Laird Ian was being held. Then, he must negotiate with the captors to return Laird Ian. If they cooperated, they might be allowed to live out their days in prison, rather than be tortured to death. The young man was quite terrified of his circumstances.

Ken told him to sit down and poured a glass of scotch for the man. "Drink this and calm down, young man. You will need to listen carefully to the directions, so you can find the place where the captors are holding their laird. You must pay close attention as you go, so they cannot follow you. I dinna want them to have their laird back until Elisa agrees to return to London with me. I know that I can convince her to go with me. She will do anything to protect her husband and her children. She will want the laird returned so he can protect his clan and her children."

Then, Ken explained what the young man had to do and where to go and described the landmarks he had to follow to get to where the captors were holding the laird. He made the man repeat the directions back to him until Ken was certain the man would not get lost in the woods; then, he knocked on the door.

The guards opened the door and pulled the young man from the room and escorted him out of the keep. Then, he was led back outside the castle and released. Hopefully, the young man would make his way to Ian and give their terms to the men holding Ian captive.

The guards ensured the door to Ken's room was locked again and took up their positions in the hall again. They would wait until Sir Duncan signaled for them to escort Ken to a dungeon cell.

Elisa asked Sir Duncan if he had ordered men to secretly follow the man.

"Aye, I did, Lady Elisa."

She dinna speak to anyone. She just sat by the fire and prayed. She prayed Ken's man knew where Ian was being held. She prayed this man would actually go to Ian's place of captivity. She prayed he would make it there safely. She prayed their men's presence would be kept secret and they would not lose the man they were following. She prayed whatever their mission was that it would be successful.

Then, Elisa prayed the captors would agree to their terms. She asked God to please return Ian to them safely. She prayed she would be brave enough to keep her word. At this point in her prayers, she became overwhelmed with emotions.

Elisa took several deep breaths to calm down, but she couldna calm down. A few tears started to run down her cheeks, so she turned more towards the fire, hoping no one would see her crying. She hated to cry and especially for anyone to see her cry. She tried biting the inside of her cheek and digging her nails into her palms. She hated it that she wasna strong enough to control her emotions. When she still couldna control her emotions, she thought about the beatings she received from her parents and the way she could endure it without making a sound and walk away as if nothing happened. After a few minutes of recalling the memories, she was able to control her emotions again.

Sir Duncan placed a stool near her and sat down staring into the fire. "M' lady, I sent the men out to check the watch." He paused and then said, "I can give you breathing room, if you would like. Unless, you would rather I escort you to your room."

"Nay, Sir Duncan, I would rather have something strenuous to do. I prefer to have more activity and hard work than to think about," but she stopped herself from completing the sentence; she added, "things." No one needed to know what she went through. She told her husband what she could bear to tell him. The rest would have to remain locked in the little box she envisioned in her mind. No one needed to know the pain her cousin and his friends and associates inflicted on her. They dinna need to know the real reason she had to go to the docks to get her shipments from the captains of the ships was so she could let them hurt her in exchange for the shipments of merchandise.

He suggested, "I could clear the tables to the sides of the room. You dinna get your training this morning. We could do so now."

"I dinna think the clanging of swords in the hall would be a good idea right now. I wouldna want to rouse the entire castle thinking the battle has moved in here. Perhaps, we could go to the kitchen and I could cook something."

He stood up and held out his hand to assist her. She stood up and they went to the kitchen. She put more wood on the fire and brewed some coffee. She placed a ham on the spit to roast. Then, Elisa started mixing ingredients to make bread. While the dough was rising, she poured coffee for both of them. She left hers on the table across from him and started mixing ingredients for some desserts and tarts. Then, she cooked some bacon and sausages. She washed and peeled potatoes between checking on the meats. She set the meat aside, at the edge of the hearth to keep it warm. She chopped up potatoes.

Elisa kneaded the bread dough and put it in a pan to rise one more time before cooking. Then, she started to cook the potatoes in the bacon and sausage grease. When the potatoes were done, she set them with the meats. She scrambled up eggs and cooked them in the same pan. She added some of the ham and bacon and sausage to the eggs and then she added some mushrooms and cheese.

When the bread was done, she set it on the table and slathered the top with butter and left it to cool. She chopped apples and mixed them with sugar, cinnamon, flour, and oatmeal. She made another pastry, stuffed it with the apple mixture and put it in a pan over the fire. Finally, she checked on the ham. When it was done, she removed it from the spit and placed it on a chopping block. She sliced it and added it to a platter and set it with the other meats. She kept everything on covered platters near the fire on the hearth so it would stay warm until she was ready to serve the food. Then, Elisa sliced up the bread and put it on a plate.

As she worked at kneading, chopping, slicing and organizing everything, she felt the tension ease from her body. It was always this way. It was why she learned to cook. It helped to remove all the emotion and anxiety from her thoughts. She could just bury herself in the work and become so engrossed in creating something that she could completely forget about anything else. She dinna do it for any praise, but she often heard someone comment on how good it was and it gave her a little bit of pride to know that she pleased someone. She mostly spent her meals in the nursery with her brother and sister, so those compliments were very seldom and never from her father or cousin.

"Blast," she swore, angry with herself for allowing those thoughts to slip back into her mind when she worked so hard to banish them and bury them in the black box.

Duncan rose from the table and approached Elisa cautiously, "Are you alright, m' lady?"

"Aye, I am fine, Sir Duncan."

"You dinna burn yourself?"

"Nay, I dinna think so. But, I wouldna notice if I did, Sir Duncan." She held her hands out so he could examine them to ensure that she dinna have any burns.

Duncan held her hands in the light of the fire and examined them to ensure that she dinna have any burns. He turned her hands over and examined the back side before he released her hands.

Elisa turned back to the food and continued to stir the food in the pans in front of her.

"Why did you say that you wouldna notice if you burned yourself?" Duncan asked. He hoped he wasna stirring up trouble by asking. But mayhap, she needed pushed to share; nay that he should be the one to push her. She wasna his wife, but she was his responsibility; so he pushed the issue.

"My mother scalded my hands in verra hot water when I was four. She was angry because I let the water get cold because it took me too long to wash the dishes. So she heated more water and held my hands in the hot water and then she made me wash all the dishes again. I dinna feel pain unless it is a deep wound or verra painful."

Duncan was hard pressed to control his anger, but he kept his emotions to himself. "If you dinna injure yourself, then why did you swear?"

"I was thinking about something and that led to me thinking about something else and I dinna want to think about that, so I swore because I was angry with myself for nay blocking out the thoughts."

She mixed together another batter and started pouring the cakes out on a couple pans. She let them cook and flipped them after a minute or so and then let them cook another minute before she moved them to a covered platter. The cakes would keep her verra busy and she could think about what fruit she would add to the top of the cakes. She eventually decided on slicing up apples and adding cinnamon and sugar to it and cooking it up with a little water to make a glaze. When that was done, she whipped up cream with sugar until it was thick and firm. She actually licked a bit of it off her finger after she purposely ran her finger around the inside of the bowl. She knew she shouldna, but whipped cream was a bit of a luxury that she was rarely allowed, usually only for a special day like when she celebrated the children's birthdays. Otherwise, she couldna justify the luxury.

She knew she had to force herself to stop cooking or she could easily cook everything in the larder and pantry. She needed to warn the cook that she occasionally did this to vent her frustration and then she could ensure that most of the stores were kept safe in the basement.

She served up a plate for Sir Duncan. "You dinna make all this for me, I hope. M' laird wouldna want me to get fat and lazy in his absence." Then, he added, "I am sorry, I dinna mean to upset you." She shook her head. "I am nay going to eat unless you sit and eat with me, m' lady."

Elisa looked at Sir Duncan, nay believing what he just said. He explained, "M' lady, you dinna eat lunch at the picnic and you havena eaten since. You made it look like you were eating dinner with your cousin, but all you really did was push the food around on your plate. M' laird said I am responsible for you until he returns. Now, sit and eat, Lady Elisa, because I dinna want to tell the laird you starved to death while he was gone. He would cut me to pieces."

Elisa just stared at him with one eyebrow raised. She couldna believe the audacity of these Scotsmen. Sir Duncan handed her a plate. She put a tiny amount of ham, potatoes and eggs on it. She grabbed a piece of bread and sat down and ate in silence. She took one of the cakes and put some of the apples and whipped cream on it. When she was finished, she said, "I can see why m' laird made you his commander in arms. If you manipulate me again with 'the laird said' comment, I will take you up on the training offer."

She stood and walked over to the hearth, where she proceeded to remove the vat of water and stopped up the sink and added the hot water to the sink. Then, she gathered all the dishes that she used to prepare the food and started washing the dishes. She scrubbed them until they shined. Then, she swept and mopped the floor. She would have been happy to clean the fireplace too, but she knew that she shouldna because she just finished cooking and she knew the coals would still be hot, even though she doubted she would notice. But Sir Duncan would insist upon examining her hands if she did that. There would probably be blisters. She wouldna care, but he would probably report it to Laird Ian.

Nay that it would matter because she wouldna go back on her word. She would do what she said she would to ensure that Laird Ian was returned to his clan, but especially to ensure that little Ian and Elsbeth were never treated as she was treated. She would find a way to accept the things that her cousin would do to her if it ensured the children's safety.

When Sir Duncan saw the pained look on her face and that she was moving towards the fireplace, he guessed she intended to clean it and set up a fresh fire. He couldna believe she would think the coals would be cool enough for that task. He quickly finished eating, and said, "The men will be changing the watch soon. Would you like to go up to your room and freshen up?"

Elisa snapped out of her morose thoughts and saw the direction she was headed. She paused and asked, "What did you say, Sir Duncan?"

"I said the men will be changing the watch soon and asked if you would like to return to your room and freshen up."

"Aye," Elisa replied and let him lead her from the kitchen.

"Were you intending to clean the fireplace, Lady Elisa?"

"I dinna think I can explain it to you in a way that you will ken, Sir Duncan."

"I will listen if you wish to try to explain."

"I know the coals are too hot, but I also know that I willna feel it. I also know that my hands will still be burned and then I will get blisters, but that pain is preferable to what I was thinking about, what I have to do later. I know that I will find the strength to do what I must, but I canna handle the thought of that, so I prefer to deal with physical pain. The one involves emotions and I dinna think I handle them well; I dinna think I control them verra well. The other is physical pain and I can take it or handle it. I prefer what I can control."

"I think you explained yourself verra well. I think I ken what you are saying, even though I dinna ken what the emotional pain is that you are referring to." He dinna think she intended to share exactly what that was with him. Perhaps, that was something between her and Ian. But they reached the door to her room; so, he dinna have time to ask further questions to see if she would share more. He really shouldna be so familiar with her. She was his brother's wife, even if she dinna know they were brothers and believed they were cousins. He really dinna ken why his mother wanted her to believe they were cousins rather than brothers. He dinna ken how that could have any effect on her plans. But, he kept those thoughts verra closely guarded so no one could read his thoughts. He dinna know what gifts she had, except she could remember everything that she saw or read or heard, even if she was sleeping.

When they reached her room, Sir Duncan entered first to ensure there wasna any danger lurking inside. He stayed near the door, which he left open a few inches so he could hear that she was safe while she was alone in the room. She opened her trunk and found another pair of leather breeches and a top. She moved the bucket of water from the hearth and went behind the dressing screen. "Tell me what you can of Hawk," she called out.

He talked while she undressed, washed with the bucket of water and a rag, and redressed. She brushed out her hair and re-braided it. She pinned it up with the special daggers. She put on her sword belt again and stepped out from behind the screen. She put on a lightweight cloak and they headed back downstairs.

"Dinna you want to change?" she asked as they descended the stairs and crossed the hall to the door.

"Nay, m' lady, I will be fine for today," he answered.

"Are you sure? I dinna mind standing in the hall while you change. I am sure a couple guards can surround me for the few minutes it would take you to change out of your dirty clothes, rinse off and redress."

He tried to nay think about her words or if she would think of him undressing. "I will keep your offer in mind," he smirked. He hoped she recalled her hesitance to accept his offer to carry Elsbeth and it would lighten her mood for a moment. He dinna think she would be too upset with him for using her words against her. He hoped she would take it as teasing. To be honest, he wasna sure if she knew what that was. He was certain that she dinna ken how to play or have fun. He was certain her parents beat that out of her if what he had seen of her childhood was any indication. He was certain that hadna changed when she returned to London. He dinna think she was the type of person to joke around or tease others, at least nay verra often.

"Verra clever, Sir Duncan," was her only reply. Elisa noticed the kitchen staff setting the food out as they headed out of the hall. Sir Duncan led her across the bailey and up the steps to the parapets. She watched across the vast open ground while Duncan spoke with the captain of the guard about the remainder of the night.

The watch changed and the relieved men headed into the hall for something to eat and then to get some sleep. Elisa spent the day watching for signs of a rider. Occasionally, Sir Duncan would ask her to walk with him around the parapets. After a few times, she asked if he did this to stretch the legs and to keep alert because it wasna good for your legs to stand still for too long.

"Aye, m' lady," Duncan replied; then, he explained in more details. He finished with, "We can all stand verra still for a verra long time, or even kneel or crouch, if it's necessary. But, it is best to keep the circulation moving by having some activity."

Elisa nodded and thanked him for answering her question. She dinna notice the pain in her feet or legs, she was too numb from worrying if Laird Ian would be alright and whether he would be returned safely. Worse, she worried about how she could keep her word to her cousin. She really dinna think she could go through with it, but she knew she must for the safety of the laird and the children. She became more withdrawn. She barely spoke at all, only what was absolutely necessary. She did eat a bit of bread and cheese and an apple when Duncan insisted. Mainly, she was worried he would force her to rest in her bed, if she dinna eat and that was something she couldna abide by.

Sir Duncan must have noticed her lack of communication throughout the day because he said, "Let's go to the chapel. I need to speak with the priest." So she followed him to the chapel. She knelt to pray at the altar, while he spoke with Father Patrick. She couldna hear them so she focused on her prayers.

Sir Duncan told Father Patrick, "I dinna ken what is happening. She was so strong yesterday, giving directions and making sound decisions. She gave us verra good and helpful information regarding her cousin and the plan. She was even able to get her cousin to tell her in my presence how many men he brought with and were camped outside our walls. Today, she is verra withdrawn, quiet; she barely answers when asked questions. She just follows me as she promised she would, but it's as if she isna really there anymore."

"I am worried about her too, but she isna eating or sleeping properly. I am certain she is worried about the laird and I imagine she is terrified of her cousin. It is too much for her to handle. I only hope this doesna go on too long and she will recover quickly when the laird returns."

"I guess all we can do is try to get the laird home quickly and pray that helps her to recover," was Sir Duncan's reply.

"Why dinna you sit in the first pew behind her and I will ask her some questions, then mayhap, her answers will give us a clue."

"Alright, that sounds like a good idea."

Father Patrick approached Elisa and sat on the floor near the kneeler, facing her. "Lady Elisa, I wonder if I might speak with you; ask you some questions. Would you mind too terribly much if I asked you some questions?"

She prayed the Lord would help her answer his questions. When she looked up at him, he continued, "How are you feeling today?"

"I am verra worried about the laird. I am sca" she let her voice trail off.

"Scared?" the priest finished for her. "It is alright to be scared, m' lady. Why are you scared?"

"Because I will have to keep my word and I dinna know how I will be able to do it," she said.

The priest looked at her, confused, "You said you were worried about the laird. Do you want him to return?"

"Aye, of course," she said. "He must return so he can provide for his children and the clan."

"And you," the priest added. "Remember, he vowed to protect you in your wedding ceremony. He always keeps his word." She dinna respond; they would ken soon enough. She dinna have the strength to explain it to them. It would be difficult to actually follow through with keeping her word to her cousin, but she dinna have the strength to explain it to them and try to make them ken. Father

Patrick continued, "If you are this worried about your husband, does this mean you care for him? Do you love him?"

"I care for the laird a great deal and I have loved him since I was three and my love has only grown stronger over the years. It is what gave me the strength to come here. But," she dinna think she could go on.

"But, what?" he asked, "please, tell me so I ken what I dinna know. I want to help if I can."

Elisa answered, "You canna help. It's too late now; I gave my word and I canna go back on my word any more than the laird would go back on his word. The only thing to do is to keep my word. It was wrong for me to come here. It only brought danger to the laird, his children, and his clan."

Father Patrick asked, "Why do you keep referring to the laird and your children this way? Why do you nay call him your husband or Ian? And the children are yours too. You raised Ian and Elsbeth. Laird Ian is your husband, they are your children, and this is your clan now."

"You ken that isna true, Father Patrick. Everything belongs to the husband. That is why you make the woman vow to obey her husband. I nay longer want to talk. Sir Duncan, may we return to the parapets?"

Sir Duncan approached from the middle aisle of the church. She couldna be sure exactly where he was during the conversation or how much he may have heard. "M' lady, I would ask for a few minutes more with Father Patrick." She nodded and continued praying, while the men moved back to the entrance of the chapel. Sir Duncan said, "Thank you for questioning her. I am certain that her fears and greatest worries are the words she said to her cousin at dinner last night. She gave her word to return to London with him if he would safely return the laird. She said she wouldna ever try to leave again, that she realized leaving was futile because she knew now that he would always come after her. She got him to promise to leave the children here. She also said she would pay whatever he wanted to get the laird back."

"If her father were alive, I would have him horse-whipped," Sir Duncan continued. "He raised her to have pride in being just like a man, as noble a character as a gentleman. Now, she feels she canna break her word to this Satan's spawn. I can only think of one solution to prevent her from this folly, but it will have to wait until m' laird returns. I willna let this be on either of their heads."

"I will pray for another solution," Father Patrick said.

"You pray, Father; and then, I will do what must be done to protect m' lady," replied Sir Duncan. Then, he marched back up the aisle to the altar. He put his hand out to take Elisa's hand to assist her as she stood up. She let him. She was quickly becoming too exhausted from her worries. She should know better than to allow herself to be emotional. She should not allow herself to be happy, bad things always happened after she experienced happiness or tried to have fun. She must try to remember that and nay try to have fun or be happy in the future. Then, mayhap, she could prevent some of these things from happening. But if not, at least she could stop herself from being happy for a little while and then being very unhappy afterwards. At least then, she wouldna have to deal with her mixed emotions and she would have better control.

Duncan stamped down his anger. He couldna act without his laird's permission; and until his laird was returned and made a decision, the Satan's spawn would have to remain locked in the dungeon. Duncan just had to ensure the man, and he used that term loosely, would have to remain secured in his cell. Duncan dinna think Cousin Ken was a man. He thought he was a coward to cause such fear in a girl. He wouldna care about the pain he inflicted on Cousin Ken if it would put Lady Elisa at ease and comfort her to know that the vile man wouldna ever hurt her again.

He glanced at Elisa, but he dinna think she could sense his thoughts. Mayhap, she dinna have the gifts everyone else seemed to have in the clan. Mayhap, she just hadna known they existed and so she dinna ken how to use them. He should still be careful to nay let anyone sense his feelings, especially right now, when they were both vulnerable with Ian away. They were both too emotional. He must ensure nothing inappropriate happened between them because he knew who she was, who Ian was and his relationship with Ian was different than Lady Elisa realized. He still dinna ken that deception, but to him it was a deception and he worried that Lady Elisa would feel the same way. He would try to convince Ian to discuss it with her. He dinna care about going behind his mother's back and spoiling her plans. It would be better for Ian and his relationship with his wife, if he told her the truth and the sooner the better.

He realized that he was walking quickly, most likely because of his anger; and he slowed his pace, so Lady Elisa dinna have to run to keep up with him. She was verra tall and had long, slender legs; but she was still considerably shorter than he was. A gentleman slowed his pace to accommodate the lady's shorter legs, so she dinna have to look like she was running or even rushing or hurrying to keep up with the man.

When they reached the stairs to the bailey, he took her arm so he could ensure that she dinna stumble on the stairs to the parapet. The stairs were steep and although he was used to running up and down them, she wasna. Not only that, but she had to contend with her skirts without showing too much ankle. He almost chuckled at the thought. He wouldna mind seeing her ankles. Hell, he wouldna mind if she cried and needed his shoulder. Her head would fit nicely under his chin. He wouldna mind holding her in his arms and caressing her back and running his hands through her hair while she cried. Nay, he told himself, that wouldna be appropriate and he dinna need to think about her height or her long, slender legs again either. He chastised himself for even thinking such thoughts. He should return to the chapel and say a penance. He would have the men take it out on him during training.

He refocused his thoughts on his guard duties and set his mind clearly to the task of protecting Lady Elisa, his brother's wife, he reminded himself again. Somehow, he dinna think this was going to be an easy assignment for him anymore. He always found the work to be easy, fun, exhilarating, sometimes challenging; but he always enjoyed it even when it was difficult or hard work. Now, he had emotions and feelings that he shouldna have, feelings he had always felt for his brother's wife. He had to keep them buried and hidden. Now, he felt like his job just became a lot more complicated and difficult than it was before.

The relationship between the three of them was quite a mess since he was really Ian's brother, but she was raised to believe they were cousins. Ian knew that he had feelings for Lady Elisa and he had known since they were ten. Ian knew that because of those feelings, Duncan would do everything in his power to protect her. But, it was insane of his brother to expect him to spend so much time around her, especially alone with her, through such difficult circumstances as the past couple days, while his brother was who knows where and going through who knows what. He had no idea if Lady Elisa had even thought about that.

He really hoped that she remained strong until Ian returned to them because if she broke down and he had to comfort her and hold her, he wasna certain he could be strong enough to nay do anything he shouldna. He definitely needed to see Father Patrick when this was over and then let the men punish him on the training field.

In the meantime, he would just have to pray for God to give him the strength to do the right thing and for his brother to be returned as quickly as possible. Then, he checked with the guards about how their shift went. Afterwards, he resumed his place next to Lady Elisa and watched for any signs of riders or the return of their laird, his brother. It was going to be a long day.

Chapter 9

ELISA STOOD GUARD all the rest of the day on the parapets. Sir Duncan forced her to at least eat some bread and cheese and an apple and drink a cup of ale a couple times during the day. As the sun was lowering to the horizon, she saw dust rising over the hills. She prayed they were returning Ian and that he was safe and healthy. When they were close enough so she could see Ian's face, she tried to give him a reassuring smile, but the world faded to black and she collapsed.

Sir Duncan caught her up in his arms. He gave orders to have the men brought into the gate but surrounded by twenty soldiers, so they had no chance of winning any battle or harming the laird. Sir Duncan sent a man ahead to request a maid be brought to Elisa's room. Then, he carried her to her room, leaving the door wide open, and laid her on the bed. He moved away from the bed and stood by the chairs by the fireplace. When the maid arrived, he told her she must stay in the room with him at all times. Then, he sent for two more guards for her door and afterwards he sent one of the guards to inform Ian his wife fainted when she saw him and they were now in the laird's room.

The laird's men captured the men who were holding Laird Ian. The laird had them sent to the dungeons to await his decision on their future. Then, he greeted his men and gave orders to continue the double guard for now. The guard updated him with what occurred in his absence. Then, he gave him the word regarding Lady Elisa. Ian excused himself to check on his wife. He climbed the stairs to his room.

Sir Duncan was pacing by the fireplace when Ian entered the room. Ian walked to the bed and checked on Elisa, but she was unresponsive. He brushed the back of his hand across her cheek and caressed her before he kissed her. Then, he crossed the room to where Duncan was. Ian asked Duncan to tell him everything.

Sir Duncan suggested they remain in the room because he was fearful what Lady Elisa would do when she awoke. They turned the chairs so they could see her while they talked. Sir Duncan explained everything to Laird Ian. He praised Lady Elisa for keeping her word to him about not going anywhere without him and not trying to rescue the laird herself. But then, Sir Duncan exclaimed, "I'll be damned, she did it. She found a way to rescue you herself. I guess she dinna keep her word to me after all."

The laird cautioned him, "Be verra careful what you say about my wife."

"Oh, nay, m' laird. It is a good thing. It makes what I have to do easier." Then, he continued to explain the plans she suggested and that he was surprised by how good the plans were. "She is verra clever and a good strategist. She was verra calm through it all. Only a person verra close to her would ever notice the fear and worry she carried or someone who could sense her feelings."

Then, Sir Duncan continued to explain what happened when her cousin came. "I could nay believe the calmness about her. One would never guess she feared him at all. She sat with him at the table and talked with him as if nothing bothered her at all, when I know she had to be cringing at his presence. She was verra brave and courageous."

Sir Duncan lowered his voice as he told the laird about his conversation with Father Patrick. "I believe when she saw you, she was so overwhelmed with the thought of returning with her cousin to London, that she fainted. I dinna ask the maid to revive her with smelling salts because she hasna slept the entire time you have been gone."

"You either, I suppose?" the laird asked.

"Nay, but I am fine, m' laird. Now, I must ask for your indulgence. I willna allow her to return to London with that fiend and I willna allow you to soil your hands in this matter, for I can see only one solution to prevent her from insisting on keeping her word. That Satan's spawn must die, and I dinna want this task to be on your hands; so, it canna come between you two."

"I will consider the matter; if it is the only solution, then I will allow you to do it."

Sir Duncan said, "I told Father Patrick I would give him time to pray and see if he could find another solution. He willna give his blessing, but he will ken if it's the only way to protect Lady Elisa."

"M' laird, I need to tell you something else about your wife. She isna the same. She has been withdrawn and quiet; she only speaks when asked a question and only answers as much as she deems absolutely necessary. I am fearful that she is resigned to keep her word; but in so doing, she has lost herself. I dinna ken what she feels exactly, but I could tell that she was very distraught over this situation. I am sorry, m' laird. I hope that she will recover from this."

"You mustna blame yourself, Sir Duncan. You have done all that you could to protect her in my absence; and, I willna blame myself for my actions were also to protect her and the children. It was a calculated risk, but I was certain I would only be taken as a ransom and in exchange for her. I was right and it worked out. I will only put the blame with her Cousin Ken. That evil monster did this to her before she ever came here. We must go talk to Father Patrick and do this before she awakens."

Ian turned to the guards at the door, "Go release the children, relieve their guards and send them to get food. You and Sir Scott can stay with the children in the nursery. Ask Sir Colin, Angus, and Alice to come sit with Lady Elisa."

"Aye, m' laird," they replied and went to carry out their orders.

As soon as Sir Colin, Angus and Alice arrived, Laird Ian greeted them and asked about the children. When he was assured they were fine and had taken it all in as some grand adventure, he gave them orders to stay with Lady Elisa. He cautioned them and ordered them to watch her carefully if she awoke because they were unsure what she might try to do. "She is to nay leave this room."

Laird Ian and Sir Duncan went to speak with Father Patrick, who had no solutions to give them. They left the chapel and Laird Ian gave Sir Duncan permission to proceed with his task. "See if the men who held me captive would be willing to return Cousin Ken's body to his father. I willna pay them the ransom, but I will pay them to return his body and also travel expenses." Ian returned to his room to sit with his wife.

Sir Duncan walked to the dungeons and entered Cousin Ken's cell. He had the guard lock him in and remove himself to a distance that he couldna hear them. He questioned Ken about what he did to Elisa while she lived in London.

Ken was verra happy to tell him about hiding and jumping out and scaring her, kissing her and fondling her. Then, he shared that her father dinna believe her when she tried to tell him what Ken did and he beat her, so he took advantage of that knowledge and caused her to be late completing a task or fail to do it, causing her father to beat her. After her father died, he beat her himself and forced his unwanted advances on her. "I was warned not to take her virginity, but I dinna need to do that to get what I wanted from her."

"Who warned you to nay take her virginity?"

Ken laughed before he answered, "Lady Isobel." He was careful how he worded his treatment of Elisa. He could see just how angry Sir Duncan was and he dinna want to provoke him too much. He was certain Duncan intended to kill him and he could accept that, but he was certain he dinna want to be tortured, so he dinna say exactly what his unwanted advances were.

"What did you do to Lady Elisa?"

"I was with her, but in a way that dinna take her virginity. She wasna willing, but she knew better than to complain or say no. Others have had the same and they will come for her when I am dead. Lady Isobel will ensure it."

"So Lady Isobel knows what you did to Lady Elisa and she approves?"

"Yes, as long as we didn't take her virginity."

"What else do you know about all this?"

"If you don't kill me, Lady Isobel will have me killed since I failed to keep Lady Elisa in London until the king could come for her."

"Which king, the King of England or Scotland?"

"They have both been with her, but they dinna take her virginity, so I don't think it was either of them. She wasn't supposed to come here and her marriage to Laird Ian wasn't supposed to be consummated; she was supposed to be saved for the king; that is all I know. This willna be over with my death. There are many others that want her and a few kings, as well," Ken warned.

"Then, they will die." Duncan replied and carried out the task necessary to protect Elisa. He would have liked to torture the vile man, but he knew that Ian wouldna approve; so he ended the Satan's spawn's miserable life quickly by driving his sword through his chest. He cleaned his sword and sheathed it. As instructed, Duncan spoke with the men who held Laird Ian. The laird's captors said they would be glad to return the body to London and receive payment for their travel expenses and told Sir Duncan, "Your laird is verra gracious. Please, thank him for his generosity."

"You will be held until m' lady awakes and can see her cousin is truly dead. Then, you will make your way straight to London where your payment will await you." Sir Duncan left them in the dungeon and returned to his laird. He informed the laird the deed was done and she could view the body. "The captives will gladly accept your gracious offer and they thank you for your generosity," Duncan said.

The laird chuckled, "I imagine they would, considering the alternative." The sound of the laird's laughter caused Lady Elisa to fret in her sleep. Sir Duncan watched her, concerned for her wellbeing. "Out with it, Duncan," Ian requested.

"I worry that your presence is causing more harm than good. Lady Elisa cares verra much for you and she did all that was necessary to gain your return. But, your return is the catalyst to her horrifying fate since she doesna ken she willna have to keep her word to return to London."

"Well, I can sit quietly by the fire and you can talk to her when she awakens." In the meantime, Ian asked Alice to bring them a tray of food and a pitcher of ale.

Sir Duncan lightly chuckled, "Your wife is a verra good cook, m' laird. What she cooked on the journey here was nothing compared to what she can do in a fully stocked kitchen. You are a verra lucky man." Then, Sir Duncan told Ian, "You must watch her closely if she is near fire, m' laird. She swore while she was cooking and I was concerned that she burned herself, but she just continued cooking. So, I approached her and asked her if she burned herself and she replied that she dinna think so, but she wouldna feel the pain most likely unless the wound was verra deep or really painful. She held her hands out to me so I could see them. I examined them in the light of the fire, but she dinna have any wounds. I asked her what she meant that she wouldna feel it and she explained that when she was four her mother scalded her hands in hot water because she let the water get too cold because it took her too long to wash the dishes. She said she doesna feel it anymore."

"Why would her mother make her wash the dishes when she was only four," Ian asked. "They had servants. They were wealthy people."

"I dinna know the answer to that," Duncan replied. "I just wanted you to be aware in case she is injured that she wouldna realize she was in pain."

"Aye, I ken. Thank you, Duncan."

"She prepared a large feast, enough to feed all the people in the castle all by herself. I suppose she did the cooking when she was in London too if she had to do the dishes. She filled a plate with food for me, but I refused to eat it. I told her I dinna want to have to tell you that she starved to death in your absence because you would cut me to pieces." They both chuckled. "It convinced her to eat, but she warned me to nay use you to manipulate her like that again or she would give me a training lesson. She was quite angry with me."

At this, Laird Ian couldna help but to laugh. Just then, Alice returned with their food and ale. "I brought a plate and a cup for Lady Elisa in case she wakes up. Enjoy. I understand that the pastry and whipped cream were made by Lady Elisa this morning while all the kitchen staff was asleep. She left them quite a feast, m' laird. Anyway, I thought you would like to finish the pastry."

Sir Duncan said with a grin, "Aye, it was verra good, too." When Alice gave him a disapproving look, he said, "Lady Elisa needed some activity to keep busy because I wouldna let her stay out on the parapets the whole night. However, I was smart enough to nay word it that way. But, I refused to eat until she sat and ate and she was quite angry with me.

That is why our dirty dishes were left on the table; so please send my apologies to the kitchen staff. I had to appease her by taking her back out to the parapets after that. You will be happy to know, Alice, she gave me a good set down."

The men filled their plates with food as Alice left the room. But when Elisa started thrashing in her sleep, both men rushed to the bed. The laird asked Sir Duncan, "Did you remove her weapons when you put her to bed?"

"Weapons? Nay, m' laird, I dinna know she was armed."

"Is she still in her breeches from yesterday?" Ian asked.

"Nay, m' laird. I suggested she come freshen up to get her to come down off the parapets before the men's change of guard. I searched the room and she took a clean set of breeches and a top from her trunk. She went behind the screen and I stood in the hall with the door ajar. She asked me to tell her about Hawk while she changed. I thought it odd at the time, but I realized she dinna know Cousin Ken had been moved to the dungeon. And so, she probably just wanted to hear my voice so she knew I was still there and she felt safe from her cousin. When she came to the door, she had on her cloak."

"You had better help me," Ian said.

"I dinna want to see your wife, m' laird. I will find Alice." Sir Duncan dashed out of the room before Ian could even respond. Ian sat on the edge of the bed and caressed Elisa's cheek and hair while he waited for Alice to return to the room.

Alice entered and approached the bed, "Aye, m' laird?"

"I need to undress Lady Elisa and get her weapons off her." They stripped off her cloak first and removed her sword belt with its dagger and set it in her trunk. Then, they removed her boots and breeches. Ian gave Alice the daggers from her boots, calves and thighs. Alice put them in the trunk. Then, Ian untied the belt that held the daggers around Elisa's waist and handed them to Alice. He covered her with the blanket. Alice helped Ian remove Elisa's dress and then her top. Ian removed the daggers from each arm and the necklace around her neck. Everything was laid in her trunk and Ian covered her up the rest of the way.

Alice went to the wardrobe and pulled out a night gown. Ian sat on the edge of the bed and lifted Elisa while Alice pulled the gown over Elisa's head and down her body. Then, Ian laid Elisa back down and covered her again. Elisa turned on her side and curled around Ian, draping her arm over his leg. She continued to sleep restfully. When she stirred in her sleep, Ian moved back to his chair by the fire. Seeing the pain she was in because of what her cousin did to her was breaking his heart.

Duncan returned to the room when Alice left. Laird Ian and Sir Duncan continued to talk quietly by the fire. The castle settled for the night and all was quiet. When Lady Elisa awoke, she was out of her mind with fear. She was confused because her mind kept screaming in her ear that she must always keep her word and do what she said she would. Too confused to think about it anymore, she threw the cover off and leapt towards her trunk. She opened it trying to get to her sword belt. It was buried under all the other daggers. She never left the trunk in this mess. She continued to search for her sword.

Sir Duncan flew out of his chair and strode across the room. "Lady Elisa, what are you after. You should be resting in bed. What are you mumbling? Please, talk to me, m' lady."

"I canna do it, I canna. Nay, I willna do it. I canna keep my word to that vile, loathsome cousin. I canna endure the horrors he will inflict on me. I canna. I canna. I would rather be dead." She finally found her sword and pulled it from its sheath. "I know I am supposed to be brave, do what is necessary to protect them, keep my word, but I canna, I willna go back."

"M' lady, I canna let you hurt yourself. I promised the laird to protect you." Sir Duncan watched her closely to see what she intended to do with her sword. He wasna sure how to proceed.

Elisa mumbled Scriptures about strength, "I can do all things through Christ Jesus, who strengthens me. With man it is not possible, but with God all things are possible. Give me the strength to do this."

Somewhere in her mind, she thought she heard Ian's voice. "Send for Father Patrick, quickly." Then, she heard the voice again, "Sir Duncan, I forgot two of the daggers in her hair. Be careful."

Sir Duncan said, "Shh, be quiet. The sound of your voice is making her worse." He turned back to Lady Elisa, "M' lady, it is me, Sir Duncan. Just listen to me, focus on me. I need you to look at me and listen carefully to what I have to tell you. Are you listening to me?" he asked.

Elisa continued to quote what Scriptures she could think of that said God strengthens you or He is your strength. Her mind was too confused to really think straight. All she knew for sure was that her parents expected her to keep her word, never break her given word or her promise or her vow to do something. She had given her word to her cousin that she would return to London with him if he allowed the children to stay here and he returned Laird Ian to his clan. Now, she had to keep her word, but she couldna do it. She would rather die before she suffered the pain her cousin would cause her. She swore, "Blast the vile coward and his debaucheries."

"Lady Elisa, are you listening to me? You dinna have to go back to London. Your cousin is dead. He is likely already in hell, so you are nay breaking your word because your cousin, Ken, is dead. He canna take you back to London. Besides, you dinna say you *would* go back to London; you said you *canna* leave here until Laird Ian is returned. You said you *willna* go with your cousin, Ken, until you see that Ian is alive and well and safe within these walls. Please dinna try to do this. Put the sword down. Just listen to me. If you try to do this, I will be forced to protect you. Remember, the laird said you were my responsibility and I have to protect you, even from yourself. Now, come out of that corner and back to bed."

Elisa swung around as she stood up with her sword in her hand. She pointed it at Sir Duncan, "I warned you to nay use the laird's words against me to manipulate me or I would teach you a lesson. Now, it is time for your lesson."

Sir Duncan stepped back a few steps as he drew his sword. "Mayhap, m' lady, it is time for your lesson. You ken that I have trained much harder and longer than you have. You canna possibly think you can win a fight against me, nor will I kill you. I'm skilled enough to disarm you without injuring you, m' lady." He swung the sword in front of him a few times and stepped back towards the foot of the bed.

Elisa took a couple steps towards Sir Duncan and swung her sword at him. He easily blocked her.

He taunted her, "You shouldna draw your sword on someone who is bigger and better than you, and far more experienced." He took a couple steps to move around the foot of the bed.

She swung at him again, "Stop taunting me. And stop running away. Are you a coward that you back away from a lass?"

"You know I am nay a coward; and you shouldna draw your sword when you are so upset, you canna focus and think clearly."

Elisa followed his steps around the end of the bed.

Sir Duncan said, "What did the laird say? 'You should be in better control of your anger.'" He gave her a smug superior look.

Elisa saw a motion on her left. She tried to reach for one of her hairpin daggers, but there wasna enough time; it was too late to react. She felt a solid thump on her jaw and the world went black again. She slumped to the floor.

It happened so quickly, but when Duncan realized Ian's intention, he started to say, "Nay, dinna do it, m' laird."

"I hope she can forgive us both, Sir Duncan. That was verra clever of you to draw her out past me, taunting her to keep her distracted."

Sir Duncan said, "I dinna do it so you could knock her out. And I dinna think she will think it was so clever of me. I dinna want to be anywhere near the training field when she is able to train again. I dinna intend for you to hit her. I would have disarmed her if you had given me a chance to wear her down. I just wanted her to stop thinking about taking her own life and focus on fighting with me long enough to get her to calm down and listen to me. Then, I would have disarmed her."

Just then, Father Patrick came in, "Oh, my goodness, what happened to Lady Elisa?"

Ian explained everything. Then, Father Patrick suggested, "I think we should remove all weapons from this room for now. You should bandage her hands so she canna grip anything. And, until we see how she is going to respond to this incident, I recommend that you tie her to the bed; give her enough rope to move about but not enough to get out of the bed."

He turned to Laird Ian, "We must bandage her head to hold her jaw in place. I just hope you dinna break it. It is going to be verra swollen and bruised." He looked back and forth between the two men, "What were you two thinking?"

Sir Duncan said, "I was thinking she was trying to take her life and that I must do everything necessary to protect her, even from herself. She was hysterical and what I did just made her angry, but at least it distracted her from throwing herself on her sword. She dinna ken that her cousin is dead and she wouldna have to return with him to London. She wouldna listen to reason. I was trying to distract her and wear her out so I could disarm her."

"Aye," Ian said. "She was praying Scripture asking God to give her the strength to do it. I only hope she will listen to reason when she awakens."

Father Patrick interrupted, "You had better be praying she forgives you. After everything her cousin did to her to make her this hysterical and unreasonable, you may have made things worse by hurting her."

"I dinna need you to tell me that, Father Patrick; I ken it already," Ian replied.

Ian removed her sword from her hand, which she still had a death grip on. He had to pry her hand open. He handed the sword to Sir Duncan. Then, he lifted Elisa in his arms and laid her in their bed again. He covered her up. He took out all the weapons he could see in her trunk and handed them to Sir Duncan. Then, he remembered the pins in her hair; so he sat on the bed and lifted her head as he removed the pins from her hair and handed them to Duncan too. "Ask Alice to bring us some bandages after you find a safe place for those. Bring back some rope, enough that I can tie her to the bed. Oh, she isna going to be happy with us, when she wakes."

Duncan did as he was told and returned with rope. Alice was right behind him with bandages. When she saw the bruising that was already showing on Elisa's jaw, Alice asked, "What happened?"

Ian explained, "She was hysterical and trying to take her own life. We did the only thing we could to prevent her. Dinna lecture me, Alice. I ken I have hurt her badly and not just because of the bruise on her face."

"Couldna you have grabbed her from behind?"

"She was going to throw herself on her sword, Alice. Duncan was trying to distract her with his words and she went after him with her sword. She was forcing him across the room. She was distracted and I just reacted. I dinna want to hurt her. If I had stepped behind her, she would have turned on me. I was unarmed. I only tapped her." Alice shook her head in disapproval. Ian said, "You dinna have to say anything, Alice. I feel awful without your disapproval. You dinna know what she has been through since she left here eleven years ago, but it dinna seem like anything improved since then. What she has told me may very well give me nightmares. I couldna even sleep for fear of what she was going through once I knew it was her cousin who took me to try to use me in exchange for her."

"In all the times the three of us went to have a little fun at the loch, did Duncan or I ever get punished for it? Nay, but she was beat every time. Do you think I dinna realize she would agree to return with him to London in exchange for my freedom? She knew what he would do to her and she still agreed to go with him. What he has done to her is so awful she couldna even tell me what it was because she canna bear to think about it. And I dinna want either of you to ever ask her about it or even imply that you have any idea about what I am talking about. I am only saying this so you will ken that I knew at least a little of the horror her life has been and I knew she would still sacrifice herself for me. I ken that I caused her a physical pain that will cause her a much more difficult emotional pain to overcome. But I dinna see any other solution at the time. There wasna time to reason it out and think of other possibilities."

"Alright, I willna say anything more about it; and I certainly willna say anything about what you have said about her cousin. She doesna need to relive any of that."

Ian took the bandages from Alice and sat on the edge of the bed and wrapped Elisa's hands. Then, he wrapped a bandage around her head. Her jaw was going to be badly bruised and it was going to take a long time to heal. He said, "She relives it in her nightmares, Alice. You dinna see how she reacted when I lifted her from her horse to my lap as we were riding here. She fell asleep in the saddle and I just wanted to let her sleep and move her to my horse. She drew her dagger and cut me before I even knew what happened. I had to drop the reins to try to stop her from fighting me. Duncan had to pull her horse away in case she slipped from my grasp, so she wouldna be trampled. Her reaction was much too violent of a reaction to what she told me the first night we were together in my tent. So, I insisted she tell me more on our wedding night." He paused and pulled one of her hands into his and held it in his lap. "I dinna want to proceed with her until I understood more of what she had been through. Since she dinna have a mother for so long, she dinna have anyone to explain things to her. She dinna want Mother to explain it to her. I tried to ask her questions but she couldna answer in a way that made sense at first; but then, when she explained what her cousin told her and what she could tell me about what he did, I finally understood and was horrified by what she has been through. So, you dinna have to worry that I dinna ken the pain I just caused her."

"Alright, I am sorry, m' laird."

"Nay, Alice, I am sorry, but it's too late now." Ian turned to Duncan, "It's a good thing that you dealt with her cousin, for I probably would have done something awful and unholy to the man. Thank you for dealing with him."

Duncan only nodded. He wasna sure what he should say and now he was struggling to keep his composure. He dinna want Ian to see how badly he was affected by what his laird was telling him about Elisa. He knew that he couldna ever let his feelings show where she was concerned. He must always keep things professional between them. He had to keep a safe and appropriate distance between them. He was the commander of Ian's guard, his first in command. Elisa was Ian's wife and had been since her first visit to Mull when she was just a newborn baby. Duncan loved her from the moment he saw her lying in her crib. He dinna understand his strong attraction to her, but it had not changed during all her visits to Mull, nor since she hadna returned when she was seven and he and Ian were ten. He wasna sure he kenned what Ian knew about Elisa and he shouldna know because he wasna her husband; but he knew with every fiber of his being that her life hadna improved when she left here. He was certain of it; and now, it seemed that Ian was confirming it. He wasna entirely sure what her cousin meant by his words; he hadna explained in detail; and he realized now that Cousin Ken had probably chosen his words carefully because he knew just how angry Duncan was and Ken was afraid.

Ian took the rope from Duncan and tied her hands to the headboard posts, but with plenty of slack so she could move about the bed. He hoped he dinna have to leave them tied for very long. He dinna want to tie her feet unless it was absolutely necessary.

He and Duncan resumed their vigil in the chairs by the fire. They sat there quietly. They never needed to talk to communicate with each other. After a long time, Ian whispered to Duncan, "I'm sorry I said anything about what she has been through. I should have kept it to myself. I promise you, you dinna want to know. I havena forgotten what you told me after she returned to London. It's why I need you to protect her, Duncan. I ken it's so unfair to you. But if something happens to me, I know you will protect her. You will ensure she is cared for as she should be. You know she doesna forget anything; she canna forget. She relives what has been done to her in her nightmares."

"I ken," Duncan whispered back. He couldna say anything more. He couldna bear Elisa being in pain. He watched her last beating and he couldna believe what her mother did to her and then she handed the whip to his mother so she could continue the beating. Duncan was horrified. Through the ordeal, Elisa held the stable door and was silent. She returned to the nursery. Duncan saw the tears in the back of her dress and her flesh and the blood. The image was seared in his memory. He couldna forget the night before and that day. He and Ian stayed beside her the rest of the summer and they refused to allow anyone but Alice to attend to Elisa. Their father had come to the door of the nursery every morning, early before anyone else in the castle was up, and he asked about her wellbeing. He respected their wishes that no one come near her.

It was the best and worst summer of his life. He blamed himself for the beating. He blamed himself for nay doing anything to prevent it. He blamed himself for nay trying to make them stop. When the summer was over and she was finally well enough to travel, her parents packed up her and her things and took her back to London. He rode down to the loch after they left and stayed there for a long time. He cried and cried. He knew then that she would not return to Mull for a very long time. Apparently, eleven years was long enough but it seemed like eternity to him.

Ian found him and tried to comfort him. Ian touched him before Duncan could block him from seeing his feelings for Elisa. Duncan was afraid his feelings for Elisa would drive a wedge between him and Ian and he would lose them both, but they grew closer than ever. They were even more inseparable. They sensed each other more closely than before. They hardly ever needed to speak out loud because they were so close they just knew what the other wanted, or felt, or needed. "I dinna know if I can be of any help to you in this, Ian. I dinna think anything I do or say would be appropriate. You know I willna do anything to interfere in your marriage; and I will do all I can to protect both of you. That is all I can say right now."

"You dinna have to worry about what is appropriate, Duncan. I know you would never hurt either of us." They sat in silence for a long time. Then, Duncan rose from his seat and clasped Ian on the shoulder and then he left the room quietly and went to his room. He wasna worried that he would miss his watch during the night. He knew Sir Thomas would take his watch, since he had been up for three days straight. He would make it up to Thomas tomorrow night. They would get back on schedule the following night. He undressed and collapsed in bed. He fell asleep quickly. He slept through the night.

Ian barred the door after Duncan left. He undressed and slipped into bed with Elisa. She cuddled up to him. He slept through the night and woke with the dawn. He rose carefully from the bed, dressed quietly, and prayed that Elisa would recover quickly from this ordeal and that she would forgive him. He slipped out of the room. He went down to the hall and ate.

Duncan joined him and ate in silence.

Ian broke the silence, "You look better rested, at least. Would you like to go to the training field? Mayhap, it will help with the scowl on your face. I know it would help my frustration."

"Aye, m' laird, if it will help with your frustration."

"Good. Then, mayhap we will return in a better mood and we can try to move on from this incident."

The hall was soon full of the guards. Their father joined them at the head of the table. "Father, I dinna have a chance to thank you for your help with the attack on Cousin Ken's men. Thank you for eliminating them. They willna be able to give us any trouble in the future."

"Nay, they willna give anyone any trouble in the future. How is Elisa?"

"She is still asleep. We are going to go to the training field. You are welcome to join us."

"I dinna think so. Would you mind if I sat with Elisa?"

"Nay, Father, I dinna mind," Ian said.

"You two enjoy getting your issues worked out on the training field. You both look like hell."

"We feel like hell, Father. But, our issues are nay with each other and we canna raise the dead to torture the coward with whom we have an issue." Finally, Duncan laughed and Ian was relieved. It was about time. They could start to recover from all this now.

They went to the training field. They battled each other harder than ever before. After more than two hours, Ian asked, "Do you feel any better yet?"

"Aye, we can call it quits whenever you wish, m' laird. I dinna think I need to continue. I still wish we could revive our *cousin*," he said it with contempt. "So I could kill him again, but my temper is simmering at least. I suppose I shouldna think or feel or say this, but at least I had the pleasure of killing the vile bastard. You will just have to console yourself with knowing he is dead," Duncan smirked.

Ian laughed and sheathed his sword. He clasped his brother on the shoulder. "I ken exactly how you feel. Funny how his name is the same as our word for understanding, yet he dinna seem to have any."

"Aye, but I dinna wish to use the Sassenach word, either. This doesna make me feel any love for any Sassenach."

"Be careful, Elisa is part Sassenach."

"She isna Sassenach. She is a Scot."

"Her mother was half English, Duncan. Her father is English."

"That wasna her father, Ian; and you ken it well enough. You've heard the arguments enough times to know who her father is. You know that is why your mother did the things she did, because he is her father; and why he couldna do anything to stop it."

"Aye, but I dinna think Elisa knows. So, we shouldna discuss it. You know how Mother is when things are revealed before she plans for them to be revealed."

"Well, I dinna care what your mother thinks. I dinna think we should keep these secrets any more. Lady Elisa isna a child any more. We should tell her everything we know now, so she doesna feel betrayed later when she finds out or figures it out on her own."

"I will think about it; and, she is your mother too," Ian corrected him.

"That has been the best thing out of all her plans is that she wanted everyone to believe I wasna her son, only your cousin. I am happy to oblige that relationship after everything she has done to Lady Elisa. I ken why Father dinna step in; he couldna; but I dinna think I can ever forgive myself for nay trying to do something."

"You must forgive yourself, brother. We were only ten and there wasna anything we could do. And, Father is right, if we had tried to do anything, they would have treated her even worse. You have to find a way to forgive yourself. You canna allow yourself to be consumed by guilt and anger and regret. I need you strong and so does Elisa. It's best if we let the childhood go and do what we must to protect her now. I would love to have Father visit here more, but I am nay going to allow Mother to spend too much time here, especially since she seems bent on hurting Elisa's feelings with every comment she makes."

"Just let me know if you want that problem eliminated. I will be more than happy to oblige you. I might even relish it."

"You would hurt Father if you did that, Duncan. We must be more like Elisa and forgive and move on."

"Aye, Lady Elisa acts as if none of it ever happened. I dinna know how she does it, but I canna. I can still see the image of her walking from the stables to the house. And I know I willna ever forgive myself. I canna; I was as much to blame for what happened and I dinna even try to prevent her from being beaten. It should have been me."

"We must try harder. I dinna want our time together spoiled by those memories."

Duncan dinna say anything, but he wondered why Ian said their time together, like he knew they wouldna be together for very long. Duncan had seen his future, all three of their futures, but he had chosen not share it with anyone. The problem was that he rarely had to share anything with Ian. He just knew. It had been like that since they were ten and Ian touched him after Elisa returned to London. He returned to the keep beside Ian in silence. What they discussed dinna need to be overheard by anyone else. Silence was best. Duncan went to his room to bathe and change into clean clothes.

Ian returned to his room. His father was sitting in a chair next to the bed. He walked to his side of the bed and looked down at Elisa. "Has she awakened?"

"Nay, son, she has stirred several times. She thrashes about in her nightmares."

"Aye, do you ken what she is dreaming about?"

"I dinna think you will want to know the answer to that."

"I have a bit of an idea. I will ask her to share with me, but I dinna think she will want to share. Would you encourage her to tell you if she wanted to?"

"Only if she came to me, Ian. I would do anything to change her past, but it isna possible now. I willna forgive myself any more than Duncan can forgive himself, even though he was only a little boy."

"We were nay that little, Father. We should have done something to stop it. But I dinna think we can keep living remembering the past and wishing we can change it when it is impossible. We should learn to forgive and try to move on. It will be better for Elisa."

His father lifted Elisa's hand and kissed the bandages. "Are you going to tell me what happened?"

"Aye, Father, do you want to know now or will later do?"

"I can wait. I will go so you can bathe. I dinna think we should be talking about all these things when she wakes up. We probably shouldna speak around her even when she is asleep unless we dinna care if she knows what we are talking about."

"What do you mean?" Ian asked concerned now about all he had said to Duncan and Alice.

"You know about the clan's gifts. Her gift, or curse as Duncan prefers to call it, is the past. She remembers everything she sees and hears or reads. She can probably hear us and will be able to recall it later." His father kissed her hand again and rose from the bed. He walked to his son and clasped his shoulder for a minute before he left the room.

Ian bathed and sat on the edge of the bed waiting for Elisa to wake up. He used the time to think about what his father told him. He thought about what to tell Elisa. He thought about his own gifts and what he knew about his own future. But, he dinna want to think about that. He finally had her only to lose her too soon. He prayed God would help him explain what happened and their reasons. He also prayed God would help her forgive him and they could be happy for the time they were together.

Chapter 10

THE ROOM WAS filled with bright sunlight when Elisa awoke to see Ian watching her. "I am glad you are finally awake. I want you to take several deep breaths and stay calm because I need to explain the past few days to you. And, it is going to require a lot of patience and understanding and forgiveness from you. Can you do that, Elisa? Can you let me talk to you without getting too upset?" Ian asked.

"Aye," Elisa tried to talk, but there was a great pain in her cheek.

"Dinna try to talk too much. I only did what I did to protect you from hurting yourself and others. You were upset to the point of hysteria. Do you remember?"

"Nay."

"I am going to go over a few things to help you remember. When you start to get upset, I want you to take several deep breaths and calm yourself down. Do you ken?"

Elisa tried to nod her head, but it hurt too much.

"We went to the loch to picnic and swim with the children. You were sent back to the castle with the children and some of the guards."

"Through the tunnel," she remembered. "You were captured."

"Aye, you went through the tunnel and I allowed them to capture me because I was certain I would be used for ransom or in exchange for you if it was your cousin. It was a calculated risk in order to protect you and the children. While I was away, your cousin, Ken, came here to ask you to return to London." Ian paused and then said, "I think you should take a few deep breaths now and try to remain calm through the next part."

After a couple breaths, Elisa said, "Go on."

"You told your cousin you would return to London with him, if he returned me to the clan and let the children stay here. Now, before you get upset again, look at me and listen carefully. You willna have to return to London, nor will you break your word. A solution was found to ensure you could accomplish both. Sir Duncan and Father Patrick figured out that what upset you so much was that your father, having raised you to a man's code of honor, forbid you from going back on your word. However, the horrifying thought of what your cousin would do to you was more than you could bear. The two conflicting emotions tore you up inside and you became verra confused and hysterical. Breathe," Ian said and he paused again.

When she was calm, he continued, "You willna be breaking your word by staying here because your cousin is dead. He canna make you go with him and he canna keep coming after you. Do you ken?"

"Aye," she tried to say, "I ken, but I am still afraid of him."

"That is why we are going to finish our conversation; and then, I am going to bring you downstairs to show you he is really dead and canna hurt you anymore."

"Now, when I was returned by the captors, Sir Duncan said you watched until you were certain it was me and then you fainted. He had no choice but to catch you and carry you to our bed. You slept nearly a whole day. But when you awoke, you were hysterical, mumbling and talking strangely. You leapt out of bed and you searched your trunk for your sword intent on killing yourself. You were praying Scripture and asking God to give you the strength to kill yourself."

"Duncan tried to explain that your cousin was dead, but you wouldna listen. You continued to pray Scripture. We were certain that you were about to throw yourself on your sword. That is why Sir Duncan taunted you, to get you to come after him, which you did. But, I needed you to calm down and listen to me so we could tell you about your cousin being dead. You were so hysterical, you were beyond reasoning with, and so I hit you in the jaw to knock you out. Father Patrick recommended the bandages on your hands and that we tie you up so you couldna try to hurt yourself or anyone else when you awoke."

"Am I just like him with his fits of rage?" She looked down at her hands and then up at the laird. She began to laugh because her hands looked ridiculous with the bandages on them. Also, she thought it would be ironic if she turned out to be just like her cousin.

Ian said, "Please, dinna become hysterical again. I am so sorry I hurt you. After everything your cousin did to you and now I hurt you too, I am verra concerned about whether you will be able to forgive me. I only did it to protect you but I still feel awful. I only hope you will forgive me someday. I canna tell you how sorry I am."

Elisa tried to reach out and touch him, forgetting about the bandages and being tied up. "It is alright, Ian. I was out of my mind with worry and fear not knowing how I could keep my word and endure the horrible things I knew he would do to me. It all became confused in my mind. I am sorry I brought all this to your door. I thought we would be safe if we could just get to you; but then, I felt like I was putting you and the children and the clan in danger and that I must go back to protect all of you. Now, I feel like I am causing too much trouble in your life and you dinna want me here. I wonder if you and the children would be better off without me here. And I am not hysterical; I was laughing because the bandages make my hands look ridiculous. I thought it was funny. And also, I wondered if it would be funny or ironic if I turned out to be just like my cousin." She paused briefly, "I am verra tired now. May I sleep some more?"

Ian chuckled, "Aye, my sweet lass, rest. I'll come get you when it's time to go downstairs." He started to rise.

"Nay, dinna go. Please, stay and hold me," she begged him.

"For a little while," he said. She snuggled up to him and fell asleep. He sat with her, stroking her hair for a while, and then gently untangled her grasp.

In the hallway, Sir Duncan asked, "How did it go?"

"She was calm through most of it. When she became upset, I stopped to allow her to take a few breaths and calm down. Then, I continued on. She seems verra calm and at peace."

"It sounds like how she was at the table when her cousin sat and ate and she talked to him. Too calm and submissive."

"Aye, that is what I was thinking too. Either she has accepted his death or she is beyond help. She will go between this calm and a raging storm. She asked if she was just like him and his fits of rage."

Sir Duncan said, "I dinna think so from what I saw of his behavior. He was smug, condescending, not a care for anyone, but himself. Not even concerned for himself, really. He thought he could walk into your castle, full of your people and walk out with her. But we know Lady Elisa cares a great deal for others. I think she was just forced to endure too much, more than she could handle. But because she has always had to take care of herself and Ian and Elsbeth, and because her father raised her to live with a man's code of honor, she felt that somehow she had to handle it, endure it. I hope she comes back to you, m' laird, to all of us. The cook said she would really enjoy having her breakfast made for her once in a while," Sir Duncan said with a smirk.

"Aye, and you wouldna mind, either. She is a good cook."

"Well, if she ever had to make it on her own, she could always be someone's cook."

Ian replied, "She willna leave here. I will find a way to deal with all this, if I can have the in-between times."

"I think you are in love, m' laird," Sir Duncan responded.

"Aye; who wouldna be? She is amazing." Then, Ian changed the subject, "How are all the arrangements below?"

"Most everyone is outside the castle. I have sent for Father Patrick and some men are bringing in the body. It will be ready shortly."

"After we see how she handles this, the children really want to see their mother. I will need to see what Father Patrick thinks about the children visiting her; how we should handle her appearance."

"With your permission, I will go talk to Father Patrick and ask him to watch her reaction to seeing her cousin with that in mind." Sir Duncan went downstairs to find Father Patrick.

Ian returned to his room to wake Elisa and carry her down to the hall. He noticed he wasna announcing his presence and she seemed to be alright without it. He knew he dinna have to worry since she dinna have any weapons in the room, but he expected her to mention it. She started to smile at him but winced from the pain in her cheek.

"I am sorry, m' darling, I really am." He untied her.

She laid her wrapped hand on his cheek and gently shook her head. Ian took her robe from the foot of the bed and helped her rise. He helped her slip her arms into the robe, wrapped it around her and tied the ribbon. Then, she wrapped her arms around his neck. He picked her up and carried her downstairs and stood in front of the box. He set her down and kept his arm around her waist to steady her, "Ready?" Ian asked.

She placed her hand over his hand that was wrapped around her waist and pressed her bandaged hand against his hand. Ian signaled for the cover to be pulled back. Sir Duncan pulled the cover back just enough to show Ken's face and shoulders. Elisa tried to be brave and look in the box. She leaned forward a bit. She looked for only a few seconds. Then, she turned and jumped into Ian's arms and wrapped her legs around his waist and her arms around his neck, like a little child.

Ian held her close, but after a bit he said, "I need you to really look, Elisa. You have to do this. I need you to look at him until you really believe that he is dead and canna hurt you anymore. You dinna need to be afraid of him. Your cousin can nay force you to return to London and he canna come after you ever again. Do you ken?"

"I ken," she whispered.

"Breathe" Ian said. "It is alright. I am right here. I have you and I willna let anything happen to you. He canna ever hurt you again, Elisa."

"He's dead. He is really dead." She wasna sure if it was a statement or a question.

"Aye, your cousin, Ken, is really dead. His body is cold and he canna hurt you ever again," Ian said to reassure her.

"Just hold me for a minute," she requested while she took a few breaths. Then, she said, "Would you turn around with your back to him so I can feel close to you, safe in your arms, while I look over your shoulder?"

So, Ian turned his back and she held him tighter while she forced herself to look. Elisa used her legs to push herself up higher so she could look over Ian's shoulder. She looked for several minutes. Then, she leaned back and rested her head against Ian's forehead, "Thank you, for protecting me, Ian." Then, she loosened her legs from around his waist and slid down his body and stood on the ground. Elisa pulled away from Ian just enough to ensure that her nightgown and robe dropped back into place over her body, but she continued to hold Ian for a minute more. They turned back around towards the body. Elisa looked at Sir Duncan and said, "Thank you, sir, for standing by my side and giving me your strength and protection in my husband's absence." She looked at Father Patrick, "Thank you, Father Patrick, for your words of guidance and encouragement, and for all the prayers I am sure you have been saying for all of us."

"You are welcome, m' lady. But, I thought you wanted a different outcome?"

"I did, but I always pray for the Lord's will to be done," Elisa said.

Finally, she turned to Sir Colin, "Thank you will never be enough for all you have done to protect me and the children all these years, Sir Colin. I couldna possibly ever repay you." She added, "You must thank Angus and Alice for me, as well. It was a great comfort to know the children were well provided for and protected through this ordeal."

Sir Colin said, "It has always been my pleasure to serve you, m' lady." Sir Colin bowed to her.

"I doubt it was always a pleasure, sir," Elisa said.

"When it wasna a pleasure, I had the horses and stables to care for and the garden to prune."

"Aye, where you spent a great deal of time." They all laughed. Then, Elisa turned back to Ian, "Can we go back to our room now?"

"Aye, Elisa," he said with a groan.

"What is wrong, m' laird?"

"Nothing is wrong, m' lady." He set her away from him and placed an arm around her shoulders and reached behind her knees and swept her up into his arms again.

"Why couldna you carry me the way you held me earlier? It's easier for me to hold onto you."

"Because I wouldna have made it up the stairs," he replied.

"Why are you angry with me? What did I do wrong?" Elisa asked.

"I am nay angry with you." Ian stopped on the stairs and gave her a look.

"How could you think about that now?" she asked.

The three men in the hall burst into laughter. Ian groaned as the sound of their laughter drifted up the stairs. He pushed their bedroom door open, entered their room, and kicked the door closed with a resounding thud. He barred the door. Then, he moved to the bed and set her down where he proceeded to kiss her.

As the sun was nearly setting, there was a knock on the door. He covered Elisa, dressed, and walked to the door. He removed the bar and opened the door. "The cook thought you could use a tray, m' laird," a maid said.

"Aye, thank you. Set it on the table by the fire and do not disturb us anymore tonight."

"Aye, m' laird," she did as she was told and was gone.

Elisa asked, "Why canna I take off these bandages?"

"That is up to Father Patrick."

"But, how can I feed myself? And besides, I want to touch you."

"For tonight, you will have to behave or I willna feed you. As for the other, you will have to be satisfied with me touching you."

Fine, for tonight or until these bandages came off, she would play his game. She would be a perfectly submissive wife. But, he would rue the day these bandages were off, for she would seek her revenge. She would figure out some way to tease him and torture him, but she wouldna relent and give in.

Ian carried her to her chair and fed her between his own bites. He held the cup to her lips after he had a drink. Anytime, he wasna paying attention when he gave her a bite, she snatched the food from his fingers and tried to suck on his fingers or flick them with her tongue. He would quickly pull his hand away and ignore her for a few bites. She tried to make the ale run down her chin, but it would catch in the bandage under her chin. She tried to get a drop or two to drip lower in the hopes that he would kiss it gone.

He finally finished eating. He fed her several more bites, until the tray was empty and asked if she wanted more to eat.

She shook her head, "Nay, I'm fine." He held the ale to her lips so she could drink. When the ale was gone, he set the tray in the hall and returned to her. He lifted her in his arms and carried her across the room. That became their game each evening and night. But most mornings, Ian was in a bad mood and he ignored her, dressed and left the room.

Elisa tried to apologize at first, but she wasna sure what she did that upset him so much. Then, she just learned to roll to her side of the bed and face the wall so he could leave without having to look at her or say anything to her. She would stay facing the wall on her side until after the maid came and left again. Then, she would rise from the bed and do her best to take care of herself. She was able to relieve herself since she wasna dressed.

Over time, she figured out how to use her bandaged hands to move her robe across the bed so she could slide her arms into it. She wasna able to tie the ribbon, but at least she had something covering her.

They had been playing this ridiculous game for at least a month now. She wondered what people thought was going on. She never left her room and no one came to talk to her or bring her food or help her dress. She supposed the maid that entered the room came for some purpose, but she never walked to Elisa's side of the bed to check on her or to ask if she needed anything or if she could help her. Since Ian dinna give her permission to have the maid help her dress, she chose to be obstinate and ignore the maid when she was in the room. She knew she was being petty and ridiculous, but she was verra upset with the situation, but she couldna do anything for herself with her hands bandaged and she dinna want to ask anyone for help. She had never needed a maid or utilized a maid when she was growing up. She felt it was ridiculous to have others do something for her when she was perfectly capable of doing it for herself.

Her head itched terribly from her hair nay being brushed and from having the bandage on her head, but she used the irritation as an opportunity to ignore the thing that was really irritating her.

At first, she spent part of her day looking out the window. But, that changed after an incident where she felt Ian was watching her and then he turned away when he saw her look his way. She went and sat in the chair by the fire to calm down. She wouldna allow herself to cry. If she couldna control her emotions, she would bite her lip. Normally, she would dig her fingernails into her palms, but she couldna do that with the bandages on her hands; so, she would think about the times when she was beat as a child and how she refused to cry and then she would walk away as if nothing bothered her; nothing and no one could ever get to her.

She realized for a while now, that the teasing game she played during dinner was irritating Ian, but she dinna allow herself to worry about that because he dinna seem to care about what she was feeling being confined to this room and nay even being allowed to bathe or dress or even brush her hair. She wondered how he could even stand to be in the same room as her. She had to smell awful since she hadna had a bath for at least a month.

During dinner one evening, Ian yelled at her "Enough, I am tired and I need to sleep tonight."

"I am sorry, m' laird," Elisa apologized, as a submissive wife should, she was sure; nay that she felt she had done anything wrong and dinna deserve to be yelled at or treated this way. But, she reminded herself that he was her husband and her laird and she was just a woman, his wife, to treat however he felt like treating her. She looked down at her lap and took a deep breath. Then, she said, "I can sleep in the chair and you can take the bed." Ian looked at her and lifted his eyebrow quizzically. "It will be alright, m' laird. I willna try anything." So, Ian went to bed. Elisa sat in the chair, staring at the fire wondering why he seemed to think that she would run away, but she supposed that was why he kept her hands bound up in these bandages and dinna dress her or ask a maid to help her.

She wasna even sure why a maid came to her room every day. She never asked Elisa if she needed help with anything. What was the point of coming into the room? She dinna bring her food or drink. Elisa couldna bathe with the bandages on her hands and she dinna help her dress. She couldna brush out her hair. Her head was still bandaged. She still had on the same bandages Ian had put on her the first day.

She was thankful for the warm weather since Ian rarely bothered to help her dress. She was grateful that she had at least figured out how to get her robe laid out on the bed and get her arms into the sleeves, but she still couldna tie it shut. She couldna even sew or knit. And she missed her children; but obviously, she couldna invite them to her room since she dinna have on any clothes. She wondered if anyone was teaching them their lessons and what they were teaching them. Were they going to training? Did they have riding lessons? Did they even ask about her or wonder about her? Did they miss her as much as she missed them?

She recalled all the time she and Ian had been together and she couldna think of anything she did or said that would indicate that she would run away. She couldna really even recall anything that she did that would make him angry with her. She was verra good at just accepting the situation. She hadna asked anything from him. She dinna even ask him to remove the bandages. She just agreed to play his game until the bandages came off. They teased each other while they ate the tray of food each evening. She would nip his fingers or try to suck on them when he fed her a bite of food and then he would refuse to feed her for a few bites. He usually ensured that she ate a good portion of the tray of food and he shared a mug of ale with her before he carried her to bed.

Elisa was used to going without food so she could ensure Ian and Elsbeth were fed when she lived in London.

She helped with the cooking and the cleaning so they dinna need too many staff to help around the house so she could save as much of the household funds as possible and she sent all the extra to her solicitor to save a portion and invest another portion. She had quite a large sum of money. Mayhap, Ian discovered her money and was worried that she kept it hidden from him for a reason and that was why he suspected she would run away.

She couldna think of any other reason he should be upset with her. She hadna complained at any time during the confinement and she hated to be confined. She hated to sit around and do nothing. Well, she dinna do nothing, she tried to exercise and she spent a good portion of her day walking around the room.

There wasna anything she could do about the situation, so she just accepted it. When she got cold, she sat on the edge of the hearth. When the fire died down, she quietly tried to add a few logs to it, nay so easy with your hands bandaged. She squeezed her hands together around the log and set it in the fireplace. She tried to nay drop it in the fire, but to be quick enough that her bandages dinna catch on fire. At least, the maid left the bucket of water on the hearth every evening so she could always submerge her hands in it if her bandages did catch on fire. She swore under her breath. Why hadna she thought to ask for a gown or a blanket? But, she knew it was because she refused to ask anything from him. Eventually, she thought of a cloak, so she crossed the room quietly. She was used to sneaking about the house at all hours of the day and night silently. She only hoped she dinna wake him and make him suspicious that she was trying to run away. She grabbed the cloak and returned to the chair. She added more logs to the fire and tried to cover up in the chair. The chair wasna verra comfortable so she moved to the floor with her back against the hearth and tried to cover herself with the cloak.

If she slept, it wasna verra restful. When the laird awoke, he dressed quickly. Elisa realized he probably saw the cloak was gone and suspected that she tried to run away, so she forced herself to sit up. He said, "Oh, there you are."

"Aye, m' laird. I told you I wouldna try anything. I just got cold and I dinna want to wake you so you could dress me. So I covered up with the cloak." She tried to pick up the cloak, but it seemed too heavy. When she tried to stand, she was weak and stumbled to the chair and slumped into it.

"I thought," he started to say.

She interrupted him, "I know what you thought, m' laird. You thought I snuck out or ran away. That is what forced me to sit up, so you wouldna be embarrassed when I was sitting here the entire time you were out searching for me. Dinna you think about the fact that my hands are bound in these bandages and I canna even dress myself? How could I possibly run away naked with my hands bandaged so?" She was verra angry with him and his thoughtlessness. She was frustrated and confused about whatever was going on between them. She was verra angry with him for treating her this way. He dinna even have enough consideration to help her dress most mornings. Her hair hadna been combed since the day they put these bandages on her head. She hadna even had a bath. More than anything, she was sick and tired of looking at these walls.

He finished dressing and strode over to the chair and tried to lift her up so he could carry her to the bed.

She swatted his hands away and said, "I dinna ask for your help. I can walk by myself."

"Then, get walking," he replied.

She only hoped her anger would give her the strength to walk to the bed. Why was she so weak, anyway? She only made it a few steps before she started to collapse, but he was right there to sweep her up. As he laid her in bed, he asked, "Can you nay make even one good decision?"

"Doubtful you would acknowledge it, even if I did." She retorted before she drifted off.

A few minutes later, she was roused by raised voices. Father Patrick was asking, "Why are her hands still bandaged? I told you a fortnight ago to remove the bandages, she isna trying to hurt herself or anyone else, m' laird. She's been trying to be the submissive wife you seem to want her to be; though, why you want that, I havena any idea. Neither of you are having any fun."

"Fine, then take off the bandages," Ian yelled back and stormed from the room, slamming the door. A few moments later, she heard the front door of the keep slam too.

"You shouldna say anything against the laird, Father, especially nay in my defense. It will only make him angrier," Elisa said.

"Here, give me your hands," Father Patrick said.

Elisa rolled towards him, but when she saw they were alone in the room and the door was closed, she said, "Wait, please. Would you send for Alice first? Would you be so kind as to leave the door open until Alice arrives?"

"Certainly, I will be right back." He opened the door and sent a guard to fetch Alice. He stayed by the open door until she arrived. They removed the bandages from her hands. She wriggled her fingers around for a long time. "Now, m' laird sent for me to figure out what was wrong with you, but we quarreled before he said anything. Can you tell me why?"

"I am nay sure, but I will try," Elisa said and explained what happened from dinner last night until this morning leaving out a great number of the details. She said, "This morning I am verra weak. I couldna even lift the cloak to put it back on the peg or walk to the bed. I was angry with him, so I dinna want his help to the bed; but when I tried to walk to the bed, I collapsed and he had to help me, anyway. So, I guess I fainted again."

Alice asked, "What do you do all day, m' lady?"

"Mostly, I just sit by the fire all day. I hardly notice if it is even day or night. I assume it is night when Ian comes in and feeds me supper and then we usually go to bed."

"Doesna anyone feed you breakfast or lunch?" Father Patrick asked.

"Nay, the laird always seems angry or disappointed with me in the morning, so I dinna want to ask him for anything."

"No wonder you fainted, you are starving to death," he replied.

"I dinna think so, Father, I think I am getting fatter."

Alice turned to the priest, "Father, will you leave us alone? I wish to speak with Lady Elisa privately."

When he left the room, Alice asked, "Why dinna you have on any clothes?"

"Because, Ian doesna dress me when he leaves upset. And, I canna dress myself with my hands bandaged."

"Why dinna you ask for assistance? Do you sit in the room naked all day?"

"Ian dinna say I could ask for assistance. I usually stay in bed with my back to the door until the maid comes and leaves again. I dinna ken why she even comes into the room. She doesna even speak to me or do anything while she is in the room that I know of, except put a fresh bucket of water by the fireplace. And then I sit by the fire or I stay in bed. Naked or clothed depends on Ian's mood. I couldna take looking out the window anymore because it made it all the more difficult to look at these walls the rest of the day." She just couldna pinpoint anything specific that she had done to upset him. She dinna ken why he was angry with her.

"Now, I need to ask you a few more personal questions. Are you two together?"

"All but last night."

"Do you recall when you had your last cycle?"

"In London, before I travelled here, I think. It isna regular. I dinna know how long I have been here because no one told me how long I was out when I fainted or when," she trailed off. She dinna want it to sound like she blamed him.

"Do you have any other symptoms besides a lack of your cycle and fainting?" Alice asked.

"I just assumed that was because of how overwhelming everything has been, travelling, the wedding, the attack, and everything after. I have been so on edge since I have been confined to this room, I havena thought about what could result from our being together. I dinna know there were symptoms to look for. I assume you mean symptoms that I might be pregnant. Do you think I might be with child?" Elisa asked.

"Aye, you might be with how much time you two have been together in this bed."

"Oh," Elisa said, kind of disappointed.

"Why would you say that, m' lady? Dinna you want a child?"

"I...I...dinna know. I am kind of scared since my mother died trying to give birth to my brother and he died with her. Then, my stepmother died trying to give birth to Elsbeth. I was barely able to save Elsbeth. I reached inside my stepmother and pulled out the baby. I just tried to clean off her face and I swatted her bottom. When she dinna cry, I blew in her face a few times and swatted her bottom again. It worked. I just kept telling her over and over again to fight."

Alice said, "As I recall, your mother was always so pale and delicate. She never did anything adventurous. Mayhap, your stepmother was the same way. Mayhap, that is why your father raised you to be like a man, strong and independent and capable of taking care of yourself, m' lady."

"Do you think it would be alright to take the bandage off my head too? Ian yelled at Father Patrick, 'Fine, then you take the bandages off.' But, I feel he only meant the ones on my hands."

"Aye, it will be alright. We can see how it looks and wash your hair and brush it out. And if we need to, we can put a new bandage on your head, m' lady." Alice proceeded to remove the bandage. Then, she went to the door and told a guard to send up several maids with hot water for a bath. She also told Father Patrick that she wanted him to return in two hours with Sir Duncan and Sir Colin.

She brushed out the mass of knots in Elisa's hair while they waited for the bath water. "I am so sorry for all the pulling, m' lady."

"Please, call me Elisa and nay Lady Elisa, either."

"Ian should be ashamed of himself. This is awful."

"It is alright, Alice. I dinna mind that much. As for the tangles, I dinna feel any pain."

When the maids arrived with water, they poured it in the bathtub. Elisa was so happy to have a warm bath. It felt glorious. Alice scrubbed her hair a couple times and rinsed it. "It's just going to tangle more, the more you scrub it," Elisa warned her. Alice helped Elisa dress and then she worked on her hair some more. She ordered a lunch for all of them to be placed by the fire. The guards were sent to bring two more chairs.

The food arrived, and the men were right behind the maid. Everyone sat down to eat. Elisa waited until everyone had food before she took anything. She wasna used to eating during the middle of the day now, so she dinna take much. Alice informed the men they were failing in their duty to provide for Lady Elisa and to protect her. She explained what had been going on. Then, she informed them that she expected them to take a stand against their laird. Elisa was completely embarrassed by the whole thing and felt Alice shared much more than was necessary. So, Elisa set her plate on the tray and went to sit on the hearth and stared into the fire. Watching the flame always calmed her and she needed to calm down.

"I dinna think you should do this, Alice," Elisa said, expecting that she would be blamed. Somehow, it seemed like she was always to blame. Most of the time, she dinna care that she was blamed; but this was one time where she felt she was trying to get them to listen to her and they wouldna hear her. She dinna want them to take a stand against their laird. She knew it was wrong. She tried to get them to listen and to nay do this thing, but no one was listening to her. She would be verra angry if she was blamed because she was the one trying to get them to stop this endeavor, but they refused to listen to her. They argued about it for several minutes before Elisa conceded. She wasna going to get anywhere with Alice, apparently.

"Well, it is their responsibility to protect you, isna it?"

"Aye, but you are asking them to go against their laird."

"Nay, I am asking them to do their duty to you, m' lady."

Elisa shook her head, "I dinna think m' laird is going to see it that way. Your own words were that you expect them to take a stand against m' laird. You canna expect me to believe that it is for my protection now that you said that. I dinna want you to do this."

"He is going to see it the way I tell him to see it, Elisa."

Elisa saw Duncan smirk. She wondered what she was missing in all this conversation. "Would it make any difference or get you to stop this, if I said I would be blamed for getting all of you to go against m' laird?"

"Nay, because it is nay alright for m' laird to treat you this way and he canna continue to do so, especially if you might be with child," Alice replied.

Elisa said, "You dinna seem to realize that by telling him I might be with child, you are giving him just the thing to continue to confine me."

Alice still refused to be persuaded, so Elisa just shook her head and threw her hands up in the air. She turned back to the fire and watched the flames. She dinna know what she could do now that Alice had convinced them to stand up for her, even though she dinna ask them to do so and she was trying to convince them to nay do this. She would just have to suffer the consequences. That was what she was supposed to do, suffer, like God told Paul he would have to suffer for His name's sake.

Chapter 11

ELISA WASNA SURPRISED when the laird barged into the room banging the door into the wall. She almost laughed out loud when he yelled, "Duncan, where have you been hiding? What is this, a proper little English tea party?"

Alice stood up and turned on the laird, "Sit down, m' laird, we have something to discuss with you."

"It will have to wait, Alice, Duncan and I have work to do."

"Nay, it willna wait, m' laird," Alice continued. "You will sit down and listen to your elders, now."

Elisa forced herself to sit perfectly still and she tried to keep staring into the fire as if nothing could get to her. It was difficult to do when she knew Ian was glaring at her. He took the chair nearest Elisa, the one she had recently vacated. "What is this about, Elisa?"

"I dinna do anything, Ian," Elisa replied. "You brought this on when you left me alone in this room, naked, with Father Patrick and told him he could remove my bandages."

"Naked?" the Father stammered. "It's nay wonder you insisted I have Alice come in to assist. She made me leave the door open, as well."

"It isna as if he has never seen a naked woman," Ian replied.

"I dinna think that is the proper response, m' laird, to show respect for your wife or your priest," Elisa responded. "Please, continue, Alice, since you are bent on this course of action." And, Elisa turned back to the fire.

Alice gave Ian a good set down and explained all that had been going on and her suspicions that Lady Elisa was with child. She informed the laird that Elisa wouldna be confined to this room during the day and nay at night, either, if he dinna start showing her some proper respect, provide for her as he should and protect her.

"You told them you were with child, before you told me?" Ian looked at Elisa and asked.

"Nay, Ian, I dinna. Alice told me. What would I know about such things? I was too young when my mother died for her to tell me anything, as I already explained to you. My stepmother never had anything to do with me. I wouldna have known there were symptoms if Alice hadna asked if I had any symptoms. Stop acting like a petulant little child, who is the last one to be told anything." She sighed, loudly and looked at the fire again until she could calm down. Then, Elisa stood up and started towards the door.

Sir Duncan started to rise, but Sir Colin stayed his hand. Sir Colin escorted Elisa out of the room and down to the hall and out the door. "Freedom, at last, m' lady."

"Nay, Sir Colin, it isna freedom. The laird will have nothing but more confinement for me. I willna be allowed to even go to the stables, let alone ride a horse, nay more swimming in the loch, nay more training, all to protect the babe. I just gave him the exact excuse he needed to insist on my confinement. But, it is fine; at least I can walk in the garden as long as I have an escort."

"I can talk to him or ask Angus or Alice to talk to him about what you should be allowed to do."

"Nay, Sir Colin, nay more talking to him. It wasna fair for all of you to stand with me against him."

"We werena standing against him; we were standing with both of you. Hurting you is hurting him in the long run."

"The laird doesna see it that way, which I ken. And, he doesna ken that hurting me is hurting himself in the long run. I dinna think he kens the effect of hitting me. I know why he did it and also that he had to do it and I dinna blame him for it. It is healing nicely. Soon, there willna be any evidence of it at all on the outside; but inside the hurt will be there, waiting and wondering what to expect in the future. Just as he is waiting for me to have another fit and try to harm myself or another."

They walked in silence for a verra long time. Elisa dinna pay attention to the time until she realized the sun would be setting soon. But then, the laird joined them and sent Sir Colin to the stables. "I am sorry, I hope you will forgive me, but I was eavesdropping earlier."

"I knew you were there. Remember, I told you I can feel your presence on my skin, it starts humming like a tight string that has been plucked. When I was first confined to our room, I spent a lot of time looking out the window. One day, I was watching out towards the woods. I wasna thinking about anything in particular except how pretty the woods are and how I would have enjoyed the sunlight gleaming on the loch. I closed my eyes and envisioned it. Then, I felt the hair raise on my arms and the strumming vibration started. I opened my eyes and turned towards the training field. I saw you were watching me, but you turned away when you saw me look at you. I would have waved." Elisa paused, but then she added, "I stopped going to the window after that because I couldna bear to look at the walls of the room when I spent any time looking out, wishing I could go out."

"I am so sor," he started to say.

"Nay, dinna say it again. I know you are sorry. I know you dinna want to hurt me. I know why you had to do it. I ken that it was the only way to stop me, the only solution at the time. You canna take it back now and I canna make the memory of it go away. I just have to figure out how to go forward from here. Just like I canna make your worry go away. But, Ian, even when Hawk came into my room unannounced that first day, even when I dinna know who he was, I dinna hurt him. And I willna intentionally hurt myself or our baby."

"Part of me knows, but part of me worries."

"I ken it. Ian, I have loved you since I was three. How could I nay want our baby, your baby? I willna harm the baby."

"The love of a three-year old is nay giving me confidence."

"My love for you has only grown since then. It is the strength I relied on to get home to you." She wanted to hold him but she wouldna make the first move after his rejection last night. After the way he had treated her for more than a month, she shouldna even want him, let alone allow him to touch her. But, she could scarcely wait for a chance to touch him and love him, but he would have to show her he wanted her first.

Ian led her deeper into the garden. He led her around a little s-curve of bushes. It was a nook with a verra large bench, longer and wider than a normal bench.

He stopped and turned towards Elisa. He drew her closer and ever so gently cupped her chin in his hand. Then, he drew her face up towards his and lowered his lips to hers. His kiss was verra gentle, at first; but then, it grew deeper and more intense. The strumming on her skin was overwhelming and the fluttering in her stomach was magnificent. She felt like she was falling, and then, he caught her up in his arms.

She focused on Ian's kisses and the way he made her feel. It was magnificent. But then, Elisa noticed something else, a tree created a canopy for their little nook. She turned and looked at the doorway, where she thought the doorway was anyway, but she couldna find it. Incredible! They were totally secluded in the nook.

Elisa turned back to Ian; he had such a sheepish grin on his face. She smiled up at him. Afterwards, she said, "I love you, Ian."

"I love you too, Elisa." He kissed her, and then he nuzzled her neck. When she protested, he said, "Shh, m' sweet wife. Just relax and focus on the feelings."

When she was relaxed, she said, "I am delirious, deliriously happy, Ian. Thank you."

"You are most welcome," he said as he cuddled up next to her. Elisa lay awake reveling in her happiness. In just a few minutes, Ian was breathing deeply and seemed completely relaxed.

"Sweet dreams, m' love," Elisa said. "I will take the first watch." Then, he was quietly snoring as he draped an arm over her and pinned her legs down with one of his. She looked up at the dark sky through the tree and realized it was well past the sunset.

Several hours later, he stirred. The sky was just getting the slightest hint of light to it. She rolled towards him; he rolled onto his back. She was just going to rest her head on his chest, but then she remembered she owed him a little revenge. So, she set her plan in motion. When he tried to free his hands, she gripped him tighter. It was sweet torture as she kissed him. She kissed his neck.

"Elisa, please, let go of my hands. I want to touch you."

"Unless someone is about to attack us, I am nay going to let you go. Now, hush, m' sweet laird, just relax and focus on the feelings." She chuckled at her use of his words. She continued since she had to wait over a month to get her hands free of those bandages.

"Elisa, stop," he growled at her.

"You knew I would seek revenge from the first night you bandaged my hands. I begged you to take the bandages off so I could touch you."

"This is your revenge?" he asked.

"Aye, and if you dinna behave, I will torture you again," she answered.

"Well, I shall never behave again, m' lady, if that is how you plan to seek your revenge and torture me."

Elisa thought she heard laughter in the garden. "I was hoping you would say that," she replied with a big smile.

Then, she was certain she heard laughter around them in the garden. "Ian, are your guards in the garden?" she asked in a low tone.

"You dinna think the laird and his wife would be unguarded, did you, m' lady?"

"I knew the castle walls were guarded. I dinna know your men would be in the garden with us. I am so embarrassed; I am mortified that your guards heard us."

Ian spoke louder, "They willna do or say anything to embarrass the laird's wife or I will trounce them on the training field." Then, he said to Elisa, "Do you want to go in to bed, m' love?"

"Nay, I am too tired to walk upstairs right now." She snuggled up beside him and laid her head on his chest.

"I could carry you, you know."

"I know, but I am perfectly happy right where I am, unless you are uncomfortable?" Then, Ian reached over the side of the bench and produced a cloak and draped it over them. She just wanted to stay and watch the sun filter through the tree canopy, but soon fell asleep.

Ian rolled Elisa over, rolling her up in the cloak. He rose. Then, he laid her garments over her and lifted her in his arms. He carried her to their room and set her in their bed and covered her up.

He washed in the tub and dressed for the day. Then, he wrote a quick note that he had clan business to attend to and would hopefully return in time to have lunch with her. He left the note on his pillow. He quietly exited the room and asked the maid to fetch anything he had left behind in the garden nook. "And then, bring Lady Elisa fresh water for a bath later."

"Aye, m' laird," the maid replied.

He sought out Sir Colin in the stables, "How was your night, m' laird?"

"I am certain the entire clan is talking about it by now. The guardsmen dinna keep their presence quiet. Now, she is mortified because they heard her torture me and inflict her revenge on me." Ian chuckled at the memory.

"It will be fine. If you recall, most of the men already saw her entice you on top of her on the hall table," Sir Colin reminded him.

"I wouldna bring that up, ever, if I were you," the laird cautioned. "But, to get to my real purpose, would you be willing to share more of your knowledge about Elisa. I want to make a romantic gesture and surprise her and I wondered if you might have any suggestions."

"I am nay sure what she would consider romantic, m' laird. I dinna think she thinks about such things. She has never said anything about that, but I wouldna expect her to discuss such things with me. It wouldna be appropriate. Most of her time in London was spent on serious matters, like raising Ian and Elsbeth, her education, and running the estates, learning to defend herself, and of course, trying to avoid her cousin or soothe his rage. I am certain she willna like to be surprised. She did warn you to nay sneak up on her. I am sure she is more focused on learning to be a laird's wife and her duties and responsibilities."

"I dinna intend to surprise her in that way. What do you ken about what her cousin did to her?"

"I only saw him pin her to the wall or the floor a couple times. He was trying to kiss her and touch her. I pulled him off her and sent him packing. To be honest, I was surprised when he left the townhouse because it was his home. I assumed he was too inebriated to realize the situation; that he had the right to be there. I think he knew he had no authority over me and that I was there for her protection. He never tried to harm me or have me fired."

"Alright, thank you. Do you know if Elisa has any favorite foods or flowers or stories?"

"I dinna know about a favorite food. I know she doesna care for beans, except green beans; she likes green beans. She doesna like liver, okra, or hominy. But, I think she eats pretty much everything else. I know she really likes strawberry, blackberry, peach, and apricot preserves. She likes strawberry shortcake and her favorite flowers are pink carnations and lilacs. She also likes hyacinth, tulips, daffodils, and iris. I told her I would do what I could to try to get them to grow here."

"We could build a greenhouse if that would help, Sir Colin. I can set the men to work on it tomorrow. I will need to go to the village and ask the carpenter what he thinks can be done. You mentioned her education and training. Do you think she really enjoys that or just did it for her protection and to be able to provide for you and the children on your journey here?"

"Oh, aye, m' laird, she truly enjoys learning and anything outside. She loves fishing, swimming and hunting. I am certain she enjoys the training too. She isna strong compared to most men, but she is clever, cunning, and strategic. If she keeps her head and isna overpowered too soon, she often bests the man. But I warn you, she will use her womanly influence to distract them, which willna be a good thing for your men to see. She enjoys learning, just for learning. She read every book in the library in the London townhouse and ordered more. She likes to learn how to do things. She just likes to know how to do everything and how things work."

"Do you think the training will endanger her or the baby?"

"I am certain you can allow her to train with her bow with minimal danger. I would recommend you, Sir Duncan or I train with her. You can push her. The workout will strengthen her muscles, which will actually be more beneficial for her during labor. If she spends too much time sitting about and resting, she will be weak during labor as her mother and stepmother were. We will need to be careful to nay stab her or the baby, and dinna shove her to the ground. So basically, we want to challenge her enough on defense, but nay really take up offense and also without it appearing that we are going too easy on her."

"That will be difficult since she is so observant," Ian said. "Does she really only sleep a few hours at night?"

"Aye, m' laird, tis true. She has been that way since the first time her cousin came to visit. She seemed to sense it would be unsafe for her or the children. She never slept more than two or three hours in the early morning when we rode here. She always had food ready when I awoke and she took the first and last of the night watch. I had to drug her the last evening so she would sleep; so I could come get you. She doesna seem to realize that she slept for over two days because it took two days to ride the rest of the way here."

Ian replied, "I think her body realizes somehow because she has been asking about how long she slept when she fainted and when I knocked her out. She knows the days are nay adding up correctly in her mind. She kens something isna quite right about the time she has been here."

"I havena any idea how she will respond when she realizes I drugged her," Sir Colin worried aloud.

Ian answered, "If she can forgive Duncan and me, she will forgive you, as well, Sir Colin."

"I dinna think so, I am the one person she has always trusted and counted on."

"We will cross that bridge when we have to, Sir Colin. If nothing else works, I will order her to forgive you, as the laird of the clan," Ian replied and he and Sir Colin laughed. "I will ensure she realizes that you knew there was danger ahead and that you needed more men to protect her and that you did what you felt was best for her safety and the children's safety. I am verra grateful that you realized the danger you were heading into and asked Argyll for assistance. And, she may already realize there was danger ahead because her cousin told her that he had run into a few obstacles and she asked how many of his men he lost. So even if she doesna completely ken, she has some idea that you were in danger when she was riding here."

"Alright, m' laird, but I really think it would be best to be straightforward with her and nay keep anything from her."

"Aye, I will think about it. She said that she doesna ken why her parents dinna just explain things to her and why they kept so many secrets." Ian went to see the cook and plan a lovely meal for his picnic with his wife and breakfast before they left. He ordered some scrambled eggs with cheese, ham and mushrooms, and bread with butter and preserves. He asked the cook to pack something special for their picnic. He returned to their room. Ian woke Elisa and asked if she would like to ride down to the loch to swim and enjoy a picnic.

"Oh, aye, I would love that, Ian," she said. "Are you bringing the children?"

"Nay, m' sweet, I just wanted it to be the two of us today."

"Oh," she said, a little disappointed.

"Do you really want the children to come with us?" he asked.

"It is alright," she replied. "It's just that I have missed them verra much. I havena seen them since they were locked in the room."

He gave her a kiss and continued his preparations as she rose from their bed and went to her trunk to get her breeches and top for swimming. When she opened the trunk, she was surprised to see her daggers and sword. "M' laird?" she questioned as she turned to look at him.

Ian had a big grin on his face. "I thought you would want your things back. I trust you to nay hurt yourself and I want you to be able to protect yourself and our family," he said.

She rose and rushed to him, giving him a big hug. "Oh, thank you, m' laird." She turned her head up to his and kissed him.

"You are welcome, m' sweet," he laughed. She gave him another hug and returned to the trunk to get ready. As Ian left the room, he said, "Come downstairs when you are ready."

After Elisa put on her daggers, she dressed and added her sword belt. Then, she brushed out her hair and braided it and pinned it up. She ate the breakfast Ian left for her. It was delicious and she couldna believe how thoughtful he was being. She loved bread with butter and preserves. She was ready and headed downstairs. She was surprised again to see the children lined up, waiting patiently by the door. She couldna believe her eyes. She let out a little sob and tears filled her eyes.

"Why are you crying, Momma?" Elsbeth asked.

"I am just verra happy, darling," Elisa answered. She gave Ian a big smile. She dinna think she could be any happier, except perhaps if she were holding Ian's baby. She hugged the children for a long time. Then, they filed out to the bailey. It dinna take long to get everyone in their saddles and they were on their way. It was a lovely ride down to the loch. They were surrounded by a large number of guards. The children were verra excited. "How did you get them to stand so patiently by the hall door when they were so excited, sweetheart?" Elisa asked.

"I told them they wouldna go if they dinna stand still and be quiet so you would be surprised," he answered with a chuckle.

"Thank you, m' love, you have made me verra happy. You are so thoughtful." She paused, "Normally, I dinna like surprises, but today has been one surprise after another," she smiled.

When they arrived at the loch, Elisa was so excited to go swimming, she dinna even wait for Ian to help her dismount. She wrapped her reins around the horn, created a loop and wrapped the rest of the reins around the horn again, so she could use the loop to step down from her saddle. It was a bit tricky to stand in the stirrup while she moved her skirts out of the way and set the reins in place, but she had practiced it a lot when she was in London and she was proficient at it now. She had her boots and cape off in a minute. She tried to contain her excitement long enough to help Elsbeth out of her dress and shift. Elisa saw that she wore her breeches and top too. The children splashed around the shallows for a while before they went in deeper to swim. Elisa and Ian were treading water just a bit farther out than the children, watching them play and swim. Several of Ian's men were watching from the shore.

Ian drifted a little farther out so he was slightly behind Elisa and gave a signal to the men so they would know that he intended what he was doing and that she wasna really in any danger. Then, he snuck up behind Elisa and pulled her under. She dove deeper and swam under him; she pushed hard off the bottom to have a bit more speed. She came up behind Ian and was higher in the water than he was. She placed her hands on his shoulders. She used her momentum and weight to press down on him until he went under. She laughed.

The children were laughing and teasing Ian and encouraging their mother to push him under again. When Ian came back up, Elisa pushed him under again, to the children's delight. They played for several minutes with the encouragement of the children to spur them on. Everyone was having a lot of fun.

Ian grabbed her and pulled her under too. She took a quick breath and held it. Ian kissed her when they were face to face. But, Elisa panicked because she knew how easily she lost all thought whenever Ian kissed her. She pushed on his shoulders and kicked with her feet to reach the surface. Ian released her. He could feel the tension and panic she felt. Elisa could see his disappointment when he came up. He turned to head back to shore.

She reached for him, "Wait, please Ian. It wasna because of you. I knew you were just having fun and I wasna worried you would hurt me. It was because I lose all thought when you kiss me and I was afraid I would forget where I was. You make me verra breathless when you kiss me and I dinna want to be underwater and be breathless and need to breathe. I was worried I would try to breathe because I would forget that I was underwater; and then, I would take in water and drown. I am sorry, I dinna mean to disappoint you. Please, I dinna want to upset you or make you upset with me. I was having fun playing with you and I want you to kiss me, just nay when I am underwater."

He took her in his arms and kissed her thoroughly. He floated on his back and pulled her on top of him.

"I love you, Ian," Elisa said between kisses, "verra much, m' laird."

"I love you too, Elisa." He continued to kiss her for a verra long time. He caressed her; but, he couldna do what he really wanted. If she hadna wanted the children with her, he would consider much more. But he was happy that she was happy; so he wouldna complain. After several minutes, Ian asked, "Elisa, how far do you think you can swim under water on one breath?"

Elisa looked at the shore. "More than halfway to the shore, mayhap, about three-quarters of the way. Why?"

"I thought I would float us a bit closer to the shore while I was still kissing you," he said with a wicked grin. "And then, we could slip under the surface and sneak up on the children and surprise them," he said with a huge smile.

Elisa smiled back at him and said, "I am game, sir." She leaned forward and they started kissing again. He caressed her with his hands. He mostly kept his hands on her back or in her hair.

He kissed her for a long time; he dinna think he could ever tire of kissing her and holding her. Then, he let them drift closer to shore while he continued to kiss her, but he only let his hands caress her back or play in her hair since they were closer to the children. She whispered to him, "That's close enough, Ian." He continued to kiss her. When she saw the children had gone back to playing and werena watching, she whispered, "Go." She took a deep breath and Ian pulled them both under and pushed her forward. They swam as deep as they could until they were close to the children. Then, they both came up near them. Ian grabbed Hawk, who screamed. Elisa came up and roared at them. Elsbeth shrieked. They all splashed about for a while. They played a game in the water with the children and everyone had fun before they swam to shore together, laughing.

Chapter 12

As they were making their way to shore, suddenly a shock ran through Elisa's body, followed by a flash of images in her mind of letters and documents and ledgers spread out on desks and bookshelves and in safes, followed by images of her mother leading her through numerous passages. Little memories in her mind that were visually stacked in a pile suddenly started to become organized. Ian grabbed her arm to steady her. It only lasted a few minutes. Ian turned towards Elisa and embraced her. No one seemed to notice what was happening. He held her in his arms and rested his forehead against hers so it appeared they were just enjoying a tender moment together.

After the vision ended, Elisa said, "Ian, I dinna know this before we left the castle. You saw it happened just now, right?" Elisa asked.

"I know, Elisa; that it happened right now. I was touching you when it happened. I saw some letters from my mother to your mother and some to you. I saw you walking dark corridors with your mother. What does this mean, Elisa?"

"I canna tell you, Ian. The more you know, the more danger you and the children, mayhap even the whole clan, will be in. Did you know that the King of England was coming here?"

"There has been word to that affect. That is why I have been so busy during the day. It's why I said I needed Sir Duncan's help when everyone was in our room yesterday. We have been preparing for a siege, just in case. But I dinna ken how those images led you to that conclusion. It doesna make sense to me."

"I just know it from the memories that were in the pile and that started forming together. I ken it doesna make sense, but I just know it. That is what happens when I need to remember something and act on some part of the plan. I dinna think I can explain it any better than that. That is what happened when I needed to start packing for our trip to Scotland. You need to take the guards and the children and get to your father's castle, Ian. You and the children canna be here when the king arrives. What I have to do must be done in private so no one hears what I have to say to the king. Otherwise, whoever hears will be in danger; and the king will verra likely have them put to death. Can you get to your father's through the woods along the loch?" she asked.

"Aye, m' lady," he replied.

"Can you get there without anyone seeing you on the road or out in the open fields?" she asked.

"Aye."

"Get changed and ensure the boys change; and I will help Elsbeth change. Then, we will talk as much as I am able. Can you have the men get our horses ready and get mounted?"

"Aye, m' love." Ian gave the orders, changed quickly, and then, ensured the boys changed. Elisa draped two plaids between Magnum and Sir Colin's horse to create some privacy so she and Elsbeth could change. She couldna change because she wasna able to remove her wet breeches and her top; it was verra difficult to get the leather off when it was wet because it shrunk a little and it clung to her skin. She knew it wouldna be easy to undress Elsbeth either. It was best to let the leather dry some before you even tried to undress.

Elisa used the time to brush out her hair and braid it and pin it up again. Then, she brushed out Elsbeth's hair and braided it. Finally, she was able to get her breeches off and then her top. She dressed quickly in her shift and dress.

Elsbeth smiled and winked back at her father, when she saw him watching her mother try to wriggle out of her clothes. Her father seemed to enjoy watching her mother struggle to get out of her wet clothes. She was careful to nay laugh since her father held his finger to his lips indicating she should be quiet. Elsbeth assumed that her mother dinna realize Ian was watching her.

Once Elisa was changed, she helped Elsbeth with her wet clothes; and finally, she was able to help her into her dress. Elsbeth noticed her father turned his back when he realized that her mother was going to undress her. "Something is wrong isna it, Momma?" Elsbeth asked.

"Aye, m' sweet girl. You must listen to your father, Sir Colin, Sir Thomas, and Angus and if your father says so, your Grandfather too. Do whatever they tell you. You must be verra grown up, now. Our lives are going to change and everything is going to be verra serious. You must let Alice or your grandmother teach you to be a lady if I am nay here to do so, but you must also learn everything your brothers learn. Do you ken, Elsbeth? I know it isna fair to do more than boys, but you must. Your life may depend upon it someday, as mine does now. You have to be capable of surviving alone in the woods and protecting yourself."

"Aye, Momma, I ken."

As soon as Elsbeth was changed, Elisa folded up the plaids and put them back in her saddle bag. Ian and the boys joined them. Ian said, "You can trust Father, Elisa."

She nodded. "I dinna think I can tell you verra much, Ian; your mother could explain when you arrive. Although, I dinna know if she will. But first, I need your father to gather as much livestock as he can into the bailey and prepare for a siege. Tell him he mustna let anyone into the castle that he doesna trust with his life. Anyone could be a spy or an assassin." She looked at the children, "Children, you must listen to the chieftain, your father, Sir Duncan, Sir Colin, Sir Thomas, and Angus. Do whatever they tell you to do. Only trust those whom your father and grandfather say to trust. Your lives are in more danger than I thought." She turned back to Ian, "Will you ensure they receive the same education that I had, without the beatings, of course?"

"Aye, of course, Elisa. I will ensure the children are educated the same as you received. I know you want Elsbeth to have the same education as the boys. I will ensure it is taken care of."

They helped the children mount, then Ian and Elisa moved away from them to talk privately. "Ian, I need you to trust me, now, that my education and knowledge will protect me. You must promise to nay follow me or try to rescue me because the children need you now. I will do everything in my power to return to you. You should stay at your father's until I send for you, but I need you to ensure that your mother doesna hurt the children; I couldna bear it if she treated them the way I was treated. I love you so much and that love will be my strength to do whatever is necessary, endure whatever I must." She reached up and touched his cheek and pulled him to her. They kissed long and hard. She dinna know when she would see him again and the memory had to last.

"I will do all I can to protect the children, Elisa. And you dinna have to worry about my mother. I willna let her hurt the children. I dinna ken what you have to do or why, but I will try to trust you. I will be waiting for your word so I can return. I canna let you do this entirely alone, m' love; so I will leave Sir Duncan to help you."

"I will send word as soon as it is safe for you to return."

Ian mounted his horse. Then, Elisa and Sir Duncan watched them until they were out of sight in the woods. "How long do you think it will take them to reach Chief Ian's?"

"An hour," Duncan replied. They waited by the loch for an hour. They listened to the sounds of the woods to ensure no one approached them until the hour was up. They used the time to discuss the plan.

Elisa directed Sir Duncan, "Just put the picnic things in the tunnel and cover the trail. You can send someone to gather the items later." Sir Duncan did as he was told and then returned to her. "You should chase me like I ran away and you are capturing me and drag me onto your horse. I will ride back to the castle with you and you can lead Magnum. We will make plans as we go, so go slowly." They did just as she said. She mounted her horse and tried to run away from Sir Duncan, but he chased her and pulled her from Magnum onto his lap. He laced Magnum's reins around his hand and also held his reins in the same hand. Then, he pulled Lady Elisa quite firmly against his chest and wrapped his free arm around her waist and held her to him. He walked Justice back to the castle. He dinna allow himself to think about what he wanted to think about. He had to respect her vows to his laird and brother, Ian.

Elisa said, "The King of England will very likely be in residence when we arrive back at the castle. You must make it appear that Ian is away and you are responsible for keeping me confined to my room. I have escaped and you are dragging me back. You need to make it look real without hurting the baby, though. No matter what the king tries to do to me, you mustna try to defend me. If possible, you shouldna be in the room when I need to confront him. It's best if no one knows what I have to say to him. It could put the entire clan at risk. I dinna want you or anyone to try to defend me. He would have you killed. I can take what he will do to me, so dinna interfere. I will survive as I have always done."

"I dinna like the sound of this, m' lady; it's my responsibility to protect you."

"It's part of the plan. You ken I have to follow the plan. It will be bad for everyone if I dinna follow the plan, Sir Duncan. You will be risking the entire clan if you dinna let me do this. You ken the welfare of the clan comes first.

I canna shirk my duty to protect myself. I have to put the clan first."

"Alright, you have made your point well enough, but I still dinna like it, Lady Elisa. This better nay cost you your life or the baby's life. I will feel that I have failed in my duty."

"It willna cost me my life or the baby's life; nothing is required of me that I canna survive. I have been beaten many times, Sir Duncan. This will be no different. I only know that there are many pieces of information, but they are all jumbled up. They are nay in any order, but when I have to do something for the plan, some of the pieces come together and make sense. But the other pieces are still jumbled up in a pile; so I know there is still more to the plan that I have to do later. So, I know that I will survive. Besides, I have to suffer for the people, Sir Duncan. That is why I was treated the way I was; so I could learn to endure the punishment that would be expected of me. You dinna have to like, but you have to accept it." She looked up at him, waiting for him to acknowledge her and agree.

Duncan shook his head, "I canna accept the way you have been treated, m' lady. I will never accept that it has to be this way. But, I willna interfere unless your life is in danger."

About halfway back to the castle a group of riders came towards them through the forest. Duncan pulled her closer to his chest and switched the reins to his left hand which he kept around Elisa as much as possible. He drew his sword so he was ready. He sheathed his sword when he saw that it was more of their guards.

"The King of England has arrived and he has been welcomed into the castle. We informed him that Laird

Ian was away." The men said as they gathered around Sir Duncan and Lady Elisa, surrounding her.

"Aye, thank you. We were just heading back. We will continue with Laird Ian is away. Also, Lady Elisa is confined to her room and has escaped and I just caught her and am returning her to her room."

"Aye, Sir Duncan, we ken."

They arrived back at the castle in the evening. Sir Duncan climbed down from his horse and lowered her to the ground. "And dinna try anything, m' lady," he said loudly in a gruff voice. He made it appear that he was irritated with her and her behavior. Elisa walked with her head down, dragging her feet; so Sir Duncan practically had to drag her as he took her by the elbow and led her into the keep. She tried to look solemn and disappointed that she hadna escaped.

Sir Duncan barged through the hall door, yelling, "M' laird isna going to be happy with you when he finds out you tried to escape again. Now, get up these stairs to your room and stay there until the laird returns, like he told you to do."

"More likely, m' laird will be angry with you because you keep letting me escape. One would think men as big as you Scots are, you could handle one wee lass better than this," she sassed him. She stumbled up the stairs. He half dragged her up the stairs. They appeared to completely ignore the guests in the great hall, when in reality, they were trying to count the number of men the king had brought into the keep. She whispered to him at the top of the stairs, "I counted about twenty-five men, Sir Duncan."

"Aye, me too." He shoved the door open and pushed her into the room, "Now, get in this room and stay there," he yelled. He stepped into the room and slammed the door. "You have been nothing but a nuisance with your constant attempts to escape, since the laird has been gone."

Sir Duncan pushed her just hard enough to make her fall on the floor. She laid there hitting the floor with her fist and yelling, "Ah."

"What is going on? Get up!" a loud, male voice boomed.

Elisa rolled over and slowly stood up. So, the King of England, himself, came; she thought to herself. Well, wasna that a pleasant surprise, she thought to herself, the tone of her voice in her head was dripping with sarcasm.

"Do you not bow before your King?" he asked, looking directly at her.

Elisa raised one eyebrow as she tipped her chin down slightly. "Nay, I dinna bow before any man," Elisa replied. "The Scriptures say to turn on bended knee only before the Lord, God."

The king slapped her face, but she refused to respond. She fisted her hand that was away from the king so he and his men couldna see it, but so only Sir Duncan could see her signal to stop. She dinna want him to respond. She dinna want anyone to think he trusted her or would protect her. She signaled for Sir Duncan to leave. He couldna hear what she needed to say or it would jeopardize his life.

Sir Duncan said, "If I may have your permission to be excused, Your Majesty, I have other duties to attend to."

The king waved him out.

Duncan bowed slightly as he backed out the door.

Then, the king turned to Lady Elisa, "You will bow before your king," he barked at her. "Or, I will have you beaten."

"First, you are nay my king. Second, I am a Scottish laird's wife, my mother was a Scot, and I am a Scot. Third, if you feel you must beat me; then do so, but the Scriptures say you canna strike me more than forty stripes. And if you kill me, you will be starting a war between our two countries that many people have worked verra hard to avoid. You will lose the support of your nobility, for they dinna wish to lose their wealth and men to fight your war, especially nay for something as petty as a woman. And, my last reason for nay bowing to you is because I willna bow to a murderer because I know what you did to try to protect your crown. You killed my mother, brother, and stepmother and you tried to kill the latter's child, as well; but I saved her. Then, you had my father killed; but my cousin still couldna get to me. You would have been better served to uphold your contracts with my parents and with me." She lowered her voice, because she dinna want Sir Duncan to hear her, "And dinna think that I dinna know that you came to my cousin's townhouse with him to force your vile debaucheries on my body. I ken verra clearly just the type of man you are."

He slapped her much harder this time before he signaled for his men to hold her. "I may collapse, but I willna bow," she said as they turned her around and then cut the back of her dress from her neck to her waist. She clinched her jaw shut and took a deep breath. She prayed for God to help her endure the beating. She prayed Sir Duncan wouldna come to her aid. She prayed the Lord would give her His strength, to endure, to persevere, without crying out. She prayed the Scripture that endurance produced perseverance, which produced character, and character produced hope. She asked Him to help her live to fight another day. She thought about the last time her mother and Lady Isobel beat her in the stable. She focused on the memory until she blacked out.

She tried just to focus on the candle flame and clench her jaw shut, but that dinna seem to be verra helpful to endure the pain. She dinna ken why she wasna able to block the pain like she normally did. But she knew she must try to block out the pain and endure it to persevere and live to fight another day. She tried counting the lashes, but she wasna sure how many times the king had struck her already. She used her memory to try to recall the number of lashes, hoping that directing her concentration elsewhere would help her endure the pain better. It helped considerably.

Elisa collapsed after about twenty lashes, a couple more mayhap. The king directed the men to lay her across the bed and to leave the room and guard the door. The king took advantage of his time alone with Elisa. He threw up her skirts and pulled her to the edge of the bed. He had never been allowed to be with her as a husband and wife before because of the strict rule that Lady Isobel insisted upon; so he took advantage now. He could always claim the king's first rights if it was an issue. When he was not satisfied, he continued with how he was accustomed to being with her.

When he finished, he dressed and lowered her skirts before he moved her back up on the bed more. He left the room with a very smug look on his face. As king, he didn't feel he had to concern himself with what other's thought. He gathered his men around him and made his excuses to Sir Duncan. Then, he left with his men and they made the arrangements to set out for their return to London.

Duncan immediately sent for Alice and they entered the room. He suggested, "I think you should find one of Ian's shirts and cut the back up the center and then across the shoulders so we can dress m' lady in the shirt, but nothing will touch her wounds. We should position her in the center of the bed. Once you have her wounds cleaned and dressed, I will have to tie her to the bedposts so she canna move. I verra much hate the idea of doing so, but I dinna want her thrashing about and ripping her wounds open again and again. Does she have a skirt that isna attached to a bodice. You could put that on her so that her lower body is always covered, even if I have her feet tied to the bedposts."

"Aye, I will just be a minute and then you can lift her while I change her. I would ask other maids to help me, but I would need at least two of them to lift her and I would be worried about them making her wounds worse. I will just be a minute to prepare Ian's shirt and find one of her skirts."

"I will do my best to keep my eyes closed as much as possible, Alice. I dinna want to see my brother's wife."

Alice gave him a look that told him she dinna believe him before she went to each of their wardrobes and found the necessary items, so they could change Elisa. She cut Ian's shirt as Duncan suggested.

"I canna change my feelings for her, Alice, if they havena changed in eighteen years, they are nay going to change. But, I can do everything possible to ensure I'm nay alone with her or at least that the door is open and other guards are in the vicinity or a maid is present. I dinna want to cause either of them any pain by doing something inappropriate." Duncan lifted Elisa by the shoulders, while Alice pulled Elisa's hands free of her bodice and slipped Ian's shirt on. Then, he lifted her by the waist as Alice removed her skirt and put the clean skirt on Elisa. Duncan closed his eyes and turned aside as much as he was able when he dinna need to see what he was doing but was just holding her. He dinna want to see his brother's wife. He said it to himself as much as to Alice. He needed to remind himself to nay step over any boundaries. She was Ian's wife; nay his and he needed to constantly remind himself of that fact. He was certain Alice knew of his feelings for Elisa and had since the first time Elisa came to Scotland, but he still wanted to try to respect Ian and Elisa's marriage. He promised to protect her and that was what he would do.

It was all Alice could do to nay gasp when she saw the evidence of the king's violence. But, she managed to keep her mouth clenched tightly shut until after Elisa was dressed. She told Duncan, "You can lower her on the bed now and then I need you to leave me alone with Elisa for a while."

Duncan looked at her.

"You will leave the room now, Sir Duncan. You willna try to see what I am doing; nor will you try to sense my thoughts. Do you ken?"

"Alright, Alice; I'm going, but I dinna ken why I need to leave the room now after she is changed." Duncan said as he shook his head. He rose from the bed and left the room. He closed the door and stood in the hallway.

Alice walked to the fireplace and took the bucket from the hearth and the cloth and lifted Elisa's skirts and did her best to wash Elisa clean. She put a little salve on her bottom and hoped that it helped her heal. She placed pads of cloths under Elisa in case she lost her baby. She lowered Elisa's skirt and returned the bucket of water to the hearth. She tried to ensure that she put it exactly where it was before she used it. She should have thought about that more closely before she moved it. She knew Duncan would be observant enough to realize what she had done if he noticed the bucket had been moved. All she could do was pray that Elisa dinna lose her baby and that Duncan was too distracted with worry for Elisa to notice the bucket. She really dinna want to have to explain anything about this to Duncan. The horror of the situation completely disgusted Alice.

She knew Duncan had feelings for Elisa and she knew that he wouldna do anything to hurt Ian or Elisa by acting on those feelings, but she dinna want to risk what he might try to do if he knew just what the king had done to Elisa. She would have to keep this a secret, most likely from both Ian and Duncan, and if possible, from Elisa as well. But she wasna sure she could keep it a secret from Elisa. She could supposedly remember things that were done or said around her even when she was asleep or unconscious, she supposed.

Alice let Duncan return to the room after she was sure that everything was in place, hopefully exactly as it was.

Duncan looked at her strangely, but he dinna say anything. He sat on the edge of the bed and held Elisa's shoulders down so she couldna move while Alice cleaned her wounds and applied a salve to them to help them heal.

Elisa awoke in great pain and gritted her teeth together and hissed, "Are we alone?"

"Nay, m' lady," Sir Duncan said, "I am only holding you down so you willna move and tear the wounds more, while Alice cleans the wounds and applies a salve to help you heal."

Elisa said, "I need some of Ian's scotch, actually, a lot of it. Will you go to the kitchen and get a bottle and a glass?"

"Aye, m' lady. I will be back shortly." He gave Alice the same strange look and left the room. He closed the door and walked down the stairs to the kitchen to get the requested items. He took his time so they could talk as he suspected they wanted to do. He dinna ken what was going on between them, but he would respect their requests.

"Tell me quickly, Alice, before he returns. He must never know, nor Ian, either."

"I believe it as you suspect, m' lady. It appears that the king took advantage of you even though you were unconscious from your beating. It appears that he abused you," Alice paused, nay sure how to explain, but then said, "in both places. I washed you as best as I could and put a little salve by the one in case it feels strange to you. I am sorry, my dear. I placed pads under you so that if you should miscarry, the pads will catch the blood. We willna know for some time. You mustna think about that. We must only think about keeping your wounds from getting infected and getting you healed up, alright?"

"Aye, Alice. I ken what the king did. You dinna have to worry about that. It isna anything," but Elisa stopped herself from saying any more. It wasna anything that he hadna already done to her many times before; but, she did her best to keep that thought to herself. She let the sobs come and she knew Alice would do what she could to comfort her and she hoped Alice would keep her secret. Nay that she had any ability to trust others.

When Elisa controlled her emotions again, she said, "You mustna let Ian or Duncan ken what happened, Alice. You will have to keep it a secret to your death. Do you ken?"

"Aye, I already knew that, m' lady. They would march off and start a war over what the king nay doubt considers his right, nay that any subjects could possibly agree with such. I am so sorry that you have suffered in this way."

Duncan knocked and waited in the hallway until he was given permission to enter. He walked to Elisa's side of the bed and poured the scotch into the glass. He set the bottle on her side table and turned to her with the glass. "How do you propose to drink this? And, do you intend to drink the entire bottle?"

"I intend to drink the entire bottle, Sir Duncan. And dinna even think about criticizing me. I could easily drink that and more and I willna pass out from it. I pulled a reed from near the water at the loch; it is in my cloak pocket. Cut both ends and put one end in the cup of scotch and the other end in my mouth. How many lashes did I take?" she asked.

"Twenty two, m' lady. He stopped when you collapsed," Sir Duncan replied.

"Thank God, I thought he would have me revived; so he could continue. Is he staying or returning to London?"

"He is preparing to leave now," Sir Duncan said. He rose from his chair and fetched the reed and cut it.

"I want him followed. I want to know when he has returned to London."

"Aye, m' lady," Sir Duncan said. "I will see to it."

"Dinna go yourself, send someone you can trust. They must be careful to nay be found out. Dinna tell Ian what happened here today. He isna to come home yet. I will send word to him myself when he may return. I dinna want him to cause a war that we have tried so hard to avoid." She paused and drank the scotch. Duncan refilled the glass when it was empty until she finished the entire bottle. "You may continue, Alice." She hoped the scotch helped her slip into oblivion quickly.

She dinna pass out, but the scotch eventually seemed to ease the pain of her wounds. At least, it seemed to be less intense after a time. Alice took her time and tried to gently clean each wound. Then, she applied the salve to each wound. When Alice finished, Elisa allowed herself to fall asleep. She hoped that she would be safe until she was healed. She dinna know how long it would take, but she hoped it wouldna take the whole summer like the last time she was whipped so severely when she was seven. But, she did her best to keep all thoughts about her past and what the king had done to her far from her mind or buried so deep that no one would ever know. She dinna know if she could trust Alice or nay, but she dinna have a choice in the matter. She could only hope Alice was the type of person whose word meant something.

Elisa thrashed about on the bed for a sennight. She suffered from her nightmares and Duncan was forced to tie her hands and feet to the bedposts in an attempt to keep her from ripping open her wounds repeatedly. He sat beside the bed as much as possible and would move to the chair by the fire for a couple hours of sleep at night, but only if Alice agreed to stay awake and sit in the chair by the bed. He made her promise to wake him if Lady Elisa stirred at all in her sleep. Then, he tried to talk to her and calm her down during her nightmares so that she dinna rip open her wounds again. It was a long and difficult sennight.

He tried to nay know what was in her nightmares, but it was impossible when she relived them out loud and so vividly and descriptively. He was appalled at what he heard and he knew that Alice was, as well. The looks she gave him were more of a warning than sympathy. He was certain she expected him to control his anger and also she expected him never to speak of anything that he heard. He gave her a nod to indicate that he wouldna speak of it, but he wasna certain he could control his anger regarding the mistreatment of Lady Elisa; that would require divine intervention, Duncan was certain.

Elisa awoke stiff and sore. She realized her limbs were tied. She tried to lift her head.

"Dinna move, m' lady," Sir Duncan rushed to her side. "I will release you, but dinna try to move on your own. I will move your arms and legs for you." He cut the ties and gently and very slowly moved her arms down by her sides. Then, he did the same with her legs. He massaged her shoulders, as much as he could touch, and her arms to relieve the pain from being tied up to the bedposts and also to try to get the blood flowing into the limbs again. "I could massage your legs too if you wish, but I am nay sure it would be appropriate."

"Drink," was all she could say because her mouth was so dry.

He held a cup full of broth close to her and put the reed in it so she could sip. Then, he lifted her head and held it to the reed.

"How long?" she asked, hoping he would figure out the rest of the question.

"A little more than a sennight, you have been in and out of consciousness nine days, m' lady," he said after a few minutes.

Sir Duncan stayed beside her. "Hand," she said after a while.

"I dinna ken, m' lady," he said.

"Squeeze my hand," Elisa grunted. "Need your strength." Sir Duncan squeezed her hand. "Tighter," she said, "need to feel pain somewhere else for a while." She struggled to make the sentence. He squeezed her hand harder until she flinched. Elisa focused on the pain in her hand for a long time so she dinna have to think about the pain in her back.

After a while, Alice came in to check on Lady Elisa. When Alice saw Lady Elisa was awake, she sent for more broth. Elisa was glad to have something to drink that would help her gain back her strength. Elisa knew it would be a long time before she would be able to fight back.

Duncan suggested, "Alice, would you massage Lady Elisa's legs to help relieve the pain from being tied up and also to get the blood flowing again? I dinna think I should do it, but I did her shoulders and arms."

"Aye, I will do that for you, Lady Elisa. Duncan shouldna be too familiar with you." She paused for a couple minutes while she worked on Elisa's legs; and then said, "M' lady, you have been crying out for Laird Ian. Should we send for him? I am certain he would return if we sent word to him.”

“Nay, Alice; I and I alone will send for Laird Ian. Duncan will explain later. I need to rest again.” Elisa couldna allow herself to think about anything but healing. She would visualize the wounds healing. She would think about the task she had to do when she was better. She couldna think of it now because she dinna want to say anything in her sleep. Her sleep wasna restful. Sir Duncan had to tie her up again, so she wouldna tear open her wounds again.

She slept a couple more days if you could call her fitful nightmares sleep. She stirred in her sleep, and said, “I am sorry, Sir Duncan.”

“Shh, it will be alright, m’ lady. You will heal quickly now.” She dinna ken him; so she tried to visualize the wounds healing until she fell asleep again. She missed Ian so much. She sobbed his name in her dreams and then she felt his presence as she always did when he was near. “Ian, you came. I am so glad. I missed you so much.”

“Shh, m’ sweet wife, just visualize your wounds healing and go back to sleep. You will be healed soon, m’ love,” Ian whispered to her mind.

“I love when you talk to me like that; it makes my heart swell with my love for you, Ian. And it makes my stomach do flips.”

“Shh, please, Elisa, I need you to focus. We dinna have time for that now. Focus on your wounds healing. Picture each wound in your mind and then envision it healing.”

“You are so bossy,” Elisa said, but she tried to really focus. She pictured in her mind what the wounds looked like and what it would look like as the wounds grew back together. Focus, she reminded herself. She could feel Ian touching her and his breath caressing her skin. She felt like she could feel the flesh growing back together. She could see the redness fading to pink, then white. Focus, she told herself, but she couldna focus because she was filled with so much energy that she couldna just lie there anymore. She struggled to get free. "Sir Duncan cut me free," she demanded.

"Nay, m' lady, you are nay healed completely and you must lie still. Dinna fight to get free. Just lie still and focus on healing." In a whisper, she heard Sir Duncan say to Ian, "Tell her to be still, m' laird."

Then, Elisa heard Ian whisper, "Sir Duncan is right, Elisa. You must lie still and focus, visualize your wounds healing. Be still. Focus, m' love, I canna do this without you. You need to stop fighting us."

"Aye, m' laird," Elisa said sarcastically, but she refocused on her wounds. She tried to only think of her wounds healing, each one growing together. Then, turning from red to pink to white. Then, she visualized the next wound healing. But, she couldna focus for very long on herself. Her body reached out to Ian and Sir Duncan. She could sense that they were exhausted and she felt so full of energy and she just wanted to share her energy with them and make them feel more energized. She dinna ken how she could feel so full of energy and she wasna sure how she knew Ian and Sir Duncan needed some of her energy; but she was certain they were verra exhausted and she felt the energy flow from her body to theirs. It made her feel better to know that they were receiving some of her energy and that they wouldna be so exhausted.

Whenever she felt like she was overflowing with energy, and she tried to share that with the two men, they snapped at her to focus, or concentrate and to help them heal her wounds.

She dinna know how long this went on but they seemed to argue about it for a verra long time, mayhap an entire day. She wasna sure if she was awake or dreaming, but the pain was subsiding and she felt so much better. She felt like she was filled with energy. She remembered the warning, so she tried to remain still and focus on her wounds.

She dinna know how long they spent trying to heal her wounds or if the entire episode was some bizarre dream. She dinna know how long she had slept or had been lying in the bed, but she awoke with the sunrise, and her hands and feet were free of the ties. She gently flexed her fingers and toes. She wasna sure if she could move her arms and legs; but miraculously, she couldna feel any pain in her back. "Sir Duncan, are you there?" she said, barely above a whisper.

Alice replied in a low voice so she wouldna disturb Sir Duncan, "Shh, he is sleeping in the chair, m' lady. He is exhausted; so try to be quiet and dinna wake him."

"Was Ian here?" she asked. "I felt him touch me, I could feel his breath on me, and I could hear him speaking to me."

"Nay, m' lady, the laird is at his father's castle, remember?" Alice questioned her.

"Aye, I remember; but I know I heard him talking to me and I felt him touching me, so I thought he came back to me. Do you know if he is alright?" Elisa asked.

"You would know if he needed you or if he was in trouble."

Nay anything Alice said made any sense, so she changed the subject. "Alice, what do my wounds look like? Could I roll over, yet? It doesna hurt."

"Aye, you may roll over. You may have a bit of tenderness; but I dinna think you will. You look all healed." Alice dinna want to say too much, but she guessed Elisa would interrogate her soon enough.

"Really, so soon?" Elisa asked, unbelieving. But, she rolled over and there wasna any pain. "Is Sir Duncan alright, Alice? He never sleeps when I am awake."

"He will be fine, he just needs to rest now and he will be better in a few days, a sennight at the most, m' lady."

Elisa had so many questions but she dinna think she should say anything just now and she wasna really sure whom she could ask or if they would give her a straight answer. "I feel like dressing, and then I think I will go to the kitchen for something to eat. But first, would you get some fresh linens and help me change the bedding? Then, we will move Sir Duncan to the bed so he can rest more comfortably."

"It wouldna be appropriate, m' lady."

"It's nay as if I am going to sleep in the bed with him, Alice. He canna sleep in the chair for a sennight in my room either. And we canna carry him to his room. I will sleep somewhere else, Alice. Now, please go get us some fresh linens so we may change the linens and move him to the bed."

While Alice went to get the linens, Elisa quickly dressed behind the dressing screen. She put on all her daggers and her black breeches and top. Then, she put on a black dress over the top. She waited to put on her sword belt until after they moved Sir Duncan. When Alice returned,

Elisa helped her change the linens. Then, they moved Sir Duncan to the bed. Elisa removed his boots.

Elisa told Alice, "I am just going to brush out my hair, and then I will come down to the kitchen. We can talk there."

When Alice left, Elisa brushed, braided and pinned up her hair. She put on her sword belt. She removed a packet of parchments from a secret compartment in her trunk. It was the evidence she needed to deal with the King of England. She placed them in the hidden pocket of her dress and another copy in the secret pocket of her cloak. She tied up Sir Duncan. She had to crawl under the bed so she could tie his right arm to his left leg and his left arm to his right leg. That way if he tried to free himself, he would only make the bindings tighter on his opposite extremity. Oh, he was going to be verra angry with her, especially when he discovered she took his horse too. She put a gag over his mouth and tied it in place. Then, she wrote a quick note in code to Ian explaining that she had to do what was necessary to end this war before it started. She begged him to nay try to follow her. She needed him here with the children to protect them and provide for them. She would find her way back to him as soon as she was able. She told them how much she loved all of them, but that now that she knew who she was, she must do this to protect them, even if it meant sacrificing herself. She told him how much she loved him and missed him and asked him to tell the children that she loved them verra much and to give each of them a hug and a kiss from her.

Elisa grabbed her black cloak, barred the door, and snuck out the secret passage. She took the exit nearest to the stairwell. She went downstairs to the kitchen. She asked Alice, "Do you really think Sir Duncan will sleep for three days?"

"Aye, m' lady, at least three days, but more likely a sennight."

Elisa insisted, "Alice, please explain what happened. How could I see, feel, and hear Ian, even though he wasna here? I dinna ken it, but I know what I felt and heard."

Alice explained, "Ian has a gift of vision that allows him to see, Elisa. He can talk to you and even touch you."

Elisa wondered, "If Ian could do all this, could he also sense my visions and thoughts?"

Alice continued, "Mayhap. Ian also has a gift of healing that goes a long way back in the line of McVeigh's. So, that was what helped you heal so quickly. Ian and Sir Duncan both helped to heal you, but it draws a lot of their energy; so they are verra weak and need a lot of rest now. That is why they will sleep for about a sennight.

"Well, I think we should let Sir Duncan sleep undisturbed for a sennight. Since Sir Duncan is Laird Ian's commander of the guard, is there someone who will take care of his responsibilities while Sir Duncan is asleep for a sennight? Someone who will ken what to do without being told? I'm concerned that Sir Duncan is going to sleep for a sennight and Laird Ian is likely asleep at his father's. There should be someone in charge here while they are both indisposed. Ian took all the guards that normally watch over me and the children with him to Chief Ian's."

"Aye, m' lady, you dinna have to concern yourself with anything regarding the safety of the castle or the clan while the two of them sleep for a sennight. All will be taken care of."

"Is there anything you think I should do in Ian's absence, as the laird's wife?"

"Nay, m' lady, you just need to focus on ensuring you are healthy."

"While I was unconscious, was there any indication that I lost the baby?"

"Nay, m' lady; there wasna any bleeding or spotting after the king beat you. There hasna been any bleeding while you were lying in bed this past sennight. I am verra sorry to bring this up, but do you recall what happened? I am sure you dinna wish to talk about it, but I need to ken if you ken it."

"I am relieved to hear that there wasna any bleeding. I hope that means Laird Ian's bairn will be fine. Aye, I ken what happened, but I dinna wish to discuss it, Alice. Do you know if word came back as to whether the King of England has returned to London yet?"

"Aye, Duncan received word that the king has returned to his court in London. He must have travelled at breakneck speed to get back to London so quickly. He must have been worried that someone would chase him and attack him. From all accounts, he has resumed his life as normal, apparently," Alice replied, her disgust for the man clear in her voice, although she dinna say that exactly. It was just evident from the words she used and the tone of her voice.

"Thank you, Alice, for everything you have done to help me and the advice you have given me, and for answering all my questions. I am going to eat something and then there is something I have to do. You shouldna worry about me; you will have to trust that I know what I am doing and

I will be alright. You may return to your other duties. You dinna need to look for me either. Do you ken?"

"Aye, I ken, m' lady."

Elisa waited until Alice left the kitchen and packed what she needed. Then, she snuck out of the kitchen and made her way to the stables. She quickly saddled and harnessed Magnum and Sir Duncan's horse, Justice. She knew this would really irritate him, as if he wasna going to be irritated enough with her for tying him up and gagging him. She left the note for Ian in Justice's stall. She knew it would be found and brought to Ian. What she had to do was something she had to do on her own and she dinna need any witnesses to her whereabouts when this plot was discovered. She was taking a huge risk and she might verra well be caught and hanged for her crimes; but, she would do what was necessary if it was within her power and she would suffer the consequences later if it was necessary. She dinna doubt that it would be necessary either. She wasna a fool when it came to Lady Isobel's plans; they were designed for Elisa's maximum pain and punishment. But, she would face that trouble when it was required of her. For now, she had to try to do what was required of her and do it to the best of her ability; although, she doubted it would be good enough. She focused on the task at hand and tried to nay get caught before she even set out to accomplish the prearranged plan.

Chapter 13

ELISA DINNA WANT to delay any longer. She snuck out through the secret garden tunnel. She worked her way down to the loch and found the path that would lead her back to Argyll Woods. She would be hidden within the woods until she reached the crossing. She only hoped that she dinna miss the low tide. She really couldna afford to sit and wait nearly twelve hours for the tide to change and she dinna think it would be a good idea to tire the horses trying to swim across. Then, she would have to light a fire and dry all her clothing. Her food might get wet; and then, she wouldna have anything to eat. All she could do was pray that she arrived at the crossing during low tide.

She was on her way back to London, a place that she had hoped nay ever to return. She would take turns riding Magnum and Justice. When one tired, she would switch to the other. She would only sleep a couple hours at night. She knew that with her head start and her ability to go so long without sleep, there was verra little chance anyone would catch up to her. No one would likely come after her or even realize she was gone until Ian and Duncan woke, except possibly that meddling Alice, but Elisa hoped Alice would be busy with her other duties. She could get her business taken care of, set her plans in motion, and be headed back to Scotland before anyone could get more than a couple days south of the border.

If she needed help on the way home, apparently, she could reach out to anyone in the clan; but she dinna want to give away her location; so, she visualized a black box in her mind. She realized after talking to Alice that Ian came to her using his gifts and healed her and that Sir Duncan helped. She was glad they would both sleep for about a sennight. After Alice told her they had this vision gift, she realized Ian had probably seen what the vision at the loch revealed to her, which meant that he would very likely figure out what she was going to do if he hadna already. But since Ian only left Sir Duncan to watch over her, she dinna think Ian realized exactly what she was about to do. Otherwise, he most likely wouldna have left her with so few to guard her. She had to be thankful for that.

Her parents kept so many secrets about her true identity, a princess of both realms; bloodlines of Scottish royalty from both her parents and bloodlines of English royalty from her mother. She was in line to receive the crown from either side of her family. Her parents tried to abdicate, but in having children, they created more danger. And suddenly, she realized why the secret compartments of her numerous trunks contained so much jewelry and tiaras and crowns and two scepters, one for each throne. It was to prove her royal lineage and heritage.

Ian's marriage to Elisa only strengthened their Scottish connections because he and his father were also royalty, probably his mother too. By sending copies of the marriage contract and adoption papers to both kings, they put themselves in greater danger because those records would be entered in the royal registries and it would acknowledge their rights to both thrones.

If her parents had nay been so secretive, then mayhap, they could have avoided this and just lived peacefully on the Isle of Mull. She could only hope that the evidence she carried would be enough to help gain her the allies of some of the nobility. She dinna know if there was enough proof to ensure their cooperation or if they would risk standing against their king. All she could do was follow the plan and place the evidence where the vision showed her to place it and hope that it was enough to gain the nobility's allegiance.

She must focus her mind on the black box; block Ian and Sir Duncan from envisioning her thoughts. It was the only way to protect them. Focus on staying alert and traveling as fast and as far as she could before anyone caught up to her.

She reached the crossing and watched the tide for a couple minutes. The low tide had come in. It was starting to recede, but there was still time to get across. She watched the tide carefully as she crossed. She dinna want the horses to be spooked by the spray of the tide. She dinna need to be unseated and dumped in the water.

After she crossed the sandbar, she climbed the bank and stayed along the ridge so she could ride in the tree line. It wasna the ideal place to ride because her silhouette could be seen through the trees in the sunlight. It allowed anyone watching her to see that she was a lone rider and that was a danger to her, but she dinna wish to ride out in the open either. She dinna stay on the ridge for verra long, only until the woods cut down into the valley too. Then, she rode down into the valley and stayed on the path that cut through Argyll Woods. She was grateful that she made it into Argyll Woods the first evening. All was going as planned so far. She tethered the two horses together and then to a bush so Magnum could get free if it was necessary. She found a secluded place to slip up into a tree with her satchel, water and bedroll. She set up her bed, ate a little meat and bread and drank a little water before she slept for two hours. Then, she gathered her things and climbed down from the tree. She put her things back on Magnum's back and took care of her personal business before she mounted Magnum and set out again. Thankfully, she had sufficient moonlight to see the path she had to take. Although, she supposed she could find her way in the dark if it was necessary and she was willing to rely on her memories to guide her.

She rode until sunrise and skirted off the road to a parallel path and rode through the woods as much as she could to avoid meeting anyone on the road. She really dinna need to meet anyone. She was skilled with weapons, but she knew she wouldna have any chance against any number of opponents. Besides, she simply dinna have time to deal with them. She ran the horses for a couple hours in the morning and then walked them until she stopped to eat lunch, switching horses every two hours. Then, she ran the horses for two more hours and walked them until she stopped to eat dinner. She ran the horses for two hours again until dark. She dinna dare run them through the wooded paths during the night. She couldna afford to injure or lame one of the horses. She needed both horses so she could get back to London quickly. She definitely needed them both once she reached London. The journey back to London was going so much faster than her trip north to Scotland with Sir Colin and the children.

A few days into her ride, Elisa heard a whisper of laughter and she knew Ian was searching for her. She reigned the horses into a secluded part of the woods and focused her mind. "Stop, Ian; stop seeking me. You mustna. You must care for the children and protect them from both kings, if necessary. Let me go. I will call for you if I absolutely need you. But for now, let me go. I love you."

She took a deep breath and focused on the black box. She hoped Ian would stop searching for her now. She set out again. A few more days and she would reach London. She was verra grateful for her ability to remember things from when she was so little. She could easily recall the paths to take to get back and forth to London from when she was a little girl and had ridden with her parents to Mull and back to London. She was also verra glad that she hadna listened to her parents when they told her to sleep during the journey. If she had slept, she wouldna know the paths so well.

It took her about a sennight to reach London. She was glad to be at the end of her journey. Elisa stopped at an inn as she reached the outskirts of London. She knew that one of the King's bastard daughters worked and lived there. Elisa asked the innkeeper if the girl might serve as her maid for the night. The innkeeper agreed, and Elisa gave him a few coins for his lost worker. She ordered a bath sent up to her room and also a warm meal. When the girl came to Elisa's room with her tray of food, several other maids brought buckets of water and filled a tub for her. Elisa waited until the other maids left the room before she asked the girl if she would like a better station in life. The girl said that she really could use whatever help she could get because she dinna make enough money here that would ever help her leave this place. Elisa told her to return to her room in two hours; that would give her time to eat and bathe. Then, she would change and give the girl her clothes and she could take her calling card to her old residence tonight and Elisa would meet her there in the morning to discuss her new position. The girl agreed. So easy to deceive her, Elisa thought. Though she dinna care for the idea of deceiving others, it was a necessity in this case so she could make it appear that she died tonight. The king betrayed and abandoned his bastard daughter; and now, Elisa would use her to betray the king.

Elisa ate quickly after the king's daughter left the room. Then, she enjoyed her bath. Afterwards, she dried off and put on all her weapons. She put on a clean pair of black breeches and top under another black dress. She brushed out her hair and braided it and pinned it up again with her dagger pins. She let the girl into her room and gave the girl her dirty dress to change into. Elisa gave her the calling card and then paid for a carriage to take the girl to Elisa's father's townhouse. Well, she supposed her Uncle Kenneth officially owned it now that her father and her cousin were both dead.

Elisa snuck into the stable of the inn and saddled her two horses and snuck out again. She relied upon the memories her mother planted in her mind with all the games and tests they had gave Elisa as she made her way through the London night. She followed the same path Sir Colin took on their way out of London, was it only two and a half months ago? She played this game many times with her mother, secretly running through dark passages. She dinna ken how the memories came to her in flashes just when she needed the correct junction. Of all the secrets her parents kept, why couldna they at least have explained the flashes of visions? So many tests and secret passages. Yet, Elisa always solved them easily. The flashes of vision just came to her at each necessary point. Since her mother played this game with Elisa from such a young age, since just after she could walk and run, Elisa learned to trust her instincts. Never once had the memories failed her, but that was why she dinna need Ian or Duncan searching for her to distract her at the wrong time. She focused her mind on the black box and then she focused on her surroundings and let the flashes of memories flow so she could rely on them to do what she needed to do as she made her way through the London night.

Elisa's mother showed her many secret passages in nearly every home of the nobility. She went to those homes that were important to the plan. She snuck into the homes through the secret passages. She made her way through the necessary corridors to the library or study where she left documents and incriminating evidence in many of their desks and ledgers and even their safes. Sometimes, she put the evidence in certain books on the bookshelves. Evidence that made it appear like the king was extorting them, evidence that they were blackmailing other men of nobility, and other more devious plots and schemes, including the murder of her mother, brother, stepmother and father.

It was a long night moving through the city as stealthily as she knew how. She was verra good at sticking to the shadows and walking quietly so no one would know she was there. She had practiced this since she could basically walk. She knew she could run through the forest in the fall without making any noise in the leaves as well. So, she wasna too concerned about anyone seeing her. She only hoped someone dinna come across Magnum and Justice while she was in someone's house. They were probably quite noticeable since they were such good horseflesh; quite a prize for someone to pilfer. But, she'd have to think about that later; she returned her thoughts to her current mission of setting all the documents in the homes of the nobility. She double checked her work before she placed it, so that she dinna leave the wrong thing in the wrong house before she slipped out of the secret passage and moved on to the next house.

Then, she left Magnum in an alley a couple blocks from her father's home. Her last stop was the castle. She left Sir Duncan's horse in an alley near the castle. She proceeded to the alley that contained the secret entrance to the castle and entered it. She snuck through many passages until she reached the King's chamber. It seemed her mother was the only one who knew of this particular passage as she had been forced into a liaison with the former king. Apparently, he dinna share this secret with his son.

The passage opened right above the King's bed. She opened the secret panel and listened carefully to ensure no one was in the room. She reached down and slit his throat while he slept. She quietly listened. No one seemed to be in the room. Elisa lowered herself onto the bed. She peaked out of the bed curtains to ensure no one was there. She took a complete outfit from the king's wardrobe, placed it in a satchel. She stole the ring from the king's hand with his crest. She left more incriminating evidence in his room, evidence proving he was extorting the nobility and he killed her family members. She was careful to nay disturb the king's body or step in his blood as she snuck back into the passage and closed it up. She made her way back through the passages.

A few blocks from the castle, Elisa donned the king's clothes and hailed a hackney. She recalled from her memories the voice of the king and his dialect of speech. She used the king's voice to direct the hackney driver to her old residence. She asked the driver to wait around the corner and entered her uncle's townhouse. She went down to the cellar where she knew her parents had probably already prepared for this. She hated the secrets, hated that she knew these things without understanding how she knew them, more games on which they had worked. Somehow, her parents planted the plans that she needed to do and the memories of the plans just came to her at the right time when she needed to do them. The unexpectedness of these flashes of visions was difficult enough to deal with but reviewing the little bits of information when it was all jumbled up, like a pile of puzzle pieces was very frustrating, especially because she liked everything to be neat and tidy and organized. She supposed that was why she mostly thought of memories and emotions as being in little compartments in the little black box. But when she needed to complete certain plans, the pieces that she needed from the pile just came together in her memory and showed her what she needed to do.

The barrels were laid out in patterns. Some of the barrels were Ian's father's scotch. Such a waste, Elisa thought.

Others contained explosive powder. She took a small one by the door, pried the cork out and poured out a pile, and then made a trail of the contents from the center barrel, which she uncorked. She created a big enough pile to reach the height of the uncorked hole. Then, she poured a trail from the barrel to the main hall. She went up to her room, where the king's daughter was sound asleep. It was then she recognized the young woman. She was the maid that helped her stepmother. Elisa was young then and concerned with her stepmother. She wanted to help any way she could. She was confused about the visitor until he entered the room shortly after the maid left and the man smothered her stepmother with a pillow. Elisa had not seen the maid again after that day. At least now, she dinna need to feel too guilty about what she was doing. The girl was nay innocent in all of this. The king's daughter helped the king to kill her stepmother and nearly killed Elsbeth in the process.

Elisa left more documents in one of her desk drawers and returned to the main hall. She continued to make the trail of powder down the front stairs to the gate. She stooped down near the bushes and poured a little pile of the powder out. She struck a flint and the spark lit the pile. She dropped the king's ringed glove next to where the pile was. She hoped it appeared that the king had removed his glove to strike the flint and start the fire. She also hoped that the explosion wouldna damage the evidence that she left in her desk drawer. Her room and desk were the farthest from the main part of the house, but she thought there might be quite a lot of explosives in the basement and also that the scotch itself might be explosive or at least flammable.

Elisa ran to the end of the block and slowed to a quick walk as she turned the corner. Using the king's voice again, she told the hackney to drive quickly back to where he picked her up and then she started to climb in. She opened the door, tossed in a bag of the king's coins. She told the driver to go before she entered the hackney. Then, she jumped down again just as the hackney lurched forward and took off. She darted into the shadows and hid in some bushes until the hackney was out of sight.

She hoped the driver dinna notice her getting off. She hoped the horses lurching forward covered the movement of her jumping off. She made her way to Magnum where she left him in an alley two blocks from her home. She removed the king's clothes, changed back into her black outfit and put the king's clothes in the satchel again. She rode back towards the castle and tethered Duncan's horse to her saddle on Magnum. She had one more stop to make.

Elisa made her way to her solicitor's office and left two letters for him; one authorizing him to transfer funds to Ian to cover the expense of sending Cousin Ken back to London and another letter authorizing funds were set aside to provide for Sir Colin.

She was on her way out of London. She prayed, "Please, God, let this plan work, let these people leave us alone. Please, help this plan to prevent war between England and Scotland. And, Lord, please help me get safely back to Ian in Scotland. Please help me stay alert during my journey. Most importantly, forgive me. I ken I shouldna have done these things but if I dinna do them, then I am putting my family in danger and at risk of being used as I was used. So, please forgive me. In Jesus' name I pray that Your will be done. Amen."

She saw two large rocks near the path to the solicitor's door and wrapped the king's clothes around them and put everything back in the satchel. She made her way through London, following the same path Sir Colin used to lead her and the children out of London two months ago. She kept her eyes on the streets and her ears focused on listening for anyone that might try to harm her. "Ian, if you can watch my surroundings and help me be alert to any danger, that would help me get back to you," Elisa whispered to Ian. She tried to focus on the right roads to take. Sometimes, she thought she could hear Ian or Sir Duncan say something. She took it as a warning and avoided any area they cautioned her against. She wasna used to anyone seeing her thoughts or knowing her so closely. It was disconcerting, but she needed their help to warn her against danger and to keep her safe; so she had to try to trust them. But, trust wasna something she had any ability to do. She had been abused too many times, by too many people to rely on or trust others, especially since a lot of her abuse came from her parents, the ones who should have loved and protected her.

As she crossed a bridge, she let Ian and Sir Duncan watch her flanks while she lowered the satchel into the water. Once the satchel was just under the surface of the water, she reached over the bridge rail and cut the rope as close to the water as she could reach. She dinna want to make a splash and attract any attention. She could only hope the rope was short enough and would become wet enough and sink too, before anyone saw it. Then, she rolled up the remaining rope and tucked it into her satchel again. She mounted Magnum and continued down the road trying to focus on the correct streets to take, watch for dangers and listen for any whispered warnings. It was exhausting, but she knew she couldna stop for at least two days. She dinna want to be anywhere near London. She avoided as many towns as she was able. Thankfully, she just took this route; so it was familiar to her now.

She followed the same schedule she used to get to London. She ran the horses for two hours in the morning and switched horses and walked until she took a break for lunch. Then, she ran the horses for two hours again, before she switched horses and walked until she stopped for dinner and a short rest. Then, she walked the horses during the dark of night. After two days, Elisa found a verra secluded grove and tethered Magnum loosely. She knew he could get loose if it was necessary to move away from her for her protection or if necessary to avoid a predator. She tethered Justice to Magnum's saddle. She climbed up and set her rope and cloak up in the treetop so she could sleep. She wasna sure how long she slept, but she knew it was at least six hours. She listened for anyone around her when she woke up. Nothing could be heard. She gathered her cloak and rope and climbed down. Magnum was nearby and Sir Duncan's horse was still attached. She put her things in the saddle pack and mounted. She was off again.

She whispered to Ian, "It's alright if you need to rest. I should be fine for a while. I will meet you at home verra soon." She was so grateful when she reached the border. She avoided the border towns for fear anyone would be looking for someone trying to escape from London. She knew it would be too risky to go through Gretna Green or Glasgow, so she stayed farther to the west.

She heard a whisper, "You are nearly home, m' sweet wife."

"You should be resting," Elisa whispered back, "but, I canna wait to get home." She returned to her schedule of sleeping two or three hours in the early morning and travelling as much as she was able during the day and most of the night. She ate what she could from her satchel or found in the woods. She found plenty of mushrooms and berries. She dinna dare to light a fire for fear of anyone being attracted to it; so that meant no game or fish to eat. She was very careful about watching her surroundings, especially while she traveled through Argyll Woods and other wooded areas. She was afraid of the woods because there were too many places to hide, but she was afraid to be seen out in the open too. It seemed that there wasna anywhere that was safe, a theme that had followed her most of her life. All she could do was hope and pray that she dinna come across any other travelers. She dinna know if she would have the strength to fight them off.

Ian took her words to mean that it was safe for him to pack up the children and return to his castle. It took about an hour to get everyone ready and it seemed like another hour for his father to say goodbye to the children. Ian was a little frustrated with the delay, but he knew Elisa wouldna be home when he reached his castle, so he tried to be patient with his father and the children. They verra much enjoyed their visit with their grandfather. It made Ian smile to see his father so happy and playing with the children. He mostly remembered his father as a serious man and always working to care for the clan or to train his children what they needed to know to be a laird or chieftain one day, and also everything they needed to know to sail a ship. He hoped being chieftain wasna anything he needed to do for a verra long time; but then, he was reminded that he wouldna be around for a verra long time, so he hoped it wasna something Duncan needed to do for a verra long time.

Ian led his family through the woods back to his castle and recalled playing at the loch with the children and Elisa. They had a lot of fun before she had her vision and sent him and the children to Chief Ian's. He would send the children to the nursery with a couple maids and several guards to watch over them so he could sit and speak with Alice and Duncan about what happened in his absence.

The gates were opened to allow their entry as soon as the guards recognized Ian and his men, and probably his children too. He helped Elsbeth dismount and hugged her and kissed the top of her head. Then, he hugged the boys too before he asked them to return to the nursery with a couple maids and several guards. He explained that he needed to speak with others about what happened in his absence. The children went to the nursery without complaining, for which he was grateful and had Elisa to thank for their good behavior.

Sir Duncan came out to greet him and waited on the stairs of the keep. He hugged each of the children before he allowed them entry. Ian was glad to see that Duncan cared for the children; they would be his responsibility soon enough. Duncan and Ian clasped hands and pounded each other on the shoulder before they entered the keep and sat at the table in the great hall.

Duncan explained everything that happened from when Ian took the children from the loch to their father's castle. Duncan told Ian about the king beating Lady Elisa and that she took twenty-two lashes before she passed out and was laid on the bed on her stomach and the king was alone in the room with Elisa for quite some time while his guards stood guard at the door. Then, the king emerged from the room with a smug look on his face. Duncan assumed that the king raped her and he hoped that she dinna lose Ian's bairn, but he dinna voice his opinions to Ian about any of that. He would let Ian draw his own conclusions regarding the matter.

Duncan described Lady Elisa's wounds and how he and Alice worked together to get her out of her dress and into one of Ian's shirts and a skirt of Elisa's, so none of her back would have any material touching any of the wounds. He told him how he had to tie her hands and feet to the posts of the bed to keep her from reopening the wounds when she thrashed about during her nightmares, which he said were quite violent. Duncan dinna intend to tell Ian about Lady Elisa's nightmares unless he asked him to, but he dinna think his brother wanted to know just how bad it was. He would probably find out on his own if Lady Elisa had them again when she returned.

Ian dinna ask about the nightmares. Duncan was right; he dinna really want to know just how bad it really was. What he knew was enough to cause him nightmares, but he needed to at least appear to be strong for Elisa's sake.

Then, Duncan explained what happened after Elisa woke from being healed by the two of them. How she and Alice carried him to the bed. How he woke tied to the bed so that whenever he moved his right arm, it tightened his grip on his left leg or if he tried to move his left arm, it pulled on his right leg. And how he was gagged and couldna even call for help.

Ian roared with laughter.

"Oh, aye, m' laird, it's verra funny to you, mayhap. It is nay funny to me to be tied up by your verra clever lass. It is humiliating to be incapacitated by such a wee lass."

"I'm sorry to laugh at you, Duncan; but you ken she couldna have moved you to the bed without Alice's help. And you have to know that she couldna have succeeded in tying you up if you hadna been asleep and weakened from healing her. You heard her; she was full of energy and fighting us trying to heal her almost the entire time. I think she was trying to heal us while we tried to heal her. She was trying to give us some of her energy."

"Aye, but my pride is still bruised, m' laird," Duncan complained, but he knew Ian would only be more pleased and more proud of his wife.

Ian laughed, "Well, you may have to just get used to having your pride bruised by the wee lass."

Duncan raised his eyebrows as he looked at Ian, but Ian wouldna tell him what he meant by his comment. Duncan shook his head and then explained how Lady Elisa went to the kitchen and asked Alice numerous questions and what Alice told her. Then, Lady Elisa told Alice that she was going to eat something and then there was something she had to do, but she dinna say what it was. She told

Alice to return to her duties. Lady Elisa ate, packed food in a satchel, and poured water into several waterskins before she snuck out to the stables and absconded with his horse.

Ian roared with laughter again.

Duncan continued to relay the events that occurred. He was embarrassed and humiliated to tell the truth of what happened, but his laird needed to know the truth, he supposed, even if it bruised his pride. "Apparently, Lady Elisa told Alice to let me sleep undisturbed for a sennight. So, I lay in your bed, struggling to get free, which only made the knots tighter, the more I struggled to free myself, while she stole my horse and snuck out of the castle. Even if I had managed to free myself, I couldna have gone after her."

Ian laughed, but said, "There were other horses in the stable, Duncan. You could have used another horse."

"Justice is my horse. She had no right to take him. She only did it to humiliate me further," Duncan complained.

"Mayhap, or mayhap she knew Justice would know how to find his way back to you if something happened to her and he would lead her and Magnum back to us," Ian said to try to ease Duncan's bruised pride. "Do you want me to punish her for taking your horse? I ken that she shouldna have taken him without your permission, but I think you ken that she only borrowed him. She dinna intend to keep him forever."

"Nay, I dinna want you to punish her, m' laird. The lass has been punished enough. It seems to me that someone has hurt her throughout her whole life. I dinna think she needs anymore of that kind of treatment. I'm sorry, I just needed to vent. I willna complain about your wife anymore."

"You ken that it's funny, dinna you?"

"Aye, I ken why you think it's funny; it's just nay funny to me because I'm the one you are laughing at."

"I'm nay laughing at you, Duncan. I'm laughing at the picture of my wee little wife getting the better of such a large man who is verra well trained. I'm sorry if you canna see the humor in the situation. I dinna mean to laugh at you, but I could really use the laughs right now. This situation with Elisa is verra tenuous. I dinna know for certain what she has done, but I think I know. I dinna know if I really want to know the truth, but I know I shouldna be such a coward. How can I protect her if I am too afraid to know the truth? I am frustrated with this situation. I feel there isna anything I can do to protect her. I am nay happy with Mother for creating all these plans."

"Schemes," Duncan corrected.

"It doesna matter to me what you call it, but it is putting Elisa and the children in danger. She just spent a month riding here with Sir Colin and two children. She was unprotected for the majority of that ride. And where is she now? She out there on the trail alone and unprotected because she feels that she has to follow Mother's plan or she is certain Mother will hurt someone she cares about."

Duncan explained, "She feels she has to suffer for everyone else; she said that was why she was treated the way she was when she was growing up, so she would be prepared for what she would have to do to follow the plan. It is nay right. It was never right for her to be punished when we were all involved. It irritates me that she canna see that how she was treated was wrong or that she thinks she has to suffer for others."

"You and I ken that the way she has been treated is wrong, Duncan; but I dinna think Elisa kens it. It's the only thing she knows. I dinna like that she feels she canna tell me about these things or that she feels she has to do everything herself and alone, but I dinna think she will ever trust me, at least nay completely. I think she will pretend like she trusts me, but she will continue to do whatever she has to in order to protect herself. Mayhap, we should discuss this another time. I think I shall have to be brave enough to force her to tell me what she did and try to convince her that she is nay alone and that she doesna have to face these things alone. It's just that she is so much braver than I am and it's so blasted intimidating. I'm as humiliated as you are, Duncan; mayhap, even more so. She is my wife and my responsibility. I should nay leave her here with you to protect her. I am a coward."

"You are nay a coward, m' laird. She had a vision at the loch, dinna she?"

"Aye," Ian answered.

"You thought she was following the plan. You ken that Mother set up these plans and that Lady Elisa is supposed to complete them, even if we dinna know or ken the plan, we know that Mother always has consequences if anyone meddles in her plans. You dinna do anything wrong. You are nay a coward."

"Well, if she has to go do these plans alone, then she needs more training. I dinna like her riding around the country unprotected, but if she has to go alone, then we need to be certain she can protect herself and survive on her own."

"I think she can survive on her own, m' laird. She managed to provide for herself, Sir Colin and two children and ride from London to Mull in one month's time. You know she would have made the trip all on her own if Sir Colin had nay drugged her and ridden here to get you. I ken that he did it because he expected trouble ahead and he wanted to ensure Lady Elisa and the children were protected; so he asked Argyll to send his men to watch over them until he returned with you. It was the right thing to do. She is still confused about the time that she was out, so I think she suspects something, but she hasna come out and asked directly. But, I agree, she needs to be trained to fight so she can protect herself if she runs into trouble when she is on one of her missions to follow your mother's schemes."

Ian chuckled, "I am glad that you have rid yourself of all relations to Mother. I think we shall have to speak with Sir Colin about what he has taught her and then discuss a training plan for her. The three of us and mayhap, Sir Thomas should probably be the only ones that work with her while she is pregnant. Sir Colin said that the training would be good to strengthen her body, but we will need to be verra careful to nay knock her to the ground or cut her or the baby. We should challenge her without going on the offensive and we should be careful to nay look like we are going too easy on her."

"That shouldna be too difficult," Duncan replied sarcastically. He and Ian both laughed.

"That was pretty much my response to Sir Colin. She is too observant to nay realize that we are nay really challenging her. It would probably be best to just explain to her what we are doing. Then, she willna be upset with us when she realizes we are nay fighting her as hard as we would fight each other. I dinna think she will like it that we are treating her so carefully because she is with child either. Mayhap, she doesna realize she is a woman and nay a man."

Duncan laughed, "That is the problem with raising her as a man; she thinks and acts like a man and expects to be treated as equally as we would a man. It simply is nay the right thing to do on the training field. You shouldna discuss it with Sir Colin; just explain to her that you want to work with her to assess where she is in her training, explain that you are treating her the same as you do one of the orphans that you take in. You start from the beginning."

"Aye, you are correct, Duncan. That would be the best way to handle the situation. Thank you."

"You are welcome, m' laird. I need to know if you are angry with me for nay protecting Lady Elisa from the King of England. I feel I failed to do my duty as your commander and her protector."

"Nay, Duncan, we all ken that it was something she had to suffer for the plan. I am nay angry with you. I am angry with myself for taking the children and going to Father's and hiding there with the children. I could have sent them with the guards or I could have taken them there and returned, but I dinna. I know I am telling you on the one hand that she had to suffer for the plan and follow the plan; but on the other hand, I am blaming myself. Sorry if I am confusing you. But nay, I dinna blame you. I blame myself; but mostly, I blame Mother for setting all this up to begin with and for all the abuse she inflicted on Elisa; so that now, Elisa feels it is her place to suffer for everyone."

"Alright," Duncan said.

"At least you dinna have to spend this past fortnight at Mother's. Although, I did verra much enjoy seeing Father with the children. I think he had fun and enjoyed playing with them. He made sure that Mother stayed away from the children too, but that really wasna much of an issue since none of the children are hers by blood."

"So, she canna love her grandchildren, simply because they are nay her blood relatives. I am nay surprised. I dinna think she loves her own children, except mayhap Fergus," Duncan replied.

Ian spent his time reviewing with his men what was done in his absence. They spent time each morning on the training field. He missed training with his brother. They always enjoyed training together. He settled into his life as laird and clan leader, but he spent much of his time trying to watch over Elisa unless he had more pressing matters to deal with.

Elisa rode for two more days, switching horses every two hours and breaking for about half an hour three times a day for meals. She rode until she dinna have enough light. She rested for two to three hours until the moon was high, if there was a moon or she let the horses rest if there wasna enough light to ride during the night.

Elisa was grateful to recognize the wooded path as she rode through Argyll Woods and two days later, she finally reached the crossing to Mull. She was thankful that it was low tide and she dinna have to wait for the tide to change and retreat. She rode through the woods and cleared a hill, and she could see her home over the next hill. "Home, Ian, I am home," she whispered to him. She galloped all the way to the gate. "I am so sorry boys," Elisa said to the horses. "I know you are exhausted too. I will see that Sir Colin gives you a wonderful bath, a good brushing, and a hearty dinner, every day this sennight."

As she topped the second hill, she heard the cry to open the gates. She kept her eyes on the woods around her. She dinna want any surprises before she reached the gate. And then, she pulled up on the reins as she entered the bailey and a moment later she was in Ian's arms. He held her tightly to him and kissed her long and hard. When he finally paused to look at her, she asked, "Miss me much?" she laughed.

"I ought to tie you to the bed and beat you myself," he said.

Elisa laughed, "I wouldna care as long as you held me and kissed me. I missed you so much, m' love." He carried her into the castle and up to their room. He ordered her a bath, but she wasna sure she could stay awake that long. He also ordered a tray of food, ale, and scotch. She bathed and dressed in a light gown. She had been in breeches so long; the dress was so soft and smooth. She stood and looked down at the dress as she ran her fingers over it, marveling at the soft texture and smoothness.

Ian saw the strange look on her face and asked, "What is it, m' lady?"

"It's just that it has been so long since I wore a fashionable dress, I dinna remember what it feels like," she said, as she walked to the chair by the fire. "I really have missed you, Ian."

"Aye, I ken, but you need to eat a big supper, then I will show you how much I have missed you. And then, you are going to stay in that bed for at least a sennight and get some rest."

"Aye, m' laird," Elisa said, "but, mayhap, you would consider letting me sit in the chair if I am nay sleeping and you have to attend to other responsibilities."

"That is the best you can do to be a submissive wife, isna it?" Ian laughed and pulled her into his arms again and kissed her for several minutes.

"I dinna think submissive is in my character, considering who I am, Ian," she said. "I am sorry, Ian, I dinna know who I was until those letters from your mother to my mother and me flashed before my eyes when we were at the loch. My parents spent their lives trying to prepare me for a role that I may have to hold one day, but I hope these plans I just executed also prepared a way for the possibility of stopping it. Only time will tell which way things will go; but for now, I just want to enjoy my husband and my family. But even if I dinna know my heritage, I dinna think I would be verra submissive considering the training and education I had, Ian."

"I ken, Elisa, when I grabbed you and saw your vision too, I knew then that you dinna know who you were until that moment. I grew up knowing that we have royal Scotch bloodlines, but the king leaves us alone as long as it is clear we are nay making plans to try to take the throne. I dinna want that role unless there isna anyone else to serve as king."

"I dinna want you to know what I have done, Ian. I feel like I had to do what I did because of the plan, but I also ken that I am responsible for my actions. I am nay proud of what I have done. I will have to see Father Patrick when I am recovered. But, please ken, I only did it to try to get them to leave me alone, so they willna keep coming after us and our children." She finished eating and Ian had her drink some scotch. Then, they went to bed. Ian was verra gentle with his kisses and caresses. "I love you, Ian," Elisa said.

"Aye, m' sweet wife, I love you too." He cuddled up next to her and held her close.

She said, "I need you by my side." Then, she slept deeply.

Ian lay awake thinking for quite some time. He had missed her verra much and he was ever so grateful that she was safely returned to him. Now, all they could do was pray the kings would leave them to live their lives. Only time would tell if the kings would leave them alone or continue to come after them.

He thought about what preparations they might need to make to ensure they were prepared if another king showed up at their castle. He would do his best to stockpile reserves of meat and grain and all that they might need to survive a verra long siege. A king would have many resources and men, so they could be held under siege for a verra long time. He could easily stockpile enough food and grain to last a year or more, so he just needed to get to work on it. He would ensure that Duncan kenned the plan. They would eat from the oldest stockpiles and continually refresh until they had enough to survive for a verra long time. He dinna think it would be expecting too much to think that a king might lay siege to their castle for at least a year, so the best thing to do was to be prepared for two years.

He really dinna want to risk losing any of his people, so it was best if they spread the word throughout the clan to let them know what to expect as well. Kings could be ruthless when they felt thwarted. They wouldna show any weakness or remorse for anything they did. They felt everyone owed them loyalty nay matter how poorly they treated their people.

If the king came here, he hoped the man dinna burn their fields and crops or slaughter their livestock. He would have to put men along the shores to watch for anyone coming their way. Then, word could be sent around to the crofters to hide or come to the castle. The livestock could be brought to several hiding places in the hills if they dinna have time to bring them into the castle.

He needed to prepare pens in the bailey to separate all the livestock so the bulls werena in with the cows and the rams werena in with the ewes. They would need cages for the roosters; otherwise, they would fight with each other. The chickens could be left to wander in the garden and they would kill the bugs; it would be better for the vegetables anyway. They would have to store a great deal of grain and hay to feed the animals for two years.

They would have to plant double or triple the crops this year if they hoped to stockpile so much grain both for their needs and the needs of the livestock. If the livestock couldna graze in the pastures, then they would need grain because they couldna survive on hay alone.

It was a lot to think about and prepare for, but he dinna mind the challenge. It was best to be prepared. He was grateful that the King of England hadna laid siege to the castle. They werena prepared for it. They could have survived many months with their current supplies, but probably nay the winter too. He and the men and probably Elisa too, would enjoy hunting so that wouldna be a problem to stockpile meat, at least.

He lay awake for quite some time thinking about his plans. He would have to discuss it with the men in the morning and get started. He would also send word to his father to let him know that he was making such preparations just in case it was necessary. If they were left alone, fine; but, if any more kings came here, he would be prepared to feast with them or to endure a long siege. The outcome would be on the king's attitude towards them and Ian really dinna care which it was. He dinna mind hard work or a good fight.

He finally allowed himself to drift off to sleep as he thanked God for Elisa's safe return to him. He prayed for her health, the baby's health and that God would help him organize all they needed to get accomplished in the next year or two. He asked God to provide them with ample crops to ensure they could withstand a two-year siege or more if it was necessary.

When Ian woke in the morning, he thanked God that Elisa slept soundly and dinna have nightmares before he slipped out of their bed without disturbing her. He quickly and quietly dressed and slipped out of the room and made his way down to the hall for breakfast.

Chapter 14

WHEN ELISA WOKE, she felt like she had slept for a whole sennight or more. She was alone in the room. She checked the bed for any signs that if she was pregnant, she might have lost the baby, but there wasna any blood. She put her hand on her stomach and whispered, "I hope that Ian's baby is in there, and if so, that you are healthy." She prayed that nothing would happen to the baby and that it would be a healthy baby.

She planned to relax for today and make plans to provide for a baby. Oh, she hoped so much for this little blessing. She would ask Ian where she could get some yarn; so she could start making some clothes and blankets. Not, just for their baby, but she wanted to make one for every baby in the clan. She snuck out of bed and opened her trunk. She took out her writing desk so she could make a list of things to do. She wrote down baby blankets; bows, arrows, and quivers for Ian, Hawk, and Elsbeth, meet all the clan, go with Ian on his rounds to visit the clan.

Ian came in, "What were you doing out of bed?"

"I am in bed," she replied.

"Aye, but you had to get out of bed to get your writing desk. What are you doing?"

"I am making a list of some things I want to do," She responded. "Ian, could we get a bow and a quiver of arrows for each of the children?"

"Aye, m' lady, I will see to it that Sir Duncan, Sir Colin, and Angus add it to their training."

"Thank you, m' laird," Elisa said.

"What else is on your list?" he asked.

"I would like to go with you when you do your rounds throughout the clan, so I can get to know the people and their families. I would also like to get some yarn so I can make some blankets for the babies. You mentioned before that you try to help out the orphaned children; I want to help too."

"That is a good idea, Elisa. I want you by my side, leading the clan with me. I would like that verra much."

"Are you sure you dinna want a submissive wife waiting in your bed?"

"Nay, I prefer the wife of my wedding day," he said with a smirk. Then, he joined her after she put her writing things away.

After her sennight of rest, Ian relented and let her out of their room; although, he quite enjoyed slipping into the room throughout the day, when he wasna needed elsewhere, and spending time with his wife. They established a routine and he let her join him and the men and the children on the training field. Ian explained to Elisa that he kenned her need to be strong enough to defend herself; especially if she might have to go somewhere alone to complete some task for the plan. But then, he needed to assess her skills and determine a training plan for her and he said they had to be careful to nay hurt her or the baby. Elisa agreed with what Ian explained to her and they spent several days training lightly until Ian felt that he could increase the intensity of the sessions. He warned her that if Sir Duncan, Sir Thomas or Sir Colin trained with her, they might go lightly for several days until they felt comfortable with her level of skill.

Since Elisa rarely slept more than a couple hours, she often rose and cooked breakfast for everyone before they went to the training field. After training, she bathed and changed and they broke their fast. She helped with many of the women's chores around the keep. She took care of most of the mending and she spent a great deal of her time making outfits and blankets for her baby and other babies and children in the clan. She started with the youngest orphans to ensure their needs were met since they dinna have parents to take care of them. She also spent as much time as possible with the children and taught them their lessons each day. Then, they spent time on their riding lessons with Sir Colin; and afterwards, they spent time with the guards on their training lessons. They were learning to handle a bow and arrow, a dagger and a sword. Elisa was happy with their progress.

One or two times a sennight, Elisa went out with Ian to visit the clan and get to know them. She asked whether there was anything they needed. She took meticulous notes because it helped her remember their names and anything she could do for them, to help them. She soon realized that she only needed to recall her previous visits to remember everyone's names. She relied on her gifts more and they seemed to get stronger because she used them. At least, she no longer worried that she couldna remember people's names or what she made for each one. She even remembered anyone who was ailing and what was bothering them. She prayed for the members of the clan especially while she was knitting items for them. She asked the Lord to work His healing into the item she was making and to provide healing for the person who would receive the project.

She had several projects going to provide clothes and blankets for her baby and many of the clan children. She dinna know if she should deliver them as she made them or wait until she had one for each baby, and then start on the older children. But one day as they were preparing to go out to visit the clan, Ian asked, "Elisa, are these clothes and blankets for our baby or for the clan? Because, I dinna think our baby will need so many."

"That pile is for the clan, I just wasna sure if I should give them out as I made them or after I had one for each baby."

"I dinna see how you can possibly keep up with the babies and make for the older children too. You may need to get some of the ladies to help you."

"Are you sure they wouldna think it was more work?" Elisa asked.

"Do you think it is work?" he asked.

"Nay, but that doesna mean they will feel the same way."

"Well, tell them they dinna have to help if they dinna want to, only if they want to," he suggested.

"Oh, thank you for the suggestions, Ian," she responded and gave him a kiss. Ian enveloped her in his arms and held her as close as he could without pressing against her stomach too much. He dinna want to hurt the baby while he kissed his wife.

When he ended the kiss, he said, "I better go tell Sir Colin to hitch a wagon, then. And I'll send some men up to bring all these things down before we have nowhere to sleep," he chuckled. "Just let them know what to bring down." Elisa smiled at Ian.

The men came and took the items to give to the families. Then, Elisa followed them downstairs. She was beginning to show and Ian came to assist her as soon as he saw her on the stairs.

"Overprotective," Elisa mumbled.

"Mother said you might have trouble keeping your balance as the baby grew bigger inside you," he reminded her.

"Dinna be calling me fat, m' laird."

"I dinna say that," he replied.

"I ken what you meant," she said.

"I dinna, I swear, Elisa," Ian said. "Mother said you would get moody and sensitive."

"Moody and sensitive?" she yelled.

"I am sorry, m' love," Ian begged, "please dinna get angry at me for everything I say. Dinna let me spoil our day together," he added the last after Alice shot him a look.

"I'm sorry, Ian," Elisa said, "I am a little sensitive now that I am showing. I feel fat and I dinna need anyone to say anything to confirm what I already feel. I am also worried that you will use it as an excuse to make me stay home. In case you dinna realize, I dinna like to be confined or have restrictions on what I can or canna do. I am used to being alone and doing things for myself."

"I havena," Ian said. "And, I am well aware that you dinna like being confined or having any restrictions. I dinna think I put too many restrictions on you. I dinna tell you that you canna do all the things you do, even though most ladies would leave the majority of the chores around the keep to the maids and would only take a supervisory role. I dinna mind that you help out. In fact, I am proud of you that you dinna think any of the chores are beneath your station."

"Nay, you havena made me stay home yet; but you have doubled the guard," she replied. "And, you have Sir Duncan and Sir Colin ride so close, I couldna fall off my horse even if I tried." When they stepped outside, Elisa dinna find Magnum. "I suppose I will have to ride in a wagon from now on too?" she sighed.

"Elisa, I am riding in the wagon with you because we have so much to deliver. Please, dinna be cross with me. I want to enjoy our day together."

"I am sorry, Ian; but, you have to warn me ahead of time that you expect me to do things differently than what we normally do. I dinna like to change from my usual routine, at least nay without a warning." She stopped complaining and let him lift her into the wagon. He walked around and climbed in and then they were off.

"I apologize, Elisa; but, I thought I did warn you when I told you I would have Sir Colin hitch a wagon."

"Oh, I see. Well, I thought you meant for all the blankets, nay for us too."

Ian chuckled and reached for her hand. He lifted it to his lips and kissed it. She was rather funny the way she saw things so differently than he did, but she was appeased easily with a little explanation and affection. And, he certainly dinna mind showing her as much affection as she needed to feel better. He doubted she even realized that she needed so much affection, but he supposed it was a product of all the abuse of her childhood, since she had suffered so many beatings and now she felt it was her place to suffer. He kissed her hand again and held it in his lap until they reached the first home.

At each home they stopped, he lifted her to the ground and spoke with the man of the house and the older son or sons while she greeted the family and gave each child a blanket. She talked with the mother and even the children for a while before they continued on to the next home. It filled Elisa with joy to give something to the people, to be of some help. The mothers and the children were all very grateful and thanked her for everything she did for them.

Ian watched her as he talked with Sir Duncan, "This is why I love her, Duncan; she gives so much, thinks of others' needs before her own, wants to help them and make their lives better. I know I should try to keep her home, but when I see her smile, her face so full of joy, I canna. My heart is filled with love for her and I canna thank you enough for helping me deal with my responsibilities in my youth."

"Your wife's beauty is so much more than her looks, m' laird. She is special. She has a special gift to see the needs of others and to fulfill their needs. Lady Elisa isna happy unless she helps others. I believe that is true beauty. And, I was glad to help you accept your responsibilities because I knew it would be good for both of you. I would do anything to ensure both of you are happy and Lady Elisa is well cared for."

"Aye, Duncan, I know you will." Then, Ian walked towards Elisa. "M' lady, we must start back now if we wish to get home before dark." He shook hands with the man of the house and clapped his shoulder. Elisa hugged the lady of the house and all the children. Then, she walked with Ian to the wagon, and he lifted her in. He walked around, climbed in, and they headed back to the castle.

Ian held the reins in one hand and reached for Elisa's hand with his other hand. He brought it to his lips and kissed her hand. "I love you, m' sweet wife. You are very sweet to think of everyone's needs. I am proud to have you at my side."

When they entered the castle, the gates were closed behind them and he handed the reins to one of the stable hands, jumped down and walked around to Elisa. He lifted her down and led her into the keep. "Do you need to go to our room to freshen up or do you want dinner now?"

"I am hungry, now that you mention it."

"I dinna ken how you can be so engrossed in your project that you forget to eat."

"I dinna know, Ian. I just prefer to do one thing at a time. I just want to finish what I am working on before I move on to the next thing. I dinna like to be interrupted."

"Aye, you are verra focused and determined, most of the time." He chuckled as he helped her into her seat and took his seat. The guards joined them at the table and the maids served dinner. Elisa ate quite heartily for a change and Ian was happy that he dinna have to constantly encourage her. He hoped that would continue throughout the pregnancy. They settled verra nicely into their life together and Ian was verra happy and he thought Elisa was too, most of the time anyways, as long as he dinna say stupid things that upset her, like earlier today. But, he dinna see how he could know everything that might upset her; so all he could do was try to think before he spoke and then apologize when he upset her. She really wasna that difficult to get along with and she dinna complain verra much.

When dinner was over, Ian helped her move to the chair by the fireplace. He spoke to her in a low voice so only she could hear him, "I want to say something, Elisa; and I dinna want you to take it the wrong way and get upset with me. I am verra glad that you ate so heartily at supper this evening and I hope that you will continue to do so. I dinna think that you are fat or that you will get fat because you are carrying our child and you need to eat more so you will have a healthy baby. I think this is the first meal we have had together that I havena had to coax you into eating more. I would like to see that continue."

"I will try to eat more, Ian, but I am used to eating verra little, having verra little, and doing lots of work. It really doesna bother me that much. I think you are more upset than I am by all of this." She picked up her project.

"I dinna ken that, Elisa. Your parents had plenty of money to pay for servants and to feed and clothe you. They should have provided for you, nay just Ian and Elsbeth, nay just for your education and then leave their education in your hands. I'm sorry, I dinna mean to bring up your childhood and upset you. And, aye, I am upset about your childhood. I dinna agree with how you were treated and I willna agree with it. Ever. It was wrong. I'm sorry; we can discuss this more later." He took her hands in his and squeezed them gently before he returned to the table before he became angry about the situation her parents and his mother created and the life she lived before coming here to fulfill their marriage. He discussed clan business with the men. They were making verra good progress on their siege plans. Ian just wanted to be aware of exactly where they were in their progress to ensure they were on schedule and so he knew what was necessary if the siege occurred sooner than they expected. Elisa listened quietly while she worked, but she dinna make any comments to the men's plans.

Elisa still woke early and often times, she snuck out of bed and made her way down to the kitchen to cook breakfast or to make candles or soaps or to assemble baskets of items that she wished to give to the families in the clan. She asked each family to make two identical baskets so she could deliver things in one basket and take the empty basket back to the castle with her so she could fill it for the next visit. It helped her to ensure that the right things went to the right household. She always had a number of projects going on to help the clan. Sometimes, it was baskets of bread, cheese, and fruit or even candles or soaps. Other times, it was clothes or blankets. Many times, it was reading to the children and teaching them to read and write. Over time, every baby had a blanket, a bonnet, and slippers. Most of the older children now had a blanket. Her latest project was a shawl for every woman.

Elisa was near her due date and Ian wouldna let her visit the clan's homes. He sent Sir Duncan, Angus, and Alice. They took her list and delivered each item as Elisa wrote it down. Elisa worried they wouldna do it correctly, that someone would receive the wrong item. She plagued them with questions when they returned.

"I am nay going to do this anymore," Alice said. "Everything will just have to wait until Lady Elisa can bring it herself, m' laird."

"I'm sorry, Alice," Elisa said as she ran, well she wished she could run up the stairs, but Sir Duncan had to assist her because she was so large and she couldna climb the stairs without help. She slammed the door to her room and kicked it too. She nearly fell into the chair by the fireplace and cried.

The laird said, "Alice, do you nay ken what is really bothering, Lady Elisa?"

"Aye, I ken it, m' laird. But I canna make her ken that she will be fine. She has to have this child soon so she can see for herself. She likes everything explained to her in detail and then she puts it in neat little lists so she can do it and then mark it off her list. But having a baby doesna work that way. I have tried to explain it to her but I dinna ken how to ease her worries."

"Alice, having this first child is nay going to calm her anxiety. Her mother and stepmother both died during their second child's labor. She lost her brother and she nearly lost Elsbeth. Our children will always cause her anxiety because she will always fear for their lives. You dinna see what she went through at the hands of her cousin. She tries to block it from me but I ken it. She will never live without worrying that someone will try to harm, not just our children, but all the children of the clan, mayhap even all of Scotland. She canna bear the thought of a child going without food and provisions. It causes her heart to suffer real pain."

"I am sorry, m' laird. I will try to be more patient with her. I should go apologize."

"Nay, Alice, no one could be more patient than you. And I believe Elisa will be the one to apologize to you."

"Aye, she willna let anyone take the blame for anything. She doesna have to be the one to sacrifice in every dispute," Alice said.

"It is who she is. It's why she fights so hard to protect the children and to try to prevent a war."

"Do you think you should send for your mother?" Alice asked. "Do you think it would be any help or comfort to her? She is near the end of her pregnancy; and mayhap, it would help her to have your mother with her."

"I dinna think that will be a good idea. Lady Elisa doesna need any conflicts with Mother right now."

"Aye, m' laird," Alice subsided.

Ian left the hall and went upstairs to check on Elisa. "Are you alright, m' love?" he asked as he entered the room. He dinna need to knock or announce his presence with her and he was verra glad of it.

"Aye, I think so," she said as she sat staring at the fire.

"What is it, then?" Ian asked.

"I just sense that something is coming," she answered.

"The baby? Is the baby coming?" he asked as he knelt by her.

"Dinna look, Ian. There isna anything to see. It isna clear," Elisa said as she pulled away still staring at the fire. "It isna the baby, well, not exactly. The baby will come whenever it's ready to come. I think it is a letter or a message or mayhap a parcel. I canna be certain and I dinna know if it is good or bad. We shall have to wait and see."

"I willna look, just let me hold you," he insisted. Ian stood up and lifted her into his arms. He sat in his chair with Elisa on his lap, so she was still facing the fire. Elisa snuggled up to him and rested her head on his shoulder. "Do you ken it," he asked in a whisper, "the way the fire comforts you?"

"Nay, I dinna ken it. It's part of the secret, one of many pieces of the puzzle, that I havena put together. So many little pieces all jumbled together. Why did they have to have so many secrets? Why dinna they just tell me?"

"I really dinna know, love. Mayhap, to help you remember it," Ian suggested. "If it was a game, it would be fun to learn and easier to remember."

"I suppose," she answered, "but, I remember that I always enjoyed learning. I still love to learn. I dinna think I was a difficult child or anything like that. And what they did, beating me, dinna make their training seem like a game. It wasna for fun. There has to be a hidden message that I havena figured out. Part of me doesna want to figure it out because it's probably safer to nay know. And mayhap, that is why I canna figure it out."

"I'm sorry, m' love; I dinna mean to turn the conversation to your childhood. I dinna mean to hurt you. You know I never wish to hurt you, Elisa."

"Aye, I know, Ian." She snuggled into him and relaxed. She could feel her body going out to him to relieve his tension and stress and worries, but she dinna say anything to him, she just let her body do what it did to heal him. He dinna say anything as he relaxed, so she wasna sure if he knew what she was doing.

Eventually, Ian dozed off. Elisa tried to see what was coming again, but she couldna make it out clearly. After, a little while, she woke Ian and insisted he go to bed. She lay down with him until he was asleep again. Then, she carefully slipped out of his grasp and rose from the bed and sat by the fire for a little while. She dozed off and slept for a couple hours; but when she woke, she had a strong urge to bake, so she went to the kitchen.

In the morning, Ian woke alone. Elisa's side of the bed was cold and empty. He rose from the bed and looked about the room. The fire was burning nicely. A warm bath awaited him, but Elisa wasna in the room. He bathed and dressed and headed down to the hall. A wonderful aroma was coming from the kitchen.

Just as he was about to enter, the cook came out grumbling and throwing her hands in the air. "Dinna go in there, m' laird."

Ian entered anyway. He couldna believe his eyes. There was bread everywhere, bread that was baked and was cooling now, bread rising, bread cooking. And pastries, too, some in various stages of preparation, others baking or cooling. There were also large platters of meats; sausages, ham, and bacon.

"Elisa, what are you doing?" Ian asked. "Were you up all night cooking?"

"Aye, Ian, I was. I canna seem to stop myself. I dinna know what is wrong with me."

"Why dinna we go set the table in the great hall with all this food? And then, let's go find Alice and talk to her; mayhap, she can explain why you feel some need to cook all our winter stores for breakfast today?" he chuckled.

"Oh, Ian, I am so sorry."

"It's alright, Elisa, I was only teasing. But mayhap, you could let the cook know ahead of time when you plan to take over her kitchen. Then, you two wouldna get upset with each other."

"I'll try, m' laird, but I dinna know ahead of time. It just came over me to come downstairs and do something, bake something."

"Well, everyone will have a lovely feast for breakfast today. I hope this isna going to last long because I dinna want the men getting too fat."

"Very funny," Elisa replied sarcastically, recalling Sir Duncan's response when she had cooked for him while Ian was taken captive. "Did you say that because of what Sir Duncan said to me when I cooked while you were being held captive? Do you think that is funny?"

"Aye, I said it because of what Duncan said; and aye, I think it's funny. You dinna?"

"Nay, I dinna think it was funny then or now." She carried several platters to the table and he helped her, knowing she wouldna want the maids or cook to help her. He dinna care for doing women's work, but he knew she would do it all herself if he dinna help. The men would likely tease him, but he would just have to deal with them on the training field.

"Do you have a sense of humor? Dinna you ever want to tease or joke around or play, just a little?"

"Nay, I prefer to have lots of work to do and a list of all the things I need to do, so I can check them off the list as I complete them. I prefer to have a schedule and follow the schedule. I dinna like if the plan or schedule changes."

When she finished setting the table, he led her to her seat and made her sit and eat. Otherwise, he was afraid she would go find something else to work on and skip the meal.

As he suspected, a number of the men teased him and gave him grief about being a pretty maid, serving them.

Elisa turned to him and said in a whisper, "I'm sorry, m' laird."

"Dinna be sorry. It isna your fault. I dinna have to carry anything to the table. You would have taken care of it if I dinna help. Besides, I will deal with them on the training field," he said with a smirk.

"I am still sorry. They wouldna be saying those things if I had done the work and nay you."

"Elisa, they are only teasing me. It's fine."

"And that is different than challenging or confronting the laird? It is alright to tease you?"

He refrained from chuckling or laughing. She wouldna take it well. "Aye, love; it's different from challenging me and is alright."

After breakfast, Elisa shooed everyone outside and she cleared the tables in the great hall and washed all the dishes from their breakfast and all the dishes she used to make the breakfast. She cleaned up the mess she made in the kitchen. She scrubbed every pot in the kitchen until it shined. She even cleaned out the fireplace and started a fresh fire. She made a stew in several of the large cauldrons for everyone's lunch. It dinna take too long to cut up all the meat and vegetables and throw everything into the pots. She cleaned up the workspace and washed the few dishes she used. Then, she cleaned the great hall; she scrubbed all the furniture, swept out the rushes, scrubbed the floors, and ordered fresh rushes brought in, but she wouldna let anyone else spread them around. She cleaned out the fireplace and set up a fresh fire before she put the new rushes down on the floor.

When she finished cleaning the hall, she went to the nursery. She sent the children to the stables to find Sir Colin to see if he could give them some lessons. She swept the nursery, scrubbed the furniture and the floors, cleaned the fireplace, and set new logs in it.

She went to her room and cleaned it too. Then, she took a bath and changed her clothes. She went through the baby's things and refolded them and put them back in the baby's trunk.

She refolded and organized all the shawls for the women of the clan. She checked her list to verify everything was recorded. She returned to the kitchen to make dinner. She tried to nay go overboard and cook too much. After supper was ready, she lined up the platters on the kitchen hearth, until the maids could bring them to the hall tables. She washed the dishes, dried them, and put them away.

If she could have, she would have cleaned the stables, but she knew Ian wouldna approve of her being around the horses. There had to be something else she could clean or organize. She thought about it for several minutes before she thought of Ian's library; yes, that would give her plenty of things to clean and organize.

Tomorrow, she could clean and organize the pantry and the larder, but she would have to tell the cook before she did it or it would upset the woman, she supposed. She snuck out of the kitchen through the secret passage and made her way to Ian's library.

When Ian and his men came into the hall, the maids were setting the platters on the tables. Ian asked Alice if she knew where his wife was.

"I dinna know, m' laird. She cleaned the kitchen, the hall, made supper and cleaned the kitchen again. She left the platters on the kitchen hearth for the maids to serve and isna in the kitchen anymore. No one knows where she went, m' laird. No one was in the castle all day except to eat lunch, because she demanded we spend the day outside."

"Thank you, Alice."

"Aye, m' laird," Sir Colin said, "she probably cleaned the nursery too because the children have been in the stables with me all afternoon."

"Do you ken what is going on with her, Alice?" Ian asked.

"Aye, m' laird, I think so. I think she may do this for a day, mayhap two. Just let her clean or organize whatever she wants as long as she isna going to hurt herself or the baby. I think it means she will have the baby soon. It might be more than a day or two, but that is how long it usually lasts with most women before the labor starts. Of course, your wife isna like other women, so I am nay certain what to expect, or how long this could last."

"I hope you are right," Ian said to Alice. "I am going to go see if she is in our room; you all go ahead and eat." He turned to Duncan, "Speak with the cook later and find out exactly how much she cooked today and how much we need to replenish our stockpile. I dinna want to be too low."

"Aye, m' laird," Duncan replied and went to the kitchen.

Ian took the stairs two at a time. He opened their bedroom door, saw how clean it was; but, dinna see Elisa. He closed the door. He wondered where she had gone.

As he started to head up the stairs to the nursery, he heard a crash down the hall in his library. He ran to the door and shoved it open. Elisa was kneeling near a pile of books that were strewn all over the floor. "Are you alright, m' sweet wife?" Ian asked her.

"Aye, Ian, I am fine; I just dropped a stack of books. I just thought I would dust the books and the shelves and reorganize the books."

"Do you want any help?"

"Nay, m' laird. Go, enjoy your dinner," she replied.

Sir Duncan knocked on the door and signaled to Ian, "M' laird, I think you should return to the hall," he whispered, hoping Lady Elisa wouldna hear.

Elisa asked, "Are your parents here, m' laird?"

Both Ian and Sir Duncan looked at her, surprised, "Aye, m' lady," Sir Duncan replied. "Are you joining us in the hall?"

"Nay, I am nay hungry. I will come down when I finish in here. I have another project I want to work on when I finish this one."

Ian told Duncan to wait for him down the hall. Then, he turned to Elisa, "Is this what you were expecting to come here, my parents?"

"Nay, Ian, I told you I think it's a message or a letter or mayhap, a parcel. That hasna changed. I assumed you sent for your mother to force me to bed, since I dinna sleep last night and I have been obsessed with cleaning and cooking all day."

"Elisa, I would never send for my mother without discussing it with you first. I dinna want her upsetting you," Ian replied.

"Well, you better go see why they are here, then, m' laird," she responded. "You will tell me about it later, willna you?"

"Aye, I will tell you what they say, I promise, Elisa. I ken you have enough to worry about." Ian left and went down the hall where Duncan was waiting.

"How did she know it was your parents? I dinna say who was here, m' laird."

"You ken how she does that, Duncan; the same way you or I do. Did they say why they are here?"

"Aye, they said they had some news they felt was important to share," Sir Duncan said.

"Well, then this might be what Lady Elisa is expecting. She said she feels a message or a letter or a parcel is coming. She has felt it for a while." Ian and Sir Duncan descended the stairs and sat at their usual places at the table when their father was visiting because of course the chief was given the head of the table. Ian filled a plate and started eating his supper. He spoke with his father.

Lady Isobel said, "Ian, when did you get a new cook? This food is delicious."

"Mother, first of all, dinna make your insulting comments about my cook. And secondly, our cook was away today because Lady Elisa gave her the day off. My wife prepared our meal."

"Where is Lady Elisa? Why isna she eating with us?" his mother asked.

"She isna hungry and she is busy right now. Let it go, now, Mother," Ian replied.

After dinner, the maids cleared the table and Ian dismissed the men. Only Sir Duncan, Sir Thomas, Sir Colin, and his parents remained at the table. "So, what is the important news you brought?" Ian asked.

"I received a letter from a friend in London," Lady Isobel said and she showed him the letter. Ian read through the letter while his mother explained, "The King of England was found dead in his bed. No one knows who killed him for certain or how they got into his guarded room. Evidence was found in his chambers that proved he was blackmailing several of the households of nobility and that he was guilty of multiple murders. Confirming evidence was also found in the households of these same nobility. But another more interesting thing has happened; Lady Elisa's London residence was destroyed and the King's ringed glove was found in the front yard. Also, a burned woman's body was found and the news is that Lady Elisa is dead."

"My wife is upstairs, Mother. She isna dead. So the woman in the London townhouse isna my wife. I dinna see how they could think it was Lady Elisa, unless she has a twin sister."

Both Ian's looked at Lady Isobel verra carefully. They scrutinized the look on her face. Both men noticed a momentary look of shock on the woman's face. But, what was she shocked about? That Elisa had a twin sister or that she had been discovered because she knew Elisa had a twin sister? Lady Isobel recovered verra quickly and masked the look of shock.

Ian continued, "This is interesting news but how will this affect the outcome of things? Obviously, if England believes she is dead, they willna seek to kill her or seek her to take over the crown. But, that mightna prevent them from seeking to harm the children."

"Well, it will certainly delay things for a while, because everything is in chaos in London. And, it may prevent them from coming after the children when they find out she isna dead. They may realize what could happen to them or their families to be set up in such an extensive plot. It may also do the same on the Scotland side," Ian's mother said.

"Well, we shall have to wait and see how it all works out, I suppose," Ian said. "They will ken Lady Elisa isna dead when I submit the birth record for our child. We shall have to prepare for a verra long siege and war, Father." He kept his thoughts to himself about the extensive plot being all Lady Isobel's doing.

Ian turned to Sir Duncan and Sir Colin, "You ken what may still need to be done, get started in the morning. I am going up to check on Lady Elisa." He turned to his father, "I assume you will stay the night, Father. Will you stay tomorrow or head home and start your own preparations?"

"I will send a rider home to ensure they ken the possibility of a siege and war is far more likely. In the meantime, mayhap, we could visit with you and Lady Elisa until the baby comes. I would enjoy seeing my grandchild," Ian said, nay thinking or implying that the child wasna Lady Isobel's grandchild. But, it was too late, the words were already said and she would catch on to the hidden meaning. Blast it, Chief Ian thought to himself. He knew he should be more careful with his words. Lady Isobel would find some way to hurt Elisa because of his comment and he dinna want that at all. He never intended for his actions or comments to cause Elisa any harm.

Ian said, "That is fine. I am sure Lady Elisa would enjoy the company, as long as you keep Mother from upsetting her. Help yourself to some scotch; you know where it is."

Ian returned to the library to talk to Elisa. He told her the message just as his mother told him. He knew she wouldna be surprised, but only a verra few people knew Elisa went to London. Only Duncan, Alice and he knew that she was healed of her wounds early. Everyone else thought she was still recovering from the beating the King of England gave her. Well, except perhaps, Sir Colin would know because the horses werena in the stables where they belonged. But he was certain Sir Colin wouldna ever do or say anything to hurt Elisa. Alice knew she was recovered, but she dinna know where Elisa was during that time, only he and Duncan knew. "We will send the birth record when the baby comes and wait and see how the King of Scotland responds. You just have to focus on having our baby. We will make preparations for a siege and a war so we are prepared if that is the king's intentions should he come here."

"By the way," Ian continued, "I dinna have time to tell you before. Alice says this obsessive cooking and cleaning is verra likely a sign the baby will start to come in a day or two. She said it could be longer; but usually, it happens a day or two before labor starts. She says it is alright to do as much cooking and cleaning as you want as long as you are careful to nay hurt yourself or the baby."

Ian approached Elisa and reached for her, "I willna see unless you want me to." He held her in his arms and kissed the top of her head. "Elisa, I ken you dinna want to put me or the children in danger, but you dinna have to bear this alone. I am here to listen and to help you any way I can. I want to help if you will let me."

Elisa turned towards Ian and let him hold her and caress her. She cried for a long time. It was a relief to let go of the stress for a while, to let her guard down just for a short time.

Ian let her cry. When she was recovered, he sat her on the sofa and went to the door. He asked one of the guards to have Alice bring a tray of tea with a sandwich and an apple.

Ian sat on the sofa next to Elisa with his arm draped around her shoulders until Alice brought the tray. He insisted that Elisa eat and have some tea. "You did all the cooking and cleaning today, but you dinna eat any of it, did you?" Ian asked.

She just shook her head, she dinna want to see the disappointment or concern in his eyes. She knew what would get him to let it go, so she took his hand and rested it on her stomach.

"That isna going to work tonight, Elisa."

She stiffened.

"You dinna think that I knew what you were doing, did you?" he asked, and laughed. "M' sweet wife, I love you so much."

"I love you too, Ian. It's just that I am afraid to show you while the baby is inside me. I dinna want the baby to feel or see or know any of that. You and I both have some ability to see things and I can only assume our child will too, so I dinna want him or her to see this."

"Aye, I ken," Ian said. "But after the baby comes, Elisa, I insist you let me see so I can help you bare this burden. That is what your husband is for."

"Hmm, I thought you were here to love me and make me deliriously happy, and so I could bear your children," she laughed.

"Well, I will see what I can do about that; but first, you have to have this one," he said and drew her closer to him. He held her for a while, hoping she would fall asleep, but after she elbowed him in the ribs a few times with her fidgeting, he loosened his hold and asked if he could help her reshelve all the books. He was surprised when she agreed. She organized the books and he placed them on the shelves. It was only a couple hours until dawn when they finished. She wanted to make a list of all the books, but Ian said to her, "Elisa, you have been up more than an entire day. I am going to bring you to our room; and if you will go to bed for at least a few hours, I will let you finish this later this morning and mayhap, even start another project. But you must sleep for a few hours and nay sneak out of bed when I'm asleep."

"I was thinking I could clean the pantry and the larder later today."

"Well, you had better discuss it with our cook so you dinna upset her two days in a row."

"Humph," she growled, but let him help her to bed. She was verra uncomfortable and couldna fall asleep. Ian of course, was sound asleep, but the clever man had pinned her down with one leg over her legs and his arm over her mid-section. How could he nay ken that she had enough weight on her stomach already? She wondered. She ranted for some time before she started to relax. Finally, after about an hour, she dozed off. She was tormented with dreams, dreams that she was being hit and kicked in the stomach and the back. The dreams were verra vivid and she fought off her attacker as best as she could, but she was pinned down and couldna get away from the attacker. She tried to fight back, but she wasna strong enough. Why wasna she stronger? She needed to be stronger so she could fight harder and protect her children. She continued to dream the nightmare and struggled to fight. If only she could break free of whoever was holding her down; then, she might be able to fight off whoever was hitting her in the stomach and the back.

Chapter 15

SHE KNEW SHE had to protect Ian's baby, live to fight. She awoke to a sharp blow, reached for one of her daggers that she kept under her pillow. It was gone.

Ian tried to hold her tighter and calm her down, "Elisa, it's only your husband, Ian. Wake up so you ken what is really happening." He continued to speak soothing words to her until she came around. "Please, love, you are confusing what is really happening with your dream. I need you to wake up. Come on, m' sweet wife, you have to wake up now. No one is fighting you; that part is just the dream." He continued to talk to her until she woke up.

"What are you doing, Ian?" she asked him.

"I am just trying to get you to wake up so you are aware of what is really happening. You were dreaming and responding to the dream."

"The pain in my stomach and back was so real," she explained as she looked at him, confused.

"The pain in your stomach and back are real; that is your labor, but no one is hitting or kicking you; that part was the dream. You went into labor a few hours ago, but you have slept through most of it since you dinna feel verra much pain. Alice was here to check on you. I sent her to make all the necessary preparations. She will be back shortly. I have been monitoring how many contractions you have had and how long they last and also how long in between the contractions."

"Is your mother going to come in here, too?"

"Only if you wish it, m' love. I would nay ever ask Mother here without your permission; nay after all she has done to you, alright?"

"Alright, mayhap, I dinna know. I dinna have a mother who could explain anything to me. Even if she werena dead, I am nay sure I would want her here anymore than I would want your mother here. She was as bad, if nay worse," she paused. "Ian? I dinna want you to leave nay matter what those two ladies say about men shouldna be in the room. I need you. I dinna want anything to happen to me; but more importantly, I dinna want anything to happen to the baby, your heir. I couldna bear that. I know I should be stronger and braver, but I am verra scared about what might happen while I am in labor and I mightna be able to protect myself or the baby. Please, dinna leave."

"I willna leave the room, but I need to dress before Alice returns," Ian said. He released her and got out of bed. He dressed quickly in a pair of breeches and a shirt before he came and sat on her side of the bed, facing her. He helped her sit up. Then, he stacked all the pillows in the center of the bed and helped her to sit up against the pillows. It wasna long before Alice returned with several maids carrying linens and men carrying buckets of water.

Elisa looked at Ian and pleaded with her eyes for him to get rid of all the people. She dinna want a lot of people around when she suffered. Ian sensed her thoughts and shooed out the men and the maids. "Is that better, m' love?"

"Aye, thank you, Ian."

Alice complained, "I canna do this alone, m' laird."

"I ken; that is why I thought you would want my mother to help." Alice glared at him and he laughed. Ian turned to Elisa, "I guess that answers your question about whether you want Mother in here."

Elisa just responded, "Aye," with a grunt because a contraction started. She tried to focus on blocking out the pain and trying to breathe through it.

Ian grabbed her hands and told her, "Squeeze my hands as hard as you want." She gripped him and squeezed verra hard.

"How many contractions has she had since I left?" Alice asked.

"Five," Ian replied. "The previous one was sharp enough to finally wake her enough I could get her to come out of her dreams. Her contractions are only a couple minutes apart and they last about a minute each."

When the pain eased Elisa asked, "Alice, I need you to explain to me exactly what is happening, what is going to happen."

Alice answered, "It is different with every woman, m' lady."

"I dinna want your vague answers. Just tell me what I need to know, how this will progress; so I can cope through the pain."

So Alice explained what she could.

"I need you to explain it to me again when it is happening, alright. It will help me focus and get through the pain."

"Aye, m' lady," Alice said.

"I am sorry I have been so difficult, Alice. I dinna mean to be; it's just that I need to know what will happen so I can handle the situation. I ken it is different for each woman; and I am nay like others but knowing what to expect and breaking it down into little steps helps me deal with the pain better. I can cope with the pain if I think about it as little steps that I mark off on my checklist."

"Aye, alright, m' lady. I just dinna want to tell you it will go a certain way and then if it doesna go that way, you willna trust me. Since you are nay like others, I dinna have any idea how this might go for you. I can only tell you what is normal for others."

Ian waited until the two of them worked everything out between them. He went to the door and asked for one maid to return to the room before he said, "Before either of you gets angry with me. I havena and willna ask mother to come in here. But, you ken that when she goes downstairs to break her fast and none of us are about, she is going to come barging in here demanding to know why she wasna summoned."

Elisa had another contraction. Alice looked at Ian, "That was too soon. I need to examine her." As soon as the contraction ended, Ian helped Elisa slide down in the bed and held her hands while Alice did what she needed to do. "She is nearly ready. Lady Elisa, dinna try to push yet, alright? We need to wait a few more contractions."

Elisa said, "Ian, can you light a candle and place it where I can see it and focus on it." Before, he could even return to the bed, she was having another contraction.

Ian glanced at Alice, "Is this normal?"

"Nay, m' laird, but your wife isna normal; she is extraordinary. So we canna expect her labor to be like other women's labor, when she isna like other women. That is why I have been reluctant to explain too much to you, Elisa." Alice examined her again. "She is ready. We need to get her moved before the next contraction." Ian lifted her in his arms so Alice could put a pad under Elisa. Then, he moved Elisa around on the pillows as Alice directed him to do, so she was half sitting and half lying down. Alice explained this would help her to bear down and push. Ian sat behind her and reached around Elisa and she held both his hands while he pushed his chest into her back to help her bear down.

Then, everything happened at once. Elisa started a contraction and was trying to push while she focused on the flame of the candle. She told herself that she was as small as the flame and the pain couldna get to her because it couldna be any bigger than she was. Ian was holding her hands and encouraging her to push as hard as she could. And, Lady Isobel barged into the room complaining no one had come to get her. "Be quiet or leave." Elisa yelled at her.

Ian told Elisa, "Just focus on the flame, m' sweet wife." Elisa refocused until Ian's mother walked around to the other side of the bed and blocked her view of the flame.

Elisa whispered to Ian, "Make her move, canna see flame."

"Mother, please move. You are blocking Elisa's view of the candle flame. She needs to see the flame to focus."

His mother started to say something, but Ian interrupted, "Just move, now."

"Please, Lady Isobel, just move," Elisa cried out. Lady Isobel moved out of the way. Elisa tried to focus again, but now the pain was intense and it was harder to get focused.

"Push, Elisa," Ian said. "Focus on the flame and push one long, hard push." He wasna sure if Elisa heard Alice's instructions, so he repeated what Alice told Elisa to do. It was convenient since his head what right near her ear and he could easily talk to Elisa.

Elisa pushed their son into the world. While Alice finished cleaning up Elisa, Lady Isobel took the baby from Alice and with the maid's help she cleaned the baby and wrapped him in a blanket. Ian held Elisa in his arms while Alice changed the bedding; then, Ian helped Alice change Elisa before he set her back against the pillows in the center of their bed. Lady Isobel handed the baby boy to her son. Ian kissed his son and welcomed him into the world and turned to Elisa. He placed their son in Elisa's arms. Elisa held her little boy and gazed into his face. She kissed him several times. She removed the blanket from around their son and caressed each of his fingers and toes and let him grip her finger. His grip was strong. Elisa took Ian's hand and held his finger out so the baby could grip his finger and their son latched onto his father's finger.

Ian was surprised how strong his son's grip was. "He's strong. I dinna know he would be able to hold my finger." Ian sat on the edge of the bed facing Elisa and smiled at her. "He doesna want to let go."

Lady Isobel interrupted them and asked, "What are you going to name him?"

Ian and Elisa looked at each other.

Elisa said, "I dinna think about it; I thought I would let you decide, Ian. If he was our first child, obviously, I would have chosen Ian. But since we already have an Ian, I just thought I would leave it up to you, dear." Elisa said to Ian, "Mayhap, there is some other family name you would like to use."

Ian smirked and teased, "Well, I guess we canna use Duncan or Colin, since you have spent so much time alone with each of them."

"That isna funny, m' laird," Elisa said, "And, I am offended you would imply such a thing, especially in front of our son."

"I was only teasing you, love. What about Malcolm Festus?" Ian suggested.

"Are you sure you want to pick the first king's name?" Elisa asked. "Dinna you think that will be proving our connection to the throne? Willna it put everyone in more danger?"

"It may, but the first Malcolm dinna seek the throne, so it may be just the message we want to send to our Scottish king."

"Alright, m' laird. Your son's name shall be Malcolm. I hope it is the result we want. Will you make the arrangements with Father Patrick to baptize Malcolm?" Elisa asked.

Ian said he would make all the arrangements and prepare the announcements.

Alice said she needed to talk to the two of them privately before he left. After Lady Isobel left, Alice told them it would be best for Elisa to rest for two months and to avoid getting pregnant for at least a year.

Ian said he would ensure that Elisa wouldna get with child for a year. "I will do my best to encourage her to rest,

Alice; but, you ken she isna going to take that verra well. She is used to doing everything herself. So if I canna be with her, then you should do all you can to be with her; otherwise, she will be out of the bed and taking care of Malcolm and training as soon as our backs are turned."

Elisa looked at him in shock that he would say such a thing.

"Aye, you will and I ken it well enough. I know you verra well, m' love. And normally, I dinna mind your spirit and determination. I dinna mind that you do for yourself and nay let the maids do everything for you; but now, you need to think about your health and the baby's health."

"Alright, Ian, but I am pretty sure I willna enjoy this. I canna just sit here all day and you know I willna sleep all day. I have to have something to do."

"Will you at least try to sleep every other time that Malcolm is sleeping, just for a day or two?"

"Aye, I will try, but can I have the mending brought here and my knitting project when I am nay sleeping? I could probably work on the ledgers too while I am confined to the bed, if you will let me." She waited for his approval.

"I will let you work on one project today, Elisa. We will see how today goes and discuss the rest later. And please dinna get upset with me. I will discuss this with you after the baptism, alright?" Ian gave her a kiss before he went to tell his father and men; and then, he went to see Father Patrick. Elisa spent several minutes holding and feeding Malcolm. After she burped him, she sang Malcolm to sleep before Alice placed him in a cradle next to the bed and Malcolm and Elisa slept after that.

When Elisa woke, she heard Malcolm making a sucking sound. No one was in the room so she sat up and scooted to the edge of the bed. She turned back and stacked all but two pillows against the headboard. Then, she leaned into the cradle and picked up Malcolm. She laid him between the two pillows and scooted back to the center of the bed and sat up against the stack of pillows. Then, she was able to pick up Malcolm and she began to feed him.

When Ian came in, he was surprised to see her sitting up and feeding Malcolm when no one was in the room. "Did you get out of bed by yourself, Elisa?"

"I wasna exactly out of the bed, m' laird. Malcolm was hungry so I scooted to the edge and put my feet down on the floor, adjusted the pillows and leaned over to lift Malcolm to the bed. Then, I scooted back against the pillows and lifted Malcolm into my arms, so I could feed him."

"Do you think that was a good idea to be up so soon?"

"It must have been," Elisa said, "because I am fine, Ian. It isna as if I am cleaning the room. I only picked up Malcolm and moved back to the center of the bed to feed him. Please, dinna make a big deal out of this."

"Alright, Elisa," Ian said calmly. "I dinna want to fight with you. I just want you to take it easy for two months and give your body time to recover like Alice said. I ken you had to take care of yourself and the children before; but I want to take care of you now, Elisa."

"You dinna really think that will happen, do you, Ian?" she asked. "I've taken care of myself for so long and I raised little Ian and Elsbeth by myself, while I ran multiple estates and businesses."

"I am simply letting you know my expectations," Ian replied. "I am nay going to allow you to disobey me on this matter. I will spend as much time with you as I am able, but for a fortnight you will be confined to this room. After that, I will allow you to work in the library. After the two months, then I will allow you to be moved to the hall, but only if you dinna do anything too strenuous. I want you to let your body heal, do you ken?"

"Aye, I ken that I am to be confined for two months while every day you go train, ride, visit the clan, and I am sitting here with my motherly duties. I think you should leave now."

"I am sorry, Elisa, but I dinna think you ken why. It isna so you can do your wifely or motherly duties. It is because once Malcolm is baptized, the announcement will be sent to the Kings of England and Scotland. We may hope that England is too busy cleaning up their own affairs to ken the meaning of the announcement. They mightna realize it means you are alive and have born another heir to the throne, one with even stronger ties to the throne. But, the King of Scotland will certainly ken the meaning of Malcolm's announcement. I am certain His Majesty will come here prepared for the worst. Therefore, we need to be prepared for his visit with a large entourage, a possible siege, and mayhap, even war. I want you healed and healthy and by my side. If anyone can negotiate or make him ken we dinna want the throne, it will be you, m' love. You are much more prepared to deal with the king than I am after all your training while you were growing up." Ian sat down on the bed next to Elisa. He caressed her arm and kissed the top of her head. "Mayhap, for the king's sake, we should fight often. I believe we can use your defiant wife role to our advantage. We dinna want him to think you are too good of a wife that he would want you for his own," Ian suggested.

"That is an excellent plan, m' laird," Elisa agreed. "And you can make it up to me when I am recovered."

"Aye, it will be my pleasure, m' sweet wife." Ian took Malcolm from Elisa when he was done eating and placed him back in his cradle. "Now, I dinna mind if you take care of the mending. I would say help, but I know that you will do all of it yourself; so I willna even try to deceive myself. But, I expect you to sleep at least every other time when Malcolm is sleeping. Can you do that?"

"Aye, I will at least try to sleep. I can close my eyes and rest if I am nay able to sleep. I will try, Ian. I am sorry to be so difficult, but it isna in my nature to just sit around and nay do anything. I canna stand to do nothing, but I will try to nay do anything strenuous."

"That is all that I ask of you, Elisa; that you try to rest." He laid his hand against her cheek and leaned down and kissed her. "You look verra beautiful, Elisa."

"Thank you, Ian."

"I want you to tell me how you feel after what you have been through this morning."

"I feel fine."

"Please, love, tell me more than that."

"My stomach muscles hurt a little and I am bleeding a lot, but otherwise, I feel fine. I am verra happy, except for our arguing. I am also worried about the king coming here and what he will expect."

"I am worried about the same thing, Elisa. I dinna think his visit will be a good thing. I am sorry, that doesna help relieve your worries any."

"Nay, I prefer to deal with the truth. I dinna need to be coddled. Do you think his coming here will be more of your mother's schemes?"

"I dinna know for sure, but most likely. She seems determined that you should suffer every chance she gets to cause you some pain, whether it is verbally or physically. I am sorry. I try to limit the amount of time she spends visiting here, but I do enjoy having Father visit and seeing him with the children. I am sorry you missed seeing him with the children when we went to his castle for a fortnight."

"I dinna think I would have enjoyed visiting there, Ian; nay even to see him playing with his grandchildren."

"I ken. You willna be upset with me because I view it with happiness?"

"Nay."

When they were done talking, Ian sent for Alice and she brushed Elisa's hair and wrapped a shawl around her shoulders and then Ian invited his parents and Father Patrick into the room so they could baptize Malcolm. Ian left the door open and Sir Duncan stood in the hall and watched the ceremony. Afterwards, Ian let everyone hold Malcolm before he handed his son to Elisa. She loosened his blanket and held her finger to his hand and he gripped her finger. She sat with her head bent to her son and sang to him in a barely audible tone.

Duncan quietly slipped down the stairs and out of the hall. He went to the stables and saddled Justice and went for a long, hard ride. He couldna bear to see the family together and nay be part of it, but he dinna want to be part of it either. He dinna want to see them so happy, but he dinna want them to be unhappy either. It was best if he wasna around them until he could control his emotions. He knew Ian would ken and nay criticize him. He sensed a few of his guards followed him, but they kept their distance so he could have his privacy.

It was a verra difficult fortnight. Elisa was good for a day and then she felt she couldna tolerate the situation the next day. They fought about the restrictions and her word that she would try. Ian was able to get her to relax and try again for another day. Elisa dinna want to be confined or have any restrictions on her and Ian dinna want her out of the bed or moving around so her body would heal as quickly as possible. So they had a good day and then a bad day.

After nearly a sennight, Ian figured out the pattern to their days and he spent the good day taking care of clan business and as much of the bad day as he was able sitting with Elisa in their room. When he wasna able to sit with her, he asked his father to sit with her.

After a fortnight, Ian carried Elisa to the library, so she could organize and categorize the bookshelves. He left her to work. Malcolm was brought to her to be fed whenever needed. Elisa had another idea to work on first. She created three lists of what they needed to do to prepare for the king's arrival. She prepared a menu for when the king was there. Then, she made a list of everything she thought they needed to prepare for a prolonged siege. And finally, she made a list of what she thought was needed if the king waged war on them. Obviously, Ian would need to review the three lists and make any necessary changes, but it was a start; and Elisa felt like she at least contributed something.

Elisa was so engrossed in making the third list, she dinna hear Ian come into the library. He read through the first list and was perusing the second list before she even noticed him. When she looked up to see if he was upset with her, he only said, "Continue."

Ian asked for lunch to be sent up and also for Sir Duncan, Sir Thomas, Sir Colin, and Angus to join them for lunch. They ate and discussed the lists. Elisa edited the lists with changes, added things they suggested that she hadna thought of, checked off anything that was already done. At least she felt she contributed something to the preparations, even if she couldna do any of it herself or oversee it personally.

When the men returned to their responsibilities, Ian said, "That was verra well done, Elisa. I dinna know you would be so knowledgeable of what would need to be done. Thank you, I am verra impressed, m' love."

"I only hope you are nay upset with me. I wanted to help, but I know I canna do any of the work right now. The preparations for the king's arrival are of nay consequence, but do you think the other two lists should be secured somewhere where they willna be found? It's one thing to prepare for a siege, but the other may look like we are going against him, defying him," Elisa asked.

"I will take care of the lists. I am nay upset with you; I'm glad for your help," Ian said. "And, I appreciate that you respected my wishes to nay do too much too soon. I know it's difficult for you to sit and let others do the work, Elisa. I just want you to be healthy."

"Aye, I ken, Ian, but I dinna have to like it. But I willna go against your wishes on this. Since we are alone, I want to bring up another matter. You said you would wait until after the baby was born, but I need you to wait until after the king leaves. I dinna want you to have to lie to the king."

"I will allow this for now, Elisa, because I believe the king will come soon. I ken your reasons, but I willna allow you to keep finding an excuse to nay tell me or show me. I mean it when I say that I want to help you. If you want to tell me now, we'll work it out."

"You said you could ensure we dinna have any children for a year, so I will tell you before then." Elisa said. "If you dinna mind, I would like to stay and work on the bookshelves."

"I hope you will tell me after the king leaves." Ian kissed her and held her for several minutes before he returned to his responsibilities and preparations and Elisa started to make a list of all the books in the library. The project kept her busy most of the rest of the afternoon.

Malcolm was brought to her whenever he needed fed and she stopped working to feed him and spend time caressing him and holding him and singing to him. When he was sound asleep, she let Alice bring him back to the laird's room. Then, Elisa continued to work on the list of books.

Since there wasna a lot of work that she could do, that dinna involve lifting, Ian asked her to handle the ledgers. He showed her where all the receipts were kept and where the ledgers were and he left her to take care of everything regarding the ledgers and balancing the accounts. He assumed since she could handle the London townhouse and her father's three estates and her uncles two businesses she wouldna need him to explain anything to her and that would alleviate him explaining anything about the accounts. She dinna ask questions and he dinna volunteer anything more about the ledgers. He thought it was a nice arrangement and it protected the interests of their business without giving away too much information.

Once again, Ian thought he was a coward for nay forcing her to show him her memories about what she did, even though he certainly suspected the truth of the situation. He wouldna accuse her or question her without her telling him directly. And now, he was keeping a secret about their family and their business and there really wasna any reason to keep it from her. He dinna know why he hadna told her from the beginning. She was a verra honest person and she expected the same in return. He knew he could trust her; she wouldna do anything to harm him or the family or the clan.

He really was a coward where Elisa was concerned. Even knowing that waiting to tell her was going to hurt her feelings, he still wasna prompted to sit down and tell her everything. He supposed that might be why she dinna share her secrets with him, but he wasna persuaded by that argument either. He just buried himself in the work that needed to be done and in his training so he and his men would be prepared if they had to face the king in a battle or a war.

There was certainly plenty to do to keep busy. They had fields to plant and hunting and fishing and then the meat to prepare to store for a long time. There were sheep and lambs to care for and cattle and calves to ensure they were moved to an area that was protected and safe. They set guards on the livestock to keep raiders and the king's men from harming them or stealing them. The men were informed to bring them to the caves if it was necessary to keep them out of sight and safe. They stockpiled supplies in the caves.

Every morning the men trained. After they broke their fast, they went out to the fields to plant more crops than normal. Then, those that were given guard duties along the shore were sent to relieve the men already there and those assigned to the livestock went to relieve the other men already in the field. Every few days, new men were sent out to relieve those in the field and along the shoreline.

Chief Ian sent word to Laird Argyll to send a runner with a message to them if the king and his entourage were headed their way. Laird Argyll agreed to send a runner and he assigned a large retinue of men to watch for the king and his entourage with the understanding that one runner would return to the keep with word and another would ride for Mull.

All the preparations were well under way. When they werena busy in the fields, they spent more time training or hunting and fishing and preparing the meat and the hides. It was a verra busy time and it was easy to immerse oneself in the work.

Elisa met daily with the housekeeper and the cook to ensure the household was being taken care of. She let them know there was a good possibility the king would visit them once he received word of Malcolm's birth and he could arrange to bring an entourage of men here. They agreed to ensure the keep received a verra thorough cleaning and that plenty of food would be prepared in the event of the king's arrival. Elisa discussed a menu with them for the meals during the king's visit so they would be prepared.

Elisa started having the children join her in the library so she could give them their lessons. She had discovered they really werena having many lessons. Alice was faithfully teaching Elsbeth how to act like a lady, but other than that, the children were just given some books to read. So Elisa reviewed what they had read so far and started teaching the children more of what she was taught and in multiple languages so they would be fluent in several languages as she was. She spoke with them in at least three languages and sometimes four or five languages.

She was verra happy being with the children each day. It made her confinement and restrictions much easier to deal with and it also alleviated Ian from having to spend every other day with her, so he could go about his business and clan business and his training. Elisa realized the children werena getting their training or riding lessons and she asked to speak with Sir Colin.

"I just want to know what your schedule for the day is like, Sir Colin, if you can tell me without it causing you an issue with Laird Ian."

"I dinna think my schedule is anything secret, m' lady." He explained his schedule and it was quite a full day.

"Thank you, Sir Colin; that will be all," she replied. She dinna wish to cause any problems between him and his laird.

"You are concerned that the children are nay getting their training or riding lessons?"

"Your schedule is already full, Sir Colin. I am nay going to ask you to do more than you are already doing. I wouldna ask you to do anything without Laird Ian's approval. Besides, Ian and Elsbeth already know how to ride. They rode all the way from London to here. I am nay certain about Hawk's skills, but I dinna think any of us will be leaving the castle until the king decides if he is coming here or nay. The preparations you and the men are making are far more important than the children's lessons. I would only ask that if something happens to me, you will speak to Laird Ian about resuming their lessons when the issue with the king is resolved."

"Aye, m' lady, I will be certain to take care of that. Are you saying we should expect something to happen to you in the future?"

"Nay, I am nay saying anything of the sort, so you dinna need to run to the laird with any tales. I am just trying to prepare for every possible outcome in the future. I just want to be certain that if I am nay here, the children will still receive the lessons they will need. You may return to your duties, Sir Colin. Thank you for your help."

"Aye, m' lady," he replied with a slight bow and left the library and returned to the stables.

She made a note to herself to bring the children with her to the garden when she was nay longer confined to her room and the library. At least, they could all walk about the garden some and she could give them some of their lessons outside if the weather was nice. They were children and should be allowed to play. They shouldna have to be confined to the nursery all day long. It wasna any fun for them, she was sure. Besides, they would become sickly and weak if they dinna have more activity and exercise.

She created a list with a number of games they could play in the garden and listed some rules for them. The children could play the games without her if for some reason she wasna here to play with them or teach them. It took her an hour or so to make the list. She gave it to the children the following morning after their lessons.

She spent the next fortnight making a list of lessons for the children to study. Once she was engrossed in the project, she was totally focused on that. In the morning, she ensured that she took care of the other responsibilities, she met with the cook and housekeeper and then she took care of the ledgers. In the afternoon, she worked on the lessons she wanted the children to learn over the next year or two. She included the training and riding lessons, as well as what they should spend time learning in the classroom. Ian could always hire tutors to take care of their lessons if he dinna have time or know what she felt they needed to learn.

She drafted a letter to her solicitor to ensure funds were transferred to Ian to pay for the tutors for the children. Then, she drafted a letter to Ian explaining her funds that she had saved as well as her investments and all the information he might need to reach her solicitors in London and Edinburgh. She explained the transfer to his ledgers to cover the cost of the payment to his captors for taking Cousin Ken's body back to London. Then, she explained the funds she authorized the solicitor to set aside for a tutor for the children if it was needed. She tucked the letter in the ledger to mark the page on which she was working. Ian would easily find it if he worked on the ledgers or if she wasna here anymore, he would have what he needed. She left a copy of the letter to the solicitor with her note to Ian.

She felt she had taken care of everything she could think of that might need to be done in her absence.

Chapter 16

Just as Ian thought, the King of Scotland packed up his entourage and headed straight for Mull when he received Malcolm's birth announcement. It had only been two months since Malcolm's baptism. Ian rode out to greet them with a large number of guards. He doubled the guards attending Elisa, the children, and the wall. All Elisa could do was pray; pray so hard that Ian would be safe and the king wasna here to wage war. She prayed that the king would choose allies over any other options and leave them in peace.

At least the waiting was over; they would know one way or the other if they could continue to live in peace or if they would have to go to war. Ian had rushed out to meet them without telling Elisa whether she should wait in her room or downstairs.

She quickly sent for Alice, to ensure food was served with ale and scotch as soon as the king entered the castle. Elisa decided to wait in their room until Ian came to get her or sent for her. Mayhap, she was being a coward, but she dinna want to be sent away if they wanted to talk amongst the men. It would be too humiliating to be sent to her room like a child. She knew she wouldna take such treatment well.

Once she was dressed and her hair was done, she sat holding Malcolm. He was so little and needed her so much; she only hoped she would be allowed to be here for him while he grew up. One can never tell the whims of kings. It was several hours before Ian came to get her. He came in and stood by the door watching his wife holding their son. She had so much love to give and so much passion. But today, she must keep her passion and her temper in check. Ian hoped she was ready for this meeting. "Elisa, it's time," Ian said softly.

Elisa stood and laid Malcolm in his cradle. She turned and walked towards Ian. "I guess this is the day my parents prepared me for. I hope I dinna disappoint anyone, especially you, m' laird."

"You willna disappoint me, Elisa; you couldna."

As they descended the stairs, Elisa said, "Malcolm is going to outgrow that cradle soon. We need to think about a new bed for him." She knew it was a simple little thing and that it would help to alleviate Ian's stress about their situation. She let her body's energy go out to him. Really, she dinna do anything. Her gifts just did what was needed to relieve Ian of what ailed him, the stress of everything he was dealing with waiting to see what the king would do. Thankfully, her body always felt so full of energy and unlike Ian and Sir Duncan, she dinna get tired when her gifts healed others. She dinna feel anything except the energy. She knew it was happening, but it dinna affect her.

They reached the bottom of the stairs and walked across the hall to where the king awaited. Ian introduced his wife. Elisa said, "Your Majesty, it is an honor to meet you," as she dipped a deep curtsy. She waited for the king's permission to rise from the curtsy as was expected of her.

"Well, I did not expect that, Lady Elisa, after what I heard about the King of England's visit."

"M' liege, I dinna know what you were told, but my allegiance can nay be to the King of England, when I am married to a Scottish laird. As I tried to explain to the King of England, my allegiance is first to God, then to the King of Scotland, the Chieftain, and finally to m' laird husband."

"So, then, the rumors that you died in England are not true."

"Nay, Your Majesty, those rumors are nay true," she answered.

"Do you know how that woman came to be living in your father's home, your home?" the king asked.

"Your Majesty, it was nay longer my home. After my father died, his properties belonged to my cousin, Ken, and then my uncle, Kenneth. Mayhap, she heard I left and thought the place empty, so she found a way in. I wasna there when she entered my uncle's home, therefore, I couldna know how she got in."

"Are you saying you were nay in England?" he asked.

"My liege, as you are aware, the King of England was here, he and I had a disagreement, which resulted in him insisting I be beaten with a whip. I was told afterwards, I took twenty-two lashes before I was rendered unconscious. I was laid up in bed healing from my wounds afterwards."

"I am surprised you could take twenty-two lashes. Most women could not take so many," His Majesty responded. "Do you have scars, my lady?"

"Your Grace, I dinna look at my back because I dinna wish to remember that time. So, I dinna know if I have scars," Elisa replied.

The king looked to Ian for confirmation. Ian said, "If m' lady would turn around." Elisa turned around. Ian lifted her ringlets up out of the way with one hand and pulled her neckline down with the other hand. Apparently, she had enough scars to satisfy the king's curiosity.

"Why wouldna you want to remember the day you defied the King of England?" he asked.

Elisa turned back around. "I am nay proud of defying a king, Your Grace, because it may cause you to nay believe my loyalty to you is true. Part of the reason I dinna care to remember that day is because of my pride. I expected to take the full thirty-nine lashes, but I couldna. I am verra disappointed in myself because I succumbed to the pain."

"Lady Elisa, I do not know any man who could withstand thirty-nine lashes. Why would you think you could take that kind of pain?"

"Your Majesty, I dinna ken the amount of pain I would have to withstand and I hadna endured that much pain before."

"So you have been beaten before, but not to that degree?" he asked.

"Aye, m' liege, I have been beaten before," she moved out of Ian's reach and looked at him, pleading that he wouldna sense the nightmares, "many times. But, the pain was too intense and I couldna endure it. I dinna like to find any weakness in me."

His Majesty laughed, "You are a woman, barely more than a child, really. Of course, you have weaknesses."

"Aye, Your Majesty, but I wasna raised to believe that."

"Why would your parents train you to think this way?"

"Your Grace, they said because I was a female, I must excel at both women's responsibilities and exceed the expectations of men. They dinna tell me things directly. I believe it was to partially conceal who I really am and also to prepare me for the role I might be required to hold one day, if I should ever have to go to court. I dinna socialize in London, neither did my parents socialize. They dinna want me to ever fulfill my role at court, but they wanted me to be prepared for it if I had to."

"So, where does that leave us?" he asked.

"Your Majesty, I dinna think that leaves us anywhere other than exactly where we are. I dinna wish to have that role. I never have and I never will, Your Grace. I was only trained for it in the event that I was the only remaining choice. If there was no one else in line to inherit, then I would be educated enough to fulfill the role. If Your Majesty would be so generous as to consider our preference on the matter, I would prefer to remain here with my husband and children and it is my greatest desire that we may form a strong allegiance." She curtsied to His Majesty.

"I will think on it and give you my decision when I am ready," he replied. "Good night, Lady Elisa, I wish to speak with your husband now."

Elisa curtsied and returned to their room and sat before the fire. Alice brought Malcolm to her so she could feed him. Elisa told Alice, "You may go to bed. I will put Malcolm to bed in a little while."

"Nay, m' lady, Ian requested that I stay with you until he returned," Alice replied.

"Thank you, Alice."

It was hours before Ian returned. He sent Alice to bed and placed Malcolm in his cradle. Elisa undressed and prepared for bed quickly. She dinna know if she should ask how it went. She supposed Ian would say something when he was ready. She sat on the edge of the bed watching Malcolm sleep.

Ian stood behind her across the bed, "His Majesty was verra impressed with how wise you are for one so young. He wants the household to swear allegiance tomorrow and he will return to Edinburgh the next day."

"But he dinna say what he intends to do with me?" she asked.

"Nay, Elisa, he dinna."

"Well, then we shall have to wait until he is ready to tell us. Will you hold me, Ian?"

"Aye, m' love, come to bed," Ian said as he lay down on the bed. He extended his arms to her. He would have to be happy with holding her and caressing her. He couldna expect to receive anything in return. He couldna be with her. They couldna take any chance that she would get with child, especially if she might have to go to Edinburgh with the king. He tried to nay get upset about that thought. It wasna Elisa's fault if the king ordered it and there wasna anything he could do. One wasna allowed to say nay to the king. If he did that, he would essentially be starting a war. He dinna wish to do that and he knew Elisa dinna either. That was the whole point of their marriage was to prevent a war between England and Scotland. The last thing they needed was a war amongst their own countrymen.

Then, Elisa suddenly had an idea, "Ian, I changed my mind. Will you lie on your stomach?"

"Alright," Ian said and rolled over.

Elisa massaged his shoulders and worked her way down each arm and up again; then, she returned to his shoulders and worked her way slowly down his back. She massaged all the way down to his toes of his right foot and back up his leg. Then, she worked her way down his left leg and back up. She spent a verra long time on each limb before she worked her way back to his torso and moved to the next limb. "Roll over, dear," she said.

Ian rolled over and Elisa massaged his arms, then his chest. She worked her way down each leg and back up again.

Elisa dinna think either of them would sleep, but Ian was soon snoring. When Malcolm fussed, she sat up, fed him and put him back in his cradle. Then, she replaced the logs on the fire and went back to bed. She must have slept, but she dinna feel rested.

She awoke to Ian dressing and Malcolm fussing. She quickly changed Malcolm and fed him again; then she put him back in his cradle. Finally, she dressed for breakfast and took care of her hair.

"Are you ready, m' sweet wife?" Ian asked.

"Aye, I just need Alice to sit with Malcolm." Just then, there was a knock at the door. Ian opened it.

"Thank you, Alice. Lady Elisa just changed Malcolm and fed him." Ian said.

"Thank you, Alice," Elisa said as Ian escorted her out of the room and down the stairs. The king awaited them. At his greeting, Ian bowed and Elisa curtsied.

The king suggested they break their fast together. He talked about all the events at court during the meal. Elisa kept her head down and tried to show as little interest as possible. She dinna want to go to court. She dinna want to leave her husband and children. She liked all the things she did to help around the castle and she dinna want to give that up either. After breakfast everyone assembled in the bailey and the king stood on the stairs of the keep so everyone could kneel and swear their allegiance to the king. The family returned to the main hall with the king and he said, "I believe I shall take Lady Elisa to court with me, since she hasna been before. I would enjoy showing her about the court."

"Aye, My King, as you wish," was all she could say. She knew she must maintain her composure. She only hoped Ian and she would have time to talk before she left. She would share everything with him before she went so she wouldna go back on her word. She went to their room when the king dismissed her and packed one trunk. She ensured she had her black set of breeches and top and cloak in the hidden bottom, several of her daggers and her sword belt. She even packed her bow and quiver. She packed three other gowns and a few smaller daggers in hidden pockets. She packed an extra set of hair pin daggers and her hair brush and mirror and her winter cloak.

She was done packing, so she went to visit the children. She spent most of the day with them and told them what was happening, and that she dinna know when she would see them again. But, she would look west and send her love to them every day. She asked them to pray for her every day to have the strength to endure and persevere until she could return to them. She gave them each a hug and a kiss and told them to behave and to study diligently.

Elisa returned to her room and held Malcolm the rest of the day. She rocked him in her arms and talked to him and reached out to him with the clan's gift of sight so she'd hopefully be able to see him while she was gone. He seemed verra calm as she did this. She told him numerous times how much she loved him and would miss him. "I hope you dinna grow up too much while I'm gone. I dinna want to miss you growing up and I shall miss you terribly, m' little man." They sat by the fire waiting for Ian.

Ian dinna return until almost dawn. "Ian," Elisa cried when he finally came to their room. She stood and walked towards him. He enveloped them in his arms.

"Elisa, m' love, he willna be persuaded otherwise. I am so sorry. If I do or say anything to prevent you from going with him, it would be treason and it would start a war because the clan would stand with us. If I do nothing, I am failing you. I have already failed you so many times. I am so sorry that I dinna do anything to try to protect you when you were little. I thought if I avoided you and dinna encourage you at all, mayhap, they wouldna beat you. I am such a coward because I couldna bear to hear it or watch it. I am sorry if you felt that I dinna care about you because I dinna want to see or hear them treat you that way. I failed you when I dinna come to London to get you; and now, I am failing you again. I am so sorry."

"Ian, it will be alright. I am strong, I can do this. It's just that I will miss you so much, m' love. I am certain he intends for me to have his child, which doesna make sense. It will only strengthen my connection to the throne.

I dinna see how he thinks it will help our allegiance to him, unless he intends to have you killed when I am gone; so he can have me for his own. Ian, I need to know that you willna hate me if I return to you after having his child?"

"I could never hate you, Elisa. You are my heart and soul. I love you verra much. I have for a long time now, but I was too stupid to show you that I cared when we were growing up."

"Aye, Ian, m' love, you are my heart and soul too. I love you verra much. Now, I have to ask if you want to see what happened. I dinna wish to go back on my word and I dinna know if I will be back before the year is up, but I dinna think so."

"Nay, m' lady. I willna hold you to that now. I dinna want our last remaining time together to be tarnished by that unless you want to free yourself of the burden of it."

"Do you think the king intends to try to get you to give him some information he thinks I may have shared with you after he has taken me with him? I dinna want you to know if it will mean more information you have to withhold or that he could try to use against you and the clan. Nay, it will be best for now if it is only my burden."

"Aye, Elisa, I agree that it may be best if it is only your burden to bear for now. I am verra sorry. I should be protecting you, nay you protecting the clan and me. I too think he has something planned for after you leave."

"I knew the consequences of my actions, Ian. I willna let any of you suffer for me so I can avoid it. Please, be verra careful, Ian, I am afraid for all of you. Kings dinna feel there are consequences for their actions. But there will be repercussions. Does he really think it is going to be acceptable to take a laird's wife, mayhap kill her husband, as if I am going to want to be his wife after he kills my husband? And all the men of the country are going to go along with this? Well, I suppose there are some husbands who would be happy to be rid of their wife." Elisa continued with her outburst.

Ian laughed and held her shoulders, "Elisa, I dinna plan to spend our remaining time together listening to your tirade, either."

"I am sorry, Ian. I just need to get it out now before I say something in front of the king. I am verra angry. I dinna think I can even tolerate his presence."

"I ken, Elisa, but now, let me kiss you and hold you until you have to leave."

"Aye, m' love."

Then, Ian put Malcolm in his cradle. He took Elisa in his arms and kissed her long and hard. She wanted him so much but they knew they couldna risk her getting with child because the king would just use the baby to hurt her. She couldna escape if it meant leaving anyone behind to be mistreated by the king. She wouldna do that to her child. Besides, Malcolm was just over two months and Alice said they needed to wait a whole year to get pregnant again. She dinna like what was coming at all. She would have to figure out a way to persuade the king to wait until her body healed for a year. But, that would mean staying with the king for at least a year, mayhap, two; and she dinna know how she could tolerate that.

Ian showered Elisa with hugs, kisses and caresses. It was all they would have to remember until she returned. They held each other and kissed and caressed each other until there was a bang on the door. Then, Elisa let out a sob and burst into tears, "Oh, Ian, how shall we survive this?" She rested her forehead against his chest.

"Shh, Elisa, you will do whatever you have to do and find your way back to me and our children and our clan. I will always love you. You mustna blame yourself for anything that happens. It is the king's fault for forcing you to go with him to Edinburgh. I ken that you canna say to nay the king; so you mustna blame yourself." He helped her put on her cloak and walked her down the stairs. "It will be alright, Elisa, we will find a way, m' love. Survive, persevere, live to fight another day," he whispered to her. Ian had to lift her onto Magnum for she hadna the strength to do it herself.

The king and his entourage set out with Elisa in the center of it. She rode in complete silence. Irritable couldna begin to describe her mood; anger and seething were closer to her emotions. No one tried to speak to Elisa for her mood was evident upon her face. But, it dinna take long before the king decided to ride with her and make idle conversation. She dinna respond unless he asked her a specific question. Then, she gave the briefest answer possible. Escape wasna an option, he would only hunt her down. Most likely, she would end up tied to the back of the horse. Nay, she preferred to ride sitting up. Think, Elisa, she told herself, you must find a way to make him realize he canna keep you here. Find a way to make him send you home. Use the time to discover whatever you can that can be used against him later. Use the time to discover all the secret passages in the castle, entrances, and so on. You must know it all, so you can find a way out or in, if necessary, later.

She refocused her mind, set aside the anger and focused on everything he said.

Eventually, the king realized she hadna responded to anything he said, "Do you not have anything to say, Lady Elisa?"

"I am sorry, m' liege, I dinna realize I had your permission to speak freely. Did you wish I should speak freely in front of your men, Your Majesty?"

"Did you intend to ride all the way to Edinburgh in silence?" he asked.

"Aye, I suppose I did, m' liege," she responded.

"Well, speak freely, then," he said. "Dinna you wish to bring any maids with to serve you?"

"My King, I havena used a maid in my entire life. There isna anything she can do that I canna do myself. And she canna protect my reputation for you have shattered that by bringing me with you without my husband. You have taken a clan laird's wife and made her your whore. Well, I suppose to be more specific you took a princess of your realm from her prince husband and made her your whore. That is the consequence of your actions, m' liege. I assume that was your intention. You do think of the consequences of your actions before you act?" Elisa asked.

"But I thought you would bring several maids with you like all the ladies at court do."

"That willna matter since you dinna bring my husband. People can only draw one conclusion from this situation and that is that you intend for me to be your mistress. How should the clan accept me and respect me as the laird's wife after this?" she asked.

"But, I thought you would enjoy the parties and dancing," the king said.

He was like a petulant boy. Ridiculous! "I canna attend the court's parties and dances, m' liege, nor any other social events. You canna flaunt your mistress in front of the entire court. Nay, I shall have to remain in my room and wait for you to visit."

"I am the king, I can do whatever I want," he cried.

"Your Majesty, I am sorry but that isna so, just ask your advisors when we arrive. They will tell you, I am nay mistaken in this matter."

"We shall see," was all he had to say.

"How long did it take you to reach Mull? You will have been gone from Edinburgh for quite some time and you will need to return to your responsibilities and take care of matters of state before you can even consider taking some time for anything else."

"It took a fortnight to reach Mull," he replied in a sulky voice. They rode in silence the rest of the day until they stopped for supper and to rest for the night. It was verra early in Elisa's opinion to stop for the night, but he was the petulant king; and apparently, he dinna care to ride too far each day. She couldna believe that it took a fortnight for him to ride from Edinburgh to Mull. She rode from Mull to London and back to Mull in that amount of time and it was eight times as far. This was going to be a verra long and tedious ride if he was going to stop for the night when he stopped for an early supper. She would be rather annoyed and frustrated by the time they reached Edinburgh for that reason alone, to nay mention the fact that she was basically being taken against her wishes. She was certain that she hated kings; kings and sailors were the worst type of characters she could ever imagine.

"Hey," Ian whispered to her, "that isna fair to lump everyone together in one group."

She heard Ian and Sir Duncan's voices in her head, but she dinna ken why they should be offended by her comment. "Fair?" Elisa whispered back. "Should I have some other opinion of kings when they have treated me horribly?"

"I ken why you feel that way, Elisa, but that doesna mean all kings are bad. And what do you have against sailors?"

"Aye, all kings are bad. They abuse their power and force people to do things they dinna want to do because they are nay allowed to say nay. And, I am nay discussing my opinion of sailors."

"Fine, I can agree with your opinion of this king, but the previous king wasna like that. And this isna the first time that you have made a comment about the lack of honor regarding sailors and I want to know why."

"I am nay discussing that."

"Elisa," Ian warned.

She shrugged and whispered to him, "I dinna have to discuss that with you." She blocked him from her mind. She wanted to add that he couldna make her, but she knew that she would just sound childish and petty. There wasna any way she was going to share anything about her experience with sailors and what they did to her and why she felt sailors dinna have any honor. Ian would just have to accept that he couldna force her to discuss that and also that she was entitled to her opinion. She felt justified considering what the captains of the ships did to her. She had Cousin Ken to thank for all that pain. Even if Cousin Ken was dead and he couldna hurt her, the captains werena dead and she dinna doubt for one minute that if they had the opportunity to capture her, they would be more than happy to inflict retribution on her. She knew without any doubt that they would be happy to continue with the vile debauchery they made her suffer in the past. She hadna any intention of ever suffering the pain and humiliation they put her through.

She was quiet and brooding. Her mood was rather apparent on her face. She knew she should school her features so it wasna so obvious to others as to what her mood was; but for now, she dinna care what these men thought about her. She hoped that if it was obvious she was angry, then they would leave her alone and nay try to do anything they shouldna.

When, the king called a halt to their ride. He ordered the tents set up for the night and Elisa put aside her morose thoughts about disreputable kings and sailors. She focused on her current situation and what she could do to help around the camp.

One of the guards approached her and asked if he might assist her dismounting. She moved her feet free of the stirrups and moved her legs free of the horns on her sidesaddle. Then, she released Magnum's reins and placed her hands on the guard's shoulders. The guard lifted her to the ground and released her waist. He kept his hands extended but wasna touching her and only long enough to ensure that she was steady on her feet. Once he was certain she wouldna collapse, he took a couple steps back.

Elisa stood on one foot and shook out the other foot. Then, she switched feet and shook out the other foot until the circulation was normal in both feet. She led Magnum to the area where they were tethering their horses. She unsaddled him and brushed him out. She would gather her bedroll and satchel when she retired for the evening.

She offered to help with the dinner preparations and suggested they gather wood first to get a fire started and then she would gladly do the cooking or at least help with the cooking. She knew she dinna need any assistance, but she dinna necessarily want to do anything to make herself look any more attractive to the king than she already was. The meal was good; Ian's cook sent the best for the king. She was proud of Ian and his cook. After the meal, she cleaned up and washed all the dishes and dried them before she returned them to the trunk they were in before she made the meal. She spoke with the guard who helped her dismount and asked questions about the guards' schedule. She explained that she would be happy to make a stew and some bread for the men so they would have something to eat when they were relieved during the night.

The guard agreed to allow her to make food for the guards and thanked her for her thoughtfulness and willingness to help.

Elisa mixed together ingredients to make bread. While it was rising, she cut meat and vegetables and added them to a couple cauldrons. She asked the guard, "Is there water to add to the pots?"

"Nay, m' lady; we would need to bring a few buckets to the nearby river. I can send some guards to take care of it for you."

"I dinna mind carrying a couple buckets of water. You could just escort me there and back. You could ask more guards to come with us if you think that is best."

He looked at her for a moment with one eyebrow raised.

She chuckled, "I ken your caution, but it would be futile to try to run away. His Majesty would just have me hunted down. When he found me, I would be tied to the back of a horse and I dinna wish to ride to Edinburgh in that manner. I prefer to ride sitting up. Also, I dinna wish to risk my husband's clan; so you dinna have to worry that I will run off."

"Give me a minute to gather a few guards, m' lady." He wasna certain he could trust her, but her argument was sound. He would try to trust her unless she gave him a reason not to. He quickly gathered a few more men to escort her to the river. "We are ready, m' lady."

She nodded and picked up two of the buckets and carried them to the river. The guards surrounded her, two on each side of her. She chuckled to herself that she must look ferocious if they needed eight men to guard one wee lass. She heard Ian and Sir Duncan's laugh in her head. She whispered to them, "Are you two going to watch me all the way to Edinburgh?"

"Aye," she heard them reply in unison.

She imagined shaking her head and chuckling. When they reached the water, she was tempted to do something inappropriate to tease Ian, but since Sir Duncan was also watching and she really shouldna behave inappropriately, she decided to nay do what she thought of. She dinna need them gathering their men and following her to Edinburgh and starting a war. Besides, she reminded herself, nay anything good could come of having fun and she shouldna need to be reminded of that fact. God only knew how many times she tried to have a little fun when her studies were done only to return to the castle and get a severe beating for her behavior. She shouldna need any reminders to nay try to have any fun after all the times she had been beaten.

She filled her two buckets and carried them back to the campfire. The guards offered to carry the buckets for her but she refused their help. She dinna need their help; she could do it herself. She returned to the campfire and moved the cauldrons to the fire and added the water. She attended to the bread again and let it rise one last time. Then, she set it over the fire to cook. She washed dishes while she waited for the bread to cook. Then, she transferred the bread to a towel and let it cool. She washed the baking pans and stirred the stew before she went to her tent to go to bed.

After everyone retired for the night, Elisa snuck out of her tent easily, for the guards patrolling the camp were loud. She climbed a nearby tree and affixed her rope and cloak so she could sleep in relative safety. She thought of Ian kissing her and whispered, "I love you, Ian." Then, she thought of each child, kissed them and told them she loved them. She envisioned herself holding and rocking Malcolm. She envisioned him reaching out his hand and grasping her finger. She kissed his hand. She tickled his toes and kissed each one and told him how much she loved him and missed him.

Elisa woke early, gathered her rope and cloak, and climbed down the tree. She gathered wood as she returned to camp.

One of the men said to her, "Where have you been, Lady Elisa? Some of the men are looking for you."

"I am sorry for their trouble; you can let them know I feel safer higher up off the ground, so I sleep in a tree." Elisa added the wood to the fire. "Can I help prepare breakfast?"

"Yes, m' lady, and I will quietly get the word around to the men."

"Dinna do anything that will get any of you in trouble with His Majesty. You dinna need to do anything to try to protect me," she said. While Elisa prepared breakfast, she thought of each family member and wished them a good morning and sent them her love, a hug, and a kiss. She finished eating first and started cleaning up. She quickly packed up and saddled Magnum. She wouldna allow the men to do anything for her. It wasna necessary and she dinna want them to risk upsetting the king in any way. She wasna sure what he might do to punish her, but she was certain he wouldna have any problems ordering one of the men to be beaten or killed. She dinna want to put any of them in danger.

The trip took a fortnight because the king dinna get an early start in the morning and he liked to stop for lunch and dinner and he dinna travel after dinner. Elisa was so frustrated with the slow progress, but she kept her thoughts to herself. She gathered wood and started the fire. Several guards would go with her and help gather wood just to ensure they were in the same vicinity as her. She cooked the meals and cleaned up afterwards. They realized after the first night that she could have easily snuck away from camp if she wanted, but she wouldna. So, they dinna bother her; they just worked with her to do whatever she did.

They set up her tent in the evening and surrounded it until she took her bedroll and went to a tree. They set up their bedrolls under the tree and she woke them when she climbed down in the morning. They put their bedrolls with their saddles as she did and followed her to gather wood or hunt and then sat around the fire while she prepared their breakfast. They took turns guarding her and spread the word as to how to handle the situation so they dinna upset her.

She basically established a routine, as that was what she preferred to do. It worked best for her and helped her to be in a better mood. The guards seemed willing to accommodate her schedule. They mostly left her alone to do as she pleased since she dinna try to run away. They simply helped with whatever task she was doing, like gathering wood and made it appear as though they were guarding her.

One particular guard stayed with her all the time and he directed the other guards to ensure they understood what was required of them while they guarded her. "I dinna know your name," Elisa said to him after a couple days.

"Alex, m' lady; I am assigned to provide your protection."

"Oh, it's for my protection that I am surrounded by the king's guards?" she teased him and chuckled. "I just wanted to thank you for letting the others know my routine. I just want to caution you and your men to nay defend me against the king. I can handle whatever he might do to me. I dinna want you to do anything that would put any of you in jeopardy. Also, you and your men shouldna approach me or touch me without letting me know first and waiting for me to acknowledge your presence. But, I really appreciate that you and your men allow me to sleep in a tree. I feel much safer up in a tree. I know no one can get to me very easily, nor any predators."

Alex lifted his eyebrow at her.

She laughed. "Aye, you ken my meaning. But if it will be a problem for any of you, then I will stay in the tent. You have only to tell me."

"I will simply explain to His Majesty that you do not feel safe on the ground because you do not want to be attacked by predators. It isna a lie. If he questions me, I will simply tell him that we might not notice a rat or snake sneaking into your tent."

Elisa laughed, "Aye, precisely my point."

Alex laughed too, "I thought you might agree."

"I hope that you are getting enough sleep, Alex. I am sorry, but I dinna sleep verra much, only a few hours a night." She couldna change her sleeping habits, or the nightmares would start. As much as possible, she preferred to nay have the nightmares.

"I will be fine, Lady Elisa. I will catch up on my sleep when we reach Edinburgh. After a long sleep, I will be recovered and I will likely be assigned to you during your stay in Edinburgh."

"Well, I am sorry for your loss of sleep. I can only sleep for three hours; otherwise, I have verra bad nightmares and it wouldna be safe for anyone to be near me during my nightmare. I might hurt someone and I wouldna want to do that to you or any of your men."

"I will explain to the men if I have your permission to do so. We will be very cautious."

"Thank you, Alex. You should also inform them to nay ever touch me or sneak up on me. I dinna think I would respond verra well to that. I havena in the past. I dinna expect that to change in the future, at least nay any time soon."

"I understand and I will ensure the other men understand as well. Should I warn His Majesty too?"

"You can try, but I think we both know that he will
do as he pleases."

Chapter 17

THE TRIP TO Edinburgh was slow and took much longer than was necessary. It made Elisa irritable to go so slowly. Even riding with the children from London to Mull had gone at a faster pace. The children complained less about their discomfort than the king. The man was worse than a six year old. It was ridiculous how badly he behaved. He wasna a gentleman and as far as Elisa could tell, he dinna have any noble qualities. He was verra much like a little two year old, selfish and petulant. He wanted everything his way and he thought he could punish anyone who stood in his way to getting what he wanted. He complained about the least little inconvenience.

On several occasions, she was tempted to turn him over her knee and give him a spanking. She had never been violent before except when she was touched inappropriately and to train, but this man made her want to respond to his bad behavior with violence. She wouldna ever strike her children, even if they misbehaved. Numerous times during their journey, she thought she might bite her tongue off to refrain from saying something she shouldna when the king was complaining. It dinna help any to hear Ian or Sir Duncan laughing in her head.

Once they arrived in Edinburgh, the king was ensconced in matters of state. Elisa was assigned a room in the castle. She asked questions, as to how to get to the kitchens and the laundry. She dinna know what else she would need access to. Alex was assigned to escort her around. She was grateful he was assigned as her guard. They had formed a good rapport during the trip and she felt comfortable around him. Other than food and clean clothes, Elisa dinna ask for much. She figured she would read a lot to pass the time. She was just thankful that they had finally arrived and she dinna have to deal with the tediously slow travel anymore. She said a prayer thanking God for their safe travels and for His attempt to teach her to be patient, though she doubted she had any success, but she had at least refrained from speaking her thoughts out loud. She supposed that was something considering the trial the king was. She chuckled and hoped that God dinna mind her sense of humor, if that was what it was. She wasna sure, since she dinna think she had a sense of humor. She dinna normally have time to play or have fun. That certainly hadna been any part of her childhood.

Games were nay for fun; they were part of her education to teach her to strategize and to find an excuse to punish her. She paced her room and ranted for several hours. She noticed Ian and Sir Duncan rarely intruded on her thoughts during her rants. She supposed they dinna want to listen to her, so they chose to nay invade her mind. Good, because she dinna need them in her head. She wouldna allow herself to fully form the thoughts she had about them abandoning her and leaving her to fend for herself because she couldna risk them hearing those thoughts and attempting to rescue her or coming to Edinburgh to start a war.

It was a month before the king was finally able to come see her. She tried to think of what to say and how to say it. Now, she only had to hope the king would let her speak.

"I have been very busy with affairs of state," he said.

"Aye, Your Majesty," Elisa replied.

"I wish I could spend more time with you, but it is not possible right now."

"Aye, m' liege, I ken."

"Is something the matter, Lady Elisa?" he asked.

She was surprised he noticed, but she looked at him questioningly. When he said she could speak freely, Elisa said, "I would like some books to read to pass the time, mayhap, some yarn and knitting needles. I would like a private time to walk in the garden when no one would be around to disturb me. But what I would really enjoy is news of the world, if you wouldna mind sharing what is going on?"

So, he told her news each day when he was able to come and visit, which wasna very often. It wasna unpleasant to visit with him, but she dreaded what else he expected of her.

One day when he came to visit, she was in a verra bad mood. He asked what was bothering her, so she said, "I really miss my family, Your Majesty; but also, I dinna know why you brought me here and I really dread what you are expecting from me, especially, since I dinna know what is expected."

He responded, "I think you know what I want."

"I think I ken, but I need you to say it out loud and I need time. I am nay ready. I dinna ken why you want me to break my marriage vows and I dinna ken if I can do that to m' laird. My faith requires me to be faithful to God and to my husband. I gave my vow, my word."

"Alright, I will say it straight; I want you to be my mistress. Would that be so bad?"

"Aye, m' liege, because I am already married. I dinna want to break my vows. I dinna want to be with anyone but my husband. You could have many other women, anyone else, why me?" she asked.

"Because I know you dinna want something from me."

"But I do want something from you. I want time to adjust to the idea and more importantly, I want a time frame that you will let me go home after the time is done."

"Alright, how much time do you need to adjust?" he asked.

Finally, Elisa felt like she was getting somewhere. "My maid said I shouldna get with child for a year from my son's birth; so I need until May before you can be with me. I also want to ask you what you intend. Is it your intention to get me with child? And if so, then what will happen?"

"I thought if we had a child together it would strengthen our ties, solidify our alliance."

"And you dinna think my husband will mind me raising your bastard child in the highlands, a constant reminder of how his king takes what he wants with no regard for others, a constant reminder of my infidelity?" Elisa asked. "Dinna you think this will have the opposite result and start a war amongst your own people? Highlanders dinna think and act like the people of your court. They value a person's given word, honor, integrity, faithfulness."

"Exactly," he replied, "your husband has sworn his allegiance and he will honor it."

"You dinna think stealing his wife for your whore is considered a breach of contract, a break in that allegiance?" she asked, knowing she was verra close to going too far, if it wasna already too late. "Scotland has enough trouble trying to keep England at bay. Why would you do this and increase your troubles within your own country? It doesna make any sense to do this. There are numerous women who would willingly be your mistress. Why do you want to be with someone who doesna want to be with you?"

"No, I do not think it is a breach of contract or a break in our alliance," the king answered. "The clans will send as many men as I require if England tries to strike because they willna want to be ruled by England. You are of no consequence in the matter."

"Alright, assuming my husband honors his allegiance to you, then how long do you intend to keep me here and what if I become pregnant? Who will raise the child? Where will the child be raised?"

"I assumed you would take the child back to the highlands with you. There is too much risk for a child to be at court."

"Well, at least we agree on that, m' liege. I would want to return as soon as it is certain I am with child before anyone here can know about it. You will provide me with an escort home. You will nay come and see the child until he or she is ready to come to court; otherwise, you will put the child at risk. Do you ken?" she asked.

"Agreed," he said.

"How long do you intend to keep me here if there isna a child? I need a time period. I canna stay here indefinitely."

"Two years," he said, defeated.

"So, if I dinna get with child in two years, you will send me home with an escort or as soon as it is certain I am with child. And you will nay visit until the child is ready to return to court. I want it written, signed, and sealed with your ring. And I want to see the contract, which will remain in my possession, Your Majesty," she said.

"Agreed, I will write it up, sign it, and seal it. I will deliver it to you at my next visit."

"Thank you, Your Majesty," Elisa replied, gratefully. She was exhausted from trying to deal with this petulant boy's attitude and keep her emotions in check. She hoped he noticed how tired she was and took his leave. Elisa tried to stifle a yawn and hide it behind her hand.

"You are tired, Lady Elisa. I shall go and let you rest."

"Thank you, Your Grace. Good night," she said and curtsied until he left the room. She really was tired. She changed into her nightgown and went to bed.

The king returned the next evening with the signed and sealed contract. She read it. It was exactly as she requested. Now, Elisa could only hope he would honor it. They had a light supper together and he shared what news he could. After he left, Elisa put on her cloak and pretended to hide the contract in her trunk; but actually, she hid it in a secret pocket inside her cloak. She dinna doubt that she was constantly watched.

As time passed, Elisa knew she had to allow the king to be closer to her, to touch her. It was like building up a tolerance to pain or heat so she dinna flinch when it happened. That is what she had to do. She had to find a way to tolerate this and make it appear as if she dinna mind it at all, mayhap even enjoy it. The thought that she could ever enjoy it was repulsive to her and she was sure she would never be able to enjoy the experience. But if she tried verra hard, she could tolerate it without appearing that she was repulsed by his touch. She tolerated much worse things from her cousin and his friends. She knew the king was part of Cousin Ken's visitors and had abused her before. But, she tried desperately to nay think about that. She dinna want him to do that to her again. She wasna sure that the king recognized her as that little girl.

Eventually, Elisa was able to tolerate him touching her hand, a caress, even a kiss on the forehead or cheek. She dinna want to be unfaithful to Ian; but she had to do this, and she needed it to be a pleasant experience. She wasna sure she could tolerate any more pain, like the pain her cousin inflicted on her. She knew he was dead; she saw his body and knew that he was cold and dead. But, the nightmares continued.

She prayed daily that God would send a more beautiful woman to court that the king would want to marry and he would send her home. Then, the king would have legitimate heirs and not force her to be unfaithful to her husband. She really dinna think she could do this, which would mean the king might take what he wanted and it might be much worse for her. But she would rather endure the pain, than enjoy pleasure with someone other than her husband.

She rose early and went to the kitchen each morning. She made her own breakfast and ate in the kitchen. Then, she cleaned up any mess that she made. She walked in the garden with her guard, Alex. He walked close enough to her that no one dared to approach her. Thankfully, there werena many people in the gardens that early in the morning, unless they were meeting someone or returning from a meeting with someone. They rarely showed her any interest. She walked for a couple hours before she returned to her room.

She ordered a bath and relaxed in the bath. Then, she dressed and read a book and worked on a project. She returned to the kitchen and made her own lunch. She ate in the kitchen and cleaned up after herself. Over time, the kitchen staff learned to tolerate her presence, but they mostly stayed away from her. No one spoke with her and she preferred it that way. She dinna want to be fodder for their gossip any more than was necessary. She was used to being alone. It was better to be alone and nay rely on anyone. Then, they wouldna disappoint her and let her down. She knew she shouldna let herself think her morose thoughts, but some days it seemed that her ranting was all that kept her sane. Although, it was quite possible that it was just as much of a sign that she wasna sane. She chuckled to herself.

Once a sennight, she went to the laundry and did her own laundry. She paid the laundress for soap. She hauled her own water and heated it herself. She usually offered to take an armload of garments back to her room to help with mending, just for something different to do other than reading or knitting. She always returned the garments the next morning on her way to the kitchen. The laundress always thanked her and praised her for the work she did. Elisa tried to nay let anyone know she was a princess. She was more mistress than princess. She tried to nay think about her identity and her high rank. It only made her more upset if she thought about what the king was doing to a princess of the realm. His comment that she was of no consequence infuriated her. The nerve! She could do more than anyone else and she had done so since she was eight years old. No consequence; she would show him no consequence. She would treat him like he was of no consequence when he came to visit the next time. She wasna going to tolerate his rude and childish behavior.

She reached out to Ian and her children each morning and evening to tell them she loved them and missed them. She was used to being alone, except she missed holding her children terribly. She missed singing to them and tucking them in at night. She wondered if Malcolm was walking or talking yet and what he might be saying. She was terribly upset and frustrated.

She would prefer to train, but she dinna want anyone to know that she had any weapons or they might take them away from her. She dinna want to give up any of her weapons. They appeared to go with the trunks and she dinna want to lose any of the set. Except she recalled that she had given one of her daggers to Hawk and she would have to get him a new one and get that one back from him one day. She should make herself a note so she dinna forget to take care of that when she returned to Mull. She supposed it was a good sign that she still expected to return to Mull someday. She supposed it was something to hope for, but mostly she was just angry.

She was angry that she had been ripped from her family, taken from her children when they were so little and needed her; but she supposed if they survived without her, they dinna really need her. They had Alice and the clan and their father to take care of them. Aye, they had their clan, their family and they dinna need her. They were busy with their plans and dinna have time for her. Fine. She dinna need them either. She was used to being alone, no one to protect her. That was just fine with her. She would face what she had to face and do what the blasted plan required of her. Why should she care what they did to her? What difference would it make? She was insignificant, just a girl, a wee lass. She wanted to rip something to shreds, but she wouldna tear up the few dresses she had and she wouldna destroy a book. She couldna kill anything or anyone even though she was pretty sure she was angry enough to do so. She pulled the covers from her bed and her pillow and wrapped up in them and scooted under her bed until she had her back against the wall under the headboard. She cried until she couldna cry anymore and finally fell asleep.

Alex knocked on her door when she dinna come out to go to the kitchen for her supper. The room was dim and he dinna see her anywhere; so he lit a candle and searched the room. He noticed the missing bedding, but dinna find Lady Elisa. He knelt down and looked under the bed and saw the bedding there. He felt around the bedding until he felt a leg.

Elisa kicked out in her sleep at the hand grabbing her leg.

Alex jumped back as quickly as he could, but she still caught him on the shoulder. He was grateful that he had moved as quickly as he did or she would have caught him in the face. He apologized, "I'm sorry, Lady Elisa. You dinna come out of your room for supper and I was worried about you. I couldna find you and I just wanted to be certain you were in the covers. I will leave you to sleep unless you wish to go to the kitchen to get something to eat. You shouldna miss any meals, especially since you hardly eat anything to begin with."

Elisa growled at him and pulled her knees up to her chest.

"I will go now. I am sorry I disturbed you." He rose from the floor and extinguished the candle. When he was certain it was out, he set it on the bedside table and retreated from the room and closed the door. He remained at her door all night. He could lean against the door and doze for a few minutes at a time until he was rested and alert again. He only needed a few hours of sleep. He could work something out with one of the other guards so he could catch up on his sleep tomorrow night, which was what he did once a sennight. He was usually fine as long as one night a sennight he got one good night of sleep.

Elisa woke in the morning in the same bad mood. She reached out to her children, but she realized that doing so was just going to upset her every day. She told the children she would reach out to them and she wouldna go back on her word even if it was painful to her. She just had to bury her feelings while she spoke with the children and that dinna take but a couple minutes.

On her way to breakfast, she apologized to Alex.

He said, "It's alright, Lady Elisa; you dinna have to apologize. You warned me to nay touch you without your permission, so it wasna your fault. I just needed to be certain that you were there and you were. I am sorry if it seems like I dinna trust you, but I have to do my duty too."

"I ken your position, Alex. I am still sorry that I kicked you. You dinna deserve to be treated like that. It isna your fault that I am here and nay where I would prefer to be. You are right; you were just doing your duty."

"Aye, but you were just trying to protect yourself since you dinna have anyone here to protect you."

Elisa cooked enough for Alex for breakfast too. They sat across from each other to eat. Then, she washed their dishes and they stopped at the laundry for her armload of mending before they returned to her room. She resumed her routine. She was here for as long as the king determined to keep her here and there wasna anything she could do about it and it wouldna help to be so upset and angry and morose about the situation. That wasna going to change anything. She just had to accept her situation and do what was expected of her. It was part of the plan and the plan always required that she had to suffer, so she needed to start preparing for that.

Then, one day, Elisa realized it had been more than a month since the king visited. She hoped this meant he found another to pursue and would send her home. She started using her free time to strengthen her muscles. She asked Alex to knock if anyone was coming down the hall and he agreed. She walked around the room most of the day, even though she spent two hours walking in the garden every morning. She just wanted to build up her strength to be able to go all day long. She sat with a pillow between her legs, without dropping it. She even tried walking with the pillow between her legs. She tried any movement she could think of that would strengthen her legs, arms and stomach. She spent most of the day exercising, except for the time she spent doing the mending. She stopped reading to pass the time; and, she quit working on knitting projects because she dinna really have anyone in particular for whom she was making the items. She was just doing it to pass the time. But, she dinna need to do that. She needed to get stronger and prepare for what was to come and that meant training and exercising.

Elisa was quite fit in a couple months when the king finally returned to her room. Apparently, God answered her prayers; a new woman arrived at court and caught his fancy. "This is verra good news, m' liege," Elisa said. She hoped it would lead to marriage and her release.

But the king dinna want to give up Elisa. She tried to reason with him, "Your Majesty, you can marry her and have legitimate heirs. You dinna need me. You already have our allegiance, you dinna have to risk the highland lairds being angry with you for taking me because they will know you dinna do anything to me. You can have legitimate heirs with her and nay illegitimate heirs with me."

"Enough," he yelled. "You will do what I say. No more pleading with me. I will have what I want."

"Then, you will have to take it," Elisa replied, angry that he wouldna see reason and do the right thing. In a way, she was getting what she wanted. The pain was so much easier to deal with than feeling like she betrayed her husband.

The first couple slaps were nay so bad, but when Elisa tried to defend herself or fight back, he closed his fists and hit her harder. She decided to put up a fight after that. And she got in a couple blows. But after several hits from the king, she was fading into the blackness. "Ian, Ian, I need you. Dinna look, just give me your strength to fight to live another day," she whispered to his mind.

She heard Ian chuckle, "I think you mean 'live to fight another day,' m' sweet wife."

"Nay, m' love, I need to fight just to live now." Elisa whispered back. "I think you may have to come get me this time."

"Ask for the priest, for last rites before you die. The priest is a friend of the family," Ian whispered to her.

"Aye, m' laird."

Just before the king withdrew from Elisa, she muttered, "Priest…last rites…before…I die."

The last thing Elisa heard before everything when black was the king telling the guard to send for a priest for last rites.

The priest came and took care of Elisa himself. When she woke from her delirium, he said, "Lady Elisa, I am Reverend John Beaton. Ian said you needed my help until he gets here. I willna let the king come here again. I told him he has to send for Ian; so Ian can take you home. I placed my own guards inside and outside this room. So no one should bother you until Ian arrives. Now, I need to tend to your wounds. Your face is verra swollen and bruised."

He called two of the guards over and asked them to hold her hands. "Lady Elisa, just squeeze their hands as tight as you need to in order to get through the pain."

"Aye," was all she could bear to say; the pain in her jaw was so bad, even that made her see flashes of light.

"Dinna try to talk. It will be at least a few days before your face begins to heal." He washed her face, her whole body. Then, he said, "Lady Elisa, I am a man of God, but you know the clan has healing powers. I have to examine you like Alice examined you after Malcolm was born, alright? I willna try to hurt you, but I need to clean you up so I can wash away his sin and so you can start to heal. Dinna fight me and I will be as gentle as I can."

He must have seen the fear on her face; or mayhap, he felt it, because he said, "It will be alright, m' lady." When he was done cleaning her, he said, "Now, I need to feel all your bones to see if he broke anything. Then, we will sit you up and get you some broth to drink."

"Canna…pain," she tried to say. She whispered to his mind, hoping he could hear her. "I canna move my mouth without great pain. I need a reed from the river's edge to suck the broth through."

"Aye, m' lady, that is a good idea," he whispered back to her. "And, this is great because we can communicate without anyone knowing." He finished checking her for broken bones. She only winced a few times but it was only bruising, nay broken bones, except for her jaw, which they couldna tell; they would have to wait until the swelling decreased before he would know if it was broken. The broth was brought and Elisa sipped it through the reed. It was still verra painful. Her face was bandaged after she drank all the broth.

She whispered, "Thank you, Reverend Beaton," before she fell into a deep sleep filled with nightmares that she was unable to wake from. It was the same nightmare she always had, but with the latest incident added to it. Sometimes, she hated that she had such a great memory. It was awful to relive the same nightmares night after night after night. The worst part was that she seemed to be incapable of waking herself from the nightmare.

The king dinna return to her room, for which she was verra grateful. Elisa hoped he would marry and have legitimate children with his wife. She also hoped she wouldna be with child, she prayed it was so. The reverend kept his word and stayed with her. She spent almost all her time sleeping and she wondered if her broth was drugged so she could sleep. It was probably necessary so she could heal properly. She was in a great deal of pain when she woke up. But after she had her broth and a mug of ale and another of water, she sat in her bed or on the sofa for an hour and slipped back into oblivion. She always woke up in her bed and had no recollection of the time of day, only that it was either light out or dark out.

Ian arrived about a sennight after the incident. He was snuck into her room through a secret passageway. He spoke with Reverend Beaton for a long time before he wrapped Elisa in her cloak and carried her out through the same passage. Sir Duncan gathered her belongings and placed them in her trunk. There wasna much to clean up, since she kept her chamber so clean to begin with. He carried her trunk out to the stables and the waiting horses. He tied her trunk onto one of the extra horses. He would keep Magnum tethered to his horse until Lady Elisa was well enough to ride. Ian carried Elisa on his horse with him. They took another passageway from the stables to a hidden gate in the castle wall.

They had to stop every time Elisa started dreaming. The nightmares were worse than before. When she remembered what the king did, she started kicking and screaming and fighting him. Ian couldna wake her from the nightmare and it was too upsetting to the horses to continue riding. He tried to see the memory so he could reach her and calm her down.

"Elisa," Ian whispered, "it's me, Ian."

"Ian, dinna look, I dinna want you to know," Elisa replied.

"Elisa, shh, listen to me. You are dreaming about what happened and I need you to wake up, now. Please, open your eyes and look at me. I am right here waiting for you to wake up. Let me help you, m' love."

"I canna, Ian. I dinna think I have the strength."

"Listen to me, Elisa. I want you to squeeze my hand as hard as you can and I will tell you if you have enough strength left."

"Alright, Ian, I will try," she said. Elisa felt Ian slide his fingers into her hands and she squeezed his hands as hard as she could, but she dinna have much energy to put any effort into it. Her muscles ached from where the king had hit her, all over her body.

"Harder, Elisa," Ian insisted. "You can do better than that. You are nay an English girl. You are a Scottish lass. Now, put some Scotland fight into it."

"I will give you some Scotland fight,:" Elisa said and she balled her fist and hit him as hard as she could.

"See, I knew you had some fight left in you. Now, come here and let me hold you. Oh, I have missed you, m' love," he said as he opened his arms to envelope her.

"Ian, careful. I am bruised all over," she said trying to push him away. She dinna want anyone to touch her. She dinna think she would ever feel clean again.

"I am nay going to let you push me away, Elisa. You are going to let me hold you and love you no matter how scared you are, do you ken?"

"Nay, I dinna ken, I dinna ken that you would want me after this or ever love me again, Ian. I am too damaged to love."

"I am nay going to let you take the blame for this, Elisa. The king is to blame and me for nay protecting you. But you are to nay blame. How could I nay love you after all you have endured just to be my wife? You are verra brave to fight and survive. You have endured and persevered through so much in such a young life. Do you ken I love you and I willna let you go?" Ian asked.

"You dinna even know how bad my face looks under these bandages. You canna know whether you would want to look at my damaged face the rest of your life," Elisa said.

"Elisa, I dinna love you for your pretty face," Ian answered. "I love you because your heart is so full of love for others, because you are always willing to sacrifice yourself to save others. Now, I am going to hold you until you can tolerate it. And, then, I am going to keep holding you until you love for me to touch you again." And with that, he wrapped her gently in his arms. They dinna travel any more that day. Ian just held Elisa until she could tolerate it without fighting him. He ensured that she took in some broth and plenty of ale.

The ale helped Elisa fall asleep but it dinna keep the nightmare away. At least, Ian could rouse her out of the nightmare now. If she tried to fight him, he hushed her and reminded her that he wasna going to let her go. He held her close until she settled down again. The nightmare started again as soon as she fell into a deep sleep again. They hardly got any rest. He doubted any of the men got any sleep either, since she cried out frequently.

He tried to be patient and understanding when she needed awakened and comforted until she calmed down again. He knew she couldna help the nightmares. Most of her life was one long nightmare or rather one nightmare after another, starting with her parents abusing her and his mother as well. And it only got worse from there.

He would have preferred if they could ride longer, but he couldna ride while she was dreaming the nightmares. She always started thrashing about and fighting him to the point that he could barely hold on to her and keep her from falling off the horse. She struggled to get free of his grasp and kicked the horse in the process. He worried if she slipped off the horse, she would be trampled, since her thrashing about startled the horses around her.

He wasna the only one having trouble controlling his horse during her nightmares. He noticed Duncan trying to control his horse and Magnum. At least, Duncan could move his horse and Magnum away from her. Then, the horses calmed down quickly.

Ian had to try to keep his seat and wake Elisa before he could focus on dealing with his horse. He could only hope that his horse dinna bolt during the episodes. But, so far, Talon had been very good through the worst of it. He would take the beast for a nice long gallop as soon as they were back on Mull and it was safe to do so.

He was so grateful for Duncan, who always knew what needed to be done and handled everything so he could devote his time to caring for Elisa. Duncan dismounted and gave the reins for Magnum and Justice to Sir Colin. Then, he stood next to Ian and kept his hands on Ian's waist to help Ian dismount while Ian still held Elisa. Duncan devoted his time to setting up camp and setting the watch, organizing their men. Some hunted and others gathered wood and soon a fire was burning and food was cooking. All Ian had to do was sit and hold Elisa and try to calm her when she started having the nightmare again. He knew she dinna want him to see, but he tried to slip into her mind and see the nightmare anyway. How else was he going to help her deal with the pain she had to face after the beating she sustained? But mostly, all she allowed him to see was a black box. Reverend Beaton told him how badly she had been beaten. Most of her body was covered in bruises and her face was too swollen to even determine if her jaw was broken. And then, the bastard had taken what she wasna willing to give him.

If he could, he would ride back to Edinburgh and kill the king with his bare hands. But, he couldna do that. He had to think about getting Elisa to safety and that meant getting back to Mull. He had to put the clan first. He had to prepare for a siege and war.

The best way to deal with the king would be to let the people see how the king treated Elisa. Every village they rode through knew who he was and what his heritage was. They knew who his wife was and her heritage too. He was a prince and she was a princess in her own right. They were heirs to the throne. His family was the highest ranked family in the highlands. Their father was the Chieftain of the Highlands. For the king to treat him and his wife this way, was appalling. The people were already talking about it and wondering if any women were safe, if the king would do this to Princess Elisa.

All they had to do was ride through every little village and city between Edinburgh and Mull. All the people would see for themselves that their women were nay safe from the hands of their king. If the king tried to wage war against the McVeigh's, he'd have a war against all the highlands. They might fight each other, raid each other, and occasionally, steal a wife, usually because they loved the woman and their families were always feuding. In times like this, the clans stood together against all others, even the King of Scotland.

So, he would ask Elisa to ride through Glasgow with her head held high and her back straight. She would show the people she was royalty and could endure, persevere. The people would gather to him without him saying one word against the king. He wouldna have to do anything that would be construed as a break in his allegiance.

Elisa was correct in her assessment; the king had acted without thinking about the consequences of his actions. His actions would be his downfall and demise. No one of any character would condone the king's behavior. It wasna right to treat women in this manner. Most men dinna beat their wives and certainly nay to this degree. So Ian was assured the people would stand with him and nay the king.

He thought about stopping to visit his cousin near Glasgow, but, decided against it. He recalled Lady Elisa's behavior after a beating from her mother or Lady Isobel. She always turned to his cousin, Daniel. She sat on his lap and he held her while she slept. He called her his little queen. Ian dinna wish to remind her of those memories. He wasna sure how she would respond. So he decided they would ride straight through Glasgow and camp several miles beyond the city.

If Elisa was in better health, he would consider riding much farther each day. But she wasna in good health and she couldna be expected to ride for long periods of time. Her body was battered and bruised. He would have to be satisfied with whatever distance they were able to ride each day until she started having the nightmares before they had to stop until he could rouse her from the nightmare and then, they had to give the horses a chance to calm down.

The situation was frustrating. The men were tired from lack of sleep because her nightmares woke them too. They couldna travel any great distance because of her nightmares. There dinna seem to be anything he could do to make the nightmares stop. He knew it was verra likely, because she never forgot anything, that she would always have the nightmares. It wasna like she wanted to remember the nightmares, but she wasna able to forget them either. He supposed that was why she rarely slept more than a few hours was so she dinna have the nightmares.

He knew it wasna her fault and he tried to nay blame her. He tried to be patient and ken what she was dealing with, but she blocked him from seeing the nightmare. So he dinna really ken what she was dealing with. He wanted to help, but she wouldna let him. It just frustrated him more.

He supposed after this latest incident, she wouldna trust him or anyone else. It would be difficult for him to deal with that because she tried to trust him when she first arrived, even though he wasna sure that she really trusted him the way she armed herself. But, she at least tried. Now, he dinna think she would even try. She wouldna want to trust anyone.

He roused himself from his morose thoughts and focused on trying to comfort Elisa. He was grateful for all that Duncan and the men did without needing any direction from him. He suspected this was eating at Duncan as much as himself, but they couldna discuss that around any of the men or Elisa. He supposed Duncan was busying himself with camp preparations and guard duty to avoid thinking about what was done to Elisa. He was probably wound tight with anger and frustration. He was certain Duncan wanted to kill the king as much as he did.

He told himself to focus on comforting Elisa again. He couldna let his mind turn to those thoughts. He needed to focus on his wife and getting her to safety. He and Duncan would have to talk later when they could be alone. Ian suspected now that his future with his wife wasna likely to be much longer. If the king wanted Elisa, he would come after them soon. Ian wouldna let the king take Elisa this time. He did enough damage already. He wasna willing to allow the king to do any more damage than what was already done. Protecting Elisa was all that mattered to him now. It should have been all that mattered to him all along.

Chapter 18

Elisa awoke at dusk, "Ian," she said.

"I am right here, Elisa. It is alright."

"I ken, Ian. Thirsty," she said. The pain in her jaw made talking unbearable, luckily for Ian and his men; they wouldna have to listen to her. Ian poured water from a skin into her mug so she could sip it through a reed.

After Elisa finished drinking, Ian started to remove her bandage on her head. She dinna want him to see her, but she knew it wouldna do any good to resist. So, she closed her eyes. But, Ian said, "Come on, now, be brave, love."

Elisa opened her eyes just a crack but kept her gaze down so she wouldna have to see his face, his reaction. "This isna my wife, who rode all the way from London, practically by herself, nursing an old man, and caring for two small children, is it?" he teased her.

"You are so irritating," Elisa whispered to him.

"So I have been told," he whispered back to her, laughing. He was finally done removing the bandage around her head. "It isna bad, Elisa. It is still a little swollen and bruised, but nothing is protruding. I dinna think anything is broken," he told her out loud.

"Aye," was all she said.

"You must have more to say than that. You are rarely this quiet unless you are plotting something," Ian teased her.

"It hurts," she replied.

Ian got up. "I will be right back," he said. He went to his satchel, near his saddle. He pulled out a shirt and ripped the bottom off. He soaked it in cold water. He returned to Elisa and laid it on her so both cheeks were covered, but so he could still see her face. "Mayhap, the cool water will help," he said.

"Did you just rip up a shirt that I made for you?" she asked him, feigning that she was angry.

"Aye, I dinna think you would mind making me a new one. You havena made me any new shirts for a year."

"Is that what you thought?" she continued to tease him. "Thank you, Ian, for coming to get me and for taking care of me."

"You are thanking me for taking care of you? Elisa, if I had taken care of you, you wouldna have been in Edinburgh and this wouldna have happened to you, so dinna thank me," Ian said.

"Nay, Ian, dinna blame yourself. You are a man who honors your word and you gave your allegiance to your king. He purposely planned that just the way he wanted so you swore your allegiance before he told you he would take me with him to Edinburgh, so you couldna naysay him after you gave your allegiance. But I am just a woman whose word isna valued among men, especially powerful men like kings. As a possible future queen, it's my responsibility to suffer for the people so they dinna have to suffer. It's how I was raised and it's something I have to do."

"Well, now there is something else you have to do, Elisa. I want you to touch me and hold me. You canna just tolerate me touching you because it is your wifely duty. I willna allow it. I ken the passion and love you have inside you and we just have to find a way to let it out again."

Ian helped Elisa sit up and he moved closer so she could touch him. He sat facing her with his left calf touching her left thigh; her calf was touching his thigh, and he leaned across her and placed his hand on the ground next to her right thigh. "Dinna panic, m' sweet wife, you are nay pinned down. I am nay on your skirt and nothing is behind you. Take your hand and rest it on my arm."

"Ian, I canna."

"Aye, you can, m' love. Dinna be afraid. You dinna betray me. You only did the king's command because you dinna have any choice. Now, look me in the eye and reach out and rest your hand on my arm."

Elisa looked at Ian; she lifted her right hand and laid it on Ian's left arm. She felt the warmth of him. Then, Ian copied her movement. Now, she could feel a little of the tingle he always caused her. As she looked at Ian's face and he looked at her, her stomach started to flutter. Elisa moved her left hand onto Ian's leg. He copied her move again. The flutter in her stomach grew stronger. She closed her eyes and just felt his body under her hands and his hands on her.

Ian said softly, "Elisa, dinna close your eyes and hide from me."

"Shh, Ian, I am nay hiding, just feeling." She sat there and enjoyed his touch. It wasna pain as others gave her. She opened her eyes again. Then, she moved her hand up his arm and touched the back of his neck, hoping he would do the same. Ian moved his hand verra slowly up her arm, barely touching her, and when he touched the back of her neck, her body started strumming. She massaged his neck; she licked her lips in anticipation of his touch. When Ian started caressing the back of her neck, the strumming became more intense and Elisa moaned out loud. "Ian, your men can see us and hear us."

"They willna pay any attention to us. They will only interrupt if it is necessary for our safety. It is just the two of us, m' love."

Elisa caught a handful of his hair and pulled Ian closer, "Kiss me, Ian."

Ian leaned down and kissed her verra gently. He wasna sure if it would hurt her and he dinna want to hurt her.

Elisa pulled her knees up as she scooted closer to Ian. Then, she wrapped her left arm around Ian's waist. She deepened the kiss until he groaned. Ian was right, her passion and love for him was still there. Now, that she was safe in his arms, it was alright to let it rise to the surface again.

She pulled back and said softly, "Lift me up, Ian." As he lifted her, she straddled him. When he set her down on his lap, she returned to kissing him. She kept her right hand on his neck, caressing him. She moved her hand to caress him. Ian couldna remember he was supposed to copy her movements, until she moved his hand for him.

"I'm sorry, m' sweet wife. You had me too distracted." He mimicked her caresses.

She moved her hand back up his neck and grasped a handful of hair.

Ian continued to copy her movements and did to her whatever she did to him. She wanted more, but she knew she couldna. "Ian, we need to stop. Please," she begged him.

"Aye, m' love. I ken, but I really dinna want to stop. I love you so much and I have missed you more than you can imagine," he said.

"I know, Ian, but we canna, until," her voice trailed off and she burst into tears.

Ian held her tightly and let her sob. He told her he loved her and he always would because she was his heart and soul. "It will be alright, Elisa; we will get through this together; just dinna turn away from me. I dinna want to lose you. I need you. Let me help you; let me be there for you. We can do this together."

"Aye, Ian, you will have to carry me now. I feel so broken and crushed. But, I know in your arms I can find myself again. You are the only one who makes me feel this way, Ian. You are my heart and soul, m' love."

"Aye, Elisa, I feel the same way about you. You should get some sleep now. We need to ride a long way tomorrow. We dinna get far today."

"I am sorry, Ian," Elisa said.

"You dinna have to be sorry; it wasna your fault," he replied.

"Ian, is there water nearby, where I could bathe?"

"Nay, Elisa, you canna go in the water this time of year. It is too cold and the rivers are too full and moving too fast, you would be swept away."

Elisa woke early in the morning, before dawn. She had the nightmare again, but this time she felt Ian's strong arms about her and heard his soothing voice. She was able to wake up without fighting him. She couldna go back to sleep, though. For one thing, she realized she wasna tired, not surprising, since she had slept for the better part of the sennight since the incident. But also, she recognized she was too afraid to sleep because she dinna want to have the nightmare anymore. Lastly, she couldna lie this close to Ian and nay want more of what they started last night. But she knew she couldna be with him until she was certain she wasna with child from the king.

She kept fidgeting, trying to get comfortable. But before she could get comfortable Ian woke up. "Elisa, what is wrong? Lie still and go back to sleep."

"I canna sleep, Ian. I am sorry I woke you early, but I think I slept for a sennight now and I am nay tired. I canna stop fidgeting when I lie next to you because I canna have what I want and I canna lie here and nay want you. I am sorry, I dinna mean to be so confusing."

"Elisa, this isna confusing. I think I ken what the problem is and I can help you if you will trust me and let me do something for you. Do you trust me?"

"Aye, I trust you, Ian."

"So, relax and dinna talk, just feel, m' sweet wife." Ian caressed her and kissed her. She dinna protest when he covered them in his plaid. She dinna think she could enjoy being with him this way again. She was verra happy, but then she felt guilty that she couldna give back to Ian until she was healed.

"Ian," she moaned.

Ian kissed her. She started giggling, so Ian kissed her even more until she was laughing. She tried to get him to stop tickling her, but he wouldna relent, "Ian, I am nay ticklish," she said sternly.

"Really?" he asked and continued to tickle her until she was laughing and shrieking. Elisa was squirming and wriggling around to try to get out of Ian's grasp when her cheek bumped into a boot.

She stiffened and cried out.

Ian stopped immediately and started to apologize, "I am so sorry, Elisa. I dinna mean to go too far or hurt you."

"You dinna hurt me, Ian. We have company. I dinna dare look up to see who it is."

Ian tried to scramble out of his plaid to see who was interrupting. He was tangled in the plaid and was uncovering Elisa every time he moved to free himself.

She grabbed the plaid and held it tightly to herself. "Ian, stop moving; just stay still or else I will be exposed too. You men may not mind, but I will mind verra much," Elisa said, all serious business now.

The intruder dropped a cloak over them. "If you two are done with your antics, mayhap we should break our fast and be off. We need to put some space between us and Edinburgh now that you have awakened the entire camp and probably half the county."

"Good morning, Sir Duncan," Elisa said, glad that it was someone she recognized, but also embarrassed to be caught in this predicament. "How are you this fine morning?"

"Lady Elisa, I would be in a better mood if my sleep wasna interrupted with shrieking and screaming and also, if we were much farther from Edinburgh. I am glad you are doing so much better, though. I was worried that you were nay going to recover from that frightful state. Now, if you can reign in m' laird, we can get moving."

"Sorry, to have awakened you and the other men, Sir Duncan. Although, I seriously doubt you were sleeping. If I know you at all, and I do, you were on guard duty. You are always on guard duty, for which I am verra grateful. I am verra sorry to have been so much trouble that you all had to come get me and that I worried you so much. As for breakfast, I will tuck an apple and a piece of bread in my cloak pocket and eat on the way. I only need a few minutes to dress in relative privacy. But, I dinna think I will be able to reign in the laird. He doesna listen to me."

Then, Ian tickled Elisa again, she shrieked and laughed. Sir Duncan threw back his head and laughed, "I think he listened to exactly what you said you wanted, m' lady." And he turned and walked back among the men.

"Seriously, Ian," Elisa said, "that was so embarrassing. We really should be on our way already. But thank you so much for making me happy again. I will try to nay go back to that bad place again."

"It was my pleasure, love," Ian said.

"Now, dinna move until I tell you." She adjusted her left leg around the outside of his right leg and hooked her toes around the plaid. "Now, lift your right leg." Ian did and Elisa was able to pull the plaid loose from under him. Then, she did the same thing on the other side. Ian was able to escape the plaid without exposing Elisa. He took the cloak and wrapped it around her as she stood up. She wrapped herself in the plaid so she could free her hands to slip on her dress. Then, she slipped the plaid down and cinched her dress strings tight. She put on her boots and her cloak. She packed up while Ian dressed.

As Ian helped Elisa mount, Sir Duncan brought her an apple and a chunk of break. "Thank you, Sir Duncan. Thank you for watching over me and taking care of me. I appreciate it."

Then, everyone was mounted and they set out. Home, Elisa couldna wait to get home. She really missed the children. She would probably barely recognize them. She hoped Malcolm recognized her and remembered her.

"What is wrong, m' lady?" Ian asked.

"I was just thinking of going home, how much I missed it and how much I missed the children. I hope I recognize them. I hope Malcolm remembers me. I canna imagine how big they must be, now," she replied.

"Dinna worry, m' lady; they remember you," Ian chuckled. "How could they forget such a wonderful mother?" He lifted her hand to his lips and kissed her hand. He held it in his for a while.

"Are you sure they wouldna be better off without me, Ian? I seem to bring a lot of trouble to the ones I love so much," Elisa said.

"Aye, I am sure; and you are nay so much trouble, if you would let me help with some of the burden. You will nay longer carry all the responsibility on your wee, little shoulders, m' lady. I am your husband and it is my responsibility now. You will nay go anywhere or do anything without discussing it with me first, except the household chores. I know you had to do it all yourself when your father died, but you are here now and I am here and I am going to help you. So you are just going to have to trust me and let me help you. Do you ken?"

"Aye, m' laird, I ken," Elisa said. "I know you want to help. I am sorry, I am nay used to asking for help or consulting others before making decisions, but I will try harder. I have a matter I need to discuss with you, privately, when you have time after we get home."

"I will find some time for us to talk, m' lady," Ian said, "What else? Something else is bothering you."

"Well, I dinna have a mirror to see what my face looks like and you dinna say anything. You probably warned the men to nay say anything, so just tell me. I need to know."

"It's bruised and a little swollen," he said.

"That isna a good enough description, Ian," she explained. "I canna let the children see my face like this if it is going to scare them."

Ian pulled his sword from its scabbard and held it out in front of her with the shiny, flat surface facing her so she could see herself in the reflection. "Oh, Ian, it's awful. How do you all bare to ride with me?" she cried. She reached up to pull the hood of her cloak up over her head.

"Nay, Elisa," he lowered his voice and spoke to her in a calm, gentle voice as he reached up and pulled the hood off her head. "You will bare it and you willna be embarrassed or ashamed. The people from Edinburgh to Mull will see the violence the king wrought upon you. I am sorry. I should have talked to you about this beforehand. We willna go around any cities or villages, but straight through them. Most of the people already know that I had to go get you from the king because he took you and abused you. They will see firsthand how he treats noble women. It will make them see what he is capable of doing. I willna have to do or say anything against him and the clans will stand together. The people know what we are, Elisa. They know of our noble births and this is how the king treated you, a princess of the realm, and how he disrespected me, a clan laird and a prince. He showed no regard for our marriage vows."

"I willna allow you to blame yourself," Ian continued. "This is all on the king. He took you against your will for you couldna say nay to your king. I know you tried to persuade him otherwise. I know you would have tried to go along with it but you couldna bear to break your marriage vows because your parents taught you never to break your word. He could have chosen another. He dinna have any need to do this, Elisa. In this way, we can get the message across to the people without breaking our allegiance or saying anything against His Majesty. I am sorry for what you will have to go through to bear this, but I will be right beside you. I will hold you if you want me to, but if you can do this as the strong princess I know you are, then I would be the proudest man in all of Scotland."

"I ken, m' laird," Elisa said. "I am sorry, Ian, I shouldna need to have so many things explained to me. I thought I was wise, smarter than this."

"Elisa, dinna be disappointed in yourself," Ian said. "You canna know everything. You expect too much of yourself. Dinna get angry with me, just listen with an open mind and let me explain." She nodded, near tears. "Remember the night I allowed myself to be taken so Sir Duncan could get you and the children safely back to the castle?"

"Aye," Elisa replied.

"Remember, you told Sir Duncan your plan in the tunnel on the way to the castle. Then, Sir Duncan sat at the table discussing the plan with several men."

"Aye, I sat by the fire, focusing on the fire, because I was terrified of what I would have to face."

Ian continued, "Only Sir Duncan and Sir Colin knew you were afraid and that was only because they have known you for so long. You were verra brave to face your enemy, especially when you knew what he was capable of doing. Did you listen to anything said at the table?"

"Nay, I just assumed they were discussing the attack on the men outside the castle."

"Sir Duncan dinna just tell the men what to do, Elisa. They all discussed it together and decided together on the best plan. That is why I told Sir Duncan to listen to what you had to say. For one thing, you had the most knowledge of your cousin's character and about what he would do, how he would act and respond. Secondly, your plan was verra good, so was your knowledge of your opponent. It was verra helpful to the men as they made their plan of attack; it was even more helpful that you were able to get your cousin to tell you how many men were in the camp outside the castle. That was verra clever of you. But, to get back to my point, no one person makes all the decisions alone. Sometimes, it is necessary when there is immediate danger, but otherwise, we discuss things and plan together. Do you ken?"

"Aye," Elisa said, a little cheered up. She dinna have to know everything; she dinna have to do anything alone any more. She had a family, a whole clan, to help her. "Thank you, Ian," she said, smiling.

"Even the king has advisors, Elisa, nay that you can trust their ulterior motives. But, a wise leader listens to advice and tries to make the best decision possible."

"I ken what you are saying. I am sorry, I dinna realize. I dinna have that growing up, raising the children, running the estates. I had to rely on Sir Colin for advice because I was just a child and some things I couldna do myself."

They rode in silence for a while. Elisa ate her bread. She tried to eat the apple but she couldna bite into it because of the pain in her jaw. Elisa dinna think she should try to cut it while she was riding so she was going to put it back in her pocket. She noticed Ian glance at her a couple times. She sighed, took a deep breath, "Ian, will you cut up my apple, please?"

"Aye," he said. He took the apple, cut off a slice and handed it to her.

She rolled her eyes. She tried to bite it but it was too painful to bite into. Elisa handed it back, "Could you do smaller pieces, please."

"I guess this wasna the best idea," Ian teased.

"Nay, asking you for help wasna the best idea," Elisa retorted. She pulled back on her reins and turned Magnum around and rode to the back of the men. She reined in next to Sir Colin, "Please, dinna say anything."

"Aye, m' lady," Sir Colin said and they rode in silence for a several minutes until Elisa realized the men were riding in an unusual manner. She watched their movements for a minute and noticed how they changed their formation around her and Laird Ian.

"Sir Colin, what are the men doing?" she asked.

"They are splitting the formation, half surrounding the laird and half surrounding you, m' lady," Sir Colin answered.

"Why? Did the laird tell them to?" she asked.

"Well, it's their responsibility to do it without being told, but the laird trained them to do this before you arrived. You usually ride with the laird or next to him, so you probably havena noticed before, m' lady."

"I see." She paused. "Thank you for answering my questions, Sir Colin." She tried to be pleasant even though she was seething with anger and hurt pride. It wasna Sir Colin's fault, so there wasna any reason to take it out on him. Besides, it was good practice to behave like a lady even in the worst of circumstances. Although, she felt like she hardly ever succeeded in behaving like a lady. She was always losing her temper with someone.

"Aye, m' lady, you are welcome," Sir Colin replied.

Duncan said, "You are a fool, Ian."

"What did I do?"

"Do you ken how difficult it was for her to swallow her pride and even ask you for help? She hates to ask anyone to do anything for her. Shite, she would cook for the entire castle if it was possible. She already does all the mending for all the men. I dinna even know how she has time to make all the things she makes for all the other members of the clan. She was actually accepting the fact that she has a family, a clan to help her and now, you went and ruined it with your stupid comment."

"I was only teasing her. Is it my fault if she canna see that?"

"Oh, is she well known for joking around and teasing everyone? I canna recall seeing her do that. She threatened me with a training session the two times I brought up the laird's rules. Or do you nay recall that?"

"Aye, I recall it, Duncan. And we used to tease each other."

"Well, she has been gone for a year and had to take care of herself for all that time and she has been through a terrible ordeal that might have killed her. You canna say your flippant comments and expect her to ken that you are only teasing after everything she has suffered."

Elisa noticed several gestures between Ian and Sir Duncan. "Sir Colin, when the laird and his men came to get me the first day, I recall Sir Duncan rode near me most of the time. Why isna he with me now?"

"I believe the laird and Sir Duncan are having a disagreement, Lady Elisa."

"Is Sir Duncan going to be in trouble for defending me?" she asked. "Will he be punished for confronting the laird?"

"Nay, m' lady. Why do you think they are arguing about you?" he asked.

"Watch their heads, they toss their head back this way every once in a while," she answered. "It seems I canna do anything right."

"It will be alright, m' lady. You two will figure it out."

"So many things keep happening that keep coming between us, Sir Colin. And then, I keep making the wrong decision and making it worse," Elisa said. "Was I independent and self-reliant in England or was I deluding myself?"

"You were nay deluding yourself, m' lady. Aye, you are independent and self-reliant, but you dinna need to be here," Sir Colin answered. "You have the members of the clan to help you now. You just need to allow them to help you."

"I ken it now. I just hope I am able to change, to trust him and ask for his help without it hurting my pride so much and making me so irritable."

"Is that what is making you so irritable or is it something else?" Sir Colin asked.

"Besides this sidesaddle?" she asked and chuckled.

"You always hated riding sidesaddle, m' lady."

"Aye, Sir Colin, it is verra uncomfortable and irritating," Elisa replied.

"You ken it's because it was the one thing your parents wouldna let you do like a man," Sir Colin advised.

"Aye, that is irritating," Elisa laughed. "You are right, Sir Colin, and that is irritating too. I dinna like to be wrong or weak or to ask for help; I feel like it's a sign of weakness. I guess it is going to take a while for me to adjust."

She rode in silence while she thought about what Ian said about the clan helping each other. She could ask for help. She could ask others for advice and then decide what she should do. She wasna alone and she dinna have to do everything alone. She dinna need to know everything. She thought about what she and Sir Colin talked about too.

The problem was that she dinna want or need anyone's help because she could do most things herself. She liked things done her way and she got frustrated and annoyed when she explained things to someone and they dinna ken or do it her way; besides, it was easier to just do it herself than to try to explain it to someone else. She could usually get it done in the time it took to explain it to someone else. In addition, she dinna feel she should ask others to do something when she was just as capable of doing it. She wouldna ask others to do something she wasna willing to do.

She still couldna ken why her parents would raise her the way they did, to do everything herself, even what others would consider to be the lowliest job, if she was possibly expected to be the queen one day. It dinna make any sense to her. She must have missed a great deal in her education and in her memories to nay ken this.

She searched her most recent memories from when they were at the loch and she saw the letters from Lady Isobel to her mother and her. She tried to see the words on the page. The pages looked like they had been stacked in someone's hand and then dropped onto the ground. Most of the pages were fanned out and she could read at least part of each page. She tried to see the words, but they seemed to be too far away to read. On one page, she caught what looked like a family tree. Ian and Isobel were listed and next to them was her mother and father and next to that was Dan, but she couldna read the rest of the page. Below Ian and Isobel was Ian and she wasna certain but it looked like Duncan and then a letter F. She couldna make out the rest of the name. It dinna make any sense to her so she tried to read some of the pages, but the words were too far away to really make them out.

She let the memory fade and focused on her current surroundings again. She dinna need to exhaust herself looking at the memories, especially if it wasna going to make any sense to her. She dinna have anyone to ask to help her clarify what she saw. She was raised to believe Duncan was Ian's cousin and the page with the family tree would imply that Duncan was Ian's brother and that he had another sibling as well, whose name started with an F. She dinna ken why that would be kept a secret from her or why someone should try to mislead her and deceive her into believing Duncan was a cousin rather than a brother. Again, she had the distinct impression she hadna followed the prearranged plan.

She knew it was her fault that she dinna figure it out correctly or in the right time or order; but, she dinna ken how her parents could expect such a thing from her when they gave her all the clues jumbled up in a pile of pieces when she was just a toddler until she was about seven years old. She loved the challenge of figuring it all out, but it was really too much to expect from such a little girl. Realizing that she made a mistake and nay followed the plan dinna help her mood any. She dinna like to be wrong. She knew it would result in negative consequences.

Besides, she had just been happy with Ian this morning and now they were upset with each other again. She knew he expected her to trust him and rely on him, but her whole life was about nay relying on anyone, nay trusting anyone. She was alone and she felt that she was supposed to be alone and nay trust anyone or rely on anyone. It was so confusing and she dinna know how to resolve the issue.

Chapter 19

By the time Sir Duncan joined her in the rear of the procession, Elisa's back was throbbing. She dinna want to stop because they stopped so early yesterday because of her. She rode in silence and tried to endure the pain without letting anyone know that she was in pain. It wasna long before her back was tight and aching. Her leg was falling asleep and twitching. After a while, she tried to roll her shoulders forwards and backwards to try to loosen up the muscles. When that dinna work, she ground her teeth together and clenched her jaw tightly shut, forgetting about her injury. She groaned. Sir Duncan and Sir Colin noticed immediately and called a halt to the procession.

"I dinna ask you to stop," she said.

"Nay, m' lady, but you are obviously in pain and shouldna continue riding for now." Sir Duncan said. "You need to stretch and walk around a bit."

"Nay, what I need is my saddle, not this contraption that men designed just to torture women."

"Aye, m' lady. Let me assist you to the ground," Sir Duncan replied. He kept his laughter and his thoughts to himself. He needed to be verra careful of his actions considering his current mood. He was upset with Ian for hurting her feelings and he was beyond angry with the king for the way he treated Elisa, but he couldna discuss that with anyone except Ian and that could only be done in private and they dinna have any privacy right now. The most important thing was to keep Elisa safe until they were home on Mull and inside the castle.

"Thank you, Sir Duncan," Lady Elisa said. He dismounted quickly and stood beside Lady Elisa. He helped her get her right foot from the stirrup and over the horn that her right leg was hooked into. She grabbed her skirt and tried to gather it all together so it wouldna catch on the saddle. She freed her left leg from its stirrup. "I am ready, Sir Duncan," she said.

Sir Duncan lifted her to the ground and held on to her until she shook some blood back into her right leg. She clenched her jaw shut from the tingling pain as the blood flow returned. Once Lady Elisa could stand on her own, Sir Duncan released her and offered her his arm and escorted her on a walk.

"Dinna you need to take care of your horse?" Lady Elisa asked Sir Duncan.

"Nay, m' lady, Sir Colin will take care of our horses," he answered.

It irritated Elisa to be a burden to others, especially since she was perfectly capable of taking care of her horse herself. "Sir Duncan, I need a tree to hide behind." He walked her to a tree a little ways away from everyone, but where they were still visible and nay entirely alone. He ensured that he wasna too close to Elisa and that he could be seen by the men at all times. She stood behind the tree and bent over to touch her toes, so she could stretch her back. Then, she asked him if he would lift her up so she could grab a branch and hang from it. It helped to relieve the tension in her neck and shoulders and back. "Is there a river nearby, Sir Duncan?"

"Nay, Lady Elisa, and you canna go in the water, anyway. It's too cold. The snow melting makes the rivers verra cold and the rivers are overflowing with all the snow melting in the highland mountains and draining into them. They are moving verra fast and anyone would be swept away and drowned."

After a few minutes, Sir Duncan warned her, "Do you want down, m' lady? The laird is on his way over here."

"What does his face look like?" she asked.

"Irritated," he said.

"Aye, you better lift me down, then," she replied. Sir Duncan quickly lifted her to the ground and stepped back.

Ian asked, "What are you two doing?"

"I needed to stretch, m' laird and I needed privacy to do it," Elisa answered.

"Are you done stretching and ready to set out again?" Ian asked.

"Aye, m' laird."

"And are you hungry, since you couldna eat the apple?"

"Aye, a little, but I will be fine for a while."

"Elisa, you dinna have to go without or suffer. We can take our time, so you can have what you need and you need to eat. You need to rest. And I guess, you need to stretch too."

"I am sorry, Ian, I just agree with Sir Duncan that we should get some distance between us and Edinburgh. I would feel much safer if we were home," she said. "I ken why you put the sidesaddle on Magnum, but I hate riding sidesaddle. My parents refused to let me ride any other way; so when they both died, I quit riding sidesaddle. So, I am nay used to sitting that way. Also, while I was in Edinburgh, I was mostly confined to my room, except to go to the kitchen to eat or to go to the laundry to wash my clothes. I dinna get much exercise, except to walk in the garden for a short time each morning before others were about."

"Aye, I ken. I will adjust our schedule. I am sorry about earlier, Elisa. I just wanted to tease you like we used to tease each other."

"I dinna want to talk about this right now, Ian. All I can tell you is I am irritable, everything is irritating me, even Sir Colin and I never get upset with him," Elisa said. "I dinna ken why; so you are just going to have to give me some time."

"Aye, I will try, Elisa. Do you want to ride with me for a while, so you can rest and then you can ride Magnum through Glasgow? We will rest again after we get through Glasgow."

"We will see. For now, will you lift me back up to the branch?" Elisa asked as she turned around with her back to him. Ian helped her up so she could reach the branch. He kept his hands on her waist in case she slipped off. "Ian, would you press your thumbs into the muscles where your thumbs are and make little circles?" she asked.

"Like this?" he asked. He made little circles with his thumbs in her lower back and gradually made the circles bigger.

"Aye, but press harder," she answered. "Just press hard and I will tell you when it is too much pressure."

"Your muscles are verra tight, m' love," Ian said. He continued to rub her lower back. He worked from the center of the circle outward making a bigger circle and then started inward. Then, he focused on her dimples.

"I know, but we dinna have the time it would take to make them relax. So, I will take what I can get for now."

"Is there anywhere else that you would like massaged?" he asked. He could think of several places he wouldna mind massaging. He already had a plan and all she had to do was cooperate, he grinned to himself.

"Are you certain we have time?" she asked, "because my right thigh fell asleep and it would feel wonderful if you rubbed it and helped to get the blood to flow again."

"Can you hold yourself up in the tree?" She was cooperating perfectly with his plan now that she agreed to let him massage her. He was verra clever every once in a while. Nay as clever as she was, but she probably wouldna be suspecting what he planned either, because she apparently dinna think about these things, at least nay the way he did. He dinna want to keep his hands off her. She was his wife. How could he nay want her when she was gone for a year. Besides, he had a pretty good idea what she suffered to protect him and his clan and that made him love her and want her all the more.

"Aye, Ian, my arms are strong enough to hang onto the branch while you massage my thigh."

Ian released her waist and moved to stand in front of her and gently massaged her where she said she needed better blood flow.

"Ian," she moaned.

"Hmm," he asked.

"Dinna blame me if I cry out," she said.

"It is only a massage and nothing more, Elisa," he said, but he couldna contain the grin on his face.

"It isna just a massage and you ken it verra well. You know exactly what you are doing, Ian." She couldna help her response. She felt like her body was a strumming, vibrating instrument.

"Are you slipping off the branch?" he asked, unsure with all her squirming.

"Nay, m' love, I am nay slipping off the branch. You are causing this response and you ken it well enough," she answered him in a husky voice.

"Does it hurt if I do this?" he asked as he adjusted his hand.

"Ian, you better catch me before I fall," she said.

Ian grabbed her behind both legs and held his other arm out for her to slip down into. "Just let go and I'll catch you."

She had to learn to trust him, so she said, "Ready," and let go. Ian caught her shoulders in his arm and drew her towards him. She put her arms around his shoulders and hugged him. She turned his head towards her and kissed him. "Thank you, Ian. That was wonderful, but you were supposed to give me a massage to relax my thigh muscles, nay make me all tense."

Ian just chuckled, "I will try to do better, next time."

"I just bet you will," Elisa said and she laughed too. She kissed him again and then she said, "We better get going. If you will behave yourself, I will ride with you." She winked at him.

Ian started to carry her back to the horses and she let him. At the moment, she was too happy to care what anyone thought. Ian whispered in her ear, "Now, if you get irritable again, just let me know and I will hang you in a tree again and I will massage away all your tension, m' love."

She turned his head forward so she could whisper in his ear, "Fine, but I may fight back." And she stuck her tongue in his ear and trailed it over the curves, then she pulled her tongue back in and blew her hot breath in his ear.

"Careful, I may drop you," Ian responded.

"Nay, I trust you willna drop me. You might throw me to the ground and pounce on me and take advantage of me here in front of all your men; but you willna drop me. I trust you," she taunted him. She intended to tease him until he forced her to ride her own horse through Glasgow.

Ian set Elisa down and mounted his horse. "Let me use your stirrup, Ian," Elisa said. She lifted her right foot instead of her left into the stirrup and straddled the horse backwards, her skirt covering the horses head. Some of the men laughed and Elisa couldna help but laugh too.

"Elisa," Ian started to complain, uncomfortable with the men teasing them. He dinna want them to embarrass her.

"Shh, Ian, ignore your men for a minute. Look at my face and tell me what you see?' she asked him.

"Besides the bruises, your eyes are brighter, the sparkle is back and you are smiling."

"Aye, and why do you suppose that is?" she asked.

"Because you are getting even with me for earlier?" he responded.

She kept her voice low, so hopefully only he would hear her, "Nay, Ian. I have been smiling since you lifted me into the tree, because you make me happy, your touch brings me pleasure. You make me forget the nightmare.

And I dinna care what they think or say, because you can make me happy again. Besides, you can punish them for their impudent comments in your next training session."

"I ken, but you canna ride like this, Elisa," he said, all serious business.

Elisa dismounted and remounted so she was sitting across his lap. "Besides, I said I would ride with you if you behaved. I havena any intention of behaving myself until we reach Glasgow. And, I did say I may fight back," she said with a sideways glance at him and they both laughed. "If you are good, I will show you a secret," she said so only he could hear, and then, they set out for Glasgow.

Elisa put one arm around Ian's waist so she could massage his back as he massaged hers while she hung in the tree. She put her other arm around his neck and played with his hair. She ran her fingers down the center of his neck. She kissed his neck and chin.

"Elisa, you canna do this all the way to Glasgow for two hours," Ian said.

"Nay? Why not?" she asked.

"For one, you will make me crazy; and two, because you will make us fall off the horse," Ian answered.

"I told you, Ian, I trust you. I know you willna drop me," she smiled at him innocently.

"If you continue, Elisa, I willna be able to control the end result," he informed her.

"Dinna worry, m' love. I will be in control."

"Aye, that is what you want. You want to be in control because you dinna want to listen to me. You are too independent and stubborn." He shouldna have said what he was thinking. He realized too late that she wouldna appreciate his comments, but why did she have to push him so much, drive him to distraction?

"Are you really angry, Ian? Do you want me to stop? Do you really think your men think less of you because you love your wife?" she asked.

"Nay, I am nay angry. I just canna do as I want. So, nay, I dinna want you to stop, but we have to. As for the men, I dinna want them to be disrespectful to you; but mostly, I ken they just say those things to tease me, but it's because they are happy for me and because they know I am happy."

Elisa laid her head on Ian's shoulder and wrapped both her arms around his waist and hugged him. "I love you, Ian. Thank you for coming to get me and for making me happy again." His comment dampened her mood, but she was still happy to be in his embrace.

"Aye, Elisa, I love you, too, and I am verra glad you are happy again. But," Ian began.

Elisa interrupted, "Ian, dinna say it. I am nay going to face that until we get home. I need this happiness now so I can survive facing that demon later." She shoved his left hand up as she kicked his horse and pushed away and slid off Ian while he struggled to control his horse. He couldna grab her and control the horse at the same time. She ran to the rear where Sir Colin had her horse.

"I can do it, Sir Colin." Sir Colin tossed her the reins. She wrapped the rein around the horn, made a long loop and wrapped the end of the rein around the horn again. This gave her a step to get up into the stirrup. "Dinna move, Magnum," she told her horse and he stood still while she mounted. She stepped up into the loop with her right foot and stood on her left foot in the long stirrup while she fixed the reins. Then, she sat in the saddle and hooked her right leg into place and put her right foot into the short stirrup. She was ready to ride shortly after Ian got Talon under control.

Sir Duncan reined in beside Elisa. "You dinna say anything this time, did you?" Elisa asked Sir Duncan.

"Nay, m' lady, I think the look I shot him was enough. Then, I shrugged and followed you," he answered. "That was verra clever how you used your reins to mount Magnum."

"When a lady doesna always have a man to help her, she has to be clever enough to overcome every situation. Magnum is such a good horse thanks to Sir Colin's train-ing. He is verra patient with his rider," Elisa said, patting Magnum's neck. "You know what I miss, Sir Colin? I miss hunting for our breakfast every morning like I did on our ride from London to Scotland." She couldna kill the one she wanted to kill because she knew it was a sin, even her thoughts were a sin; so, she asked her heavenly Father to for-give her and to help stop having such thoughts. Also, to help her recover from what she suffered and endured. She asked Him to show her that her perseverance had some purpose.

Elisa sat her own horse until they were through Glasgow. Ian found a place to rest after they were away from the city as he said he would. Elisa let Sir Duncan lift her down. Then, she turned back to Magnum and pet-ted him. She asked Sir Colin for a brush and she brushed Magnum out as much as she could. She dinna know if there was time to remove his saddle, but Sir Colin told her to go ahead. So she removed the saddle and brushed him until he was dry. Then, she saddled him again. Sir Colin checked to ensure the saddle was tight enough. "You have learned well, m' lady. Well done."

"Thank you, Sir Colin, I had the best teacher. I couldna have done much growing up without your help. I am sorry you had to miss all this," she waved her hand over the land, "to be my protector. But I shall never be sorry to have such a dear friend and teacher. I know I can never hope to repay you for all you have done, especially, for helping me escape from London." She gave Sir Colin a hug.

Elisa tied two plaids to her horse and Sir Colin's horse, creating an enclosure between the horses. She opened her saddle pack and slid on her breeches under her dress. Then, she removed her dress and put on the top. She put on her dress and boots again. She added a dagger to her waist. She put on her cloak again and untied the plaids, folded them, and returned them to her saddle pack. She mounted Magnum and ate while she waited for everyone else to mount up.

Sir Colin pulled Sir Duncan aside, out of Elisa's hearing, "Did you hear her comments to me?"

"Aye, that was a little strange."

"Aye, more than a little strange. I think we should double her guard without her knowing. I am worried about her. I think she is going to try something."

"She has been asking about water nearby to go swimming or more likely to bathe. Ian told her the water would be too cold this time of year and too full with all the winter snow melting. You dinna think she will try to jump in a river?" Sir Duncan asked.

"Aye," Sir Colin answered, "I think that is exactly what she will try to do. Do you ken why? Can you see?"

"I think I ken," Sir Duncan replied, "she has been running the gauntlet with her emotions, verra irritable one minute, calm and plotting the next, then happy as can be with Ian, until he messes up her good mood with his bossing her around. This is how women are when they are with child."

Sir Coin asked, "Wouldna it be too soon to tell?"

"Nay, not if you have the sight and healing gifts that she has. She could've known when it happened, especially since she has already been pregnant with the laird's child and also the circumstances of her captivity and the nightmare, as she calls it."

"I definitely think we need to double the watch without her realizing. Should we say anything to Laird Ian?"

"I will take responsibility for her, Sir Colin. I am nay going to tell him so he can boss her around. It will push her right over the bridge. She will jump for sure, then. I will try to see without her knowing, but she is too clever and observant for that to work. It may be best to just talk to her, but I am nay sure we have the time right now. She is already mounted and we have been here long enough."

"Well, try now. I will try to keep Ian away. Go for a walk quickly before everyone mounts," Sir Colin said to Sir Duncan.

Sir Duncan returned to Lady Elisa, "M' lady, would you take a walk with me. I would like to ask a favor of you."

"Verra unusual, Sir Duncan," she replied. "Willna Laird Ian be angry if we delay our start?"

"M' laird is going to be angry nay matter what happens today."

"I dinna ken?"

"Dinna you?" he asked. He lifted her down from her horse again. Then, they moved into the open but away from everyone's hearing. He turned to face her, placing his hand on her arm to stop her and to get her to turn towards him. "Do you know if you are with child or nay, Lady Elisa?"

"Aye, I think so," she answered, shocked anyone had figured it out. "How did you know?"

"Sir Colin and I are concerned about your overly gracious comments to him; it was verra out of character for you. And, your moods are changing rather frequently. We are concerned you might try to take your life, you have been asking about the rivers. Do you intend to throw yourself in and try to drown yourself? Do you think the cold water will end the pregnancy?"

"Aye, I hoped to end the pregnancy. I canna explain the pain and grief this is causing me," she sobbed.

"Will you allow me to see?"

"I canna. I have to talk to Ian first. He will feel betrayed if I show you first. You know how he reacted the last time. I dinna want Ian to know until we are home on Mull. I fear he will return to Edinburgh and try to kill the king. Then, I will lose him. I canna lose him or I willna be able to survive this. I need him even if I dinna want to need him or anyone else," she pleaded with Sir Duncan.

"I ken, but then I need your word you willna do anything to harm yourself or the child until you let me see, Lady Elisa."

"I promise I willna hurt myself until we reach Mull," Elisa said.

"That isna what I said," Sir Duncan protested.

"Well, that is the promise you are getting, Sir Duncan," she snapped at him. Then, she turned to walk back to her horse.

Sir Duncan grabbed her arm, "I am sorry, m' lady. I dinna mean to upset you further; but, you ken it's my responsibility to protect you, even if it's from yourself." He quickly looked to see the future, while she was angry and distracted, hoping she wouldna realize. When he released her, she returned to Magnum and mounted.

Sir Duncan returned to Sir Colin, "She thinks she is and she was hoping the icy water would end the child's life. She willna let me look until she lets Ian see because she doesna want to betray him. She promised to nay harm herself until we reach Mull. We have to cross plenty of water after we reach Mull. I will force her to show Ian before we get to Mull if I can find an opportunity to do so. I willna let you do anything to betray her, Sir Colin. I will take full responsibility. She needs to trust you and the laird. You are the only faith she has in her childhood. You are the only one who was there for her, protected her, and helped her. She trusts you. If you betray her, she will have nay faith in anything, nay trust in anyone. She needs the laird to survive this; he has to find a way to be what she needs him to be. I dinna think I can help with that."

"You have feelings for Lady Elisa, dinna you, Duncan?"

"Aye, Colin, I have since the first summer she came to Mull. I dinna ken how I could feel for her as I do since I was three, nearly four, and since she was only a few months old. But, she is married to my brother and laird and has been since that same summer. My feelings for her havena changed in all this time, so I dinna think they will ever change. But, I canna act on my feelings; I wouldna want to hurt Ian or Lady Elisa. You must keep this between us. Ian knows. He has known since we were ten, her last summer on Mull. After she left for London, I rode down to the loch and cried for a long time because I knew she wouldna return to Mull for a long time. Ian followed me to the loch and he touched me and saw my thoughts before I realized he was there. I was worried that it would cause a problem and we would grow apart, but it has actually drawn us closer. Something happened when he touched me and saw my feelings; we can sense each other more closely. We hardly ever have to speak to each other because we usually know what the other is thinking."

"This situation must be verra difficult for you to see them together," Sir Colin said. "I am sure you want them to be happy, but that must be hurting you. But then, when they are nay happy, you know it is hurting them and that hurts you too. It must be verra confusing and frustrating. I am sorry that you have to deal with this situation. You can speak to me anytime you need someone to talk to Duncan. I ken what you are going through." Colin smiled at Duncan, "I asked Chief Ian to send me to London. Everyone thinks he sent me to protect Elisa and that I have missed Scotland to be her protector. But the truth is that I had to go before I did something I would verra much regret later. I felt for Alice as you feel for Lady Elisa, but I knew that she cared for my brother, Angus. I dinna want to spend my life watching them together, seeing their happiness and knowing I wouldna ever have that because I knew I wouldna marry if I couldna be with Alice. She was the only woman I was ever going to marry. So I ken what you are going through and if you ever wish to talk, I will do my best to listen. I am nay sure I have any advice for you, but at least you know that there is another who kens with what you are dealing."

"Thank you for telling me this, Colin. I appreciate it and I will keep it in mind. I just might spend a lot more time in the stable than the training field, if you are certain you dinna mind."

"I willna mind, Duncan. I am verra good at burying myself in my work until I get over what ails me." The two men shook hands and clasped each other on the shoulder. Then, they returned to their horses.

The men mounted their horses, one on each side of Lady Elisa. She dinna want to see them or talk to them. She just wanted to be alone, but she knew that wouldna happen. They would watch her closely now and even more so once they reached Mull. Elisa was beyond irritated. Hopefully, they just had a few more days to ride. Soon, they would be home. She could lock herself in the tower room and have some privacy. So she continued to ride in silence.

She let her thoughts stray to her memories and tried to figure out what was in the plan that she was missing, what she was doing wrong. She dinna have to watch where she was going because the guards were riding so close to her that she couldna fall off her horse even if she wanted to or tried to. She sat up straight and stared straight ahead as if nothing was wrong. That was what her parents expected her to do, continue on as if nothing was wrong. Dinna let anyone in to see the real her. She focused on a small focal point on the back of the person in front of her and let her memories flow through her mind trying to see what she was supposed to do to get to Mull. All she could see was the memories of her childhood when her parents rode in a carriage from London to Mull. They repeatedly told her to try to sleep so she wouldna be tired when they reached Mull. She lowered her eyelids, but dinna close them, so she could continue to look out the window and watch the countryside. She recalled the people as they passed them. She could feel what they felt and she smiled at them and wished they were well.

She realized now, that was her gift of sight sensing their ailments and her body was sending its energy out to them to try to heal them. She heard her parents whispering when they thought she was asleep, so she tried to sense what they were saying, but they only spoke in whispers and she couldna really hear the words clearly, but she continued to listen. Mayhap, she would learn something useful.

At one point in her parents' conversation, their voices were a little louder and she heard her mother say, "I think you enjoy this just a bit more than you should."

"I enjoy it a bit much? Are you kidding me? She is your child and you dinna seem to have any qualms about what you do to her," her father replied.

"I dinna have a choice. Isobel expects it to make up for what I did with," her voice trailed off.

"Ian," her father finished her mother's sentence and turned to look out the window.

"She told me I had to do that so she would have the right bloodlines. This has been her plan all along. She wanted you to marry me from the beginning. Then, she convinced me that being with him was the only way to produce the necessary bloodlines. I am sorry. I dinna know how many times I can say I am sorry. I would do anything to make things better between us, just tell what to do and I will do it."

"There isna anything you can do now. It is what it is. It's a complete mess now and nothing can be done to fix it. I love Isobel and Isobel loves Daniel and Daniel loves her. He wouldna marry Isobel, even after he got her with child and he convinced Ian to marry her because he knew Ian loved Isobel. Apparently, Daniel dinna realize my feelings for Isobel or mayhap, I dinna have enough credentials for Isobel. If she canna be queen, at least she can be the wife of the Chieftain of the Highlands; or mayhap, she dinna want to be sent away to London. If I had to raise someone's bastard, I would have preferred that it was Isobel's; but nay, that wasna the plan. So nay, there isna anything you can do to fix this situation now. Damn you and Isobel for your plans and schemes. But since I have to raise your bastard child, I am going to make damn sure she can do everything to provide for me when she is old enough and capable of doing so. And you are nay going to complain about what methods I use to train her up because you forced this on us with your scheming with Isobel. Now, move away and stay on your side of the carriage or I will rent a horse at the next inn and you can pay for it out of your money. Leave me in peace."

Elisa was shocked by their conversation, but it explained why her father had been so diligent at training her to run everything and also why he beat her. It explained why she was expected to do so much for herself and why he provided for Ian and Elsbeth and nay for her, why he left her to fend for herself, why he dinna care what his nephew did to her.

From the sounds of it, Chief Ian was her father, but she couldna be certain from their conversation, but that was what it sounded like her father was saying. It also sounded like her father was saying that Ian was Isobel's son and someone named Daniel. That might be who the Dan was on the document with the family tree. She wasna certain and she certainly couldna go to Chief Ian and ask him to explain it. It certainly wasna her place to question the Chieftain of the Highlands.

What dinna make sense was that her father said Isobel loved Daniel and Daniel loved her, but then Daniel wouldna marry Isobel. It dinna make any sense. If he loved her, why dinna he marry her, even after he got her with child? Why would he have her marry Ian if he knew she was carrying his child? She hated her parents and all their secrets. She apparently wasna as smart as they thought she should be and she certainly wasna capable of figuring out all of this mess, nay when they gave her only little clips of memories and nay in any order. They were expecting too much from her.

She continued to ride in silence and think about this new information. She tried to think about the black box in her mind so that no one would know what she was thinking about. She hoped they couldna sense her thoughts.

Several of her childhood memories crashed through her thoughts, but they were mostly of her training and the testing and the punishment and none of it helped to explain anything anymore than what she already knew. She did her best to keep her composure and nay cry during the memories. She dinna want anyone to know what she was going through. She recalled her thoughts while she was in Edinburgh that she was supposed to be alone and suffer alone.

So she dinna think she wanted the guards around her to sense her thoughts. She kept the image of the black box in her mind and hoped that was what they saw if they tried to sense her thoughts. She reviewed her memories in a small corner of her mind.

She had the distinct impression that she still hadna followed the plan correctly and then to top it off, she felt she was supposed to be alone, suffer alone. She was so confused and frustrated. Realizing that she did something wrong only added to her anxiety and confusion. She hated to be wrong because she knew that meant there would be some form of punishment.

When they stopped for a break, she tried to box up all her thoughts and bury them for now. The last thing she needed was Sir Duncan sensing her thoughts while he helped her.

Chapter 20

EVENTUALLY, THEY STOPPED for the night. Elisa took care of Magnum first. Then, she prepared a fire and started to make something for everyone to eat. She took some of the bread and crumbled it up. She sliced some apples and cooked them with the bread and some sugar and water to make a cobbler. She sliced more apples and some onions and meat and cooked it all together. It wasna great, but it was something to eat.

Elisa made sure everyone had food before she ate. She did eat a small portion of apples, onions, and meat. Then, she cleaned up the dishes and added more wood to the fire. No one stopped her from working; they just watched her or helped her gather wood, which was really just an excuse to watch her closely. She wasna stupid or ignorant of what was going on around her, but she chose to ignore them and let them believe she dinna ken.

Elisa knew she had to call it a night soon, or Ian would hunt her down and drag her off to bed. She would have liked to help with the watch, but she knew Ian wouldna allow it. She could ask, but it would require more than one word answers and she wasna willing to go that far. So she went to check on Magnum. Then, she picked up her bedroll.

She placed her bedroll by the fire and lay down facing the fire. She watched the fire until Ian approached. He whispered her name as he came near her. "You dinna have to announce your presence to me anymore, Ian. I ken when you are there," she whispered to him. Ian snuggled up to her and wrapped his arms around her; he laid one leg over hers. He draped his plaid over them.

Elisa slept soundly for her usual three hours safe in Ian's arms. She was able to wake herself from the nightmare without waking the whole camp. She took several deep breaths to calm herself. She focused on the fire, which always calmed her. Elisa visualized stomping the dust from her sandals, as the Scriptures said to do when you werena received and you couldna convince the people to receive the message. She knew the Scripture referred to trying to persuade others to receive Jesus as their Lord and Savior, but if she couldna convince the king that stealing her from her husband and forcing her to be his mistress, and raping her, was wrong; then, she certainly wouldna be able to convince him to accept the Lord. May he never have a good night's rest; let his enemies be at his court all day long, hounding him from every direction. But mostly, she wished he would marry that woman and she would bear him a dozen children, all strapping boys; so he would never need to come to Mull.

When she became fitful from trying to lay still too long, she gently rolled towards Ian knowing he would roll onto his back. Then, she waited until he was snoring again and she escaped his grasp. She rolled up her bedroll along Ian's side so he would roll towards it thinking it was her. Then, he wouldna snore so loudly.

Elisa sat watching the fire, but what she really wanted was to go hunting, to do her training, resume her normal life before kings tried so desperately to control her. She hated the mess they made of the past two years of her life. More, really, counting all the time since her mother was killed birthing her brother. She hated that she couldna trust others. Sir Colin seemed to be the only one who seemed to be her friend, even if it was his duty. He gave up his life and home in Scotland to come take care of her in England. She was glad she thought to have the solicitor set aside money to ensure his provision. He would have been such a sweet and gentle husband, a patient father. But because of his responsibility and duty to her, he was robbed of that opportunity.

As she watched the fire, she occasionally caught a glimpse of a shadow moving within the camp. She tried to focus on the movement. She realized it was an animal and it was moving closer. She pulled her dagger from its leather sheath. She dinna think she could get her sword out of the scabbard without waking the camp. "Ian," she said in a low tone, but got no response. She whispered to him, "Ian, an animal is in camp and it's coming this way." He still dinna respond. Now, she was getting angry; they were supposed to protect her, she mumbled to herself.

"Shh, Elisa, listen carefully," Ian whispered to her. "Do exactly what I tell you. Take several deep breaths and let them out slowly. Hold your dagger with both hands; rest it along your left thigh with the tip up but be sure it isna caught in your dress. Now, slowly and quietly lower your right knee to the side. The boar is coming in from your left. If he charges at you jab the dagger up into his stomach as hard as you can. His momentum will push you backwards. Try to use the momentum to roll to your right and roll on top of him. Then, slit his throat. I have your back if you need it, but I think you can do this."

She did just as he said. It happened just like he described. They dragged the carcass away from camp and dug a hole for the waste. She immediately started gutting and skinning the boar. "What should I do with all the innards?" she asked Ian. Elisa set aside the heart, liver, stomach and intestines, as Ian instructed her. Then, she skinned the boar and laid the skin out to dry. She started cutting up the meat so it could be cooked. It would cook faster if it was cut smaller.

She asked Ian to add all the wood to the fire, so it could burn down and she would have a lot of really hot coals to cook on. When all the meat was prepared and cooking, Ian brought a satchel of Elisa's clothes and escorted her to a nearby stream so she could clean up. Ian instructed her to bring the stomach and the intestines so they could be washed in the stream, as well. These would be used to pack some of the meat in.

Elisa was verra happy to finally be allowed to bathe. Ian dinna want her in the water because it was so cold, but she dinna think it would hurt her, but she wouldna care if it caused her to lose the king's child that she suspected grew in her womb. She couldna bear to think about what he'd done or what he expected her to do with the consequences of their actions. When they reached the stream, she laid out the stomach and intestines. Then she removed her clothes and waded in the water until it was mid-thigh. She dug her feet into the bottom of the stream and knelt down and scrubbed herself clean, she washed out her hair and wrung it out. She took her time washing so she could stay in the cold water until she was numb from the waist down. But, she had a feeling of being watched; so she quickly dressed and washed out her dress. She laid it out to dry.

She took the stomach and intestines out into the water so they could be washed out by the flow of the water running through it. She held it tightly so it wouldna slip away. Her hands and feet were numb from the cold water. After she let the water flow through the intestines for a while, she draped it back and forth over her arms so she could keep it up off the ground and clean as they walked back to camp. The camp was awake and busy preparing to pack up. She hoped this would be their last day before they reached Mull.

Elisa laid her dress out near the fire to dry. Then, she returned to cooking the meat. She mashed some of the meat with bread and seasoning and stuffed it in the intestines. Then, she cooked it in a pan and then set most of it aside for their supper.

The men had a hearty breakfast. The camp was cleaned up and they continued on their journey home. Elisa was grateful for the breeches, and her regular saddle was a relief. She was glad to be on the move again. The feeling of being watched was still there. She whispered her concern to Ian and Sir Duncan. They both confirmed her feeling; they had the same feeling of being watched. She hoped Ian would pick up the pace. She was anxious now and she just wanted to reach Mull. They rode for a couple hours and rested the horses before they mounted again. Then, when the horses needed to rest again, they found a clearing to stop for lunch. They took a little longer break so the horses would be well rested. Then, they rode in two hour increments and rested the horses, until it was dark. Finally, they stopped for the night and Ian and Duncan supervised the guard schedule and the setup of camp.

Elisa busied herself with caring for Magnum first and then making dinner at the campfire for everyone. She dinna gather wood because she was too afraid to be away from the fire. She wanted to be certain the guards surrounded her as much as possible, especially after the comment Cousin Ken said about Milliner still wanting her, mayhap more than her cousin did, came to her mind. She dinna want to be abducted by that fiend. He wouldna treat her any better than her cousin or the king. After she cleaned up the dishes from dinner, she set up her bedroll by the fire and lay down. She watched the flames and tried to calm down.

Ian assigned a number of men to sit around the fire as an extra precaution while some of the men slept. Then, they would rotate positions and sleep while the men who just slept watched the perimeter. The perimeter men would move closer to the fire. They would rotate one more time before the morning to ensure everyone got a couple hours of sleep.

Ian, Sir Duncan, and Sir Colin each took a watch near Elisa to ensure that she was closely watched and kept safe. Ian knew that even if they were sleeping, they would be close enough to protect her if she was in any danger during the night. No one would be able to slip into the camp and get that close to the fire to get to her.

Elisa had a difficult time falling asleep, but she watched the fire until she finally dozed off. She vaguely recalled Ian's presence at her back for the couple hours that she slept. She watched the fire again after he rose and took his next watch. She was grateful when the sky turned gray and everyone rose from their bedrolls and ate a quick breakfast before they saddled their horses and mounted before the sun breached the horizon.

They followed the same riding schedule as the day before; they rode two hours, rested the horses and mounted again.

In the early afternoon, she could feel they were being watched with a much stronger presence. She was verra worried for their safety and she became more afraid as the afternoon continued. Finally, she reached out to Ian to share her concerns with him. "Ian, I am scared," she whispered to Ian.

"It will be alright, m' sweet wife. "We are almost there," Ian whispered back. She noticed the men closing ranks around her as they started to gallop. She was happy to ride faster.

Elisa saw the arrow coming towards her in her mind. She gathered a length of the reins and put it in her mouth. She reached out to grab the arrow just before she felt the sharp pain in her left thigh. She prevented the arrow from going in too deep. She whispered to Sir Duncan, "Exactly how much farther?"

"Over one more rise and down to the beach and across the sand bar," he whispered back.

"Pull it out," she said and she bit down hard on her reins.

"Dinna cry out to Ian, Lady Elisa," Sir Duncan replied.

"I willna; m' laird has to protect the clan now," she replied. She turned to Sir Colin and gripped his hand as tightly as she could. It took every bit of her strength to nay cry out from the pain as Sir Duncan wrenched the arrow from her leg. Then, Lady Elisa covered the wound with her hand and took several deep breaths to calm down and to try to control the pain. She told Sir Colin, "Take Magnum's reins when we cross the sandbar and dinna stop until we reach the castle." Lady Elisa turned to Sir Duncan, "Please, dinna cross over without me."

"I willna, m' lady. You will follow Sir Colin and I will follow you. I willna cross over until you are across."

Lady Elisa was still biting the reins when they reached the sandbar and Sir Colin had to pry them out of her mouth. She held the pummel of her saddle with one hand and applied pressure to her leg with the other hand. She glanced down to ensure her cloak covered her leg so Ian couldna see the blood pouring out of her wound. She pulled her cloak tighter around her and reapplied pressure to the wound. Sir Colin led her horse across the sand bar and Sir Duncan wasna far behind.

Ian and half the men were set up on the beach and turned back towards the hill she had just come down. Ian saw Elisa cross and whispered to her, "M' lady, are you alright? What happened?"

Elisa whispered back, "M' laird, I will be fine. Your duty is to the clan now, dinna think of me, protect the clan. Be safe because I need you when you get home." She slumped over Magnum's back as soon as they were hidden in the tree line. She let Sir Colin lead Magnum and focused her breathing to control the pain.

"Aye, m' love," Ian whispered back and turned back to the shore. Nearly all his men were across. He dinna know if those who were following them would dare to come down to the shore and attempt to cross over. Ian knew Sir Colin or Sir Duncan would send reinforcements as soon as they reached the castle. Elisa and her men had already disappeared into the forest. Ian sent half his men to spread out in the forest to ensure Elisa's party made it through and to watch for anyone trying to swim the channel and make their crossing somewhere other than here at the sandbar.

Ian knew he would have to ask his father if his men could patrol the shoreline; so he could have his own men to double the guard at his castle. He was going to need more men, but the issue with that now was who could he trust? Obviously, Lady Elisa's life would always be a threat to the king; and therefore, she would always be in danger.

As men cleared the rise, they were dispatched by the archers in Ian's party. None of them reached the shore or the sandbar. When reinforcements arrived, Ian gave them their orders. He sent men to his father's to ask him for men to patrol the shore and requested his father meet him at home.

Ian knew it would be a few hours before his father's men would arrive. Ian ensured his men had the area secured. He wanted to get home to his castle; so he could ensure the watch was doubled and all was secure. But mostly, he wanted to check on Elisa. He knew something was wrong but she blocked him from seeing what it was. He knew Sir Duncan and Sir Colin would take care of her and protect her, but he was uncomfortable not knowing her situation.

He would have to wait for his father's men to arrive, give his orders. Then, he could get home to check on Elisa. He dinna like waiting. He was a man of action. Blast it, he finally accepted his marriage to her and his mother refused to allow him to go get her after her father died. He should have taken Duncan, Sir Thomas, Michael and a few other men and gone anyway. They were finally happy and settling into their life. Elisa was adapting to the clan life. She still had a lot to learn about her role, but she absorbed knowledge quickly and did what was necessary. Then, these blasted kings just wouldna leave them alone. He finally had her back again and he wasna willing to lose her again. Today's attack had proven to him how verra much he loved her. He checked on his men again and waited.

Sir Duncan dropped the reins and dismounted quickly to assist Lady Elisa. He knew she would try to walk on her own and might even try to dismount. She was already testing her weight on her leg as she tried to stand in the stirrup. "I dinna think I can dismount on my own, but I think I will be able to walk with someone to lean on."

Sir Duncan lifted her down, but when he tried to carry her into the castle, she barked at him, "Blast it, Duncan, put me down. I can walk. I need to do it myself."

"M' laird is nay going to be happy, Lady Elisa," he replied as he lowered her to the ground and held her arm until he was certain she had her balance. "It was our job to protect you, which we failed to do. And now, you will make matters worse with your stubbornness."

"Mayhap, you should be more concerned about whether I am happy," she replied.

"Aye, m' lady," Sir Duncan mumbled.

Lady Elisa walked into the castle, home at last and hopefully, for good. She asked Alice to bring her hot water, a needle and a bottle of scotch. She started up the stairs but couldna put enough weight on the impaired leg to step up.

When Alice saw she was injured, she said, "Sir Duncan, carry Lady Elisa up to her bed."

"I dinna need carried," Lady Elisa protested, but no one listened to her. Sir Duncan picked her up anyway and carried her up to her room and laid her on the bed.

Alice was right behind them carrying a tray with cups and scotch. She poured Lady Elisa some scotch, which Elisa drank down. Sir Duncan explained what happened. Alice left the room, leaving the door wide open. Sir Thomas and Sir Scott took up posts just outside the door. Sir Duncan stood guard next to the bed.

While Sir Duncan assisted Lady Elisa inside the keep, Sir Colin gave orders for reinforcements to be sent to the laird at the crossing and ensured the guard was doubled and ready for an attack. Once his orders were given, he attended to their horses.

Alice returned to Elisa with hot water, bandages and a needle and thread. She set to work on Lady Elisa's wound on her thigh. Alice asked Sir Duncan to sit on the bed next to Lady Elisa, so he could hold her down. Then, Alice removed Elisa's breeches and draped a blanket over as much of Elisa as she could and still have access to the wound.

"Ready?" Alice asked.

"I would prefer to sit by the fire," Lady Elisa said.

"Well, that isna going to happen," Alice snapped.

"Wait," Sir Duncan said, "Laird Ian said she likes to focus on the flames." So he lit a candle and placed it near the bed so Lady Elisa could focus on the flame.

"Thank you, Sir Duncan," Lady Elisa said. "Ready, Alice." Lady Elisa hissed and flinched at the first moment of pain, but then she trained her focus on the flame and was able to block out the rest.

When Alice was done, she gathered up the supplies and removed them from the room. Sir Duncan sat with Lady Elisa. He moved a chair next to the bed to sit on. "Do you mind if I ask how you do that, Lady Elisa?"

"I learned when I was little that the smaller I was, the smaller the area for my father to hit me. So when I have to endure pain, I focus on being small. The candle flame is perfect because of its size. I make myself feel as small as the flame; then there is only a tiny place where it hurts. If the pain is small, I can endure it; I just have to focus."

"Aye, I ken," Sir Duncan said.

"Can I ask you to do something for me?" Lady Elisa asked. "I dinna want to distract Ian with my injury, so I have been blocking him from seeing me and what happened; so he could focus on defending the castle and protecting the clan. But I need to know if he is alright, that he is safe."

"Aye, m' lady," Sir Duncan said and he was quiet for a while as he focused on his laird and determined what he was doing, where he was. "He will arrive shortly. He has several of the men from the journey with him, which means our reinforcements made it out to the crossing and are standing guard watching for anyone who tries to cross the sandbar. He will likely go to the parapets to ensure the guard has been doubled, which it has been. He may need to meet with some of the men and explain what is going on before he comes to see you."

"Thank you, Sir Duncan," Lady Elisa responded.

"You should rest, m' lady, until m' laird comes to see you. I will talk to the guards at your door, then I will sit by the fire until m' laird arrives. Let me know if you need anything, m' lady."

"Thank you, Sir Duncan."

Elisa tried to sleep until Ian arrived, but she couldna let go of the fact that only one arrow was shot and she was the only one injured. Clearly, it was an attempt on her life, which likely meant the king was trying to have her eliminated. She knew the castle walls would be all she saw for the greater part of this pregnancy. No riding or swimming. She wasna happy about that and she dinna think she could stand to hear Ian dictate these restrictions to her.

She had to come up with a strategy to raise this child; to somehow love him and raise him to be equipped to be a king but one who puts his people's needs first. Not a selfish king like the King of England and the King of Scotland. She dinna want him to hate his father, but she dinna want him to be like him, either.

Ian was glad when his father's men arrived at the beach and he gave them their orders. He explained what happened and why he needed them to watch the shoreline. Then, he gathered his men and rode to his castle. He dismounted Talon and left him with Sir Colin. The two men talked for several minutes and Ian thanked him for sending the guards out to the shoreline and for doubling the guards on the castle walls. Then, he ascended the stairs to the parapet and spoke with the guard for several minutes. Ian let him know that his father had been summoned and to watch for him. Then, Ian turned back to the stairs and made his way to the keep. He climbed the stairs and entered his room. The door was wide open and he knew Sir Duncan would be guarding Elisa.

"She only dozed off a few minutes ago, m' laird," Sir Duncan said to Ian as he entered the room.

Ian glanced at Elisa and saw she was asleep; so he sat by the fire and talked to Sir Duncan. "What happened? She dinna look alright when you crossed over the sandbar, but she blocked me from seeing what happened."

"She was shot in the left thigh with an arrow. Somehow, she knew it was coming and slipped the reins into her mouth to bite down on. And, she grabbed the arrow while it was still in flight. I think it prevented the arrow from going verra deep. She dinna want to cry out from the pain, but I dinna think she realized how much it would hurt. She dinna want you to stop to check on her; she just wanted to get home. She had me pull out the arrow as we were riding. She wouldna stop. She dinna want you distracted by her; she wanted you to focus on protecting the clan."

"I dinna know if she is verra brave or just too stubborn. I can tell you that was the only shot. No one else was injured so that likely means she was the target. The only thing we dinna ken for sure is who sent these men to harm her, but my guess is it was the king."

"Aye, m' laird; I feel the same."

Elisa interrupted, "Dinna say it, Ian, I canna bear to hear it." She tried to sit up. "I ken it has to be this way, but I canna bear it."

Ian moved to the bed, "Aye, m' sweet wife, I know." He tried to soothe her. He helped her to sit up and then he sat on the bed next to her. "How do you feel?"

"Like I was shot in the leg," she answered, "and annoyed with being confined to this bed again."

"Aye, I am sorry, but you willna have to stay in bed as long as you stay off your leg. You can sit by the fire or sit in the library, as long as you take it easy so you dinna tear your stitches."

"Are you ready for me to show you? We might as well do it now and get it over with. Every time we wait something else happens."

"Aye, if you feel up to it," Ian said.

"Do you want Sir Duncan to see it as well?"

"Are you alright with that?"

"If you trust him, so do I," she agreed. She knew Ian would probably tell Sir Duncan anyway; so it would be easier to just show them both at once. She knew Ian relied on Sir Duncan's advice so she kenned Ian's need to share things with Sir Duncan.

Ian indicated for Sir Duncan to join them. He resumed his chair next to the bed. Ian sat on the bed facing her. Elisa held out her hands so they could hold them, but then she let go of Sir Duncan's hand and whispered to Ian, "If you canna love me after this is done, please just tell me; so I can deal with it."

"Aye," Ian said.

Then, Lady Elisa took Sir Duncan's hand and showed them everything her parents taught her, her mother's death, her brother's deaths, her stepmother's death, how she saved Elsbeth. Her father's abuse if she dinna do something right after he taught her how to do it, or if she dinna do it quickly enough. She squeezed Ian's hand tighter as she showed them what her cousin, Ken, did to her, how he molested her and beat her whenever he visited; his fits of rage. But she couldna bear to show them everything; it was too difficult for her to face. She showed them what happened when the King of England came here after her cousin died. She dinna want to, but she showed them the horrible things she did when she returned to London, how she manipulated and used the king's daughter, the evidence she left within the homes of the nobility to put suspicion on all of them, how she killed the king and left the evidence in his bedchamber and took his clothes, glove and ring. Then, finally, she showed them what happened in Edinburgh.

Ian asked her if she could show them what happened today. So she tried to show him how she felt the arrow coming, but because of all the noise they were making she dinna hear when the arrow was released. If she had heard it, she would have been able to catch it or avoid it.

Ian asked her to show him anything else she could remember from the scene.

"I dinna ken what you want, Ian," she said.

"Can you show me what was going on all around you, not just your guards, but farther off in the woods?" he explained. "Can you show me all the surrounding area, including the area where the arrow came from?"

Elisa tried to replay the scene for them to see. She wasna sure what they were looking for. She tried to look slowly at the landscape around them as they were travel-ing through the woods so they could see more details. She lingered when she reached the area above them where the arrow came from. She dinna see anything that was help-ful, but she hoped what she showed them would be useful to them.

When they were done, Ian suggested she get some rest.

Elisa rested her hand on Ian's arm to hold him back. She hoped he would give her a few minutes more. "Wait, Ian, can I talk to you alone?" she asked.

"Aye, m' lady," he said and sat with her until Sir Duncan left the room.

"I want to know what you were looking for. I dinna want you to be angry with the men. I dinna think they did anything wrong. If anything, I was upset with Sir Colin and Sir Duncan and was probably to blame."

"Nay, Elisa, that wasna what I was looking for. I dinna think you or the men did anything wrong. You told me you were afraid and felt we were being watched. No one in our party was to blame. I was looking to see where the arrow came from so we can go search the area for clues as to who attacked you. Obviously, I feel it has something to do with the king, but it wasna his men. I need to know who actually attacked you. I need to know who our enemies are; who can and canna be trusted because I think we are going to need more guards and I need to know who I can trust to choose more men."

"Thank you for telling me, Ian," Elisa said.

Ian helped her to lie down. "Aye, m' love. It will be alright." Ian said.

"I dinna think anything will be alright ever again," Elisa said. "And I canna spend the rest of my life confined within the castle."

"I ken," Ian said and kissed her. Then, he rose from the bed and left the room to talk with Sir Duncan.

Alice came in to see if she was alright shortly after Ian left. She brought a tray of food and some ale. Elisa ate and drank. Her leg was throbbing and she knew she wouldna be able to sleep, so she asked Alice for some scotch.

"I dinna think you should drink too much, m' lady," Alice tried to make it sound like a suggestion. She dinna want to upset Elisa.

"I ken, Alice, but my leg is throbbing and I willna be able to sleep."

So Alice gave Elisa some scotch to help relieve her pain so she could sleep. She would prefer to drink until she dinna feel anything, but that would require her to drink at least a bottle of Scotch. It took a long time, but eventually, Elisa fell asleep.

Chapter 21

Elisa woke in the early morning. Ian wasna in bed. She reached over to his side of the bed; it hadna been slept in. "Ian," she cried out, in a panic.

Ian whispered back to Elisa, "I will be there in a couple minutes, Elisa."

"It is alright, Ian, I just woke up and was in a panic because you werena there. I am alright. You dinna have to come here," Elisa whispered back. Then, she burst into tears. She carefully crawled out of bed and tested her leg to see if she could stand on it and walk. She made her way to her chair by the fire. She pulled her knees up to her chest and wrapped her arms around her legs.

Ian finished his discussion with the guards and returned to his room to check on Elisa. He quietly opened the bedroom door to find Elisa sitting in the chair with her face buried in her knees, crying. Ian rushed to Elisa's side and wrapped his arms around her. He held her close until she stopped crying. "What is it, m' love?" he asked.

"I woke up and you werena there when I reached over to your side of the bed. It dinna seem like you had even been to bed; so I was worried that you werena going to come to our bed anymore, because of what you saw earlier." She started crying again.

When she stopped crying, Ian cupped her chin with his hand and turned her face up towards his, "Nay, m' sweet wife, I dinna want to disturb your sleep because Alice said your leg was bothering you and you had trouble falling asleep. Also, I wanted to work with Duncan regarding the watch and some other preparations, so we were talking. I dinna leave our bed, m' love, I couldna do that. It's difficult enough trying to leave you alone."

"Are you sure, Ian, even after what I have done?"

"Aye, Elisa, very much so and I still love you verra much. I have done things just as bad. So how could I nay love you when you would do what you did to protect your family, our family? I love you still. I love you verra much."

"I love you too, Ian. I am sorry I panicked. I am sorry I dinna trust you. I just dinna know how to trust people. My whole childhood feels like a lie, the constant testing and the little bits of information. I dinna even know if I have it all figured out or nay. I dinna know what my parents were trying to teach me or what they want from me. If I canna trust my own parents, then who can I trust? Certainly, nay my uncle and cousin. I dinna know if I can trust anyone, not even you, Ian. I am sorry, but I dinna know if I will ever get there."

"I ken, Elisa, how could you trust anyone after all the things your parents put you through, what your cousin did to you, what both the King of England and the King of Scotland did to you? I am sorry you had to suffer through all the things those people put you through. I am going to try to protect you from now on, m' love. I know you canna trust others. I ken why. I hope someday you will trust me. I know your inability to trust is why you do everything yourself so you dinna have to rely on anyone else or trust anyone else. I also know that you have a great love for all of our children, all the children of the clan. You will do anything necessary to protect them. You give so much of yourself and take so little from others, Elisa. I ken you, m' love. You are nay putting me through something I dinna want to go through. I want you, Elisa, and I will take whatever I can get because I love you. I will help you if you will let me. I need you to let me help you. I need you to let me take care of you like you take care of us."

"I am trying, Ian, but I just dinna know how."

"I ken, Elisa, trust me to hold you for now," Ian said. "I ken that it is difficult for you to trust even me. I am trying to be patient, especially because we havena had time to work on our marriage without something happening that separates us. But we are here now and I am nay going to let you leave again. We just need to talk to each other and we will be able to work it out, Elisa. So, even if all you can do is tell me your plans for the day or if you have a bad feeling something is going to happen or that you are scared; I want you to tell me. I need that from you because then I will know you are trying to trust me."

"Alright, Ian, I will try. For now, can you just hold me?"

"Aye," Ian answered and pulled her into his arms. "Do you want to sit with me so you can see the fire?"

"I just want to sit with you, but I dinna need the fire. I just need you. I know I am supposed to be brave, never show my fear, but I canna help it; I am scared all the time that it willna ever stop. That they willna ever stop coming after me. I only feel safe when you hold me. When you kiss me, all I think about are the feelings you make me feel and I can forget the other things for a while."

Ian held her tighter. He kissed the top of her head. "Thank you for telling me, Elisa. I will do what I can to protect you. And I would love to make you feel only me touching you."

She turned her face up to his. He bent down and kissed her, "Ian, I willna want to stop if you do this."

"Aye, Elisa, me either."

"Are you sure it will be alright?" she asked.

"Aye, it will be more than alright," he said. Ian picked up his wife and carried her across the room. He kissed her gently.

"Ian, thank you. You make me feel so wonderful," Elisa said.

"Thank you, Elisa, you make me feel wonderful too. It was my pleasure." He spoke with the guards at the door to send a maid up with a tray of food. They talked until the tray arrived and ate together on the bed. Then, he insisted she rest during the afternoon. He did his best to reassure her that he loved her, even if he couldna spend the entire day with her. He caressed her until she fell asleep. He ensured that she was sleeping for half an hour before he rose from the bed and slipped quietly out of the room.

He spent the afternoon with his most trusted men preparing for a siege and war, if it should be necessary. He met with the men that went to investigate the attack on Elisa. They dinna find verra much that could prove who they were or for whom they worked. They dinna find anything that showed they were the king's men or with any particular clan.

At dinner time, he returned to his room with a maid carrying a tray of food. He had her set it on the table between their chairs by the fire. When the maid left the room, he approached Elisa's side of the bed.

He pulled back the covers and helped her up. Then, he reached for her robe at the foot of the bed and held it out to her. She turned around with her back to him as she first slipped one arm into its sleeve and then the other. Ian wrapped the robe around her and found the ribbon and tied her robe shut. He liked that she was caught in his arms when he finished tying the ribbon. He bent his head down and nuzzled her neck for several minutes before he caught her chin and turned her more towards him so he could kiss her lips. Elisa turned to face him as Ian deepened the kiss and wrapped her arms around his waist. She let him kiss her for as long as he liked because it helped her forget all the other memories in her mind.

After several minutes, Ian pulled back and released Elisa. He took her hand in his and walked with her to their chairs by the fire and he ensured that she ate a healthy portion for dinner. After they finished eating, Ian held her on his lap. He wrapped his arms around her and held her close. He kissed her and caressed her; and then, he carried her to their bed again. He missed her so verra much while she was in Edinburgh. He was glad that they had so much work to do to prepare for a siege and a war because that was all that kept him from marching across Scotland and starting a war.

The year passed quickly since he was so busy working in the fields, hunting, fishing, taking care of the clan, and making preparations that he dinna have much time to think about what he really missed. At least, it kept him from thinking about her every moment once he buried himself in his work.

"I love you verra much, Elisa; but now, we should get some sleep. It's almost dawn."

"Aye," was all she mumbled before she fell asleep. Ian cuddled up next to her with a chuckle. He wrapped his arms around her as he always did. He draped a leg over her legs and fell asleep.

A few hours later, Ian woke and dressed quietly. He slipped out of the room and went downstairs to the hall to eat. Then, he went to the training field.

When Elisa awoke, she rolled over and reached for Ian. He wasna there. She reminded herself that Ian loved her. He would try to protect her and their children. She dinna need to panic, but she knew the fear was lurking just below the surface. She had to put on a brave face, dinna let anyone but Ian know that she was afraid. She could do this; it was what she was trained to do.

She carefully got out of bed. She tested her leg to see if it was going to hold her up. She dressed and grabbed a proj-ect to work on and made her way to the chair by the fire. She concentrated on her project. If her mind drifted to the nightmare or fear of the king coming after her, she focused on the fire and thought about the way Ian made her feel.

After a sennight of staying in their room, working on her projects, reading Scripture and praying, she couldna take looking at the bedroom walls anymore; so she decided to head down to the hall for something to eat. She got up slowly to ensure her leg would support her. She thanked God that her leg was already starting to heal enough to walk on her own. She decided she would add time to her schedule every day to read Scripture and pray. She knew putting God first was the right thing to do and that He would help her through even the worst of situations, as He had already done on many occasions. She thanked God for all the times He helped her as she left the room and started down the stairs. Ian and some of his men were just coming into the hall from training.

Ian went up the stairs to meet Elisa. "M' lady," he said as he lifted her into his arms and carried her the rest of the way down the stairs.

"I dinna need carried, m' laird," Elisa protested. "I just need to go slowly."

"I dinna mind carrying my wife down the stairs because I can do this," Ian said and he kissed her.

"Ian," she could barely speak, "you shouldna do that in front of everyone."

"Since when is my wife shy? As I recall, you were more than happy to lie on the table for me on our wedding day," his whispered, his breath into her ear making her shiver in his arms.

"That isna fair, Ian, I drank too much scotch and ale and you were purposely annoying me to get a reaction out of me and your father was antagonizing me just to see how far he could push me. Apparently, I can be pushed to behave verra badly."

"Hmm," Ian mumbled as he nibbled her ear, "and mayhap, I just want a little reaction out of you now."

"You dinna get enough reaction earlier?" she asked.

"I will never have enough of you, m' love," he answered.

"Well, I suppose you can carry me back upstairs after I eat breakfast," she told him.

"Aye, m' love, it would be my pleasure."

Elisa was excited for later and her face was probably verra red. Ian's whispers in her ear already had her stomach fluttering. "Ian, if you dinna stop I willna be able to eat."

"I will try to behave myself then. You need to eat and take care of yourself," Ian said. He set her down on their bench at the head of the table. He went to the kitchen and brought her a plate of food. Then, he sat next to her. Ian couldna keep his hands off her. He rested his hand on her leg and caressed her.

Elisa couldna eat with Ian caressing her leg. So she ate with her left hand, so she could hold his left hand with her right hand. She tried to focus on eating and not everything she was feeling. She slipped her hand palm up under his hand and locked her fingers with his, hoping she could eat without his hand caressing and touching her and making her stomach flutter.

"Ian, if you dinna stop, I canna eat." Elisa said in a low voice. She caught a glimpse of Sir Duncan, who had a big grin on his face. "Is something amusing to you, Sir Duncan?" Elisa asked.

"Aye, m' lady, I am verra glad to see you two so happy together," he answered.

"Thank you," Elisa said, blushing.

"You shouldna be embarrassed, m' lady." Sir Duncan tried to encourage her.

Elisa tried to eat again, but Ian was moving his fingers up and down her leg. Apparently, he dinna care if she ate. "So what have you been up to this morning?" Elisa asked.

"Training and more preparations," Sir Duncan answered.

"Preparations for what?" Elisa asked.

Sir Duncan dinna respond. Instead, he took a drink and looked at Ian over his cup. He whispered his apology to Ian, "Sorry, m' laird. I dinna mean to say something I shouldna. I would have expected you to tell her what we have been doing for the past year."

"Ian, what preparations?" she asked.

"Are you done eating, m' sweet wife?" Ian moved his fingers up and down her leg until he could touch her bare leg. He caressed her bare skin. He tried to be patient because he knew he should let her eat. He tried to control himself, but he dinna think he could nay touch her, nay after a year without her.

Elisa was so startled by his hand touching her bare leg, she jumped. She hadna realized he was even pulling up her skirt. "That isna going to work, Ian." Elisa stood up, yanked her skirt from Ian's hand and turned to walk away. But then, her injury dinna like the way she turned and stressed her leg. "Blast," she cried out in pain.

Ian was up and lifted her into his arms before she could even take a step. "Put me down, Ian, I am fine. I am serious, put me down, now," she demanded. He set her down but held her to ensure she had her balance. She turned to him and said quietly, hoping none of the men heard, "I am not a child that needs to be carried. I can walk, I just twisted and my leg wasna ready for it. Go, sit and talk about your preparations with your men. I think I will take a walk." This time, Elisa carefully turned and headed out the hall door.

She told the guards outside the door, "When they come looking for me, I will be in the stables or the garden." She went to the stable to see Magnum. She asked Sir Colin for brushes and spent a good hour thoroughly brushing out her horse. When she finished brushing him, she shared her apple with him.

Then, she asked Sir Colin if he had time to walk in the garden. So they strolled in the garden for about an hour. Sir Colin stopped to take care of an area of the garden and she sat in the grass near him or helped him weed the section of garden.

"Are you alright, Lady Elisa?" Sir Colin finally asked.

"Aye, I am just angry. I thought it would be better to take a walk that to fight with Ian in front of all his men."

They continued working in the garden for a while before Elisa asked, "Sir Colin, I havena seen Alice since I returned. Do you know where she is? Is she alright?"

"Aye, she is fine, m' lady." Sir Colin answered.

"Have you seen Ian, Hawk, Elsbeth, and Malcolm since we arrived home?"

"They are doing fine, m' lady."

"I would like to go see them but I am worried about my face and the bruising and swelling. I dinna want them to see it," she tried to explain her concerns.

"It isna that bad, Lady Elisa," Sir Colin replied.

"Would it be asking too much for you to escort me back?"

"Nay, m' lady, it would be my pleasure."

"We should go the way we came, so we willna miss Ian if he is looking for me," she suggested. He agreed. "Thank you, Sir Colin, for spending this time with me, I am sure you had other responsibilities to attend to and I am sorry if I interrupted them."

"Dinna worry, m' lady. I enjoyed our time together. I miss all the time we used to spend together in England."

"Aye, me too. But I also feel responsible for you missing out on a part of your life. If you hadna to come watch over me, you might have had a wife and children too, like Angus and Alice. I am sorry," Elisa said, tears welling up in her eyes.

"Nay, m' lady, I would have been like Sir Duncan, thinking that the only possible life for me would be m' laird's first in command," he answered. "Please, dinna feel sorry for me or feel like you are to blame for me missing out on a part of my life. I served my laird and I was happy to do so in whatever capacity he needed me."

"Sir Duncan doesna believe he can have both his command and a wife and children?" she asked.

"Nay, he doesna, but he could if he found the right woman who could ken and respect his responsibilities."

"Aye, I will think about it," Elisa said with a grin.

"Now, dinna get me involved in your women's plotting and scheming to see every man happily chained to a woman," Sir Colin protested.

"You wouldna want to tease Sir Duncan, then?" she asked skeptically, with one eyebrow raised.

"Aye, I will do that, but dinna ask me to set up anything."

"Alright, I willna ask you to do anything to set him up with any women. Mayhap, I will see if I canna find someone to keep you warm in your old age while I am looking," Elisa said.

Sir Colin had a look of horror on his face and Elisa laughed. "I am only teasing you, Sir Colin; well mostly.

Thank you, again, Sir Colin, for spending this time with me." They reached the steps to the hall and Elisa knew Sir Colin would return to the stables. She gently squeezed his hand and watched him walk back towards the stables.

"You are welcome, m' lady, my pleasure. Have fun with your scheming," he called over his shoulder as he made his way back to the stable. He buried himself in his work, as there was plenty to do while they waited to see if the king would follow them back to Mull. He knew the king showed up at the London townhouse on more than one occasion and he suspected the king treated her as her cousin did. He dinna see anything and so he wasna put in a position to go against his allegiance to the king. Part of him was thankful for that; but part of him worried about what exactly Lady Elisa suffered at the hands of her cousin, his captains and shipmates and the two kings that came to the townhouse on numerous occasions since her father died. He definitely felt he failed in his duty.

One of those kings was dead now; and you might think the other king would worry that the same might happen to him, but he dinna seem to be the least bit concerned that it was a possibility. The evidence that he abused Lady Elisa was clear upon her face. Colin dinna doubt that her body was also covered in bruises or what else the king most likely did to her with the way she suffered in her nightmares. He was glad that Ian found a way to help alleviate the nightmares while they travelled. The first few nights none of them got much sleep because Lady Elisa cried out so frequently during her nightmares. He wasna sure that Ian should be intimate with her so soon after, but Ian was gentle with Lady Elisa and it seemed to help her stop crying out during her sleep.

It dinna take long for Colin to realize that the true situation was that she dinna stop having the nightmares, but rather, she stopped sleeping more than two or three hours so the nightmares wouldna start. He ensured that he had the watch when he thought she would wake up after a few hours of sleep. Then, he could escort her if she wished to hunt or gather wood for the fire or prepare their breakfast. He would ken what she needed and she wouldna have to explain anything to him. He was happy to be of help if he was able to do so.

He realized that he hadna prevented her cousin from harming her, but mayhap a few times. Her cousin found other times to inflict his harm on her. With the number of times that he invited his friends to the townhouse, Colin guessed that they also harmed Lady Elisa. He felt that he hadna been a verra good protector. He failed in his duty to Lady Elisa. He would live with that blame for the rest of his life. He knew there was a lot of regret for nay protecting Lady Elisa running through this family, starting with her father, Chief Ian, and also with Ian and Duncan and himself, of course. The one person who should regret all of this dinna seem to have any concern for her well-being at all. And, Sir Colin really hoped that he was gone from this earth if the day ever came to pass when the plan was finalized; he dinna think he could swear his allegiance to the man if he became king; nay at the expense it cost Lady Elisa.

Ian hadna asked him as much as he expected him to ask about her childhood. He wasna sure why when Lady

Elisa was his wife; but then, neither did Chief Ian and he was Lady Elisa's father, even though she dinna know it. He wasna asked to send reports back, but he guessed that someone sent reports because he knew that Chief Ian believed that Lady Elisa was well and that Laird Ian informed the chief that he dinna think that was the case. From her reaction to Laird Ian lifting her onto his lap on his horse, Colin had to agree with the younger man. And that was all the proof that he needed that he failed in his responsibilities to protect Lady Elisa. He was certain that she was harmed by her cousin when he wasna there to protect her or was unaware that she needed him, but he dinna feel that was an acceptable excuse for failing in his duties.

Sir Colin buried himself in his work caring for the horses. He couldna change the past. He just had to live with his failure. He dinna ken how Chief Ian could to stand by and see what Lady Isobel and the other two did to Lady Elisa, because he couldna tolerate it when he saw what her cousin tried to do to her. He did all he could to send the man packing, even though the townhouse was Cousin Ken's home. Colin was grateful when her cousin left the townhouse and left Lady Elisa alone for a while. But, he realized now that he wasna as aware of what was going on as he should have been and he would have to live with that on his soul. Knowing that he dinna spend much time inside the townhouse wasna any consolation either; he was rarely inside the house except to eat meals and then he only walked through the garden entrance to the kitchen and back to the garden entrance.

Chapter 22

Ian was just coming out of the hall, "What was that about?" he demanded.

"Nothing that concerns you, m' laird," Elisa replied.

"I will nay have you scheming and stirring up trouble, Elisa," he said.

"Aye, m' laird, but it willna be any trouble to you," she answered. "I wish to go see the children, Ian."

"You are nay longer worried about them seeing your bruised face?" he asked.

"Nay, Sir Colin says it doesna look that bad," she replied. "I need to see them, hold them, and tell them how much I love them and missed them."

"Aye, I ken, but I thought we would go to our room when you came back in and talk about a few things."

"Talk?" she paused, "alright, because to be honest, I dinna have the energy to argue. So please carry me up the stairs, Ian."

"Are you alright? Why are you so tired?" Ian asked as he swept her up in his arms. He carried her up the stairs and into their room. He sat in his chair by the fire with her on his lap.

"I just gave Magnum a verra thorough brushing and then I helped Sir Colin in the garden. I just needed to do something more strenuous because it helps me work out my anger. Neither of those two activities put any strain on my injury," Elisa answered him.

"Well, I hope you are nay too tired to listen. Duncan wanted me to tell you from the beginning, but I dinna see it yet; so I dinna quite believe it myself. I should have listened to him. Your mother and my mother are distant cousins, but they grew up together. They were so close, they decided my mother would have a son and your mother would have a daughter and we would be married. I dinna know what gifts of sight either of them have, but they must have them. At some point, my mother decided to have twins. I dinna know how she made that happen."

"You have a twin brother? All the times we came to visit you when I was growing up, I never knew that," Elisa said. "Who?" she started to ask, but a vision flashed through her. Ian saw what she saw. All their childhood playing together when Elisa came to Scotland. "Sir Duncan is really your twin brother? Why did I always think he was your cousin? It always annoyed me that your cousin was always visiting when I came to visit."

"I dinna know why you were told that he was my cousin and we were told to just play along with it. Somehow, our mothers had all this planned out from their youth. You have the gift of sight, Elisa, but you recall things from the past. That is how you did all the things that your parents taught you from such a young age. Learning was always easy for you because you learned these things when you were so young; you only had to recall them from memory later."

"I have the gift of sight for the present, the things that will happen in just a few days. Dinna focus on this for now. I will talk about this more in a little while, but the King of Scotland is coming for you. It was part of our mothers' plans from the beginning. That is why my mother had twins. They had to have a gift of future sight and that is why my mother had twins and why your mother gave you the memories she did. So you could do what you had to do to expose the corruption in the English court, I suppose. It is why I wanted you to let Duncan see what you showed me because it will affect his future too."

"I dinna ken what you are trying to say, Ian."

"I am sorry if I dinna explain things well, Elisa. Duncan was always better at this than me. I was groomed to be my father's replacement as Laird of the Clan, but mother insisted Duncan should always be at my side and learn all that I learned. I suppose she knew the future. Duncan sees the future too. You are the past, I am the present and Duncan is the future."

Ian continued, "You must remember that, Elisa; Duncan is the future. You said it always annoyed you that he was always around. That is because he has always loved you. I dinna know then he could see the future or how far he can see into the future, but I know now he can see from an infant to an adult. He used to sit by your cradle and hold your hand. Mother was always telling him to let you be and to nay meddle in her plans. I dinna know until I was ten that he cared so much for you. When you returned home after your seventh summer here, he was verra sad while we sat beside your bed keeping everyone away from you while you healed from a verra bad beating your mother and mine gave you. After you left, he rode down to the loch and I followed him; he was really distracted by his sadness, I reached out and touched him. He was upset because he knew you were nay coming back for a verra long time. I dinna understand his sadness, but he told me it was because he loved you; that he has loved you since the first time you came to Mull, the summer you and I were wed the first time. You were only an infant and he and I were three, almost four. He has always wanted to be around you. I dinna really want to spend the summers with you, but he always convinced me to spend time with you and include you. I think it was to help me grow to love you, but also because he loved you and wanted to be near you. I cared for you, Elisa, but I couldna stand what they did to you. I know they all think that I was being selfish, immature, irresponsible, but it was really because I just couldna stand to hear them or watch them beat you."

"Mother dinna want Duncan to be so close to you; she thought he was going to mess up her plans. He convinced her that he wouldna interfere but that he could help me accept the marriage to you and that it would be best in the end. He was right, I suppose."

"You dinna come back after that summer, but he did what he could to help me see that my marriage to you would be a good thing and that I would be happy. He has always been my advisor since that summer. I knew if anything happened to me, he would always protect you and take care of you."

"That is why he is always at my side when you have clan business to take care of?" Elisa asked. "I knew he had feelings for me, but I dinna know they were so strong. I always felt I shouldna be alone with him. It's why I made sure he always left the door open."

"Aye, I know and he tries to remember to do the same, to never step over the lines of propriety," Ian said.

Elisa said, "It's why I think we should find someone he can love, who loves him back."

"Nay, Elisa, I dinna know if I can make you ken this, but when the king comes, I willna let you go back with him to Edinburgh. But if something happens to me, you must do whatever Duncan tells you to do. There is another contract that Father had the kings sign. After you returned to London and Duncan told me you wouldna return for a long time, I went to Father and insisted that if anything happens to me, you must marry Duncan because I know he loves you and he will do all that he can to protect you and take care of you. He willna let anyone hurt you like you have been hurt in the past and he'll be good to you. Father agreed, went to the kings and made them sign the agreement that you marry Duncan if anything happens to me."

"You canna be serious, Ian?"

"Aye, Elisa, I am verra serious. Listen to me, the king could take you back to Edinburgh with him if you were a widow. You dinna want that, I know. You must marry Duncan, so he can prevent the king from taking you. Do you ken, Elisa?"

"Aye, I ken, Ian. I will do what you say, but you have to tell Duncan I dinna love him. I love you, Ian. I have always loved you."

"I know, m' sweet wife." Ian kissed her. "Your parents nurtured your love for me because they were worried about Duncan too. But I think if you recall your memories, you will see that you dinna want Duncan around because he made you feel your love for him too. You were trying to honor our marriage, so you tried to avoid him. Dinna think about that right now, you can think about that later. I know you willna want to hear this, Elisa, but you must. When the king comes, I will go out to meet him. I believe he will act with treachery. It will bring war to our clan. You must marry Duncan and consummate the marriage immediately after the contract is signed. There must be witnesses to the marriage and the consummation, Elisa. I know this will be difficult for you, but you have to do this. Do you promise?" Ian asked.

"Aye, I promise, Ian," Elisa said and she kissed the palm of his hand and closed his fingers over the kiss, the clan's vow to keep their promise and to protect the clan and the family. Elisa was overcome with tears. She dinna want to hear any of this. She dinna want this life. All she wanted was her marriage to Ian and their children. Blasted meddling kings, she thought. She pushed herself up off of Ian's lap and lay down on the bed; she hugged her pillow and cried.

A moment later, she felt Ian lie down on the bed beside her. He wrapped his arms around her and held her. "I know, m' sweet wife, I know you dinna want this. It will be alright. We will each do what we have to do and we will do it to the best of our ability as we were trained to do. You can be happy with Duncan if you let yourself remember your love for him. He loves you, Elisa, and you can trust him too, just like you trust me and our love."

"But you need to know one thing more, Elisa. He isna going to give you the freedom I gave you. I let you have more freedom than other wives because you raised your-self and your raised your half-siblings. You ran your father's estates and businesses after he was gone. But when Duncan is laird, he isna going to let you do these things. You have had this time with me to help you transition to your role as laird's wife. With Duncan, you will have to submit to his authority. Do you ken, Elisa?"

"Aye, I ken," she said and she burst into tears again. Ian held her and caressed her and kissed her. He dinna want to see her cry, but he couldna leave her. He knew it would be abandoning her and she couldna deal with it. It would break her heart and possibly her mind. She might never be the same if he left her to cry it out on her own. He couldna do that to her or Duncan.

He hoped that if he held her and caressed her and kissed her, that eventually, she would be too tired to cry and mayhap, she would even turn to him for love and he could try to make her happy again.

When Duncan knocked on the door, Elisa said, "It's alright, Ian, go talk to Duncan. You can wake me when you get back."

"Are you sure?"

"Aye, I will be alright," Elisa said.

Ian got up and went to the door. He went down to the hall with Duncan. "She knows what is coming, she gave me her word she will do what you say. She will marry you. But she is verra upset. I hope you will have the patience to work things out with her. I fear she is going to need a long time to come to terms with this." Ian told Duncan.

"Aye, m' laird. I ken. I just wanted to update you that the king has only one more day before he will arrive here."

"Well, then, that is it, I suppose. Thank you, Brother, for everything. I know you will do well as laird. You always anticipate exactly what I would do and take care of it for me. No one could have asked for a better commander. Thank you, Duncan. And I wish you two the verra best. I know you have always loved her. I am sorry that this is how it worked out. But I thank you for helping me accept our marriage and to make the best of it for what time we had together. All the necessary documents you need are in the safe in our room. Another set of copies are in the library safe. Do you need anything else, my brother?"

"Nay, m' laird, I will cover things here so you can say goodbye to Lady Elisa. I will come get you when he arrives."

"Well, I want to explain a few things about Elisa before I leave her in your care because I dinna think she showed us what her childhood was really like. She showed us that her cousin touched her and kissed her and pinned her down; but I dinna think that would cause her to fear him the way she did. I could sense a great fear in her and I think he did much worse things to her. She couldna bear to tell me what he did to her, but she did say that he took advantage of her and that he entered her, but in a way that dinna take her virginity because he wasna allowed to take her virginity. She was a virgin when I lay with her, so what she said was the truth. I hope that you ken what I mean without me saying it."

"Aye, Ian, I ken what she suffered at her cousin's hands. I dinna tell you when you returned from Father's because I dinna think you wanted to know how much I really knew. I dinna think you wanted to know what she suffered. I dinna think I should know what she had been through since she wasna my wife, but I sat with her during her nightmares while you took the children to Father's. I hope you are nay upset with me that I knew or that I kept it from you."

"Nay, I am nay upset with you, Duncan. I am glad that you ken what she has been through because I know you will help her try to deal with the nightmares and you will be good to her and try to keep her safe."

"Aye, I will do everything in my power to keep her safe, Ian. Goodnight, Brother." Sir Duncan said. They hugged and pounded the other on the back.

Ian returned to their room. Elisa was asleep in the bed. He barred the door and climbed into bed with his wife.

"Ian," Elisa said as she rolled towards him.

"Aye, m' love," Ian said. He enveloped her in his arms, dipped his head down to hers and kissed her. He was hungry. He deepened the kiss.

He would never have enough; but now, he would have to leave her in Duncan's care come the morning. She was so beautiful, so passionate, so loving. She gave so much of herself in everything she did. Seeing how much she cared for others and tried to help others that dinna have as much as her had sealed the deal for him. He had fallen deeply in love with his wife.

"Elisa, I love you. So verra much." He lay beside her and wrapped her in his arms with one leg draped over her, like he always did. Then, he fell asleep.

List of Characters' Names (Relationship)

Cousin Ken
Uncle Kenneth
Cousin Richard (Elisa's mother's cousin)
Jonathan (little Ian) and Ginger Elisabeth (Elsbeth) (Elisa's
    stepsiblings)
Laird Ian, (Elisa's husband)
Sir Duncan (Laird Ian's commander of the guard, cousin
    or brother)
Angus (guard, married to Alice)
Alice (Ian's nanny)
Chief Ian & Lady Isobel McVeigh (Laird Ian's parents)
Father Patrick (Laird Ian's priest)
Talon (Laird Ian's horse)
Magnum (Lady Elisa' horse)
Justice (Sir Duncan's horse)
Fergus (Duncan's youngest brother)
Sir Thomas, Sir Scott, Michael (guards)
Alex (the King of Scotland's guard assigned to Elisa on the
    way to and during her stay in Edinburgh Castle)

About the Author

Alyssa McBath is married, with two adult children and three dogs. She grew up in a rural, farm community. She spent much of her childhood reading any book she could get her hands on, including her Bible. She gave her life to Christ at age 8 after a series of abusive situations and she realized she could not rely on or trust members of her family or the parents of her friends. Her family traveled much of the Pacific Northwest during her childhood which led to her living in several states and continuing to travel, especially with her daughter. So far, she has lived in six states and traveled to forty-one states. She loves camping, bike riding, hiking, especially to waterfalls. Her greatest passion is serving in children's ministries and crocheting, knitting and sewing more items than she could possibly count.

Further Reading – Coming Soon

www.ingramcontent.com/pod-product-compliance
Lightning Source LLC
Chambersburg PA
CBHW071956190726
48293CB00001B/58